The Fork

A. Parise

Amy —
what gets us through
this, is us.
Alex

Cover Art by Mareika Glenn

This book is dedicated to everyone who I lived with,

in various houses,

in New Brunswick, New Jersey, from 2003 to 2009,

but particularly the remarkable residents of our little collective

at Hale Street from 2003 to 2005.

Thank you all for two of the best, most magical years of my life.

Audrey A.

Lauren V.

Rita S.

Scott N.

Emily Z.

Eryn L.

Erin F.

Luis R.

Memory is a snatch of tune, floating in the dusty air. Memory is a clenched hand, slamming against a cracked windowpane. Memory is a lock of hair in a dented tin box, voices in a boardroom, the flash of steel in the sun. Memory is a length of vibrating sisal twine, humming in the afternoon, a cold drop of rain or sweat inching down the spine.

Memory is hoofbeats sundering the world, the smell of mildew in a shadowed room. Memories can be ordered, but that is not what memory is. Memories can be set down in a place, conspicuously and meticulously laid out, a skeleton on a table. Conversations can be recalled imperfectly and laid to rest on a page, images devolved from curves into polygons, people pared down to their essentials and described. But this is not memory.

Something lies between memory and recollection, between the living past and dead words on a page. Memory is alive, changing, vibrant; words stand still. While living, memories collide, join, recombine, and break apart again; one informs the next. What lies between memory and recollection is anamnesis, the bringing together of the separate bricks of memory and building a proper house. Once the house is built, anamnesis ends; the door leads from the front path to the foyer and windows overlook the gardens. The rugs lay on the floor and the dry paint sticks in sheets to the walls.

The process of building the house is not neat. Doors wind up on the roof and windows in the basement, gutters are mistakenly laid on the inside of walls instead of along the eaves.

2

The house is built brick by brick, and every brick is important. Any forgotten brick, and the edifice will collapse. However, each brick cares only that it has neighbors, not which neighbors it has. The bricks will suffice in any order that the mason chooses to place them, and every person is their own mason, building their own house.

The top of Liberty Place One had been shorn off as if with God's own chainsaw.

A collection of Freemans were reflected in the shack-sized sheets of glass littering the road. Freeman dodged left and right, leaving behind callouses and blood on the street behind him. The footslaps and shouts of pursuit chased behind him, the sounds drawing nearer as he swung past brittle edges sharper than any knives.

If his guess was right, the four leaders of the pack behind him would be Scotto, Ricky, Dawn, and Legitimate. It was sad to say, but Scotto would probably be the easiest of the batch to deal with; Dawn led the cavalry and would be the hardest to chase off. Ricky, Legitimate, and the gendarmes pursuing didn't matter. They were just bodies, just extra feet and arms to help bring him down.

His heart and lungs pounded from the unaccustomed work. Years of management and direction and delegation had left him unathletic; the suddenness of the pursuit was also unexpected. He had thought that he'd have far more time between dropping the packages and their arrival at the furnace, far more time before the chain-reaction had gone too far to stop. Far more time before anyone noticed, and anyone blamed...

But he hadn't.

A dagger of glass taller than he rose out of a lump of something organic on the street. He was approaching the true maze on the far side of Liberty Place, the area where he would lose these pursuers.

This was the one thing they'd all forgotten, if they'd ever known it at all: sometimes, the environment was not something to be fought. Sometimes the world around you could be used strictly as it was, without the requirement that you fight it and bend it into a new shape. They were all so busy reconfiguring the world that they forgot that it had a shape already.

He had started to forget that. No more.

A quick right turn, and he was heading towards where the glass on the road changed from house-sized and clear to house-sized and mirrored. Here the true labyrinth began.

"I found a place for the next Full Moon party."

"Wonderful. Where?"

"Over on Arch Street, there's a place with a huge courtyard and a fountain. There's a sign that says it's the Betsy Ross house."

"We've had parties there before, Freeman. It's fine during the summer, that courtyard is, but it sucks during the autumn and winter. It's too damned cold to be holding outdoor parties now."

"Ah, but there's a way in."

"Really?"

"Yep. And I checked it out, the walls and ceilings are solid enough that we'll be able to make about as much of a ruckus as we want."

"How'd this happen? Gleaners check that place over all the time. It's so obvious that it's a good place, I can't imagine that no one has found it before."

"Remember those floods? A doorway in the street was uncovered. The basement isn't dry, of course, but the roof was made of very flat rocks, of all things, and when it fell in they made a sort-of floor on top of the old basement floor. So it's mildewed, but the top layer of rocks are dry, if a little shifty."

"Basement? You mean, well, yeah, right, it's only one story, isn't it?"

"Yeah. Which means there'll be plenty of light when the sun goes down."

"Protected from the wind, dry, and lots of light, huh?"

"Yep."

“I think I'll put the word out.”

“I already started.”

“Freeman, why would you do that?”

“It seemed like a good place, it seemed like something we'd all want to do.”

“It was your idea that you-and-I start getting people to agree on things through the Full Moon parties. What in dust's name were you thinking?”

“Well, that's been going okay, you've been successful, and you said you were really busy this moon, so it seemed, I don't know, like the best thing to do.”

“We're busy every moon. Freeman, you know what we're trying to start here, you know what's arrayed against us. We're trying to get this decision-making process started and, and, Freeman, this was your idea.”

“Wasn't it yours?”

“Yes, it was, but you said, let's start it up with the Full Moon parties, remember? Why start working against it now? It's something new, Freeman, something that's just starting, something fragile. Why?”

“It didn't seem like a big deal. I didn't think I'd be damaging anything. I'm sorry, Molly, I really didn't think I was doing anything wrong.”

“Whatever.”

The wagons always smelled better on the way back from Philadelphia than they did on the way in.

It amazed Freeman that cheese from Philadelphia should smell so different from the cheese made at home, that the red basil should be so much spicier than the green his family planted, that the peppers should bite back so. But they all did. Everything from the markets was different from what their little community grew. As the son of the drovers, he was the lucky child of the village who got to go to Philadelphia every year; this was his twelfth year and his tenth trip to the City.

Goods trickled into Philadelphia from up and down the coast, from the mountains to the west and sometimes even beyond, from the bays to the south to the islands and capes to the north. Goods came from cities with names like Brooklyn, Boston, and Washington. And, of course, from the farms in Jersey.

They bartered the village's produce, trading tomatoes and jerkies, rose hips and woodcuts and leather for everything imaginable. This year, coming back were pepper seeds from the peppers that bit back, there was dried sage and corn and oil. The tomato wagon was filled with sharp-smelling wood that would give new flavors to the smoked fish and beef that were village staples during the winter. There were yards of light cotton cloth and sqwacking geese covered with feathers far softer than seagull feathers. There were jams, jars sealed tight with beeswax, and honey, and pickled vegetables, and small satchels of fragrant spices whose names he didn't know and whose smells he didn't recognize.

Which was all nothing compared to what could be found at the market, and nothing, he suspected, compared to what he had purchased for himself, trading carefully hoarded utensils, black with age, gathered from the basements of ruined buildings.

His family lived on the sands of the peninsula far to the south, near what was once known as Cape May. Cold during the winters and warm during the summers, but almost always with mild weather, and only minimal work to do during the winters; keeping the firewood piled high and occasionally fishing, reading lessons and sewing and weaving and indoor repairs, water to be carried and floors to be swept. There was plenty of free time. When the snow did come through there was little to be done outdoors, and the snow would indeed come.

To work on while the snows came through, he had acquired three metal boxes, all once identical, bearing the crypic word Techtronics. What exactly they once did were beyond both his ken and the knowledge of the junk dealer who traded them to him for some beach glass. They were all broken now, the large discs on top of them stuck in place, the buttons seized, wires coming out of cracks in their cases in random directions. But even young Freeman knew what you could do with three of something that were broken.

Old Farley at the farm had once broken a shovel handle. Rummaging in his shed for a busted adze, he pulled the handle off and replaced the shovel handle with it, then resumed digging.

With three broken things, you could sometimes make one thing that worked.

"You know, I've been to dozens of these little markets and I've never heard prerecorded music at one before."

"It's not common, no, but there's music everywhere. All you need is to know where to look and to have the right tools."

"Is that right?"

"Da. For example, you could buy this device right here, which is playing this disc here, from me, and you'd be able to play music in your own home. And these discs, which are called records, are to be found all over the place. They're not always clean, but water and a rag will clean one up well, and then you can have this in your house. If you don't feel like looking for records yourself, I have a small supply of cleaned-up records that you can buy here also."

"But the machine doesn't work by itself, does it?"

"Hah. Of course not. Look here. This box, with these two wires coming out of it? There's a demon inside. The demon's angry about being trapped in there, and so he jumps around a lot. When he jumps, we can tap him for energy, and when you hook it up to the record player —like so—he'll supply enough motive power to run the record player for hours."

"What happens when the demon runs out of energy?"

"When the demon gets tired you bring the box back to me. For a small fee I trade you the old box for a new box with a new demon in it. Then I can feed the demon in your box and get him ready for the next time you come by."

"Fascinating."

"Thank you. Are you interested in one? The record players cost four bushels of vegetables apiece, and a new demon-box, special price today only, is two bushels of grains. The trade-in on a demon-box is only a quarter bushel, just so you know. I also have this lovely device, which can also be run off the same demon-box, which you can bring home for your woman to do her sewing on. The seams are far straighter than hand-stitching and take far less time."

"I'll have to think on it. So what do you run the generator on?"

"…

"You have the better of me, sir."

"Look kid, the demon bit is good, but I recognize a battery when I see one."

"I have a small generator farm that runs on the artificial rivers under the city."

"Have you shared electric light with these yokels yet?"

"Thank you sir, but I am one of these yokels. And I haven't yet figured out how to manufacture new light bulbs, so, no, I haven't. I'm working on it, though."

"I see. There's some people across the river I think you'll be interested in meeting, and who I think may be interested in meeting you. Are you amenable to perhaps going to Camden one of these days? They're looking for someone with experience with electricity, and they can provide quite well when their needs are met."

"That is a fine shirt you wear, sir."

"Please, kid, call me Scotto."

"I am called Freeman."

"How does this thing work?"

"Ask a simple question..."

"No, seriously."

"There's a lot of gears and heavy things."

"Of course. You're not being very forthcoming."

"You're asking a question that's a lot like 'Why does the Sun stay in the sky?' Alright, fair, not that hard, but still."

"What do you mean?"

"'How does this thing work?' It's very complex. I can hardly answer that in only a few breaths. To answer it properly, I'd have to get into physics, into density differentials, into mechanics, into optics, hell, into social structures."

"Fine. Describe one piece of its operation."

"Look, that's no good either. No part of this will make sense without being taken as a part of the whole. Describing it piecemeal will give you no concept of the scale, the complexity, the fine poetry of the intermeshing parts."

"Pretend I know nothing of the poetry of machines."

"Fine. Alright. See that third segment there?"

"Yeah."

"Alright. By that point in the machine, the rubble has passed through both the jaws and two sets of presses to crush the materials into relatively small bits."

"Okay."

"After passing through a bottleneck to sort everything into a relatively narrow pile, the conveyor belt passes under a large magnet.

This will pick up metals such as tin, iron, and steel. These metals then pass off to the side, where they're dropped onto a new conveyor system that carries them back to the smelters. Before going into the smelters, however, the tin has to be separated from the iron. The tin is less dense, however, so there's a density gauge that measures the density of each piece of metal by weighing each, and then measuring displacement in a water column. If it's tin, then it gets sorted into one bin; if steel or iron, another bin. Once the bins are full, a new conveyor pushes the full bin into the smelter. The scrap is melted together into pigs, and then the pigs are dropped onto the conveyor belt that carries the newly-recycled materials across the bridge and over to Camden."

"You lost me. What are pigs?"

"Steel bars. And I know. I knew I was going to lose you. And you want to know how the whole thing works? This machine is all I've done for the last five years, and you expect to understand it in a day."

"It's just a machine."

"Trust me on this one. It's not just a machine."

"Trust you simply because you designed it?"

"No. Because this carries the future with it. This machine is our future, our hopes, and our dreams, and the ashes of what we dreamt before this machine came along."

"A poet and an engineer."

"No. Just someone who knows their responsibility. I don't know what yours is, sir, but this is mine."

Early summer evenings were the best time to walk out onto the broken roadbed of the Walt Whitman Bridge. Freeman and Molly and Steve and Crissa were coming out to celebrate a good day at the markets.

There was a bar out on the bridge, a place called the Spectra. It was one of the few places in Philadelphia to have not changed families for longer than Freeman can imagine. While he enjoyed the place, he had to take issue with such a word being put to such a small use.

The bridge no longer reached all the way to Jersey; only the Benjamin Franklin did. But the roadbed of the Walt Whitman was solid out to midriver, where it suddenly disappeared into the brown waters of the Delaware. One could walk out onto the bridge; one could not walk across it.

The roadbed slanted slightly near the ground of Philadelphia; the Spectra was out near the cracked edge of the bridge. When did the bridge break? Who knows? Certainly not any of them. They'd found mouldered postcards and pictures of the bridge back when it still went all the way to Jersey, all grey and gleaming and beautiful. Now it's orange with rust, spiky with fraying cables and chunks of shattered asphalt.

The Spectra was built where Whitman's Palace once was. The Gleaners, who prided themselves on the pretense that they knew more of the history of their city than most of its other inhabitants, knew that the bridge wasn't named after the leader of the Whitman Brigade, as the city generally assumed, but that it was the other way around. Who this Whitman was, well, that was anyone's guess, wasn't it? But the bridge was hardly named after the petty warlord who was smashed by the Spectrum Sprawlers.

The Spectra itself was more patch than building. It occupied the most coveted spot on the bridge, near the jagged teeth of the slanting ramp down into the Delaware River.

In the last winter, when a storm blew away a few of the shanties erected on the bridge, Jase had considered moving the Gleaners' base here to the bridge. It had a wonderful view, and container-gardened vines grew well on the thin cables reaching up to the main bridge supports, but it was decided that too many of them would have to stay behind each day in the compound to keep out squatters, who were next to impossible to get rid of once they had taken over a place. Squatters were a problem even on not-very-desirable South Street. South Street was nice and central to the markets, but also in the no-man's land between the Duchy of Fishtown and South Philadelphia. But there, with the threat of Fishtown and the Sprawlers on both sides should the Gleaner population get too large, squatters were easy enough to shoo off, seldom requiring violence. Tales told in the Spectra, on the other hand, were bloodcurdling, even to people who lived with the threat of bleeding daily.

Jase had finally dropped it, because even though their house wasn't terribly great, it wasn't awful, either, and it had the benefit of not being sought after by any of the major power structures in the city. The middle of the road was the best place for a small group to stay; they could only use and protect so much, and it was best to hold it as well as they could, to not reach for more than they could grasp in their hands.

"This is disgusting."

"You wanted to come down here."

"It wasn't so much that I wanted to come down here. I have to come down here."

"Right. Nonetheless. Can we get a move on?"

"Ugh. I'll never get used to the way the smoke from these torches gets in your eyes when you're underground – what is that?"

"What? Oh. Yeah. Well. I don't recognize him."

"How could you?"

"Well, he's been down here a bit, that's for sure. Oh, don't get sick."

"Sorry."

"If it's that big a deal to you, check his clothes. In fact, if we can get the rats away, he might have something useful."

"I'm not gleaning something that looks like that. Besides, look at his chest. There's a damn spear sticking out of it. If someone did that, then they've taken everything worth taking from him."

"Yeah."

"The rats are ignoring us."

"They do that. That's a feast they're munching on, and feasts don't come along too often down here. I wish I'd brought a sling, there's a few on him that wouldn't be too bad."

"Yeah. But the farm's coming in well."

"You can never have too much food."

"True enough. We'll have to come back down and see if we can bag some of them. Since they're here and all."

"Yeah. It is amazing the way they just stand there, though, isn't it?"

"Sure is. Where's the compound from here?"

"A few blocks. Stick to the walls, watch out for where the railing has snapped off. You don't want to cut yourself down here, especially on the feet."

"Good call."

"Why did you want to come down here anyway?"

"I need a source of running water. The stream that runs down Pine isn't constant enough, or strong enough really. And we can't defend it from the compound. But this sewer runs right under South Street. We might be able to access it from the basement if we knocked a hole through the wall."

"Woah, hold up. Who's talking about knocking a hole through a wall?"

"I need something that will turn a generator. Windmills are too conspicuous, you can see them from the street. We've already got the one. If we have more, people will know that we've got something valuable. They wouldn't know a generator, but they could well think that we have a surplus grain supply. And you know how that goes."

"Sure do. We'll appear to be worth robbing."

"Exactly. To run the generators I need something that's inconspicuous. And people don't come down here. If we can break through the basement to here, we can run a generator without anyone else being the wiser."

If you could read, you read any piece of paper you happened to come across. What you found may have been nonsensical, it may simply be a shopping list or a receipt or a purchase order, or it may be a fragment of something larger which makes no sense in this world. Nonetheless, if you could read, you read it. There were few sensible strings connecting this world to the one that came before, and words were one of the strings that tied the times together.

So when Freeman found the scrap of paper about cities and gates, it made perfect sense to him.

This unknown author stated that every city had four gates going into it, one in each of the cardinal directions. Even should time pass and the city grow too large for the gates to be physical, those four gates still exist.

Before the Hemorrhage, Philadelphia was absolutely too large for those gates to still exist in physical form, but these days, one of those mythical gates still exist.

The north, south, and west of Philadelphia merge with swamps and forests, but the east of Philadelphia was then and for all time bounded by the Delaware River. The Delaware describes one of Philadelphia's limits, perhaps its only limit, and that limit is unbreached for now and all time.

But there is a gate.

Once, bridges ran into the city from the far side of the river in magnificent arches, caternaries suspended in graceful defiance of the river, gravity, and perhaps the world itself. Freeman had always considered them pure physics, and pure beauty. Those bridges, by and large, no longer exist. The Walt Whitman Bridge ends halfway across the river; the Camden side is a pile of rubble, the eastern-most supports a rusting reef in the center of the river. The Betsy Ross Bridge, which seemed to have no relation to the house in Old City, formed one terminus of a shipping industry which simply brought goods from the ruins of the bridge to whatever was upriver. The roadbed ran under the waters of the river, and even the captains of the flattest-bottomed boats refused to be holed by sailing over where the bridge used to be. The Commodore Barry, to the south, was split down the middle, the roadbed hanging between the two towers sticking out of the river like two hands unable to clasp.

Which left the Ben Franklin Bridge.

The Ben Franklin Bridge was the only way into Philadelphia from the east, and it was taken by cavalry brigades and traders and vagabonds and musicians and, well, anyone wishing to visit Philadelphia from more-or-less anywhere to the north. Though there were no doors, it was the eastern gate to the city, and for most of his life, this was the only gate that Freeman entered or left by. Trading with his family, running from his parents' killers, raiding into Haddon for sheep, meeting with the Fork, working on the Fork... The eastern gate, the Ben Franklin Bridge, was his route in and out of the city. This ancient, unknown writer, said that the eastern gate of the city was the gate of acceptance of responsibility.

And this evening, standing on the edge of the Walt Whitman, staring at the Ben Franklin and the Fork and the gleaming towers of Camden and the dark city of Philadelphia, Freeman realized that not only had he accepted his responsibility, but also that the last time he left Philadelphia, it could not be by the eastern gate.

The markets in Philadelphia—Freeman was slowly learning—were a grand argument, a treasure and a delusion, a map that was hard to keep straight in its ever-changing byways. There were markets that were open to his family, back—*hoofbeats sundering the world*—when he would come with his parents as independent traders, that were closed to him now that he was with the Gleaners. There were markets closed then that were now open to him.

The markets were controlled by geography more than anything else. There was a market, sometimes, at Thirtieth Street Station that would serve the Schuylkill trade, or at least some of it. Some of the Schuylkill trade stopped at a temporary market in Fairmount Park; a small waterfall in the river kept any but flat-bottomed boats from traveling down it.

The flat-bottomed boats that did go all the way to the Thirtieth Street docks—little more than collapsed architecture hammered by feet into a rough ramp—were usually boats that would never travel back upstream. A frame and bed of sawn planks, resting on a roped-together mass of tied, inflated goatskins; room for cargo and a tent pitched on top. These traders were in Philadelphia for the market fiercely contested by Upenn and Drexel, for the finished goods from their workshops, for the tools, for whatever books the undergraduates had copied that had any meaning to the farmers up the river. The traders would return on horse or foot, lugging their goods along with them.

The smaller market at the foot of the waterfall would often see its goods winding up back at Thirtieth Street. The river traders would trade with middlemen, who would haul the goods up to the main market and trade them with, well, whoever they were aligned with. Being a middleman in the middle of the rivalry between Upenn and Drexel was a dangerous game, though—in theory—market peace should keep those middlemen safe. It didn't always, and thus the Gleaners kept themselves closed off from that particular market.

On the Delaware River, there were three markets: one at the foot of the Betsy Ross Bridge, a private market completely controlled by the Duchy of Fishtown, one public market at Penn's Landing, and one down in the old Navy Yard, near the delta of the Schuylkill and the Delaware.

No one really knew what went on in the Navy Yard. It was closed, and those few trading boat captains who went to both the Navy Yard and Penn's Landing would turn purse-lipped and silent at any mention of that market. No one knew anyone from the Navy Yard. Sometimes people would go there. No one would ever hear from them again.

When the Betsy Ross Bridge collapsed, whenever it actually did, it blocked the Delaware almost entirely. The artificial reef of the bridge wrecked up most boats that tried to pass it; there were rumors that Fishtown did their best to keep that particular reef intact. Boats from the north, be they coal-or-tire barges, steel, or consumable traders, would sell to Fishtown at the captive market at the foot of the bridge, and some of those goods would eventually make their way into the city at large.

The Gleaners stuck to the free markets, though; these were the most interesting, and the least dangerous, market-peace notwithstanding. The three free markets—some freer than others—were the market at Penn's Landing, the market at the Spectrum, and the market that Freeman was most familiar with, where his family used to trade: the market at City Hall.

"Lemme in there."

"You're gonna get your clothes dustier. I know you hate it."

"Doesn't matter. Rittenhouse has the coolest marble fountain in the city."

"What do you think the future holds for us?"

"I don't know."

"What do you mean?"

"I mean, well, I mean"—*hoofbeats sundering the world*—"everything can change so quickly, you know?"

"With what we've been doing they won't stay the same, that's for certain."

"We can only hope. Can you imagine this as it once was? When it was first built? Tables out in front of that cafe. The awnings covered in actual cloth. Light streaming from the windows, and horses on the streets. The buildings clean, not covered in dirt and soot and smoke and vines, but bare clean rock."

"I think I like it better this way."

"How?"

"You know where you stand here. I know where I stand here. I don't know if I could have found a place in that world. What possible use could someone who can only farm a little, and can only hunt a little, and can only cook a little, find in a world that's shiny and well-lit? All I can do is convince people to do things, sometimes, and I don't know if I could do that in that kind of world."

"They probably wouldn't have needed someone to fix their record players, either."

"Nah, you would have been building them in the first place.

Designing them."

"Maybe."

"Is this what the future is going to hold for us? How long can we stand between the Southies and Fishtown?"

"No. That's not the question. We've got a generator now. We have to keep it quiet, sure, but that won't be for too much longer. We're going to change Philadelphia." Push the hoofbeats away. "Who knows what we can do once we're generating more electricity than we are now." Think about Molly on the sewing machine. "What if we could find a loom that weaves by itself? It has to be possible. Maybe I could even build one, who knows?"

"Am I in your little future world?"

"There is no future world without you."

Freeman stopped running abruptly. A turn to the left, followed by a quick right, then a few steps forward, then again to the left. Here, the rising sun was filtered into the small cavity in the mirror-structure through cracks and jags in the leaning pieces of glass, dimmed by smoked glass and dappled by the leaves of trees growing out of the street. The pursuing voices came quickly to him, echoing crazily through the sheer walls.

They'd be here soon. They had bows, maybe guns.

Time to move. He pulled a handful of ball-bearings from his pocket, started scattering them behind him. Their falls onto the asphalt were loud, but not as loud as his footsteps. A moment of hesitation, then his boots were unlaced and thrown over his shoulder.

Glass poked into his feet. A lifetime of callouses would be sliced off by this flight, he knew. Infections? Maybe. He could probably still get some 'shine from some distillers he knew on the north side of town. Maybe. If he got there.

Shaking his head, he started moving, dropping ball bearings behind him onto the ground. Move move move stop. Move move move stop. Footfalls thudded past him, going the wrong direction, on the far side of a huge chunk of mirrored glass; he could see the face through the one-way mirror, and it wasn't a face he recognized. They'd recognize him for sure, though, of that he was certain.

Move move move left move stop. Every now and again, drop ball bearings. Not enough that he could be tracked, if they figured out how he was moving, how he was choosing his path, but a breadcrumb path still.

Pass one tunnel, pass another, now turn left. Move where pieces of mirrored glass faced outside, or where at least one did. One side smoked, one mirrored; if he kept the

mirrors on the far side of where he stood, he could watch his pursuers unseen. Look down at the wrist compass, get moving in the general direction that the needle points. Move.

A lifetime of a few minutes and several new wounds later, there was a scream from back where he was earlier. The scream was accompanied seconds later by a horrendous shattering of glass. That's part of the labyrinth and one pursuer gone for certain; if he was still alive the screams would certainly still be echoing through these artificial canyons. With the amount of glass around, silence equaled death.

Alright, part of the ball-bearing trail has been found. That's okay, most of the bearings are gone now, just one more handful to drop onto a sheet of glass at his feet and then move.

This mirror-labyrinth would not hide him forever. He was eventually going to have to come out into the open, and then move. He winced as his foot was cut again. And he was going to have to get out of here so he could actually put his shoes on, that was that.

He didn't realize that his blood made a far better breadcrumb trail than the ball bearings until he'd come to the end of the labyrinth.

Time to start running again.

"Wanna go explorin?" This is from a girl his age, a girl with mud and rust smeared on her face and grease in her hair.

"I have to watch the wagons. Pa told me to."

"Pish. There's good places to look through only a few blocks from here. We can get up the stairs that the growedups can't cause they're too heavy. Maybe we can find good things in some of these buildings."

"But I have to watch the wagons." Even at nine, responsibilities are responsibilities.

"I'll watch the wagon while you find your dad and ask him if someone else can watch it for a bit. I'm sure your mom wants to get into the shade, she looks preggers."

"What?"

"Your mom's pregnant, you got a new sister or brother coming along. You got any brothers or sisters?"

"No."

"Me neither. They all died babies."

"Mine too."

"Go get your dad, we'll look through that brownstone there."

"Brownstone?"

"Those houses usedta be called brownstones cause they're made of brown stone, right?"

"Those are called bricks."

"Oh. But the house is still a brownstone."

"Okay."

"Go get your dad. Tell him you wanna look through the building."

"But I'm supposed to keep strangers away from the wagons. You're a stranger."

"I'm not a stranger. I'm your friend."

"But I don't even know your name. How can we be friends if we don't know each others' names?"

"Well, that's easy, innit?" She drew herself up straighter and thrust out a stained hand at the end of a thin arm. "I'm Molly."

He took her hand gravely. "Freeman."

"Now we're friends, so go get your pa."

"He's coming already. I'll talk to him when, oh, hold on." And he started running.

It was a late fall afternoon, and the last light of the sun poured through the split roof, painting the walls of the basement a sepiatone brown and gold. People were starting to pile into the basement of the Ross house through the newly-uncovered doorway from the street, carrying with them food and kindling and instruments and blankets.

A figure in a dark, holed sweater was arranging a firepit in the center of the room, shifting the fallen roof-slates with a broom, clearing a lens-shaped scoop on the basement floor; another figure was piling up wood in a teepee shape for the fire. As long as the walls and floor were damp, and the roof was holed, fires in abandoned buildings were mostly safe. Mostly, though everyone here had carried in an old plastic or glass bottle filled with water just in case – fires did sometimes spread through the city, and those were bad times. No one wanted another great fire like the one still talked about, the one that swept through the dockyards in South Philadelphia.

A bottle of moonshine, probably produced by the Duchy of Fishtown, was passed to Freeman by a farmer who he knew wanted to join the Collective. He nodded his thanks and pulled a swig from the flask, then passed it to Molly, who drank and sent it back with another nod for the farmer.

Since they started selling the batteries, since they grabbed the compound on Chestnut Street and enlarged their area of control, more and more people wanted to join in. And, somehow, they were important enough to the local economy that they had full freedom of movement throughout the city; plenty in here were jealous of their wealth and home, but knew that one wrong move would mean that their demons would never be fed, and they'd lose their music, or their sewing machines, their spinning wheels, their pumps.

No one wanted to risk that.

Molly's arm through his, they made their way through the basement over to where the food was, gliding on the shifting slates like nobles at Versailles. These Full Moon parties, though they'd been going on for longer than he'd been alive, had become important recruiting grounds for the Collective. If you saw someone at the markets, and they made useful things or had useful skills, well, that was one thing. But almost as useful, and truly as important, was skill with a musical instrument, or with singing, or with epic poems; unprinted paper was still scarce, and they couldn't waste any of what small stock they had. People with memories good enough to remember multiple songs, or singing and playing at the same time, or ten-minute long poems, would likely make good students. And the Collective was all about learning.

Also, skills with music or art meant that the potential Collective member—and everyone here was either a potential or a current member—was not content to waste their downtime hours with sleep, or with boredom, but sought to improve themselves. There were always chores to be done, of course. Folding the laundry, or canning vegetables, or darning the socks; everyone did these things. The Collective did these things. But there had to be more to life than chores; this was one of the Collective's deepest institutional beliefs. And if people chose to spend their downtime doing something other than sleeping, that showed excellent taste.

And the Collective wanted to bring them all into itself.

"Alright girls, get out of the wagon. C'mon, you know you want to. Hey Matt, how's it going?"

"Not too bad, nice day for the grazing, how bout you Steve?"

"It's going fine. Glad spring's finally here."

"And how."

"How are the teeth?"

"Tightening up. Yours?"

"Just fine. Just fine."

"C'mon you. Get down. The ramp ain't that bad, you do this all the time, atta girl."

"Is this all Matt and Lydia's? It can't be."

"It ain't. This used to be Independence Park, as it was called, and oh people have tried to control it but it's just too big. You couldn't wall it off if you wanted to – and plenty have wanted to, but too many people count on it for grazing space to let that go. You know, walls falling in the middle of the night, that kind of thing. Hey, John-o, what's up? How's the wife?"

"She's great. Third son's on the way."

"Excellent! No daughters again, right?"

"If I'm lucky."

"Anyhow. There's no like schedule or anything?"

"No schedule but... everyone sort of comes when they do. And that gets habitual. It's not set or anything but, well, you know when you come. It works out. Sometimes people change when they come, and that can get dicey, but, oh look, those two over there are working it out now."

"Alright, so, if you don't want to get punched...."

"Don't come when it's not your day."

"Do we get involved?"

"Hell no. It's between the two of them. If it looks like it's getting out of hand, maybe, or if someone goes for their sheep. But that all looks like it'll be ok."

"Alright. What do we do now?"

"Sit down and let the sheep graze."

"Right on. I brought a book."

"Oh, right, you can read, I forgot. Well, I'm gonna go get some water from that spring over there, you make sure the sheep stay where they're supposed to."

"Hey kid, don't think I know you."

"You're, um, Matt, right?"

"Yessir. You a new Gleaner?"

"Yep, they agreed to let me stay on."

"You're not from the city are you?"

"No, I'm from down the Jersey Shore."

"What brings you to the city?"

"Oh, um, well. You know. Parents and so forth. Become a man or something."

"Sure, sure. Well, you need anything, you just let me know. I'm down at Third and Bainbridge with my wife Lydia. You come on by if you need anything."

"Thanks very much, sir."

"And don't sir me."

"We need to get everyone together like *ligne nu*."

Freeman looked up from the wires he was soldering. Molly was flushed, dripping with rain, and standing in the doorway. She never hurried this way; something was up.

"What's happening?"

"We need to get the group together right now. Something important is happening a

few streets over, and I think we can take advantage of it."

"What's happening?"

"I don't know why, or how, or when it started, but Fishtown is pulling out of Chestnut Street."

"Pulling out? But they've got some of the biggest farms in the city there, and there's a well, and..."

"Right. They're pulling out, and I don't know if anyone else has noticed, but we're the strongest group nearby and they're abandoning some serious property. If we can seize it, then we can hold it if they ever want it back. And with a defensible hold of that size, we can finally come out into the open with your machines. This is what we've been waiting for, and it's happening now, so help me get everyone together so we can start moving."

There were ten people to bring together past him and Molly. "Right. You start with Crissa, I'll get Steve, we should be able to meet downstairs in less than twenty. Start telling everyone what you told me."

"Are you in or out?"

"Are you kidding me? I'm as in as possible. And I want in for securing the place. Why are they doing this?"

"I don't know. I don't know what's happening to them, but if they're going to abandon anything, Chestnut Street makes the most sense. It's not quite as rich, or as big, or as defensible as their main hold in Fishtown, right, but it's a close second. Their other holds are far closer to their main hold, though. They must be consolidating for some reason. Whatever that is, their loss is our gain, but only if we move. Now move."

She was already out the door while shouting the last bit. Freeman dumped water onto the brazier that was heating his soldering iron and followed right behind her.

Freeman unlocked the door of his apartment on Spring Garden, dropped his keys on the floor and went around lighting every oil lamp that he had in the place. There were a few, a very few, precious electric bulbs; after the lamps were all lit he moved slowly through the apartment plugging in and lighting each one in turn. He was mildly pleased to see that the batteries still held a charge after the, oh, easily six moons since he'd last used them.

He had no reason these days to light the entire apartment; the bulbs were far more precious than the electricity stored in the batteries, so he just used lamps to prepare his meals. The records he so loved in his youth were gone; he hadn't listened to music in five and some years.

Had it been so long? Yes. It had been five years since he listened to music last. He set down his lamp and his ass on the floor and looked around at his apartment: it was clean, and that was the only sign that it wasn't abandoned. Most apartments in this area had about this much furniture, clothing, stuff, though most of the stuff was rotting and his was in no danger of disintegrating any time soon.

Is that all he was looking for these days?

The walls were a greyish color; the apartment still held a small smell of mildew no matter how often he aired the place out. Back in his last life, and in the life before that, Byron had mixed paints and dyes from fruits and vegetables and metals and stones; the walls of the room Freeman used to share with Molly were covered in inexpert paintings, full of color and light and life. Old posters were on the walls, the shelves full of books and blankets and things that Molly found in the buildings she searched through. The air always smelled of mildew, of course, the whole world did; but on top of the mildew was food and baking bread and brewing beer and paint and life.

That was what it all came down to, didn't it? He had been alive in his past lives. Surrounded by people, by music, by smells and colors. Now he was surrounded by people who may as well have been automata, by the smells of machine oil and rubbish and burning organic matter and melting plastics, by the clanking and grinding of gears and wheels and conveyor belts. The only colors were grey and beige and black.

He looked about at his life. The Fork wanted him to live in Camden, of course, and perhaps after all the time and sweat and blood and tears that Camden had gotten from him, he should live there. But he had tried living in the apartments that the Fork had supplied materials for and the Fork had supplied to him in turn, lived there for a few moons after leaving the Collective, and it just wasn't right. After living in the post-Hemorrhage rubbish for his entire life, it was too late for him to move to the shining city that progress was building.

He could hear, in the distance, that machine, the Fork, that he had just today referred to as “his responsibility,” chewing up yet another building, or another roadbed, or another tree. As he looked about, he wondered who had made what. He knew that he had built the Fork, that was obvious, but had the Fork built him too? And whose responsibility did that make him?

"Catch!"

Freeman snagged the hemp sack Molly pitched to him out of the air and tossed it in the back of the wagon with the other bags, boxes, and crates of the dried leaves. This was the first year of any sort of mass-production of the storage batteries and he was drafting help from all over the Collective for it. This fine day of Injun Summer found him by the banks of the Schuylkill River, down in Fairmount Park, gathering fallen oak leaves with Molly. They gathered acorns, too, but they went into baskets, and there were far fewer of those than there were leaves.

Freeman grabbed an empty sack, walked over to the slowly-clearing ground with a rake, and began raking the leaves into a pile. There was a fevered rustling and a shout and he turned, thinking something must have happened to Jake, when Molly careened into him and knocked him down into the pile of leaves.

"What the—" and then he couldn't talk as she started tickling. Choking back laughter, he immediately launched an offensive against her left flank, and the leaves flew as they rolled around, not able to keep their hands off one another in the bright autumn sun.

When neither of them could breathe anymore from a combination of inhaled humus and laughter, they stopped, holding each other in their arms, still shaking a little.

"Truce?" Freeman managed to say.

Molly rolled on top of him, legs around his trunk, her hair suddenly cascading in its red glory around his face. "A truce isn't what I had in mind, mister." She paused thoughtfully. "And apparently not you, either."

Her face descended to his. After a moment, he had his hands up and was tickling her again. She snorted and rolled off him. "What was that for?"

"Jake."

"Never mind me, kids, I'm just here watching for trouble while you guys do important work for the Gleaners, excuse me, the Collective, and I'd hardly be the one to get in the way of the important work you're doing now." Jake's sense of humor was, well, dry at best. Freeman was never able to tell whether he was kidding or not. "You two need to bring us some kids." So, not.

"Perhaps he's right." Molly's mouth made a little moue of disappointment. "But it's such a beautiful day, and we're almost all alone..."

How else could he answer? He kissed her, and she kissed him back.

Freeman swung the beam of the flashlight around the tunnel. He was on his hands and knees, climbing along one of the conveyor belts of the Fork, searching for a broken linkage in the system. They had just powered it up for the first time, and something had snapped in the rear aluminum tunnel; there were a few other people qualified to look for the breakage in question, but after all, he had built the machine.

The light started growing dim. He stopped to crank the flashlight. The bulbs were costly enough, and an actual battery like these things used to have was beyond their ability to build. This small handlamp was worth half of most of the market merchants Inventories.

He played the beam through the slats of the conveyor belt. No apparent break; time to keep crawling. Eventually he'd figure out a way to make it all small enough to fit into a headband. Not today.

The tunnel was beginning more and more to smell of hot oil, of melted metal. It reminded him of the old days, crawling with Molly through buildings looking for, well, stuff, like they did back then. Back when a non-broken record was cause for celebration, back when. He cut that train of thought—*a clenched fist beating against a broken window*—off.

Task at hand. Right. Task at hand.

He closed his eyes in the near darkness and centered himself, inhaling the smells of metal and oil and plastic and smoke deeply. No musing on the dead past.

Though... He pulled a grease pencil out of his pocket and tagged the wall. Artists signed their work in the old days, right? Well, if he was an artist, this would be his masterwork, this giant metallic caterpillar, this machine, the Fork.

He wasn't sure who named the device; it hadn't been him. He'd been too busy working on it. And while the Fork were plenty self-aggrandizing, it didn't seem like their style to name a mere machine after themselves.

He crawled farther into the tunnel. When had the machine been named the Fork? It didn't look like a fork, that was certain; more like a worm, a snake, a wheeled caterpillar. There were forks aplenty in it, though. Every ten feet or so a new conveyor belt ran off from the main line, for different materials. There were so many different technologies sorting out one thing from the next that even he had trouble keeping it straight sometimes; that there was no one else around who either did or could understand it was certain. Magnetism wasn't beyond most of them, and neither were the densitometers, but the spectroscopy was past them all. They could understand the results, sure, but setting up a spectrograph? Never. Not even Cooper, his closest disciple, the only one to leave the Collective with him.

Freeman realized that he'd paused in his work and shook his head to clear it. He had to keep working, and not get sucked into these musings, reminiscences, whatever they were. Keep the thoughts on the tracks.

He crawled forward and shone the light down into the lower track. Down there, under this portion of the track, was the breakage. Gotcha. It was time to get to work on fixing this monstrosity. He swung to the access crawlspace under the belt and got to working.

"Things are moving perfectly along schedule, gentlemen."

"Excellent."

"What is the status of the Fork?"

Freeman stood and addressed the directors of the Fork. This was hardly the first time. "We're completely finished the construction of the superstructure. The cargo containers we recycled from the Camden docks have worked as well as we assumed, and they're stripped free of rust and are completely assembled. We're moving into the conveyor installation phase, and then the different sorting sites, crushing machinery, and recycling facilities will be built. I've got teams working on the furnaces on the bridge surface, and we'll be installing these once the conveyor belt structures are in place."

"Excellent. Do we have an estimated time of completion?"

"If we keep pushing at the rate that we've been pushing at, the furnaces should be able to be moved into the superstructure before the first snowfall. If that happens, we'll be able to work inside the Fork during the winter moons, which is a luxury we haven't had before. There are still materials that need to be assembled, however; we don't have enough spectrographs, for example, and we're still running short of wiring. We'll have to gather at least all of those materials. I expect that it will likely be two more years before the machine is fully completed. Which isn't such a problem if you consider that there's still about two years worth of raw materials in Camden proper, and the construction of the new buildings with the materials we already have in Camden should take about three years. We'll have a surplus of material ready before you know it."

"Can that timetable be moved up?"

Freeman knew this was coming, but let out his breath in a rush anyhow. “I'm really not sure how. We're at the point of diminishing returns for our current assembly team size, and bringing enough people in to make new crews to, say, work overnight, will sap the current team strength severely. There is little in the way of unskilled jobs, and more time lost on training new construction personnel will not serve us well—unless you want to build another of these things later on.”

"No, no, hopefully one will be enough."

"That was my way of thinking."

"No problems with raiders?"

"You'd be amazed at how even the toughest raider can be blinded with an arc welder. The teams have been pretty well self-protecting up until now, and the few gendarmes working with us haven't been that necessary. The night watch, of course, is still necessary. Once the more delicate machinery is installed, we'll need more gendarme shifts, but the current construction is all coarse enough that it's unlikely to be damaged. Unless, of course, we run into raiding parties at a similar tech level to where we're at. Which seems unlikely."

"Good. What's the status of the Riverfront buildings?"

Freeman sat down, silently relieved.

"I still say it was plague. Why else would so many buildings be standing?"

"You and your plague. Be more creative here – we don't know what happened, let's be creative."

"Plague."

"God did it. He swept down and took all the good people up to heaven."

"Then why's Molly still here?"

"Hah. If that's it then I know why you're still here."

"Why's that?"

"Coupla merchant's daughters could tell ya."

"I'm saying it was civil war."

"Civil war? Then why's so much of the city still standing?"

"The big boatyards south of the Walt Whitman burned didn't they?"

"Sure, but something's gotta burn."

"What about all those craters?"

"Something fell from the sky and killed most everyone like, what were they called, Freeman?"

"Dinosaurs? Unlikely."

"Where else did the craters come from?"

"Explosions."

"Explosions of what?"

"They used, what, gasoline? To power all the cars we see on the streets. They stored the gasoline in big tanks. The craters are all too regular and too closely packed for it to have been from the air. They're from explosions, believe me."

"I'm still saying it was God."

"Maybe the whole city ran out of food. There's no farms here."

"They would have eaten the animals from the zoo instead of letting them go."

"Maybe they were picky eaters."

"When starving? Unlikely."

"Speaking of, pass me those grubs."

"Get 'em yourself."

"I say it just all fell apart. Something that they needed went missing and everything else just... crumbled."

"Something like what?"

"I dunno. Gasoline? Electricity? Bricks? Suddenly it wasn't there and they just didn't know what to do without it."

"Plague makes more sense. Black marks painted on doors. Midwives in white dresses going house to house like angels until the angels sicken too. No one going out. The whole big machine just grinding to a halt. And then when it's over everyone's to scared to go out or too tired to rebuild, and here we are."

"Wild animals came out of the woods and ate everyone."

"No. They'd bother us if that were the case."

"Once there were less humans they stopped caring and went back to grazing."

"God did it. Don't you all read the Bible? It's the only thing that makes sense."

"But the rivers aren't running with blood."

"They only needed to do that once."

"Plague. Y'all should stop arguing with me, you know I'm right."

From the back of the boxes, there was this weird string. Even after cleaning the boxes thoroughly with soap and water, the string felt greasy, like Freeman could never get it clean. The string was made in two parts, with a thin divide running between the two parallel sides, like the rusting train tracks behind the farm. He would have thought that it was a string made of two pieces, but every string like that that he'd seen was braided together for strength. While this string didn't appear braided for strength, if he grasped it in both hands and pulled, he was unable to either stretch it or snap it. So that was that.

The end of the thick black string ended in a flare of the same greasy but solid material, with two pieces of metal coming out of it. Both pieces, for some unknown reason, had holes drilled in them, and one was wider than the other. Eventually, he'd have to dissect one. But for now, it was time to inspect the rest of the boxes.

The boxes were thin, and gleamed silver in the harsh winter's light that came through the patched window. Freeman had little enough light here; that the windowpane was intact was surprising at best, and it leaked cold air like a sieve. Heavy, multilayer curtains were drawn almost all the way closed over the window; only a handswidth separated the two curtains and let in very little light. There were a few raised portions on the boxes, some of which would depress and some of which wouldn't. Quick extrapolation implied that all of the wide raised portions should depress, but at least one was stuck on all three of the boxes.

The center of the box was a raised circular platform. Two of the boxes had a flexible black pad on the top of the platform, the third was bare. The edge of the circular platform was black with small white ticks painted onto it in regular, nonsensical, intervals. The platform was about two hands in diameter, and there was a shiny metal post sticking out of the center of the circular platform.

Of the three boxes, two of the platforms were immobile. On the third, the platform spun if pushed. Freeman looked at the spinning black platform and thought of the greasy black discs that they often threw to one another in a catching game, that time Joey cut his hand something fierce on the chipped edge of one. The refuse from cardboard sources of kindling covered in half-rotted, indistinct printed text, with colorful snatches of picture that seemed to portend a better place. Greasy black discs with a small hole in the center, greasy black discs that were ridged almost as finely as their fingertips, that were about two hands in length.

But the spinning platform wasn't the most interesting part of the boxes. All three of them had this bent metal arm sticking out the top, a bent metal arm on a swivel joint.

They ended in small black rectangles, with a few screws and multicolored ropes going in, a small rectangle with a tiny tube sticking out. The action on the arm went from a post it rested on to just shy of the metal pole sticking from the central platform.

Well, he didn't have any of the discs, so he'd figured out as much as he could from the outside of these things. Flipping the one in the worst apparent shape over, he grabbed a screwdriver and began to take the bottom off the box. Who knew what would be inside?

"Where are you going to go?"

"I don't know. I don't know what I'm going to eat, where I'm going to live, how I'm going to stay warm this winter. All I have is what's on my body now. A sling, so I can probably get myself a cat or two, maybe some squirrels, and I can maybe dig some tubers and still collect some apples to dry. But I don't know what I'm going to do. You're the only person I know in this city."

Molly and Freeman walked down a dusty road. That had been his first trip over the Ben Franklin Bridge by himself. Haddon's cavalry had stopped pursuing him at the foot of the bridge. Fortunately he remembered where last night's Full Moon Party had been. It had been a harrowing trip, and he was covered in mud and muck and dust, roadburns and scrapes and cuts. The gash in his arm was bleeding again.

"Well, I've been living with some friends this year. My, uh, my dad wants me out of the house so he can start trading south. He doesn't want to take me out on the roads, says I'm too young, but I'm not too young to join up with some people I know. You might be able to join up too. Problem is, you have to pull your share, and I don't know what you can pull."

"Well, I'm good at digging holes. Weeding tomatoes. I can process jam."

"Yeah, assume that they can all do that. What can you do that they can't do?"

"Bring down game? Make bread? Read? I don't know. What do they need?"

Molly stopped in her tracks and stared at him. "That's right. You can read."

"Yeah."

"What does that sign say?" She pointed at a red and white sign on the street.

"No parking at any time."

Molly sat on the curb.

"You ignoring what the sign says?""Shut up, I'm thinking. Can you teach us how to read?"

"I can sure try."

"How are you with math?"

"Better than most."

"I think I can get them to take you. Steve and Crissa have been looking for a tutor; their mom was going to teach them but she died last year, and they've been wanting to learn how to read as a memorial of some kind to her that I don't understand. I'll bet that they'll trade you some food, or some part of your rent, for lessons. But it won't cover all of it. You'll have to bring in food, or you'll still starve."

"Do they have a small colony set up?"

"We all live with a small group called the Gleaners. Crissa is Jase, the leader's, woman. He likes making her happy. He might agree to take you in if I vouch for you. Can you smoke fish?"

"If you've got the right type of pipe."

"Funny."

"Not really. I've helped set up a smokehouse before. I can do it again."

"I think they'll like you just fine. Let's go and talk to them. I think we'll be able to work this out somehow."

He'd just pulled his boots on when he heard a voice yell out "Freeman!"

Which was his cue to throw himself back into the exit from the labyrinth he'd just come out of, and start rolling towards the back of the glass passage. This came not a moment too soon; the powder in the pan of the matchlock that his pursuer was apparently carrying took an extra second to ignite—thanks be to humid days—and he had just enough time to get away before a shot rang out, a shot that was quickly lost in a roar of shattering glass.

He flung his arm over his eyes but still felt the glass shards that cut his face and tore his clothing. But once the ringing of falling glass shards ended, he was up on his wounded feet, moving back into the labyrinth, dodging between the glass shards, now following his gingerblood trail back into the center. From there he could find a new path out.

Except that maybe he couldn't. He scoped one of the tunnels he'd come through to find one of the Fork's men walking up the path. Jack from the furnace crews. Shit. He'd counted on not knowing his pursuers, that would have been easier. But there was no time.

He whipped a hammer from his belt, cringed, then took three quick steps backwards and hurled the hammer at the glass close to where Jack was standing. The sheet of glass shattered instantly upon the hammer's strike, and Jack was screaming as he was cut, but it didn't last long as the second sheet of the passage, which had been resting against that first sheet for so many years, finally got to stop fighting gravity and collapsed. The roar crushed Jack's cry as surely as the sheet of glass crushed Jack's body.

Freeman closed his eyes for a moment—*hoofbeats sundering the world*—but came back quickly. Then it was out into the new valley in the glass, quickly scraping his booted feet through the uncountable shards, dragging for the hammer he'd just lost.

Dammit, he'd need that later, and he couldn't search long, for he'd just caused enough noise to make every soul for blocks turn and stare into the labyrinth, and anyone in the labyrinth would be coming this way.

His foot finally struck something. He hooked underneath it with his toe, and pulled the hammer out from under the glassfall. Ignoring the mirrordust on the handle, he grabbed the shaft and stuck it through a belt loop. Then he was off back down a new corridor, this one with the mirrors facing inside. Damn damn damn. If they were on either side of the glass, they'd now know where he was, and he couldn't see them.

He kept moving, his plans on hiatus for a moment. He kept moving, in the general direction of away from where he was now. There were at least seven people after him at the beginning, and the unknown chaser who fell earlier and Jack brought that down to five. Five workers, and cavalry, versus one pudgy, out-of-shape engineer.

He looked up at the skeleton of Liberty Place above him. And had an idea.

He started running into the heart of the labyrinth, inside the bare ribcage of the skyscraper.

"Jase, I want you to meet Freeman."

"I've seen you around, haven't I? You're at the market every year."

"Yessir, that's me. I go... went with my family every year."

"I see. Well, Freeman, it's nice to meet you. But I'm in the middle of something."

"Jase, Freeman needs a place to go, and I think he'll fit in here."

"A place to go, huh? What can you bring us?"

"What do you need?"

"We need less mouths to feed. You'll be an extra burden on us unless you can do things the rest of us can't."

"I can do a few things that you can't do. First of all, I know more about machines than you do."

"Really. And why do you think this?"

"You know you're using the wrong kind of bit in that brace, right?"

Jase looked at the brace in his hand; he'd been doing some sort of unspecified repair when Kevin brought Molly and Freeman into the compound. Kevin was now watching them silently. "No, I didn't. What sort of bit should I be using?"

"That bit has a round shaft, right? Right. There should have been some bits, probably very rusty, with a squarish end, near where you found the brace. Those bits will slip less, but do need to be sharpened to work properly. Do you know how to sharpen bits?"

"No. We do have some of those bits but they're too dull to use."

"And that one slips. There's one thing. I've a few other things I can do with machines, and more complex machines than that one. I can make decent preserves, and I don't mind bee stings to gather honey and wax, which I'm sure you know are necessary for preserving berries.

“Your clothes are rather plain—though the cloth is excellent—and don't appear well taken care of. My fa...” Freeman closed his eyes. “My gramma didn't believe in us not knowing how to darn clothes, so she taught me some needlework. She also taught me to make mordants.”

"Mordants?”

"Do you do any dyeing of cloth?”

"We've tried, but the colors fade quickly.”

"I thought. Your shirt appears to have been colored with, what, mulberries?”

"What are they?”

"Those clumpy purple berries that grow on trees, and are harvested at solstice?”

"How'd you know?”

"We dyed a shirt a few years ago, and didn't use a mordant, and it turned that color. I told gramma that I didn't think we needed the mordant, and she decided to show me I was wrong.”

"This is all impressive, but it won't help us eat. What else?”

"I can read.”

Jase was suddenly as silent, appraising. “Can you teach us?”

He was in.

"Molly, you know we're shy on food. If he can't bring enough in before the year ends, we're all going to be short. You're bringing him in. Will you go with less if we're not going to have enough?”

"Yeah, I will. I've seen some of what he does. If he can keep it up, it'll be good.”

"I didn't know about the brace. That's a start. Molly, you can show him around?”

It took two days to gather enough oak leaves for their tannin needs that year.

Each year since he'd joined the Gleaners, they gathered oak leaves to extract the tannins to use as a mordant in dyeing cloth. They kept their production small, but they were able to sell their cloth and yarn dyeing services to others in the city, and from the surrounding countryside, to help supplement their food supplies. It turned out that very few people in this area knew about mordants, and now that dyed cloth from southern New Jersey wasn't coming up anymore—*hoofbeats sundering the world*—the quality of the dyed cloth in the area had dropped significantly. This year was different in a few ways, however. One of Freeman's experiments the previous year had worked, and now they had a new plan.

The first step on that plan was tannic acid. The second step was pectin. They were already gathering spoiled apples from under trees for pectin extractions, which was more difficult than the tannin extractions. But, first things first.

There were two huge bonfires in the garden; one had a sanded drum on it filled with water, which was approaching the boil, and the other was setting, waiting to be filled.

A sharpened shovel was used to tear the oak leaves, and then the oak mulch was dumped into the boiling water. Steve was helping Freeman with this stage of the process, as he did most years. They both had several sleepless nights in front of them tending the fires and keeping everything running properly. For now, Steve was watching over the fire while Freeman prepped the next set of leaves.

After the leaves boiled in the water for half an hour, they

manhandled the drum off of the fire and strained the water into the other drum, waiting on the next fire. A third drum was filled with water and sitting next to the fire; this was added to the mulch for a secondary extraction. Water went to a boil, wait half an hour, strain off the leaves. Then dump the leaves on a clean bolt of undyed cloth, put more hot water in the barrel, and add a new batch of leaf mulch. The twice-boiled mulch was spread out with rakes into an even layer on the bolt of cloth, and more water was added to the barrel next to the fires, and then the process continued.

Each time they strained the water into the second drum, the one for the boiling off, they noticed that the brownish crust on the sides of the drum was growing thicker.

Which was exactly what they wanted. Eventually they would scrape this off and dump it into jars for later grinding into powder.

The sun rose, and the sun set, and they kept going, the world drawing down until everything was just these fires, these leaves, and these drums.

During the days, Kevin came and took the prepared bolts of cloth for dyeing. At this time of year, they would dye yellow cloth with onion skins, pinkish cloth with honeysuckle fruits, and red and purple cloth with the leavings of aronia berries left over from the earlier jamming.

But for now, in Freeman and Steve's world, there was just these bonfires, and these drums. And there was no end in sight to the oak leaves. For this year, they needed a lot of tannic acid, far more than they needed for their small cloth business.

Far more.

"Well, Scotto, is this the young man you told us that you met at the market."

"Sure is, Drake. Drake, meet Freeman. Freeman, Drake."

"Good to meet you, Mr. Drake."

"No, no, no mister. Just call me Drake."

"All right then, Drake. Scotto tells me that you're looking for... well, he didn't tell me what you were looking for. He just told me that you would want to meet me. I presume that this has something to do with my batteries?"

"Sure does."

"Thanks, Scotto. Yes, Freeman, we're looking for someone to do some work for us. We're looking to do a bit of electrical generation ourselves, and possibly have some machines repaired and built. Do you do any of that?"

"Yes. I can both build and repair machines. Which I do depends on the availability of the machines in question."

"Scotto tells me that you were selling, what, batteries, sewing machines, and record players at the market. Is this right?"

"Yes, sir. I have a few other machines, but I don't sell them unless I know I have enough spare parts. There's other things, too; I haven't been able to make new light bulbs yet."

"Unsurprising, Freeman. I've been around a lot, and there are a few other people who have managed to achieve electrical generation, but most manufactories are not up to the scale I'd hope. Few have spare parts, and no one has light bulbs. Nor, I must add, storage batteries with any sort of shelf life, which Scotto tells me that you have. And, don't call me sir."

"Yes, s—um, Drake.Yes, I can manufacture batteries, though I fear at this point that it's all with recycled materials. I use glass bottles that we find in the city for the cells, and cut down anodes and cathodes from the rusted hulks around the city for, well, the anodes and cathodes."

"Good use of materials at hand. There's no lead mine around here, huh?"

"Unless you count the structures full of the hulks."

"Point. And what do you use for the electrolyte?"

"Demon blood."

"Excuse me?"

"Trade secret, Drake."

"Fair, fair. Can't tell me everything at once, right?"

"'Spose."

"Did you bring any samples with you?"

"No, Scotto over there didn't tell me that I should."

"Sorry, sir."

"Well, Freeman, when can you come back with some samples? I will have some free time two days from now."

"I should be able to get here then."

"Capital. Then, in two days, noon, when the sun is centered in the sky, right here."

Motes of dust spin in the air, golden in the late afternoon sunlight shining through cracks in the walls and holes in the ceiling. A shape in the center of the room strikes sparks to tinder, convincing a small pile of paper, rags, twigs, and unidentifiable debris to turn into crawling red sparks of fire. Dryish blankets and cushions have been brought from homes and rooms and sheds and dropped onto the cracked slates piled on the basement floor; everyone keeps well away from the walls, walls that are primarily made of rot and termites and bricks in deep need of pointing. The sepiatone light coming through the cracks in the walls and ceiling fights the newly-born fire for prominence; soot-dark hands raise ancient bottles filled with new moonshine to lips.

Near the fire, three men in many layers of clothing, bearded and with long hair tied back, play songs with instruments half-homemade, half-home restored. Keith has the upright bass, Steve the guitar, and Allan the banjo. All of their voices, and all the voices of the people surrounding them, are raised in song, songs that were old when the new world was young, songs learned despite the changes in the language, songs that teach the current Philadelphians to speak and read what the old Philadelphians spoke.

They are singing a song about *mi corazón*, a song in a language that both none and all of them understand.

Freeman sits on the shifting slates, arm around Molly's shoulders. Molly grips her bottle of 'shine in one hand, holding Crissa's hand in the other. Crissa has her head on Janna's breast, and her eyes follow every move that Steve makes, ears twitching when his tenor raises above the other voices in the room. Janna is holding hands with someone who isn't one of the Gleaners, a slightly older man whose name Freeman can never remember. He's leaning against someone else, who leans against someone else, in a circle that seems to never end, everyone basking in the last warmth of the afternoon and the newly-disturbed chill of the damp basement. And while most of them just nod along with the verses, everyone sings the chorus, not knowing what the words mean, but knowing that *mi corazón* is what they have around them.

When the song ends, Byron enters, a brace of cats and rabbits at his belt and a guitar on his back. The animals are already cleaned, and they're chopped and put on spits, set above the fire for shashlik. Byron tunes up his guitar as best as he can; Molly's the best gleaner in the batch, and she hasn't found any guitar strings recently. Byron's e-string is a piece of sisal twine which needs replacement every few songs. The other strings on the guitar are green with age and finger oils.

They all start in on a song they learned off one of Freeman's repaired record players, "Knocking on Heaven's Door." Everyone knows this song, it's in English and is simple enough for most of them to remember. Freeman sits around, basking in the glow of the fire, the sunset, and his friends, and hopes, as always, that this particular Full Moon party never ends.

A moment of tuning later, and they launch into another of Freeman's songs, which has had the dubious honor of having its chorus modified for him. Everyone around laughs, and he blushes, as they sing "Freeman is just another word, for nothing left to lose."

Freeman ducks his head to cover his blush, and knows full well that, here, surrounded by *mi corazón*, he once again has plenty to lose.

"Once you've got the fruit all sliced like this, you lay them out on a sheet and stretch a fine mesh over top. Then they have to go out in the sun. Let's, hmm, we want to keep squirrels away from them, cause the mesh won't keep them away. How about up on the bridge that goes to the building next door?"

"Freeman, look, this is great and all, but I hate dried fruit. Why are we doing this?"

"Have you heard of a disease called Skorbut, Jase?"

"No."

"I think it was also called scurvy, at least according to Joe the farmhand, but my family always called it Skorbut. I guarantee you've had it."

"I don't get sick."

"Right. But. Sometime around, oh, say, March, you probably get really tired, right? And your teeth, your teeth might feel a little loose, like they're knocking around in your jaws?"

"Yeah, but it always goes away again."

"Right. And you've had some other problems too, hair falling out if the winter stretches too long, your skin gets kind of scaly, and if you manage to cut yourself it doesn't heal right away, it festers, right?"

"Yeah, we always thought it was the bad air in the winter, at least, that was what my parents said."

"No, it's a disease called Skorbut. And it's caused by not eating enough vegetables. Most everyone in the city gets it, right? Cause you all eat so much meat?"

"Yeah, yeah we do. So, you're saying it's because of not enough vegetables?"

"Sadly enough, yes it is. That's why it's important to can fruit, and dry fruit, and if we can we'll try to freeze some greens. If you pack them tight in the snow you can keep them through the winter. Do you grow kale?"

"I don't know."

"One of the nice things about kale is that, if you prep it right, it will live through the winter so you can have a source of greens all winter long. Greens will help with Skorbut as well. Now, aside from having to sleep too much in the winter, if you don't get the disease, you'll be a more effective farmer—and hunter—in the spring, right?"

"Of course."

"And if everyone in the city gets Skorbut, and we don't, it means we get a jump on them, which puts us in a good spot, especially if we can keep it up year after year."

"Huh. I wouldn't have thought of it like that, but you're right. We'll have more disposable food. Which means we get more trade crops."

"To say nothing of keeping vegetables longer, which means even more trade crops, because we can preserve and sell fruit when other people need it fresh. That's why we're doing this."

"Well, I guess I'm sold, or at least I'll buy it til the winter. If I don't get loose teeth this winter then I'll definitely believe you. Unless it's a short winter, because I don't get it those winters."

"I'm guessing a long one, but let's you-and-I hope for short. Let's get these up on that fire escape and then set up a few more trays to dry."

"*Devai.*"

"Alright everyone, we need to take the quickest vote in history. This is possibly the most important thing that has ever happened to us."

The room was abuzz. Twelve people can make a room buzz, if the room is small enough and the news momentous enough. And the speed with which the meeting was called convinced everyone that the news was, indeed, of great import.

Freeman had found Kimya and Steve in the same room, down threshing grains in the basement storeroom. He'd sent Steve to find John, and sent Kimya up to the gathering room. Then, since he knew Molly would forget, he grabbed the two bags of black and white beans.

James was in the subbasement cleaning muck out of the sump chute. Freeman grabbed James and hauled him upstairs; James was the last one in the basement, and they headed upstairs to the kitchen in a pair to find that everyone else was already gathered there.

"Okay. Here's what's going on. Fishtown is in the process of abandoning their compound on Chestnut Street."

And that set the room on fire.

"Why?" Kimya finally yelled over the debate.

"I have no idea. That's not the point. They're pulling out, and moving all their equipment back to Spring Garden. As of yet, no one is poised to take their old digs. Their stronghold at Chestnut Street is what's been keeping us from expanding our territory; even if they weren't strong enough to smack us down after we took it, we aren't strong enough to take it from them. But they're pulling out, which means that whoever gets there first gets the buildings *and the gardens.* That compound's got easily twice the arable land than we have here, and, from what I've heard, better wells. And while we may not be strong enough to take it, four people can hold it. And there are far better than four of us here. The Duchy of Fishtown is shrinking. We have yet to grow, and when we do grow we're going to grow big. So I put this question out to all of you: do we let one of the most desirable properties in Philadelphia slip through our fingers, or do we move, right here and right now, and grasp our future in our hands? Do I have a second on the vote?"

"Aye!" John, James, and Steve all shouted.

"Freeman, pass out the beans. Any questions, as per precedent you've got until the beans are passed."

Freeman started passing out the beans. The room was full of noise, but no questions were asked, or at least none that could be heard over the din. Everyone got one black and one white bean; a black bean meant "aye" and a white bean meant "nay." There was a jar on the kitchen table that was what they traditionally dropped their votes in, and Molly dropped her black bean into it as soon as Freeman handed the beans to her.

Everyone lined up, and began dropping beans into the jar. Most everyone covered up their votes, so no one knew how anyone else voted, but at the end there were ten ayes and two nays.

It was time to move.

Only new buildings in Philadelphia keep the names that their owners give them; those names tend to be as fleeting as the structures themselves. Even when a structure is built and it manages to hold up for more than a few years, it will often change owners through starvation, violence, or both. When the ownership changes, the name changes with it.

There are two important classes of architecture here in the city: pre-Hemorrhage, and post-Hemorrhage. The names of pre-Hemorrhage buildings tend to change as they're brought under new ownership, but the name almost inevitably reverts back to the original name. City Hall, as a perfect example, has been both Southie Central, Craig's Keep, and Central Hall. Even when the building was in the hands of these groups, the name began to revert back to City Hall even before the name was changed to reflect the new ownership.

City Hall is now occupied only by the market; when the short-lived Central Kingdom decided to wage war against the Duchy of Fishtown, one of the things that they lost was City Hall. It burned in a fire that the local denizens of Philadelphia, both allied and free, tried to put out, not so much to save the building, but to save the buildings around it, quite a few of which were full of people.

Now, the fire-blackened bricks of the once-grand building stand as a mute testament to the inability of anyone to change the city. And as a market, of course.

Things tend to keep the same names as they once had because of the weight of history. Even now, the signs and brochures and photos and postcards and guidebooks run rampant over the city; each time one is destroyed, another is found to replace it. The map of the city is roughly the same now as it was before the Hemorrhage, and the guidebooks are still accurate, even if the restaurant recommendations are hopelessly out of date. The geography of the city of Philadelphia is as unchanging as it can be in a completely changed sociography. And the names of the buildings were fixed at the time of the Hemorrhage, as fixed as the streets themselves. The building names have become a part of the spiritual landscape of the city, a part of the dream of the land itself.

By tying themselves to the land, the names have caused their meanings to erode, so now the names signify nothing. City Hall now represents the failure of independence, and the Free Library is now where people go to barter for horses. But the names, the names are still the same, and are unchanging, and shall never change.

Not until and unless the map itself changes.

"Okay, take this stick. And always poke the floor in front of you to make sure it's solid. You-and-I're going up to the fifth floor of this building, where that sign there is. If the floor has any give to it at all, and you really want to go that way, lay down, and make sure you tap the floor hard with your stick while you crawl out, okay?"

"Okay. What are we looking for?"

"You'll see. There's still some good stuff up there, and the stairway is pretty solid for three floors, so it's mostly easy to get up to."

The building they were going into was on Arch Street, and was built of grey, soot-darkened stone. Its entry had once been a metal-framed glass door, or so Freeman assumed as they stepped over the doorframe and into the building. The floors were green tiles, and the walls were mildewed. There were three double metal doors, aged but not rusted, to the right, and a doorway with no door in it behind a desk. Molly lit the lamp she held in her hand, throwing new shadows into the dim room. "When we're on the steps, if you see any red marks like that one there, don't step there. It's either cracked or too soft to support weight well. In fact, if you can skip over any steps with a marking like that, you'll be happier."

"Why are we here?"

"Still good pickins. And it's fun. *Devai.*"

They went through the doorway into a room with a stairwell going upwards. There was once a skylight above, long since shattered and now choked with vines, but the former window let enough light in that Molly's lamp wasn't the only light in the room, and helped wash out the shadows.

Molly started up the stairs, lamp in one hand, stick in the other, knocking each step twice and listening carefully to the sound, her young face grave in the lamplight.

Then, apparently happy with the sound, she took a step up. It became a litany as they slowly ascended the double staircase, tap-tap-step, tap-tap-step, as they climbed the slowly brightening staircase. She skipped any step that sounded like a ripe melon.

Birds had made their home here, and were apparently too high for easy pickings, since the steps were covered in white and black splotches and feathers of many kinds.

The coos of birdsong echoed in counterpoint to Molly and Freeman's tapping. A the second story they began to find steps painted with red boxes. Taking Molly's stretching legs as the proper thing to do, Freeman also avoided the red steps. Up and up they went.

There were two half-stairs per story, and at the third-and-a-half story stairwell, Freeman felt his first true sense of fear since entering. The stairwell was halfway gone, and the platform at the top of where the stairs should have been was cracked and damaged, or at least it looked like that from here. Molly, on the other hand, just grabbed the banister and began climbing the stringer that ran at a thirty-degree angle up into space. Since it appeared safe, Freeman followed when she was up to the fourth story.

"One more floor and you-and-I're there."

"Can we get back down?"

"I can. If I can do it, so can you."

"Sure."

Molly started climbing, and Freeman followed.

"This is a disaster."

"That one generator's on its side, the other ones are all still in place. What do you mean? You can get them running again."

"They're all soaked through. I didn't realize... I didn't realize how much water would pour through here during the summer storms."

"You've got more at the house, though, don't you?"

"I do but... I mean, this is all of our working generators. And it's our only source of electricity. This is... This is bad."

"Freeman, you got them running once, you can do it again. We're all amazed at what you've done. Surely they can't be that hard to fix."

"I don't know. But it also means that the mounts we've been using will have to be redesigned. Which means that the mounts I've got ready up in the shop won't work either."

"You trying to give up there boy?"

"No. No, certainly not that. Just.... alright. Let's leave the cables here, they're fine, they won't have been damaged. But you're right, we need to get these generators back up to the shop. Dust. This is a disaster."

"Freeman. Stop. Did the batteries get damaged?"

"I don't think so."

"And you have more generators?"

"Yes."

"Then you're in better shape than you were this time last year. No one is going to starve. No one is going to die because of this."

"Right. Right. Okay. Let's get the generators off their mounts. Designing new mounts shouldn't be too hard."

"That's the Freeman I know. What first?"

"Take a wrench and let's get the vanes off the generators first. If they're broken, toss 'em, no, they'll burn. You know what? I wanted to get bigger vanes on anyway. You're right, this isn't a problem."

"But the pipes are in the way."

"They're plastic. They'll smash. Or we can cut through them and use them as planters. They don't really carry much water anymore anyhow. And if they are carrying water, well, we'll make sure we break them further up too so that they'll let water into the river upstream. We get some deeper water going right here where the generators are and we'll get more power out of them."

"Alright. Vanes first it is."

"You just work on those, I'll go behind you and get the generators themselves off after I unplug them all."

"Oh, and Freeman? Keep an eye out for rats. Delicious."

"But it's not tomato season yet. How can we eat rats without tomatoes?"

The docks to the north of the bridge embankment in Camden turned out to be a fine source of construction materials.

Sometime, probably a few days before the Hemorrhage—started? finished?—some huge ship had disgorged a pile of huge steel shipping cartons. Most of these cartons stood, undisturbed and full, behind a razor-wire fence at the docks. Some, of course, had been plundered; some showed signs of having been inhabited. Most stood locked shut, cargoes slowly mouldering on the docks.

Few of them were full of useful materials, of course. Some had been full of clothing; these were emptied, their contents sent to the furnaces and papermakers by packhorse and wagon. Some were full of machines; if their purpose could not be determined, the best twentieth of the full number were kept aside for future study, and the rest were sent for recycling. Two, in the center of the mountain of shipping cartons, were full of reams of blank paper, and had lain undisturbed and undamaged since the world ended. These were considered one of the richest finds by any gleaner, anywhere in the world, and the containers were carefully closed up again so that the paper could be parceled out as it was needed.

Whatever their contents, Freeman sent out teams to sandblast each container down to the bare metal once they were emptied. If a container was intact and watertight, with no rust running all the way through the skin, that container was moved by mule team and human power to the center of the bridge. These, suitably modified, of course, would form the backbone of the Fork. Damaged containers were taken apart by different methods depending on what the damage to them had been. Most were cut down the middle, lengthwise, and rolled slowly onto a flatbed carriage, to be towed by a team of mules, again, to the bridge, to form the outer skin and sorting passages of the Fork. The disassembly of the crates was carried out with torch and grinding wheel.

The doors of all the shipping crates were sent to the furnaces for recycling. Any severely damaged crates were disassembled and also sent to the furnaces for recycling.

The crates, of course, couldn't form the Fork itself. But they did serve as a framework in which to build the Fork. Many holes would have to be cut in the shipping cartons, many conveyor belts installed, many furnaces and boilers and far more complex machines added before the Fork could actually make choices, make decisions, and, more to the point, make recycled objects.

But the shipping containers were a good start. Very little steel was needed in the construction of the Camden dwellings, seeing as how the Fork preferred short buildings, and tended to go with concrete and cinderblock construction whenever they could.

Sometimes I-beams were necessary, of course, but the highly-damaged crates that they disassembled and sent back to the foundries were sufficient for those purposes.

Freeman only occasionally supervised the work. His workers, and his lieutenants, well knew what they were doing. He was busy through most of that summer finalizing the plans for the Fork, ensuring that he'd covered as many classes of material as he thought they were likely to find.

All the while, while he dithered with design constraints in the office, the Fork began to take shape on the Ben Franklin Bridge.

"All right. So, what you-and-I're doing here today, is turning over a new bed. Got it?"

"Sure."

"Right. You got your shovel, right? What you-and-I're gonna do is this. If you get a shovelful that's mostly dirt, you drop it in this pile. And if you hit a rock, which you're gonna do, most of the time, you're gonna drop the rocks over in this pile over here. And you-and-I're gonna dig down about six feet."

"But we're planting annuals, and their roots only go down what, four feet?"

"There's a method to the madness, you see, which will become more clear the more we work. Start digging, you'll see how it goes."

...shoveling ensued...

"There's a lot of rocks here."

"Indeed. There used to be a building here. We've been reclaiming the ground, turning it back into the garden that it once was."

"Some sort of biblical metaphor?"

"Biblical?"

"Right. Forgot. Haven't taught you to read enough for the Bible yet, eh?"

"What?"

"Never mind. We'll get there. There's a method to the madness, you'll see as you dig deeper."

"What?"

"Never mind."

...lots of shoveling...

...hours of shoveling, to tell the truth...

"Alright. Now you-and-I've got the bed down to a good six feet, right?"

"Right."

"Well, there's a lot of stones. More brick and concrete than dirt, in truth. So, you-and-I're going deeper. Let's go down another foot, we want the plants to have the best bed possible."

"Sure," Freeman said, panting, "What's another foot?"

...the shoveling was endless...

"Alright. Now the rocks go back."

"What?"

"The point here is to get a good four-foot bed for the annuals. There's about three feet of rocks in that pile. You-and-I're gonna sort the rocks, pack them into the ground in such a way that there isn't much space between each one. Then, the dirt gets sifted through that screen over there, and the rocks that come out get put into the lower layer, and the dirt gets dumped back on top of the rocks. That way, we get a good bed, full of dirt and not rocks. And if it's a little deeper than we expected, that's just fine. The goal here is to get a good bed for the vegetables for next year, and no lie."

"That's terrible."

"That's gardening. Help me dump some rocks in here, and you-and-I'll get them sorted out properly."

“That orchard over there is full of apples. Why are we skirting so far on this side of the street?”

"You got your telescope thingy on you? Hand it over."

“Hmmm. Okay. There she is. See that maple tree right there? Look a little to the left of it.”

"I don't see... ohhhhhh. That's a big cat."

"And two big kittens."

"Yeah. What are they?"

“Lions. They live inside that building and sun themselves in their little private orchard. And keep your voice down. They won't bother us if you-and-I don't bother them, but they're just one more reason why we keep spears up at all times."

“Where did they come from?”

“Same place as the zebras, same place as the nutria. All the animals either escaped the zoo or were let out from the zoo during the Hemorrhage. Dunno which one it was. But there's all sorts of animals around the city that, well, really shouldn't be here. Other big cats. Some birds. Rumors of a tiger in the west of the city past Upenn."

“And they don't bother people?”

“They don't bother people who don't walk into their homes. You always have to be careful. And watch how you bend over to pick things up in the streets; if you're in the open tigers will attack if they think you're prey. Up on two legs, you're fine; lean over to pick something up and stay that way too long they'll think you're a deer. And deer are definitely supper."

"Wait a second, though, aren't lions from like the jungle or whatever? Isn't it too cold here for them? My grandmother loved to talk about all the animals from the old days..."

"Winters aren't as cold as they used to be, and I guess they find places out from the wind. I mean, you've seen the elephants around, you've seen the giraffes; they're here, and they do their thing, and we ignore them, and they probably just find places they can hide out from the winter storms. I don't know where that is. What's that pink stuff you see in buildings called again?"

"Fiberglass."

"Right, can't you just see her bedding down in a pile of fiberglass to wait out the winter, burrowing down inside it to stay warm?"

"I guess. Seems pretty unlikely to me, though."

"Maybe that's why there are so few of them. You'll find them around sometimes in the winter, dead and frozen. Fishtown collects them, I sold one last year for a goodly pile of grain to Fishtown at the markets."

"She's looking at us."

"Let's get going. I don't want her thinking she's threatened."

"Good plan."

"At least we've got the harbor seals in the river. The meat ain't great but it's better than rat, and the tallow does a fine job in the oil lamps, much better than corn or soya oil."

"True that. Oh good, she's ignoring us."

"Let's go get some deer. They don't bite back."

"Alright, you, let's show you around the place. This, obviously, is the farm, and these two bitches here are Stella and Bainbridge. They've got a few pups over in the toolshed, and don't worry that they're growling at you now, that's what they do with strangers. They'll get used to you soon enough."

"They don't seem too friendly."

"Eventually they will be. And you smell bad, anyhow. They'll like you better once we get you cleaned up. Just not right now. And for strangers they're not meant to be. Come check out the house. We've got these two buildings here."

"But the one is outside the wall."

"The stairwell on the first two floors is gone. We've got access to the top two floors from that exterior stair and platform that goes between them. It's about as safe as buildings come; no one can get upstairs to where we live. Sometimes we'll get a hollering vagrant or something in the basement, but we ignore them. Anyways, out there in the field is Steve, Crissa, and Byron. Crissa is Jase's woman, Byron is the group's hunter, and Steve is the butcher. Steve ain't a bad shot, either; he'll help bring in meat as well as butchering it. Jase, as I'm sure you figured out, runs the place.

"Hey Lara, meet Freeman. Freeman's moving in with us."

"Hey Freeman. Molly, do we have the food to do it?"

"Freeman knows how to preserve fruit, so I think we'll be able to do it. We always get more apples than we can eat. That should help."

"Should. We'll see."

"True enough. Anyways, Lara's the cook, and if you're wanting to use the kitchen for any of your preserves, get in good with her. She's hard to get along with."

"Outta my kitchen if you're gonna disrespect me—you look worse for wear, son."

"Watch it with that spoon!"

"Shoo! I've got some cooking to do. Git!—and get him cleaned up."

"This is the map of the city."

"This is..."

"Yeah. You'll figure it out eventually, but this marks where and when fruit we can eat comes in. Fruit's a, well, a thing in this city. You'll figure it out when it comes along. No one has private orchards, we all just carefully share what's out there wild.

"That door goes to the root cellar. That's where we keep all the vegetables we harvest for the winter, and also dry the meat. We eat a lot of meat. I like vegetables better, but what can you do?"

"Oh, there's ways."

"Good to hear. So, up the steps here, that's Crissa's weaving room, she's got her loom and wheel set up there. She makes all our clothes. That over there is her and Jase's room, and let me tell you it's the warmest in the house. Mine's just over top of it, and we get some of the heat up there.

"Outside that window, below there is the greenhouse you saw."

"The greenhouse is something else, it is."

"That right there is Steve's room, that's Byron's, and that's ours."

"Where's mine?"

"You're with me. No objections, right? It'll be better with two, warmer and stuff. Do you mind?"

"Um. Not at all."

Feet screaming, boots snapping and shattering flat-laying glass behind him, Freeman ran towards the rusted superstructure of Liberty Place One, the complex paths of the labyrinth of glass slowly collapsing into a iron-red framework. The leaning sheets of glass ended at the steel frame of the building; the floors and former shops of the building stretched in front of him as he skidded to a halt in a rain of shards of smoked glass.

Off to the left, a bundle of fabric that might have been a derelict shifted. Freeman looked for the steps while keeping his attention behind him, fearing pursuers whose arrival was simply a matter of time.

It took a few seconds for Freeman to orient himself. There was a double metal stairwell in front of him. He knew from multiple gleaning trips through here that they were missing steps. He started moving to the left, moving through the building widdershins. There was an intact, if not functional, stairwell on the east side of the building; as he was on the west, and was eventually trying to get north, widdershins was the proper direction to turn.

Scotto and the rest would show up soon enough, he knew, and the only way to dodge them was to keep running, and hopefully drop some sort of trap on top of them.

But what kind of trap to drop here? He'd planned for the glass labyrinth, and for the alley maze, and for the bridge, but he hadn't planned to have to run through the tunnels.

He had no plan for flight through this dense mass of architecture.

He was three-quarters of the way across the northern face of the building when something told him to roll. He dropped about a split second before an arrow went through where his head would have been.

The spent arrow shattered against the tile walls of the building. He swung back up and looked to the west; Scotto and Lars were standing over near where he had come into the building. They were shouting; echoes from the well in the center of the ground floor made the words meaningless. Neither of them were carrying a map of the underground in their head, though, and that was one up on his front.

Freeman came around the corner just as Lars nocked an arrow. Freeman kept running—a moving target was harder to hit than a still target. He approached the steps that, by convention, led downwards, and paused, and Lars let an arrow fly. Freeman immediately darted downwards on the steps, letting Lars' arrow skip across the marble of the floor. He leapt the last few steps down, and quickly ran under the overhang that Lars and Scotto were now perched upon.

Even though he knew the way, he let his brain shut off and just followed the arrows pointing the way to the subway. Truly, any second now he'd be required, under pain of death, to find his way through the tunnels flawlessly; for now, he was happy to just follow the terrible, ancient signs to the subway station.

The underground here was full of shops, stands, restaurants. He could hardly imagine a city with enough people to support this, but it was here. Would it have been important if his goal hadn't been to build a city that could support this? Probably not.

Nonetheless, now, staring at what his goal was, his overworked heart knew that this was what he had been looking for just a week ago.

Now, he didn't know what he was looking for at all. Except that it likely had nothing to do with the Fork. And not just because the Fork's cavalry and gendarmes and workers were trying to kill him.

"Do you remember when this was simpler?"

The wash of meaningless sound caresses Freeman's body. He looks down and over at Molly, voice low, pitched only to carry to her ears.

Molly sighs a rolling breath. "Yeah, I do. But what are we supposed to do? The Collective has a food surplus even in lean years, which this is supposedly one of. Our time of plenty is thanks to you and Steve, and, unfortunately, also thanks to the Fork. No matter how they help our food supplies, I still hate that you work for them. It would be better if you were working only for us, but you're bringing in more food than anyone else. So, would I prefer that we could be sitting, and perhaps necking, while listening to music, like we used to be? Yes, yes I would. But we can't be.

"Fishtown is dead. The Sprawlers were only ever a real problem for us in their opposition to Fishtown; as soon as we moved into the Chestnut Street building, they stopped being an issue. Then they stopped being a power entirely. The burning of the Spectra proved that; even if it wasn't arson, that was their bar, and it shouldn't have been allowed to burn. They showed their weakness, and that left only us and the Fork and the remnants of Fishtown. But hey, the Fishtowners hardly count as a power, at this point, so it's us and the Fork. And you work for them, while being one of us. On one level they push, and make themselves stronger. On the other level, they give us food like dust-loving fanatics, which allows us strength in opposition to them. And we make sure that we can keep up with their donations in case it all falls apart.

"But that isn't your question. So, do I remember what it was like before now? Of course. But we have more important things to do, like making sure our little corner of the city survives properly. Note the qualifier, please. Survives properly. If the Fork had their choice, they'd smack us down. But they don't. Why? Cause you live here, that's the only reason."

"Why do you think the Fork would try to ruin us?"

"Come on, Freeman, look at what they've done. Two years before they show up, Fishtown starts pulling back into itself. The year before they show up, Haddon's raiders stopped being a problem. The year they come, the off-property haunts of the Southies and the Nor'easters start burning down. Things are happening quickly in this city, and things haven't happened this quickly in anyone's memory. Now they're over there in Camden, building their sterile new glowing beautiful city, all to some sort of central plan, and all to one specification.

"The way things are going, I'm surprised that one of these Full Moon parties haven't been attacked, and I'm pretty sure that the only reason why is that you come to them habitually. If they could make you stay back from one of them, I'd put down a barrel of moonshine on the house burning down sometime in the course of the party. And it would, of course, be accidental, just like the Spectra, just like the Brewery, and just like Smithson's. But it would burn just the same."

"I still don't think we're a big enough group that the Fork cares about us."

"You're still so naive, Freeman." She tiptoed up to kiss his cheek. "It's beautiful, and it's one of the things that I love about you, your trustingness, but it's dangerous, and it's going to get us in trouble one of these days."

The South Street Gleaners' mule was named Sal. Steve, who was the guitarist of the group, and had an excellent memory for lyrics despite his semiliteracy, had managed to shout down Kevin and Jase when they wanted other names, and forced this one onto them. Sal had been with the Gleaners a long, long time, longer than anyone but the three of them, having been acquired well before the summer Molly joined up. And the Gleaners didn't begin to thrive until after Molly, and later Freeman, joined up.

After the harvest had been brought in, and there was some time and warmth before the winter came, Freeman and Steve went out to scour the city for batteries, bringing Sal, a cart, and hammers and crowbars.

The rusted hulks of automobiles sat around the city streets and in parking garages around town. Most of them were completely stripped and useless, but some of them still had batteries—not that they'd held a charge for years— and if they were inaccessible by normal means, the crowbars would get them out.

The stash of books that Freeman had found years ago showed the proper operation of the vehicles' hoods. Most of the cars on the streets were so rusted through that they simply had to punch holes in the hoods with the crowbars, sometimes yielding a battery underneath, and sometimes not. Sometimes the batteries were melted, sometimes cracked; they took these too. If the plastic was damaged, they'd be that much easier to get into.

While they worked, they sang, their breath steaming in the cold air. While they walked, they sang. *Me and a mule named Sal, out on the Erie Canal*. Whatever the Erie Canal was, they sang the song anyway.

The parking garages were dark, even though they tried to pick the ones with open sides. The cars in these buildings weren't as rusted as the ones out on the streets, and many of their hoods were actually openable, though they still had to use the crowbars sometimes. The violent opening of the cars echoed strangely through the tilted ramps and ceilings of the building. There tended to be more batteries in these cars than there were in the cars on the streets, which Steve and Freeman were thankful for. As the day progressed, they slowly filled Sal's cart with the black boxes, black boxes that had been useless since the Hemorrhage years ago. Boxes that would never be useful again, but would yield up the materials to start bringing the world back to life. And, incidentally, to allow them all to eat more frequently, and hopefully better.

The theory they were operating under was sound. Homemade batteries ran sewing machines, record players, pumps, and presses at their home on South Street. The time that Freeman had invested into fixing machines and making the new batteries had led them to have more free time than anyone else in the city, meaning they had more time for better gleaning. This gleaning, however, wasn't for themselves, not directly.

This was for trade.

No one else in the city knew how to make batteries; no one else had learned to repair machines. No one else had a generator. The Gleaners were going to go into business, supplying electricity to the city of Philadelphia. And the Gleaners, and by extension Freeman, were going to become rich.

The sun was rising before them as Freeman and his father drove the family wagon out of Philadelphia across the Free Lane of the Ben Franklin Bridge on the early October morning. It had been a good year of trading; the wagon was full of new tools, bolts of particularly fine cloth, salt, potash and sulfur and saltpeter. Freeman's mother slept in the back of the wagon; they were all tired from the ruckus of the market, and she had drawn the short straw, which meant she got to sleep late today.

"Good year at the market."

"Sure was."

"Got quite a deal on the saltpeter, huh?"

"Sure did."

"You're quiet."

"It's early."

"Not thinking about that girl, are you?"

"What?" Freeman, who'd been doing just that, jerked his head at his father.

"That girl. Molly. Thinking about her?"

"A little."

"Don't think too much about her, that's what I'd do. The girls in the city are fun, but you're only going to be here a week out of every year. You're from the farm, and you belong on the farm; she's from the city, and she belongs there. There was a city girl I fancied when I was your age, and it doesn't work. I'm sure that I'm happier with your mother than I would have been with that girl."

"Who was she?"

"Merchant Harry's wife."

"That harridan? Dust. You fancied her?"

"Don't tell your mother. Yes, I did. She was about as good looking back then as your Molly, and about as fun to play with as your Molly seems. But city folk and country folk ain't meant to mix for too long; it's like water and ghee. You can stir them up, and they seem to be mixed, but let them stand, and they'll separate. And there's no use keeping the bowl stirred at all times—takes too much energy that's better spent farming."

"I guess."

"What all did you find in the buildings? What with one thing and the other, I didn't get to see what you had in that bag of yours."

"I don't even know what it all is. No more of those 'record players,' but something that just looks like it needs greasing called a slide rule, and some more of those lenses, and a couple of books that aren't too badly damaged, and then a bunch of machines that I don't even know what they do. But there's a lot of copper wire in them."

"Well, you'll have your winter spare time cut out for you, won't you?"

"Sure will."

Then they were silent as his father steered the horse-drawn wagon around a gaping hole in the surface of the bridge. Freeman just sat and thought about Molly, no matter what his father's advice was. Cause that kissing thing she had done with him last night had been the best thing he'd ever done.

Freeman was surrounded by little cups, sheets of paper, sketches drawn with pencil. The cups were labeled, labels referring back to the sketches, all describing which screws came from which holes, which piece attached to which part of the arm, which lump of machinery attached to which piece of metal or plastic. The metal boxes he'd bought from the trader in Philadelphia the previous autumn were completely disassembled, and he didn't know what to do with what.

It was obvious, looking at the boxes, that they were all broken. It just wasn't obvious why they were broken.

For example: in this one to the left, there was a skein of multicolored strings that were all ripped through. So it would seem to make sense that they pushed or pulled something, and that when they were ripped, it couldn't push or pull anymore. But there were two problems. First, the small device the ropes went to was anchored with screws to the bottom plate of the box, and didn't seem able to be pushed or pulled anywhere.

Second, the ropes were made of metal coated in some sort of solid greasy stuff; Freeman had never before heard of metal ropes.

Too many other questions: each box had a, well, a device in the center, a device that was a solid block with the ropes running into it, and a pole that stuck out of the top of the center. A device that in one case spun and in the other two cases was frozen in place. Other questions, and less answers: what was the piece of green board with all the things stuck into it? What did all the small cylindrical things, with metal sticking out of them and different patterns of banding on them, do? Okay, so the one green board that was split in half probably was broken, but could it be fixed? Or could one green board be swapped for a different board? Freeman didn't know, but he knew that the nibs of metal sticking out of the bottom felt good under his thumbs.

The small box, with the point sticking out of it, that affixed with a screw-mount to the arm. What did it do? Why were there ropes of sticking out of it, of definitely fixed length, that would never push or pull anything, and weren't there to keep the assembly in place?

What did it all do?

Freeman figured that asking what it all did was not what had to be dealt with right now. What he had to do right now was to take the pieces of each of these devices that looked to be in the best condition, and reassemble one of the boxes, putting the best-looking of each part into it. Just follow the directions, the directions he'd written down, and try to make something whole out of this assemblage of pieces.

At least the one thingy that still spun had its ropes intact. He had no interest in figuring out how to tie ropes that small, and that slippery, together.

"Morning, Freeman."

"Good morning, Drake."

"So what do you have for us today?"

Freeman gestured behind him at the small pile of equipment, equipment that he'd thoroughly checked over the night before. "Got a few things you might be interested in, since you wanted to see the old technology I've made work."

"Let's see what you've got."

"Alright. This is called a record player, as near as we can tell. How familiar are you with mass storage media?"

"Somewhat. Explain."

Freeman fiddled with connections as he talked. "There were other types of mass storage media, back in the old days: acetate film, CDs, DVDs, magnetic tape, USB drives, and a plethora more. Of these, some have controllers too hard to restore, like the USB drives, and the others have decayed over time. Acetate film is destroyed when it gets wet, magnetic tape can't handle temperature variation, and the various 'Ds' all have backings that have worn out; when moisture finally penetrates them, they rot. Records, on the other hand, are collections of grooves cut in this black material called vinyl. Some of these records have been warped by heat, others crushed by falling debris; some are scratched and some are so clogged with mildew and mold and dirt and dust that they never play right. But some were recoverable."

"Other people in other cities have found similar things, you know."

"Really?"

"Yes. Not many, and not many know as much about the different storage types as you do. But do go on."

"Well, as near as I can tell, you can't store much information on a record. But because the information is stored large enough that you can actually feel the information with your fingertips, a remarkable amount has survived the Hemorrhage. Like so." And he turned on the player. Salsa music filled the room.

"Very nice. How are you powering it?"

Freeman grabbed a damaged box from the pile. "Mrs. Goody managed to damage this battery, so I figured to cut it open and show you. As you can see, there are eight separate cells in the battery. Each puts out a certain amount of energy. In each battery, which we make ourselves, we find bottles of approximately similar size, make new plates for them out of the old, scrubbed plates from automobile batteries, and fill the containers with jellied acid. The we charge them on generators powered by wind, and by the water in the sewers after rainstorms."

"Any generators?"

"You expect me to give up all my secrets all at once?"

"A sharp mind indeed. These have given you an edge over the rest of the town?"

"Not these. These."

And Freeman flipped on the two electric lights carefully scavenged and carried into Camden.

Drake's face lit up with the bulbs.

The market at Penn's Landing was not an everymoon market for the Gleaners. The market ran from the day of the waxing quarter of each moon, during the warm moons, to two days before the day of the full moon. It wasn't the sort of market that the Gleaners often had call to go to, except for around the harvests.

Unlike the market at City Hall, there were no sellers of roast meat, of small amounts of cloth, of bread. The market at Penn's Landing was for bulk sales. Ships would set in at Penn's Landing, where the water was deep enough for the boats that would ply the coast and the rivers, and people would come with samples and amounts of, well, whatever they produced. Sometimes, it was cloth; sometimes dyes, tools, arrows; the ships would bring in spices, other cloths, animals, even sugar.

While it wasn't generally a good market for the Gleaners, sometimes it could be. Molly would watch, on the first day of the market, for boats with tall sails coming in with, well, a limp. She could always see it, and could never explain to Freeman properly what it was. But on those rare days she'd be down at the docks almost instantly, ready to meet and chat up the sailors of boats missing crew, missing a captain, or damaged in some way; those boats were the ones where bargains could be had if one was willing and knew what to look for.

Even Jase had to let Molly just stand back. He didn't love it—most bulk purchases or sales he brokered—but she'd bring amazing things back from the boats for grains on the bushel. Sometimes it would be a load of belt buckles, sometimes a cartload of tallow.

Any way it went, it would always be useful later. Like the bushels of buttons that were a straight trade for grain. Freeman was sure that some First Mate, recently promoted, had to answer to a sick captain for that trade.

The limping boats rarely came back to the city. Whether because of what they lost on the trades, or because of piracy or storms, or because of whatever made them flail down the river in the first place, Freeman had no clear idea.

You had to be careful at the Penn's Landing market, though. Freeman loved going to it, but stories were told. Never get on the boats. Never accept a drink. Always be in a group of at least two, preferably more. Press-ganging was common, or so it was said; either way, people would sometimes disappear with the boats after the market days.

Whether that was because they were press-ganged or families just said that to cover up missing sons or daughters, well, who really knew?

Molly had to be doubly careful, of course; she'd have a second on all her watches, and their most important job was to head back to South Street immediately and get one or two of the larger men to get down there immediately. There had never been a problem, but... her skills at both trading and gleaning made her too valuable to risk. For Freeman, there was no such calculus of risk: she simply couldn't be lost.

They never went to that market was at night. Whatever happened down there after sundown, well, that was when the roast-meat sellers and the whores and the thieves would converge on the dirty, disgusting watering holes that only opened one week a moon during the warm months. When fires would leap and the Gleaners would sometimes sneak down to the roofs of buildings that were known to be safe to see, from a distance, what parties they were too weak to join.

The Full Moon Parties were better, or at least that's what they told each other.

The July evening was mild; the thunderstorm that lit up the city earlier had blown past. Freeman stood on the wet roadbed of the Walt Whitman and looked out across the city, and the new city, and the bridge, and the Fork.

The setting sun cast red and orange light across the twinned cities; light glinted off of fragments of windows in Philadelphia, and the glass-filled windows of the Camden waterfront shone with the sun.

Even after the Spectra burned down, the community of homes on the Walt Whitman still clung to its marginal existence. It had gotten shabbier in the last few years; Freeman realized, as he stood clinging to a support cable, how long it had been since he had come here to look over the cities. Most of the actual carpentry and masonry had fallen into disrepair; where wood and brick used to reign supreme, now lean-tos and houses of layered plastic sheeting were more the rule than the exception. Each winter must see a serious changeover in the property holders. Still, the property was wanted; the reasons had changed. While the view was still one of the best in the city, what you could see had changed. And it was far from the reach of the Fork. For now.

Philadelphia's noisy, dangerous, living vibrancy had changed in the last few years. Where people were once loud and boisterous, keeping the fear of danger and death and rape at bay by going out in large groups, keeping the noise up to keep prowlers away, movement was now more furtive, more secretive. Houses were made to look more run-down to keep burglars away. These changes had been slow enough, and Freeman busy enough, that he didn't realize the silence that had descended over Philadelphia in the last years. Had it really been five years since the Collective he knew ended? Six years since—*a clenched fist slamming against a windowpane*—everything had changed?

Freeman shook his head to clear it, for clarity was what he sought tonight. What had he wrought in the last half decade?

Camden was a cleared black, blank, flat field. Rising from the field, in the center of the city, surrounded by squares of farmland, were the new apartments and homes, streets and factories and docks that the Fork had built. The buildings were fresh and square and undecorated; born of mass-produced blocks in the furnaces and built into stamped-out, soulless squares by the teams of navvies.

Philadelphia soaked the sunlight away invisibly while Camden gleamed in it. Except for the scar, the gap in the buildings fanning out from the base of the bridge. The hole in the city, moving closer to where the heart used to be. And between the two cities, the Ben Franklin Bridge, rusty and blue, the bridge that used to connect them, and the Fork. Once, not long ago, horses had galloped down the wide avenue between the towers, pulling wagons and carts and drivers, dodging gaps in the disintegrating roadbed of the free lane down the center of the bridge. Now, the bridge was only passable to walkers, and even walkers had to carefully step around rust-rotted holes in the walkways above the roadbed.

Now, in gleaming contrast to the rust of the bridge itself, the Fork stretched across it, the segmented, smoking body of the vast machine stretching from Philadelphia, from the scar, causing the scar, all the way to Camden.

The bridge had become secondary to the vehicle that rode on it; the bridge was completely suborned by the Fork.

As was Freeman.

"What the dust's going on?"

"Didn't you hear the bell? There's raiders over the fences. Grab a spear and let's move it."

"Dust!"

"Got torches?"

"I got 'em. It's goddamn raining? Who raids in the dusting rain?"

"People who think defenses slip. Shit—get the hell out of here."

"I got your back, I got his back, damn, what are you thinking coming in this shit?"

"I dunno what they're thinking. I got the rope, lets tie this one up. Don't know how many there are. Stand to my back while I do this."

"Sure thing."

"Shit!"

"You okay?"

"Get your goddamn spear, I can't get mine out of this guy."

"Damn! Put your foot on his chest and pull."

"Right. You almost done tying? Fucker!"

"He cut you bad?"

"Just in the leg where I was trying to get the spear out. Thanks for the second blow. I was hoping not to kill, but they're trying to."

—hoofbeats sundering the world—

"Can't have too much mercy with these fuckers."

"Who sent them?"

"Oh, they could be allied with anyone. Or, they could just think the compound was unguarded. Lord knows we do our best to make it look like the place only has a few people in it, and not much worth stealing. Let's check the gardens, Molly and Steve have the gates."

"Steve! How many got in?"

"Don't know. At least four. We've got two tied up. None got in the house that we saw. But there's a problem."

"What's that."

"Jase. They. Yeah. He's. Over by the fence."

"Oh shit. Jase? JASE!"

"He can't hear you, Byron. They got him. They got him bad."

"We can't stay here. Are there more of them? We don't know if we got them all."

"Crissa's on the door, she'll ring if something happens. Go for the garden."

"Good plan."

"Shitfuck. The garden's..."

"We've already harvested most of it. What grain we didn't get would be ruined by this rainstorm anyway. But this means there's another around, be careful."

"Got my eyes open. These fuckers ain't—there he is!"

"Good shot."

"Thanks. Too close to the window for my taste. You see any others?"

"No. Let's drag the bodies out."

"What about Jase?"

"... I. I don't know. You-and-I had best bring him inside."

"What are we going to do?"

"The lesser consensus stands. Can we all stand, for the greater consensus? This is important enough."

All twelve people in the room stood, some more slowly than others. Then, the course set, everyone started moving.

Molly picked out Steve, Kevin, James, and Freeman to accompany her to the Chestnut Street compound, and set everyone not on guard duty to start packing up the two carts that Sal would draw behind him. It was a good day to start the move; the rain had stopped and the sky was mostly clear, the wind was low, there was no sign of rain for days ahead.

Freeman and Steve grabbed bows and spears for the group. There was the possibility that taking the Chestnut Street compound would occur in some sort of struggle; not with the Fishtowners, they were out, but with someone else—maybe the Sprawlers, maybe the Southies—who wanted the rich ground that they were abandoning.

Lord knew, everyone in the city should want it. But the Gleaners were in the best spot to take it.

He left instructions for no one to touch his workshop, instructions which people were quick to agree to, and they set out to cover the fifteen blocks to Chestnut Street.

They moved quickly and silently. The only noise they made was the clacking of their shoes on the broken streets. After the frenzy of activity at their home on South, the streets seemed both lifeless and listless; though there were people out, they wandered seemingly aimlessly, at least compared to the Gleaners' purposeful walk.

They reached Chestnut Street, and the gate in the wall was standing open. None of them had ever been inside. This was quickly rectified. The remains of the gardens had been torched, of course, that was only to be expected. The gate hardware was missing, and they propped slabs of wood up against the doorway; Steve stayed behind at the gate to guard it. The rest of them quickly fanned out to figure out what the lay of the place was.

A shouting derelict had already moved in, but Kevin and Freeman were quickly able to bundle him up and shove him out the door. Freeman passed him a chunk of bread; it quickly disappeared into one pocket or another in his greasy outfit. It did not quiet his noises one bit.

Unsurprisingly, the Fishtowners had taken everything they could strip from the place. Old light fixtures, wall sockets, doors, windows, furniture; everything even potentially useful that wasn't part of the landscape was removed. The tall stone walls, with busted bottles sticking out from concrete in the tops, and the brown brick buildings, and the gardens dug through the street; these things still stood tall and stretched wide.

There were forty Fishtowners who had lived here, and now the twelve members of the Gleaners were going to take it over.

Which was going to be okay. Word had spread about Freeman's batteries, and the things that they could do with them, and people were slowly wanting to join up with them. Here, they'd be able to slowly, slowly, take people in, and make their little group larger, stronger, more of a power in the city.

This was fertile ground in which their little consensus could grow.

The dust on the floor of the fourth-story landing burst up around their feet like water from a puddle.

"Alright. Tap carefully; the floor is soft and it could go, but we're light enough that it shouldn't be a problem."

The remains of a door in front of them, rotted wood spilling in a damp brown waterfall across the entry. The landing was cracked down the middle, fragmentary concrete and rebar stretching like teeth downwards, apparently the source of the rubble on the stairs below. The building stretched several stories higher, but the stairwell leading up to the fourth floor was mostly gone; what wasn't gone was inaccessible from here.

"What is this place?"

"I dunno what they did here. But there's stuff worth collecting. Don't fill your bag, though, 'cause it'll knock you off balance when you climb down. Just take a few things that look useful." Molly unclipped the lamp from her belt, the snap loud in the emptiness, and headed into the open doorframe. Freeman followed her closely, tapping the stick on the ground more often than necessary.

Molly ignored the contents of the first room and made a right turn, stepping over another pile of splinters and into another room. This room was well-lit, light and wind coming though the burst windows on the street-side of the building. And inside was a workshop.

Freeman instantly understood why Molly came here. Tapping carefully, he trod lightly over to a workbench against the wall. Its surface was bent, but intact; there were many discs of dusty glass spilling from a drawer marked "blanks." He wiped one clean; it was both the thickest was both the thickest and clearest glass he'd ever seen. He set the blank down and kept looking. Here, there was a drill on a stand, a grinding wheel; he tried a quick spin, but it was frozen. Here, a collection of discs of glass carved into a bent shape. He picked one up and looked through it; the world bent weirdly. Molly walked over and rummaged, picking up a disc curved on both sides. "Come here, look." She walked to the window.

"Hold the glass in the sunlight above this piece of paper, and watch."

A small spot of light appeared on the paper, which began, incredulously, to smoke and char. "What's doing that?"

"Dunno. But you can use them to light fires. The ones curved on both sides work better, but you can use a lot of them to do it. You should take some for your family, they're really useful. My family sells them sometimes, when I can get up here."

"Are they good for trading?"

"Oh yeah. And since we don't farm too much we need to make as many good trades as we can during the market seasons to eat enough. We can gather some food during the summer but so few things last that you can gather…"

"Yeah. And you can only eat so much jam."

"Jam?"

"Your family doesn't preserve fruit as jam?"

"No. How do you do that?"

"I'll give you a jar when we get back to the wagon," Freeman said recklessly. "It's the least I can do for showing me this."

Freeman jumped the turnstile as if it were any other piece of rubbish in his way.

Once he was into the station, he slowed down. Scotto and the rest had no idea what his plan was, so he had to move quietly now; from this station, he could transfer to three different underground railways. Three different tunnels. Three different escape routes. He hoped that they'd think he was following one of the lines that went under the Schuylkill river; he also hoped that the dirt on the floor was hard enough that it wouldn't take his footprints and make him trackable.

His side was itching. He reached up to scratch it and he was suddenly on fire. A hiss of pain escaped his lips; his hand came away wet and sticky. He pumped the hand flashlight, for just a bit of dim light, and saw his hand was slicked wet and red. The glass he slid across when Scotto shot at him must have sliced him. No time for that now.

He started walking, pumping the flashlight slowly, careful to make as little noise as possible. Half-imagined, half-shadow shapes spun out of the darkness at him as he walked. Every so often, the click and scrape of rats echoed strangely; splashes from a hidden pool of water, noises from behind, more human noises. Either the Fork or someone who lived here.

He walked on. For the first time since he started running, he finally started asking himself: was he making the right choice? Plodding in the almost-absolute dark, split only by the weak beam of his flashlight, this seemed the right place to ask himself. Up until now, the future had been his choice. Up until now, the path he walked was in his control.

Now, while there were other possibilities of path, he was staring at the path he was walking, and there were no forks he could control.

He realized that he was using the wrong tense. He had made his choice. Had he made the right choice? That was the question.

A yawning hole opened up out of the darkness; the septic smell of the sewer assaulted him. He turned left, quickly, circled the hole in the ground. Then climbed the steps, and there was a sign in front of him, silently shouting "Market Street Station" into the darkness.

Alright. Down to the tracks. He looked behind him, and saw the brief glimmer of a lantern behind him. How were they following him? Was it the hand light? Was he not moving fast enough? Did it matter at this point?

He had no choice now. Down to the subway, go south one station, retrieve his cache of food and equipment, and get across the Chestnut Street Bridge, into the territory controlled by the Upenners.

There was sunlight here, where shafts, slightly clogged with leaves and rubbish, let air and light down into the subway. He skirted the edges of the pools of brightness, using this light to see and letting his cramping hand rest. He moved quickly, he needed to get back to his plan before he could pull anything else on his pursuers.

There was a train at the subway station. He avoided looking in the windows, knowing what he would see in there. Even after all this time, the skeletons bothered him.

And then he passed the train's engine, conductor still in his blue uniform. He could never look away from the conductor, who steered his ship with no choice of destination.

And then he was down on the tracks and moving towards Chestnut Street.

"So, I've been thinking..."

"Oh Freeman, it's too late for thinking. It's time for sleep."

"No, hold on, let me try. We've got some machines working, right?"

"Yes..."

"Well, I can make more, or fix more, of all the kinds. So, um, maybe we should think about selling them."

"Freeman, that's a terrible idea."

"Really?"

"Yes."

"Why?"

"Oh God, any number of reasons. We're here between Fishtown and the Sprawlers and we have to lay low, right? If we start introducing new things into the markets we will be absorbed by one or the other of those groups. And after what happened to Jase, do you really want us attacked again?"

"Word's already getting out. You heard Haddon's men. If they knew, Fishtown knows."

"I'm sure. But, we're doing good in the city now. People will leave us alone since we dealt with Haddon. They'll be scared enough that they won't come around. But if people think we have a surplus of machines they will come and take it. But, that's not the real reason."

"What is it then?"

"Freeman, if you made a bow and some arrows and they were used to kill another human, would you feel responsible for it?"

"Um. I don't know."

"Well, you would be. What if it wasn't in self-defense?"

"Uh."

"Right. You made a tool and intended it to be used for hunting. Instead it was used for violence against other humans. And it could be used against you, right?"

"I guess?"

"And that man had that bow because you sold it to him."

"Okay. But lots of people make bows."

"But no one else has running machines, no one else has electricity. You would be solely responsible for handing someone, say, a pump large enough that they could set it up in the sewers and erode someone's wall. We all know how little defense of the sewers there is. And you'd be responsible because it couldn't happen without you, whatever your intentions were. When any tool is used for ill the builder and the user share responsibility. And your tools, frankly, are potentially a lot more dangerous than a bow and arrow."

"I see what you're saying."

"We're doing well right now. With what we produce from your tools we'll be doing better than ever. We simply don't need to do it. And we don't need to change the power balance in the city right now. We need to lay low, and we need to appear to be doing well while not appearing to thrive, otherwise we will be attacked again. And we don't need another attack."

"Alright. I'll go with you on this."

"Thanks, Freeman. I'm glad you agree. Now, get the candle."

The Gleaners had always known that one day they might have to move quickly to a new home. In preparation for this they kept crates in the basement of the compound on South Street. All through the day they brought the crates upstairs and loaded everything they could into them. If something was fragile, it was packed in clothes, or empty cloth sacks, or hay from Sal's feedpile. The feed had to be moved too, of course.

There was a lot to move. Enough food, and firewood, to get twelve people through the winter and early spring moons. Books. Clothes. Furniture. Beds. Chairs. Even the stones of the firepit itself. The kitchen container garden, packed in hay to protect the fragile herbs from the cold. And all the tools and raw materials that were kept in the workshop. And the greenhouse.

The vast majority of their possessions had to be moved today and tomorrow; likely, no one would sleep tonight. It had to be obvious to the streets that something was happening, some balance of power in Center City was shifting, and when power shifts there's always something for an enterprising gleaner to grab. They knew this well, for this had been their life source for years. Suddenly, they found themselves on both sides of the fence, picking up what Fishtown dropped while doing their damnedest to not drop anything themselves.

Freeman got back from Chestnut Street after unloading the first wagonload of materials. The outside stocks were being moved first, while there was light, to conserve oil and candles for moving the things from inside. As soon as he and Steve drove the wagon to its parking spot, Crissa immediately began filling the wagon with bales of hay.

"Don't just sit there, do something. There's bags of grain piled by the door, start loading."

"Dust, girl, we just got here. Calm down."

"Too much to do, not enough light, and I don't like the way the clouds look."

Freeman lifted the first bag. "Crissa, you always think it's gonna rain when there are clouds. It doesn't feel like rain."

"It's gonna rain, mark my words. We need to get this stuff moved, and like *ligne nu*."

The first bag was in the cart, Freeman was going for the second, but diverted himself to meet Lana at the door and take a sack from her. "Has Crissa been like this all day?"

"Isn't she always?"

Freeman snorted a laugh and headed back to the wagon. "Even Lana thinks you should calm down, Crissa."

"I'll get calm when everything's moved. I can't believe we're moving after the equinox. It's a bad sign to be moving now, when the world is shutting down for the winter. What if Fishtown is leaving because the roof leaks? Or collapsed?"

"I was just there, the roof is intact. It might leak, but then, so does ours. It's going to be good. Don't worry about it." Freeman was immediately seized with the certainty that Crissa had voted against the move. But true to form for their group, now that the decision was made, she was working as hard as she could to bring the decision about.

The wagon was filling rapidly. But they were dropping grain sacks and bales of hay into it, they could pile it up as high as Sal could pull it, which was high enough. And the fewer trips they took, the better off they'd be. Freeman kept stacking.

The geometry of the city had changed, since the Hemorrhage. Here, a building had fallen over, here a building sunk stories into the ground, here the engulfing ground had risen. The land once changed by humans was now changing what humans had wrought; a new spring feeding a new stream that now ran linear through a gutter, here a tunnel collapse forming a lake in the middle of a street, here a forest spiraling out from where a park had once stood.

Here, in the city, the present, past, and future intermingled with no respect for one another, and no boundaries between them.

Freeman walked down Third Street, away from his home in the compound on South Street, clambering over fallen-down buildings, looking for someplace that looked worth checking out. The chores at the compound were done enough for the day, and it was midsummer, sunny and warm. It was high time he lived up to the name that the little group gave themselves. He was looking for a building where he could glean some fragments of the past to turn into his future.

He wasn't the gleaner that Molly was, that was certain; she was amazing. But his few gleaning trips, when there was no fruit on the trees and no ice on the ground, had gone well enough. So now he gleaned.

It was easy enough to tell an inhabited building from an empty one; it was usually marked by the front door. If the front door was open, or non-existent, that building was probably empty. Either way, any building was enter-at-your-own-risk. He'd been working his way through these buildings on Second Street, mostly trying to get into their attics. It could be dangerous; he'd fallen once, and found only an angry raccoon a different time, but many of the attics hadn't been gleaned; whether from of a lack of light, or a lack of interest, or a presumption that there wasn't anything interesting, Freeman didn't know.

But he'd found crates of Harlequin Romance books in one attic, books that had come in quite handy during the winter, and plenty of the old coins that people used to use as money and were now used as food for the forges.

So this building here. This one had no door to speak of; it had sunk into the ground and the second-floor windows were now just a few feet above Freeman's head. He jumped and hoisted himself up to the window; the glass was long gone, and a quick scan indicated that the building was indeed empty.

Mildew assaulted his nostrils. Like everywhere else in the city, must and age and water had taken their toll; the floor here was bent and peeling. Freeman put his foot down on a line of nails in the wood floor; the stringer underneath was still solid. He made his way around the room, quickly looking over everything. Most of it had been overturned already. Nothing too much here. He searched the apartment quickly. A fork and spoon, sitting under a cabinet, and a few glass jars, empty and dusty. These went into his backpack. He made his way out the door and into the stairwell. There were three more apartments on this floor, apartments that yielded little in the way of useful material. But the wood floors might be useful later, he'd have to tell Kevin about them.

He made his way up the steps, all the way to the fourth floor, where the stairwell was clogged with the remains of the fifth floor stairs. Always.

He had a rope. Time to use it.

"I can't believe you haven't helped with the acorns before. Odd. Anyway, here's two different oak leaves. You see how this one has points coming out of it?"

"Yeah?"

"The acorns off of trees that have the pointy leaves are usually fatter, and have more meat on them. But there's a trade off; they don't taste as good. They're really bitter."

"Right."

"This one's got rounded edges, the leaves aren't all pokey. These oaks have more narrow nuts, but they taste better. These don't have to be soaked as long to get all the nasty out."

"Right."

"So, you've got your two sacks, if you're under an oak with the pokey leaves, put them in one sack, and if you're under a tree with the rounded leaves, put them into the other sack. They need to be prepared differently."

"Okay."

"Good. Start collecting."

"Are we taking the ones with worm-holes in them?"

"Gather them all. We'll cut out the bad parts of the acorns."

"Sure thing. What are we going to do with them?"

"Flour. Add it to the wheat flour we grow, it tastes good, it's got more, stuff, whatever, oils and things. It gives you more energy than just the wheat flour."

"Sounds good."

They gathered in silence for a while, moving to new trees as the trees they gleaned were depleted.

"So, um, how do you think Crissa's holding up after Jase?"

"Uh, she seems to be dealing with it. Why?"

"Oh, I don't know. You've got your Molly, and I was sorta thinking, well..."

"You already live with her. You should know she's a good choice. A deft hand with a needle and loom, and pretty to boot. Does she like you?"

"Well enough to live in a house with, I guess, but I don't know about past that."

"What about Shell?"

"No more an issue. She's left the city for the countryside, some farmer at the market asked her to go with him and he's got a house, and stuff. She said she'd had enough of the scrounging life, just wanted to settle and farm."

"We farm."

"She doesn't care for all the scrounging, though. Said that the smells of mildew and rust had finally gotten to her."

"Well, I can see that. It stinks around here sometimes."

"Yeah, I guess. I like it, though, when I notice it. I've been out of the city before and coming back to the mildew and rust always feels like coming home."

"Cherry jam does that for me."

"Mildew, man. It doesn't smell good, but it's what I've lived with for so long it seems like a part of me."

"I've always said you had a black heart." And then Freeman ducked from the stick Kevin threw at him.

Freeman had been raised to believe that there was no God, nor Gods. Not because it was impossible or because it was nonexistent in theory, but because no higher power worthy of worship would have allowed the Hemorrhage to happen. Whether his family was right or not was almost unimportant now, though.

Since joining the Gleaners he had found himself beset on all sides by people wanting him to go to church. It didn't really seem to matter which one he picked; he was going to offend someone, some group, and he didn't really look forward to it.

Molly was the only other person in the Gleaners who didn't go to church, and he was never sure why people didn't bother her about it.

The Gleaners were split down the middle, religion-wise. Jase and Crissa were both Christian and wanted everyone else to be so, but... Jase's authority over physical matters was about as far as he could go. It was obvious to everyone that he couldn't survive either if anyone else left and even the other Christians in the house wanted the others to choose God, not have Him chosen for them.

They went to services on the quarter-moons, and it was only a problem with the rest of the group when that quarter-moon would fall on the solstices and equinoxes.

The rest of the group went to a local Grove, as they called themselves, and they didn't bother with the Christian God. They had a Great Mother and a host of other Gods; Freeman wasn't bothered by them that much. He went to those services because they were less boring than the Christian services, and happened far less frequently.

But it seemed like everyone knew that, somehow; the heathens asked when he was going to dedicate himself to a certain godling or another, and the Christians asked when he was actually going to start believing in anything, and when he did, he should believe in the Truth.

Outside the Gleaners, there were other groups, and he spent a lot of time considering joining one of those. There were the Jews, who he liked; their focus on intense intellectualism was one he appreciated. He just didn't like that so much of his reading time would have to be spent on theology. There was a small community of Copts, a small group of Zoroastrians, but he didn't hold out any hope on joining those—too much importance on family in the city for him to join those.

The Orthodox of North Philadelphia were too far away, and the obeisance of the Muslims was too much for him. There were too many Gods among the Hindu for him to feel comfortable, though he did really like the trappings of their rituals and would occasionally go for the food; he felt perfectly justified in this since they'd come to the Full Moon Parties for the food themselves, and an occasional gift of food of his own from the Gleaners set off his debt to them nicely.

Most of the groups of the city also had private religions; Fishtown deified its founder and its kings, as he assumed was an easy thing to do. There was a cup in the Spectrum that the Sprawlers claimed was the Grail, and their own particular strange form of Christianity where Jesus was the sun and was drawn across the sky in a wagon pulled by the saints. Where they got that from was perfectly beyond Freeman.

Where a lot of the religions agreed, though, was that the Hemorrhage happened because their own God or Gods had wished it. And that was where Freeman lost his interest: he had no need to appease a God who had wiped out the earth once, and no need to worship one who wasn't doing it again because he didn't feel like it.

The Fork is many things.

The Fork is many things.

The Fork is a machine straddling the bridge.

The Fork is a triangular building, straddling the junction of two roads.

The Fork is a tined utensil laying beside a plate.

The Fork is group of black-suited men, sitting around a table.

The Fork is the choice between a dark moldy future and a bright clean one.

The Fork is a gate.

The Fork is power.

The Fork is a machine.

The Fork is people.

The Fork is a choice.

The Fork is a decision.

The Fork is before us at all times.

"Shouldn't there be birds chirping?"

"Quiet. You have to be quiet here."

"Okay. Why?"

"You just do, you'll see."

"Oh, oh there are so many bones."

"This is where all the biggest monsters from the zoo died. There are still predators around sometimes."

"This is really creepy. I don't like this."

"There are plums. We need plums."

"You're squeezing my hand."

"I am. I don't want you to be scared."

"I'm not."

"Good. Neither am I."

"Of course. Should we start with the yellow plums?"

"Taste and see how they are."

"Sour. They're good for you."

"Let's do it."

"I can't walk without stepping on bones."

"No. They're everywhere."

"Why did they all come here?"

"Who knows? Maybe they were trying to winter here and just couldn't. Too cold, maybe? I don't know. I never did. No one does. But this is where they are."

"There must have been fifteen, twenty of them."

"Or more. Maybe they didn't all die here at once. The more religious Christians think they were demons and don't come here at all. They think that the angels and demons had a fight here and the angels won."

"They're just animal bones though. Just so big. Like elephants or something."

"Elephants?"

"Real big animals."

"Oh."

"These black plums are delicious. Perfect."

"That's why we come here. There's no plums anything like these anywhere else in the city."

"I've never had a plum that tasted this good. I don't expect to ever again."

"Only what we pick today, and next year."

"I want to hold this in my head, and never forget this. Never forget the quiet, never forget you standing there, the sun in your hair, never forget the taste of this plum on my lips. Never forget your hand in mine."

"Freeman...."

"Molly. There's plenty of time to pick. Just hold this. Hold this moment."

"Hush, Freeman. We have time."

"But this moment, this moment we want to hold. Last winter was hard, this will keep us warm through the next. Just hold this moment, beautiful. Just hold it in your head, now and forever."

At least she said us, thought Freeman.

"I still don't think that we're anything the Fork has to worry about. There's only, what, forty of us at the compound? We're not a power."

"No, we're not a power. Yet. But we do have strengths. Two, in particular. The first strength that we have is electricity. The only other group around who has that regularly is the Fork. Yes, I know, we trade in electricity, but that's not the same. People have to come to us to use their sewing machines. Which we also traded them. That gave us a food surplus. Now that the Fork is paying you on a weekly basis, and you're doing most of your work for them, we've got much more of a food surplus, which means we can take more people into our group. And there aren't forty of us, there are almost fifty-five, not counting kids. Which, you might not realize, is almost five times the size we moved into the compound with. We have kids in the compound, Freeman! We've been able to step down the pennyroyal lottery. We're becoming something, something that could hurt the Fork.

"But that's not our real strength. Sure, the Fork won't hurt us because then you might stop working for them, and you're the only engineer they've got down here, but that's just a side point. Our real strength is that we're free. They don't tell us what to do. Fishtown doesn't tell us what to do. We don't have a mystical leader, like the Upenners. We all decide what to do, and we move. You remember why Fishtown pulled out of Chestnut Street?"

"Of course. Leopold died of a sudden illness."

"A sudden illness that sounded like hemlock poisoning. And then there was an internal struggle for who would be king next, and they had to pull inwards. Which gave us the compound. We don't do that, and we won't do that. If the voting goes in a way that people don't like, we work it out. Any close vote is tossed, and a new pair of options is determined until we get something that more than just a simple majority of our people think is a good idea. This is a strength, Freeman, and it's a strength that doesn't exist in a large group like what we have. The Fork is, what, despotic? Who even runs it? Do you know? Fishtown had Leopold, the Upenners have the Swami. Do you know who the Fork are, Freeman? We know who everyone else in this city is. What about them?"

"I always assumed it was Drake, but I don't know."

"There you are, then. Drake runs the Fork."

"And I'm pretty sure we run the Collective, you and I. And I'm not sure about me."

Molly stared at him, mouth open, eyes wide. The party raged around her.

The brick factory was a continual thorn in Freeman's side.

Nothing here was electrified. Every machine, every automation, was driven by a steam engine that also heated the kiln to bake the bricks. There were four particular parts to it, and none of them would work properly for more than three days at a time.

First there was the crusher, where the broken bricks and cinderblocks and concrete were mashed into powder by a press. Some wit had painted a giant set of teeth on the faces of both the top and bottom plates of the crusher. Rust had eaten through the chipped paint on the plates, making the teeth seem as rotten as most of the wooden structures here in Camden. The fine dust that resulted from the grinding plates was then swept into a vat and mixed with river water to form a thick paste. The workers on the next stage would scoop out the finished sludge and slap it into a form, using a knife to cut off the excess and then unhinging the form and placing the completed brick onto a metal conveyor belt that would drive a full load of bricks into the kiln.

The problems were myriad. The fine dust from the grinder would work its way into the geared machinery of the crusher, making the gears seize and switches stick. The same dust would clog the gears of the mixer. The wet slurry would be too thin or too thick, making the bricks come out malformed or the mixer scream with punishment. The wet slurry would rust the hinges of the brick-forms. The heat of the kiln would cause the oil of the conveyor system to volatilize, leading to rusted scrabblies in the production line. And the steam engine driving the entire mess was prone to seizures.

Some of these things could be fixed by the linemen; they always—in theory—oiled the gears of the conveyor belt and the hinges of the forms. Today, though, the chain that drew the belt through the kiln had snapped.

Fortunately, the chain had snapped as it cooled, after it had been drawn out of the kiln, which meant that the kiln and the steam engine didn't have to be shut down. The linemen had already disconnected the conveyor belt from the long spinning drive train that ran through the building, so Freeman was able to just get started. The linkage that had broken was the size of his thumb, a long figure-eight of metal. He set his portable anvil down on the ground near the breakage, and brought the free end of the chain around. Three hits with a hammer and die and the pin was out; fortunately, the spinning widget that sat between the two links was undamaged. He pocketed it. The other end of the chain had shot through the machinery; it took some time, but Freeman threaded the chain back over the drive gears on the underside of the kiln. By now he could do this in his sleep. Then the end of that link in the chain was hammered out; this widget was shot.

Its edge was chipped, which was remachinable, but there was a crack running though one face of it, which wasn't. Freeman spun it off into the darkness of the factory. He had more.

Installation, as it was, was the opposite of disassembly. The two new figure-eight plates were lined up with the ends of the chain, the widgets were slipped in, and pins set through the holes. Three whacks with the hammer on both pins and they were solid. A little oil, and then the slack in the chain taken up by tightening a gear on a pivot, and the factory was back up and running.

And he'd never get his hands clean for dinner.

The water in the sewers under South Street ran down to the river, that much Freeman knew. Where it came from when it wasn't storming was a small mystery, but one that was solved with only a little searching.

The sewer was a domed stone passage with narrow footpaths on either side. Through the center ran a sluggish, trash-filled river of water and worse, with thick pipes running under the level of the water.

Before the Hemorrhage, all the waste in the city had run through those pipes, some of them down to the river, some elsewhere. Between then and now, though, the water flow had changed. In some places, new springs had come up, flooding the tunnels and turning the contained flow into an underground creek flowing gently down to the river. Aboveground, a new stream fed from a spring at South and Twelfth, and ran down to a collapsed manhole at Tenth Street. That source provided most of the water in the sewer system.

Almost every storm drain in the city had clogged with trash and leaves, and the pipes that they fed into burst, and now, with storms came huge torrents of water into the now-open sewer system. It was during one of those storms that the water wrecked his generator farm.

The thing was, those torrents of water would produce massive amounts of electricity, but if every storm ruined the farms there was no way they'd be able to keep a constant supply of electricity going.

That's what they were down here fixing today. A week ago most of the Gleaners had come down to the sewers on a dry, hot day to cut the old pipes out of the waterway.

The compost inside them was exquisite, and they'd planned on installing the new generators that day, but were instead tied up bringing up pipe and compost for the garden.

Since the pipes were mostly dry they didn't bother breaking the upstream ends as they'd originally planned.

The new mounts were pallets with holes drilled at the four corners. Freeman had strapped as many styrofoam blocks as he could find to the bottom, and then added a few inflated goat skins to others for comparison testing. They'd float in a basin, he just hoped they'd float in a river.

They drove foot-long pieces of sharpened rebar halfway into the walkway floor, then put the pallets in place. On top of the rebar they drove six-foot wooden poles with holes drilled in their bases, which would in theory let the pallet bases float up and down with rising storm surge—and the holes in the pallets were far larger than the poles so that they wouldn't get bound up on one side.

They installed six generators this time, three more than they'd had before. Two of the old ones were wrecked beyond repair by the storm but with the five new ones they'd be able to generate more electricity than anyone had done in the city in years.

The generators were mounted to the top of the pallets. The new vanes on the end of the mill portion of the generator were far larger than the previous ones, to allow the generators to get more of the deeper flow of the water. Unhooked, they spun lazily in the low flow of the river. Freeman also had one waterwheel built; he wasn't sure which would generate more current, but the new voltmeter he'd gotten working would tell him with the first storm.

Things were looking up.

"Hi, Drake, can I come in?"

"Absolutely, Freeman. What can I do for you?"

"I wanted to talk to you about our most recent crop of trainees."

"How are they doing?"

"Some of them are doing really well, some of them not. There's one person specifically though that I wanted to talk to you about."

"Who's that."

"Dawn. Do you know her?"

"The really easy to look at blonde?"

"That's her. She's in the wrong program."

"What do you mean?"

"Have you seen her with horses?"

"No, no I haven't."

"Look, Drake, I know you wanted her on the machines, but... I've been taking the students out for a little bit of fieldwork, and I have never seen someone able to deal with a horse like her. She's amazing with animals. And I've seen her ride, and... stunning. Absolutely a fantastic rider. But..."

"But?"

"Not so much with the machines. It's not because she's a girl, I mean we have Kelly and Etta and they're doing just fine with the maths. Dawn just doesn't have the patience, I fear, for dealing with the machines."

"You know she really wants to do it, right?"

"I do, but... Look, I can't make a hammer put in a screw, right?"

"Right. I see what you're saying. What do you think I should do with her?"

"Seriously? Put her in command of the cavalry. She's excellent with people, and she's excellent with horses."

"In command?"

"Train her for it and you won't be disappointed. She's too good at it."

"What about our command when she gets pregnant?"

"Well... give her a unit, then. Or rotate her through. She's got a good intuitive grasp of tactics, near as I can tell from how she can direct people around, and as I said, she's a damn good rider. She'll serve you much better with the cavalry than she will with the machines."

"Ah... Have you talked to her about this?"

"I've hinted that she might want to try a new path, and she just works harder. Unfortunately, she just doesn't have it."

"Can she fight?"

"I don't know. But she can sure ride."

"I'll put it in. You tell Scotto that I think it's a good plan. Who else do you have?"

"I've been pushing them really hard, and I've had pretty good success at getting the ones who shouldn't be machinists out. Dawn's the only one who's sticking with it."

"She's not going to just stop then, either?"

"Nope. Once she gets over not working with machines I bet she's the best cavalryman you have."

"Consider it done. Just as soon as you talk to Scotto."

"Jase? You wanted to see me?"

"Yah, Freeman, come in and close th' door behind ya."

"What's going on? Was there a problem in the gardens, or with the jam?"

"Freeman, what are you doing here?"

"What do you mean, Jase?"

"I mean, Freeman, dust. You obviously know more than we do about a lot of things. You could pick a place to live. But you're here. Why?"

"I want to eat. I can't eat on what I can do, all alone; I especially can't eat and work on research, and I can't protect myself. We're all here because we like to eat, and we need protection. Otherwise we'd all live by ourselves."

"But you could name your price and live anywhere. Most any stead would be happy to have you. Why are you here, and what are you planning to do?"

"You know why I'm here, don't you Jase? Do you have to ask?"

"So it's true."

"Yes, Jase, it is. I'm here because Molly is here."

"...oh."

"What did you think?"

"There's been... mutterings. People saying that you should lead us."

"That's crazy. I'm the youngest one here. I know nothing of leading people."

"And you haven't been egging these people on."

"No, Jase, why would I do that? I mean, I mean, I know that I'm here because you suffer me to be. If I was really trying to take over, well, I know that you could overpower me. And I know that you've killed people who tried to take over before. I know that you could kill me, that really, anyone here could. I have no need to face death over something so... unimportant to me. All I care about is Molly, and eating, and studying."

"So..."

"So you have nothing to worry about from me. I give you my word that I have no interest in taking over the Gleaners, and I never shall. Leadership of a group would mean that I would have less time to work, and to research, and that's what's important for me right now."

"Good, Freeman, good."

"Now, could you put the sword down?"

"This? I didn't realize you could see it."

"What's your plan then?"

"Plans? To keep eating. And since that's at your suffrage, my plans are whatever you plan for me. Just as long as I can keep researching."

"Is your research really that important?"

"It's more important than any of us. Me included."

"Why?"

"Because it's what built this city in the first place, and it is what can restore it. I'm working towards making this city what it once was. And Jase, remember, when I build these tools, they will all be at your disposal. You can do what you want with them. And you'll be strong, because the Skorbut won't bother you, and the jaundice, and... well. Now, can I get back to what I was doing, please?"

"Sure thing."

"...which has resulted in a 30% reduction on bandit activity on our northern supply route through the Trenton region."

"Excellent. Now, Freeman, what's going on with the Fork?"

"There was some damage sustained to the front of the Fork when we took down the buildings at Seventh and Arch. However, this was expected after a manual inspection from the building before. It was the largest building we had so far attempted to take down. Therefore, we had previously made a new armored plate that was floated across the Delaware, and installation of it was completed last night. The Fork has been restarted now, and we expect no problems with the next building we take down, Drake."

"Excellent."

"Forgive me, sir, but which building is the next one we plan on taking down?"

"Scotto, what's the plan?"

"We need, well, we need everything. But we particularly right now need concrete and steel. As such, there is a car park that is relatively full of junked vehicles at Eighth and Arch, and that should be the next building we take down."

"Eighth and Arch it is, then."

"Excuse me, sir, but I thought that we weren't going to take the car park because there's a nest of people inside who won't leave."

"Scotto, how has the removal program on the tribals gone?"

"They refuse to leave, sir. We've tried bribing them with food, giving them a new place in northeast Philadelphia, we've even offered them a rather advanced place on the wait list for an apartment in Camden. They won't budge."

"Hmmm." Drake steepled his fingers. "These aren't the first batch of people to not move, are they?"

"No, sir."

"What other buildings in the area are suitable?"

"None, sir. We'll have to back the Fork up. The next building behind the one that we've already taken is the mall, sir; the Fork can take down most buildings, but the mall has a large open area below it, and there isn't a good foundation to get the machine down on. If we want the mall, we'll have to take it down by hand and feed the materials into the Fork. There are some buildings close to Vine Street that are worth taking, but the Fork moves very slowly in reverse and it will take three days to get it realigned."

"And it's been down a week already? How's our timetable?"

"We're running behind already, sir."

"Alright. They'll leave when we knock the building down."

There was silence around the table. Matt began to clap, quietly.

"Drake, are you certain? We said that we wouldn't take down any buildings that had occupants when we built the Fork."

"Freeman, I understand your concern. But you of all people should know that the future cannot be stopped. These small people are trying to stand in the way of what we are doing, and if we are seen to be stopped by them then other people will try the same thing. No, these vermin must be moved. Scotto, see that the Fork is set to take the building down tomorrow. Freeman, help him. Matt, warn the tribals in the car park tonight. If they don't leave, it's their fault, not ours. We warned them."

At the mercy of the seasons as they were, Freeman still wasn't finished unpacking his workshop when he had to get started working on the gathered batteries.

The batteries had to be cut open; it was grueling, sweaty work in the cold November air. His breath steamed as he ran the rusty steel backsaw back and forth against the tops of the black plastic battery boxes. Shards of the black plastic shaved around the outside work table, far from the garden and storage areas of the Gleaners' new digs on Chestnut Street. One after the next he cut the top of the batteries off, then ran the saw down one of the long sides of the batteries. Freeman cut each battery with the positive terminal facing away from him. White powder scattered with the black shavings from the sides. Once the batteries were cut open, he set them aside. The pile of batteries grew as the hours marched along, the stack growing darkly and dully, soaking up the available light.

It took the better part of the day to cut all the boxes open. When it was done, he got to the real work on each battery. The anodes and cathodes had to be separated and gathered in separate storage crates.

Each battery was made of eight cells. Each cell had a series of plates in it. The plates were divided evenly in half; half were lead oxide and half were lead. The plates were arranged lead, lead oxide, lead, lead oxide, ten to twenty per cell depending on the battery size. All of the lead plates were soldered together across the top, as were the lead oxide plates.

White powder coated everything. The white powder was dry hydrochloric acid, which had been the batteries' original electrolyte. Freeman had a bucket and three wooden crates.

He started on the first battery. He grabbed the lead plates from the first cell and worked them out, pulling by the soldered wire that held the plates together. After the plates were removed, he knocked them against the side of the bucket, trying to collect as much of the acid as possible. Then the plates went into the first crate.

He worked his way down the cells of the battery, pulling each set of lead plates out and knocking the acid off of them, then storing them in the first wooden crate. Then it was time to get started on the lead oxide plates, following the same sequence. The lead oxide plates went into the second crate.

After he'd removed all of the anodes and cathodes from the battery, he tilted the plastic box that the cells were arranged in over the bucket and tipped out the white powder, storing as much of it as he could in the bucket. Then the housing went into the third crate. The tops of all the batteries went into the same crate—one never knew when one would need, well, anything.

When the first battery was done, and the next sixty or so were staring at him, he realized he was in for a long winter.

Freeman picked up the second battery and got started.

"Ready to start up again?"

"Sure. I'm really tired though."

"We won't read long."

"*Devai.*"

"'Real wealth consists in things of utility and beauty, in things that help to create strong, beautiful bodies and surroundings inspiring to live in. But if man is doomed to wind cotton around a spool, or dig coal, or build roads for thirty years of his life, there can be no talk of wealth.'"

"Okay, stop. What is this wealth Emma is talking about?"

"Lemme grab the dictionary. 'Riches, large possessions of money, goods, or land; that abundance of worldly goods which exceeds the possessions of the greater part of the community.'"

"Okay. Keep going."

"'What he gives to the world is only grey and hideous things, reflecting a dull and hideous existence—too weak to live, too cowardly to die. Strange to say, there are people who extol this deadening method of centralized production as the proudest achievement of our age. They fail utterly to realize that if we are to continue in machine subserviency, our slavery is more complete than was our bondage to the King.'"

"How does this apply to us?"

"Don't you see? This is what you were talking about the other night. With Jase and us. We produce things, and we give them to Jase, and he doles them out to us. When he goes trading, we don't see what he brings back. When you go trading, where does the lion's share go?"

"Are you saying that we're, what, grey and hideous?"

"Not at all, just that... it could happen. You see it too. That's why you want us to start in some group decision making, right?"

"Right. Ehhhhh... keep going."

"'...A perfect personality, then, is only possible in a state of society where man is free to choose the mode of work, the conditions of work, and the freedom to work. One to whom the making of a table, the building of a house, or the tilling of the soil, is what the painting is to the artist and the discovery to the scientist—the result of inspiration, of intense longing, and deep interest in work as a creative force. That being the ideal of Anarchism, its economic arrangements must consist of voluntary productive and distributive associations, gradually developing into free communism, as the best means of producing with the least waste of human energy.'"

"Communism?"

"Like your Quaker roots. But with everything. We'll read Marx if we find it."

"Ahhh. Okay. So. But. We all choose to do what we do. If we don't, we don't eat."

"Right, but... we do a number of things because Jase tells us to. Most things. Like, I don't know, why am I only letting slip one-two things a year that will help us?"

"Because Jase is afraid of you."

"Right. Things could be more beautiful, but Jase is afraid, so we don't do it."

"So you are saying things are grey and hideous."

"Oh, I don't know. Not always. You aren't."

"Put down that book and come here, you."

"Hey."

"Hey."

Freeman's feet shuffled in the dirt. At least, for that matter, so did Molly's.

"Your dad won't stay the two days?"

"No. He says we need to be on the road, that the weather looks to be turning and that he doesn't want to get trapped in storms all the way home."

"But the party's going to be good. The September party is always one of the best! His merchant friends are going to be there too!"

"I know. But he won't stay. He wants to leave at first light tomorrow."

"Oh."

"Yeah."

Molly looked down. Freeman's feet scuffled the dirt.

"Well... If you have to go, then I guess you-and-I'll just have to do something cool tonight."

"Like what?"

"Wanna go to the old museum?"

"Which one? I read an old tourist guide and it said there were lots around here."

"No, there's only one museum. The art museum."

"Didn't that burn when Fishtown took power from the Centrallers?"

"Parts of it did, but it's a big old stone building, the whole thing couldn't burn. You can still see some of the art around, like this huge statue hanging in the entry above the steps, and an old foreign town up on the top stories. It's really cool! You wanna go?"

"Sure. I've got my chores done, and dad has someone watching the wagon for the night. We can go now if you want."

"Let's go. *Devai*!"

They set off through Central City to the art museum. While they walked Molly chattered away. "You can still see some of the old street poking up here and there around here. This forest used to be a big wide street that ran from City Hall to the Art Museum.

"See the light poles? Mum said that her gramma used to tell her that the light poles used to have all different countries' flags hanging off of them. They used to change them out when they had things going on, like parades and marathons and stuff. Now it's all trees. But there's some good picking on the trees. That's a white cherry we like to hit in the summer, and these are all chokecherries that are a little bitter but taste good. Here, let's stop a second and pick some apples."

"Okay. I'll climb up and throw them down to you?"

"No, let's both climb. Ready set go."

"No fair, you started before I did!"

"Whine whine, climb faster or I'm gonna eat them all!"

After they filled their pockets—and a bag, you always brought a bag with you—with small green apples that were just starting to turn red, they set off back to the art museum, munching while they walked.

"And this pile of rocks here used to be a fountain. They took water from the river and forced it up through the big center sculpture there. We've sure lost a lot, huh?"

"We sure have. I can't imagine using even river water for that."

Had it all been set before him, his path leading out in vision like the rails he ran down, gleaming dully in the fitful beam of his flashlight, or did he have a choice the whole time? Until two days ago, every decision had seemed natural, everything had played out in a pattern that seemed foreordained, and he had simply walked down the paths that lay before him.

But now. Now, his feet pounding, finally drowning out the sound of the hoofbeats in his head, the fires set in the night still burning behind him, he wondered. Had it all been straight lines? Or was every moment a choice? Were his decisions right, or were they wrong? Had he even made a decision until now? And was his final decision the correct one?

For now, it was no matter. His feet pounded the ground, his even strides taking the sleepers two at a time, drawing him towards the next station on the rail lines under the city. Every few breaths he permitted himself a glance backwards; there were still no lights behind him, no flickering glimpses of pursuit. But they were back there, oh they were, and they would catch up with him soon enough.

He ran onwards, knowing full well that he was leaving some sort of trail behind him for Scotto to follow. Whether that trail was made of footprints or blood, he didn't know, but there was a trail. And there was absolutely nothing he could do about it now.

Here in the tunnel, he knew where he was going. If—and here was where the uncertainty crept in—the Fork's forces left him alone long enough, he was going to follow the slightly left-bearing rails to the station at Chestnut Street—always Chestnut Street—and emerge into the light. For right now, that was his future and this darkness was his past.

His feet pounded the rails, dodging the occasional puddles of murky water between the sleepers. Occasionally in the tunnel, just beyond the shaky beam of the flashlight, he'd see green dots in the dark, the eyes of whatever tunnel scavengers and predators were lurking and waiting for him to pass before resuming their eternal, pointless dance of death and life.

Was that what they looked like, from a distance? Were the Fork and the Collective, or even the Fork and Fishtown, locked into some sort of stupid, pointless dance of advancement and landgrabs and land losses and death that to some sort of cosmic entity, or to history, would look like the silly squabbles of the rats and cats and lord-knew-what-else that lived, loved, fought, and died in these tunnels?

There was a flash of light behind, nearer this time. It was too much to hope that they hadn't seen the glow of his flashlight. They appeared to have a torch, which was good news in a way; their technology level might be lower than his. Of course, he had little enough technology, and they had flintlocks. He could only fight flintlocks if he was lucky, like he'd been back in the labyrinth. They could shoot farther with those than he could with his sling, even if they could do it with less accuracy.

Wait. Freeman stopped running for a second, and grabbed one satchel away from his belt. Looking straight into one of the pairs of eyes in the tunnel, he poured out grains and watched as they spiralled away into the darkness. It wasn't much, but he could use aspects of the territory against them.

He wished he had more bombs. They'd come in useful when or if he ever reached the subway station.

Sometimes, at certain houses, even in these days, knocking at a door would bring you results that kicking it in wouldn't.

"Yes?"

"Hello, Lydia."

It took a few minutes, but the door opened eventually.

"Well, hello, Freeman. Matt and I were just sitting down to supper. Would you care for anything? Water? Food?"

"No, Lydia, though I thank you. I have too much to do this evening. I have come instead to offer you something."

Lydia inhaled deeply, her ample bosom raising swiftly. "Something? What might that be?"

"I understand that you and Matt have been requested membership in the South Street Gleaners but have been refused on at least one occasion. The reason stated was a lack of space in our home."

"That is indeed the case."

"Lydia, I hereby have the pleasure to offer you and your husband Matt a space in our group, with all the responsibilities and benefits commended by such a position."

Lydia looked him in the eyes. "Who died?"

"No one."

"Then what has changed?"

And that was confirmation for Freeman that Lydia and Matt should join the Gleaners straightaway. Most of the applicants to the Gleaners would have agreed, and then asked why they were now being accepted. The request for information was indicative of more critical thought than was expected of people these days.

"What changed was not within us, if that is what you were asking. Something, we're not sure what yet, happened to Fishtown, and Fishtown has abandoned their colony on Chestnut Street."

Lydia's eyes went wide. “Really?”

"Yes. We have secured the location on Chestnut, and are currently beginning to move our home base over to that compound now. We have fourteen members now; we would like to expand our complement to sixteen by tomorrow morning. Would you like to move in with us, knowing full well how we operate, knowing full well how we make decisions, in the Gleaners?”

"Do you really hold the compound at Chestnut Street?"

"For the moment. Do you care to help us hold the compound there?"

"Hell yes. We, Matt and I, agree to join the Gleaners, accepting full well the decision making process, and knowing that while the individual is important, the group is more important than the individual. We agree to acquiesce to the will of the majority.

“When shall we move?”

Freeman was amazed that she had memorized the ritual form. Molly must have prepped her for it.

"We will continue moving throughout the night. Will you have your things packed by dawn? If you will, the wagon will come by to get you."

"We will be ready to do our part."

Meat over an open fire. Mildew. Fresh bread. Sweat. Bubbling cheese. Dust. Spices. Mold. Brewing tea. Fresh water. Old burn. Horses. Shit. These are the smells that are the City Hall market.

An island in the middle of a river of road, the City Hall market has long since overgrown the courtyard in the center of the building and spilled over through its four exits into the surrounding plaza. When the sun is high, sellers of cloth have bolts hung over the railings of the spiral stairs down to the underground, where no one goes if they can help it. Gleaners have piles of junk reclaimed and sometimes cleaned piled in heaps on blankets and salvaged tarps. There are animals and cordwood and tomatoes and peppers and planks and tools and books —all in all a bewildering, ever-changing array of small mercantilism.

If one wanted to count the people in Philadelphia, the City Hall market during the summer moons would be the time to do it.

This market is where the small farmers from all directions come; this market is where the ship-captains come to sell the small treasures they bring in, or the leftovers of their bulk transports; this is where the small groups of the city come to sell their excess.

The cloth in Philadelphia is the best made anywhere, for reasons varied, but partially related to Crissa and Freeman. Crissa weaves some of the best cloth in a city known for cloth, and Freeman's country upbringing—and his grandmother's wisdom—let them dye it the brightest colors that last the longest. Their cloth demands premium prices in grain and other foodstuffs, some of which they preserve and sell again later, to the same people who sold it to them in the first place, at a windfall profit.

This market is where the Gleaners are totally safe, where they can buy, sell, trade with everyone else, and everyone is on the same terms.

Everything trades for barter, of course; there's no standard unit of value. Even if you consider a plain white teacup, its price changes depending on its thickness, the quality of the glaze, the chips in its finish. And the changing prices, even on a day-to-day basis, mean that you have to be good, real good, to get the best deals. Which is where Molly came in, and how she truly kept her place in the Gleaners.

No one else could look at a pile of metal and judge, based on the barters she watched earlier, exactly how much it should go for, and if they should pay over that, or if they should wait and see. She could tell at a glance how much of any particular commodity there was available that day, and whether they should hold or sell or what.

Generally, they would only bring a portion of their goods to the market, and when Molly made one of her sales, they would send Sal and the cart back to the house to fetch the rest of what was needed.

And no one would ever renege on a deal with Molly. They knew she would never cheat or overstate the quality of the goods they sold.

Freeman could never understand how she did it, how she could keep track of so many different sales and trades and quantities and portions in her head. How she could tell when to buy the wheat early and when late. How she could tell Crissa to keep the lesser cloths out or away and when to put them all out and when to put it all away. But she did. And Freeman loved her all the more for it.

These markets, so full of anarchy and bustle, was how they survived in the city. The gleaning, the farming, sure—that kept them going. These markets allowed them to thrive, and thrive they did with Molly at the helm of the trade.

How far does responsibility extend?

Freeman stared off the roadbed of the Walt Whitman. There were three things to see from here, three things that mattered: Philadelphia, Camden, and the Fork. And the Fork was Freeman's responsibility.

The Fork stretched across the bridge, its caterpillar-segmented steel body gleaming mirror-bright in the evening sun. Freeman hadn't built the Fork, no, but he had designed it, and overseen its construction, and directed its traffic. And, like most architects of tools, he didn't direct it. That responsibility fell to the people who paid for the Fork.

A pall of smoke always hung over it. There were smokestacks all down its length; they belched a thick stream of black smoke at all hours of the day. The Fork never shut down. The smoke came from the kilns inside. These furnaces not only baked new bricks and cinderblocks and melted down plastics and glass, but they also powered steam engines, generators, and the drive train of the Fork. They were fed by the materials that poured into the giant mouth of the Fork on the Philadelphia side, they were fed tires and coal and wood and charcoal by teamsters driving fuel-laden carriages down the bridge.

A caterpillar. Yes. The gnashing teeth of the Fork, now busy chewing through the detritus shoveled into its mouth, tore down buildings and mashed the masonry and woodwork down to small fragments. These were sorted as they passed through the Fork, until they finally reached their proper destinations inside. There, giant machines formed them into new bricks, slagged them together, or used them as fuel to power and move and bake.

The Fork was the opposite of a caterpillar. Caterpillars eat organized material, and use the organization in the food to reorganize themselves, and only dump out the homogenized material once organization is stripped. From its rear end in Camden, the Fork shat out cinderblocks, bricks, blocks of thermoform plastic, slagged glass, steel I-beams, and pigs of rarer metals. The Fork took disorganization, with its giant teeth that tore through buildings and cars and trees and people, and and reordered it into new materials. Where caterpillars dump entropy, the Fork shat out only organization.

The Fork's leavings were being built into Camden slowly. For a certain mindset, what the Fork was doing made sense; Camden was already bombed-out, so it was a blank slate, a tabula rasa. Philadelphia was still crowned with tall buildings, still home to many; it was much harder to rebuild, especially in a new image. Whereas Camden was both source and sink. And they both, of course, shared the same excellent deep-water port.

And Camden gleamed in the sunlight, oh yes it did, it gleamed like a dream. But what was that dream built on? How many bones were built into the foundations of the new city? And what share of the responsibility for that was Freeman's?

He had only built the machine, had only given the Fork a tool. How much responsibility did the builder of a tool bear for the use to which that tool was put?

The scar that the Fork had chewed into Philadelphia stared at him in the setting sun. It seemed to stare into him with Molly's eyes.

He shut his eyes, but still heard her voice in his head: "*The builder shares equal responsibility with the user.*"

He had a decision to make.

On the first market day that they were ready, Molly and Crissa helped Freeman sell, and Matt came along to run security. Granted, market truce held; anyone stealing or threatening here wouldn't be allowed back—or worse—but still, but still. That didn't affect the trip to and from the market, and they were hoping to come back far more laden than they had come.

They set up early, even though they knew that the gleaming pumps, record players, sewing machines, and spinning wheels wouldn't draw that much of a crowd. At first. The batteries they left in the wagon for now. This was the third City Hall Market of the spring, and Molly thought it the best time to try to sell the machines.

They'd already done a fine business on the first two market days with the few leftover jams from last winter, trading them for herbs and early fruit and cloth, but now the rains were coming through and it was the time to try for some real trading.

A few people they knew went past, saying hi, surprised at their offerings. Molly turned to Freeman mischievously. "Not as surprised as they're going to be. The sun is up. Let's get set."

Hooking up one of each of the devices they'd brought along to batteries was, of course, pathetically easy. When they were ready, Molly dropped the needle onto Pink Floyd's "Dark Side of the Moon." It played perfectly, of course, and the sounds that no one in the market had ever heard before caused every head within hearing radius to turn their head and look at them. Molly jumped onto the table.

"Ladies and gentlemen, step right up and hear what hasn't been heard in public since the Hemorrhage. That's right! The Chestnut Street Collective would like to bring to you a fragment of the old world. Not one of the dead fragments that surrounds us, but an actual moving working functional fragment! Step around and hear what the ancients listened to, and know that it can be yours!"

Molly jumped down. People gathered. Freeman smiled.

"Nice trick, Molly, but what's it good for?"

"Ah, so Jim here doesn't appreciate entertainment and culture. What's culture good for in this world, right Jim? Right. You're absolutely correct. However, I'd like to draw your attention right now over here to Crissa. You will notice that Crissa is sitting at a device called a sewing machine. What is this good for? Please, again, see that the sewing machine is hooked up to the same type of box that the record player is hooked to. These boxes are called batteries, and one of these boxes will run any number of different devices. Crissa, would you like to demonstrate the sewing machine for Jim here?"

Crissa zipped two pieces of cloth together. Every single woman in the crowd, and a few of the men, too, stepped forward with their mouths agape. "This sewing machine will run stitches through two pieces of fabric smaller than most hands can, and it does it in a fraction of the time. And that's not all – Crissa, show these fine people one of the decorative stitches."

This time everyone stepped forward. "So, Jim, can you see how this would be useful? How much time does Deborah spend sewing each night? Two hours? Imagine if she could get all of her sewing for one week done in two hours one night. What is this good for? You tell me, Jim?"

People actually clapped. Freeman smiled. No table nearby even had a vendor at it.

It was written in red paint, faded slightly to brown, on the wall: "I hope you get this message. I hope you read. I hope you think. The books are in the attic. Good luck."

The apartment on the fifth floor of the building was, Freeman realized the second he entered it, a treasure trove. Somehow, this apartment had remained untouched. What was here was worth more than most any other building he'd ever gleaned. Getting everything down to the second floor, that was another story. But for now...

The Pre-Hemorrhage Philadelphians lived in some crazy luxury, that was for certain. He'd had to kick the termite-eaten door open, something that he always felt bad doing. It didn't always mean that the apartment blocked by the door hadn't been gleaned, but it was a good sign. This apartment, though, was pristine.

Part of him thought that he should go get Molly, and Steve, and Sal and the cart. The rest of him was too excited to leave yet. He started looking around.

First was the windows. They were older wooden windows; panes of glass were intact in three of them. This was a treasure in and of itself. There were still screens in the windows; these would be useful as well. The frames around the windows were intact, meaning that the window weights were still there; that meant chains, possibly, and if not then iron blocks that were eminently salable to the smithies.

The furniture was, of course, all decrepit. Freeman pulled some of the old, rotted padding out from the chair in the corner. The springs were intact. There was a plastic box with a curved glass piece in it, the curved glass intact. There were a number of boxes with buttons and knobs on the front that Freeman knew he could disassemble, but he didn't know what was inside. He went into the kitchen.

The drawers were full of silverware, a king's ransom of forks and spoons. There were eight—*eight*—knives in a knife block against the wall. Eight knives alone would make this house worthwhile; that was enough to save them from having to go to the smiths for this year, assuming the rust would come off. There were plates, glasses, bowls... Freeman had never seen so much intact pottery and glass in one place before, even at his parents'—*hoofbeats sundering the world*—home. There were pots and pans under the cabinets, there was... he was overwhelmed. He stepped out into the hallway.

Alright. No obvious signs of struggle in the apartment. Nothing was packed. He knew what he'd find. Despite this, he had to catalogue it all and then get back to South Street and get the rest of the Gleaners over here to get the contents of the house back. But first, keep going.

The bathroom had a bunch of bottles and cans in it, the remains of towels, a tiled floor, the sink and tub and toilet were all intact. The fixtures were there, which meant there were pipes in the walls. Hopefully they were copper. The closet was full of rotting organics; that would have to be sorted after the fact.

The bedroom was where they were. Of course. The late afternoon sunlight streamed though the dirty window in slacker Jacob's Ladders, spotlighting certain parts of the mausoleum. Two skeletons lay in the bed, leathery skin pulled tight over them, still locked in a final embrace, as if they could stave off the dark by holding one another.

After a few seconds, Freeman could look away. And that was when he saw, next to the intact mirror—*intact mirror*—the writing on the wall.

The attic had to be next.

"Why did we gather all the unripe apples again?"

"We're making pectin."

"What's that for?"

"It makes the fruit preserves that we're making better."

"But the apples aren't ripe yet, it's only July."

"I know. But you know how you didn't like the serviceberry jam because it was too thin?"

"Yeah. What does that have to do with crabapples?"

"Are those washed? Good. Grind them. Unripe apples are high in pectin. It will help the jams we're going to make later in the summer gel up properly so we can spread them on bread. It's a little on the luxurious side, for us, but I think we can stand a bit of luxury, don't you?"

"A bit, I guess."

"Alright. Dump those apples into the boiling water. I'll add mine too. Besides, this tree is too bitter to eat, right?"

"Yeah, this tree sucks. I'm surprised it hasn't been chopped for firewood yet."

"Well, for this year we're getting pectin from it, so that's something."

"How does this stuff work?"

"Lord, I don't know. Gramma didn't tell me that part. All I know is that you mix some of the reduced liquid in with the jam you're making and it helps the jam be properly spreadable and not run off the bread. We're getting cherries tomorrow, right?"

"Right, tomorrow is cherries and hopefully some peaches."

"Then tomorrow we'll use some of the pectin, and you'll see why we're using it."

"Alright, then, I'll believe you."

"Give yours a bit of a stir. The boiling water pulls the pectin out from the apples and it winds up in the liquid. Also, the acidity of the pectin will help preserve low acid fruits like, say, sweet cherries and peaches."

"Ah. Things we're going to pick soon."

"Yep. High acid fruits, like cornelian cherries and raspberries don't need the acid, but they're both low-pectin, so it will help them set properly. And fruit jams just work far better when they're pectined. Alright. Have they been in for twenty minutes yet?"

"Sure."

"Good. Okay, now, that sack. Hold it over top of my pot. Good. Now I'll pour your pot's worth of apples and liquid through. Like that. Now we'll put the bag over your pot and dump mine through. Okay. Wow, that steam's hot. Alright. We've got the frame set up, so we'll hang the bag over top of the pot while we let the liquid boil down to half."

"We're making a lot of this, huh?"

"We're going to preserve a lot of fruit, right?"

"That's the plan."

"Okay, now the liquid's boiled down, so we'll remove it from the heat, and hang the bag over top of the pot. See how the liquid that's draining from the bag is clinging to it? That's the pectin coming out. We'll get it just fine."

Freeman dropped off of his bike. The full moon shining over Camden was both a benefit and a detraction. He wrapped his chain around the tire of the bike and pretended to lock it. A quick readjustment of his backpack, a quick wave to Smite-Them-Mightily, the gate guard, and he was into the Fork.

Smite-Them-Mightily and the rest of the gendarmes were more than comfortable with him coming in late at night to work on one thing or another. When a machine needed servicing, or when he just couldn't sleep, there was no other place for him to come but the Fork. And he came here plenty.

The engineers' office, his office, was on the top floor of the plant, above the main machinist floor. He lit the eight oil lamps scattered across the room and set his backpack down on the ground, then headed back down to the assembly floor. The storeroom was on the left side of the floor. He threaded his way through the giant machines, touching each one briefly. These machines, and the machines of the rest of the Fork, milled their way through tires and coal and charcoal and wood, but that wasn't what they ran on. These machines had milled his time thin, mincing every second and every day into the fodder that they needed to run. And Lord, did he love these machines. This furnace was the only furnace hot enough to make glass, this kiln both ran that steam engine and made the finest bricks, this drill press, this anvil; his present was bound up in these machines just as his past was bound up with Molly.

And none of these machines was the Fork itself. That was coming.

He unlocked the storeroom door, set his lamp down on a desk, and lit a few lamps around the place. Quickly now: five barrels into the wheelbarrow, drop one barrel on the machinist floor, then out the side door quietly, park the wheelbarrow just out of sight of the guard. Nudge the door shut, silently.

The Fork was lost without him. Oh, sure, given the paperwork, and the plans, and the machines themselves, Joyce and Cooper could probably keep everything running. But there was a shortage of people who could be properly educated to make everything work. And he hadn't been training Joyce and Cooper for long enough. They started looking at machines, seriously looking at machines, seriously learning, at eighteen and twenty. He'd started at eight. They'd been in training for less than five years. The Fork needed him.

Grab the barrel, and back up to the engineers' office. He set the barrel from the storeroom on the table, then took the barrel of oil out from his backpack and set it down next to the first barrel. Then he grabbed all the plats, all the plans, all the blueprints, and deposited them in the center of the huge drafting table that dominated the room.

His library. All his important books weren't here, of course, but he dropped the physics text and a few of the electronics texts into his bag anyway. The rest went onto the table with the scrolls of paper.

He knocked the bung out of the barrel, played the stream of oil across the plats. That was the true moment of choice, gone and done before he could do anything but plow forward. Save the Collective, or save the Fork. The choice was made, and that quickly.

Then the barrel on top of the oil-soaked plats. He cut down a candle quickly and set it on the table with a piece of paper sitting next to it. That should give him fifteen minutes. He broke his key off in the lock of the door, just to make sure, then set off for the outside world.

"Alright people, settle down. I know that we're all busy, but Molly insists that this will be a short voting session, though ultimately very important. She hasn't even told me everything she intends, but remember, any member of the Gleaners has the authority to call a vote if she has three others behind her. As per our custom, before Molly can bring her vote about, anyone else wishing anything voted on now has the right to speak. Any votes, stand.

"Then I yield the floor to Molly."

Freeman dropped to the floor in the spot in the circle that Molly had just vacated. Steve looked at him, questioning. Freeman shrugged.

"People of the Gleaners, I come to talk about the future. I ask, just for a short time, that you think about the future with me.

"The last five days have seen more upheaval in all of our lives than we're used to dealing with in a year. We have moved our home these last few days. We are short of sleep, and our muscles burn with the work of moving our lives to this new compound where we all will see our lives blossom in ways we have never considered before."

Molly looked at Freeman. Her eyes burned. Those nighttime conversations on the pallet they shared all rose up in his mind. *Is she going to talk about it all now?*

"People of the Gleaners, we've added more of you to our rolls in the last five days than we usually add in a year. We have room for more besides, and when we find people who can play guitar as well as you play harp, Lydia, we'll add them too. When we find as good a fruit-gleaner as you, Eric, we'll bring them in too. There are five new members in our new consensus, and for the first time, now, we consider how a child gets to vote in our family. Tiff is the first child that the

Gleaners have had in our, admittedly short, but particularly fruitful times.

"Here is what I wish you to consider, Gleaners all.

"There are two things wrong with our name. First, we have always called ourselves the South Street Gleaners. Well, we no longer live on South Street. And when we did, calling ourselves after the street that we simply lived on was silly, in truth. We had as little to do with greater South Street as we did with Camden.

"Now, we hold the most profitable *two blocks* on Chestnut Street that we can. We have more land than we can work. And when we find people who agree with us, they will be clamoring to join us. And we will expand what we control, and we will expand with the same love for ourselves and others that we live with now.

"The second thing wrong with the name is just that. We are no longer gleaners. Will we still glean? Yes. Yes we will. We will never stop gleaning as long as there is more to learn, more to eat, more to rebuild. But we have all this space that was once burned-out, that was once Fishtown's productive farmland, and that will be our productive farmland. We have an orchard which has been transplanted here, an orchard that will grow over the course of the fall and spring as we dig out new trees to plant.

"We have cisterns. We have a well. People, friends, family, we are no longer at the mercy of anyone but ourselves. Will we still call ourselves the Gleaners?

"I hereby call a vote. As before, our name will reflect what we are, and how we live. From now on, I say that we are the Chestnut Street Collective. Who will stand with me?"

Not a soul was left sitting.

The whole 'why' of the Hemorrhage was something that the Churches loved to debate. No one knew for certain, no one had any proof, everyone had their own theory.

But the Churches, they loved to pontificate on the whys and the hows and, in some of them, on what you had to do to keep it from happening again.

The Hindus were probably the most honest. They had a belief that the world moved in cycles, as per the Gods' will, and that it just happened when it was time for a cycle to end. Once the Hemorrhage happened, the world was in a new cycle, and it was time for humans to remake the world that the Gods wanted. Since this was the closest to the 'I have no idea but...' that Freeman saw as the most proper theory on the Hemorrhage, Freeman liked this one an awful lot.

The Christians had their book of Revelations, and they liked to say that the Hemorrhage had occurred in concert with the apocalypse laid out line by line in that book. Which may have been true. No one had any proof, and there was no real record left behind of the final days of the old world beyond some graffiti that still stood in out-of-the-way places that said 'The End is Here.'

No, Freeman couldn't buy that one because if the Hemorrhage had happened like they claimed, there was a whole chapter that was missing from reality, but not from the book. And since he had never seen a Kingdom of God, well, what was there to say?

The heathens all said that the Earth Mother became angry at the world for its treatment of her—as evidenced by the city around them and its current state. Depending on which Grove or person you talked to, that was as much agreement as could be found there. Plagues, floods, fires, drought, locusts... There was evidence for most of these; piles of human bones with no obvious violence visited upon them past the actions of scavengers, the blasted remains of the factories south of the Schuylkill on the Delaware and the heat-twisted carcass of the bridge you'd use to get to them, the water stains halfway up the walls of some houses in Old City. All of these were possible answers. Freeman didn't really buy any of them because the signs just weren't consistent enough.

And then there were the insane ramblings of the private religions; the Fishtowners were the best example. That Duke Fishtown I was born into the last world and was displeased by it so he slaughtered everyone who disagreed with him by axe. Freeman had seen more of the world than most Philadelphians, and knew it was larger than people thought, thousands of square miles, and that would just be too much work for one man, even if he became a God at some point in the process.

And that was the problem. If the churches had all ignored the Hemorrhage and just got on with other religious nonsense, fine. But since they didn't... why follow a God who loved the world, and so did this, or who hated the world—and particularly man—and did all this in a spasm of rage?

He never said any of this, though. Smile and be silent when people asked him. Or say he was going to three different rituals on the same day to three different groups and not go to any of them. It was better, easier to not rain on anyone's parade, and instead to spend that time reading and studying and thinking. He always got more comfort out of focusing on the real than he did out of faking belief in some mysterious mythology, one that may well have been made up anyhow.

"Alright, everyone gather round. We've added Freeman this year, and I've reviewed our food supplies. We'll be able to make it through the winter, I think."

"Praise be!"

"Yes. It's a good thing indeed. There's a catch, though."

"What's that?"

"We'll be able to squeak by, but... we can't afford any surprises this winter. We're likely to be on short rations by March, and that's alright because we'll start getting greens then, but we still can't afford anything like a child. We're going to have to suspend the pennyroyal lottery this winter, and all the women will have to just drink the tea."

"No!"

"I'm sorry, Crissa, but we're going to have to do it this way. We don't have a choice for survival, and what Freeman's bringing in is just too valuable."

"But Jase... you know..."

"I know, Crissa."

"Why wouldn't you tell me this in person you... you..."

"Crissa."

"..."

"Anyone else?"

"Jase you bastard you know I'm a month late!"

"We can kick Freeman out."

"And we should!"

"Crissa, he's already taught us canning. That's the only reason we've got enough of a surplus to bring another person on. You know what the hunting in the winter looks like. We don't have much of a choice. And you're only a month in. You know this has happened before."

"But that was the lottery!"

"Crissa."

"Yes, Jase."

"Lara? Molly? Meghan? Any objections?"

"No, Jase. Makes sense to me."

"You know I'm not getting pregnant anytime soon."

"Still and all, you're drinking the tea. I'm sorry about this. It is not something I want to do but there's no way we'll survive the winter if we have a pregnancy, and you all know what happens to the kids whose parents were on starvation rations during their term. If we have kids here we need to have healthy ones who can do their share once they're big enough, four-five winters old. We just can't risk it now."

"All this for reading, Jase? All this for words? You'd risk your son for words?"

"No, Crissa. Not until we can provide an actual future. Freeman hasn't been here long but we need what he knows. If we can provide a better future next year than this, then that's what we need to do. And you have no way of knowing you wouldn't pick the white bean today. There was never any guarantee."

"This is a guarantee."

"Yes. Here's your cup. Drink up."

Can a machine be truly said to make choices, or can it only discriminate?

Freeman stood on the bridge walkway with Drake and Scotto and watched the Fork slowly make its way towards the first building it would be taking down, watched as it approached its first real test. Granted, it had been ingesting everything that the sweepers threw into its mouth, the giant conveyor belts of its esophagus dragging the matter down to the forking paths where steel and glass and plastic and concrete and brick and ceramic and paper and leaves and trees would all be separated from one another, and fed to separate holding bins until a heavy enough a store was built up. Then each bin would drop its material into the proper forms or furnaces or shredders or crucibles.

But what was the separation process? And did it matter? Did the Fork actually choose which pathway each separate mote of material would find its way down? When the iron was slagged into pigs, was the separated-out concrete sent to the grinder to be mixed with new lime and water and turned into cinderblocks, was that the machine's choice?

What was the Fork?

The front of the Fork, hungrily chomping down on whatever it came across, whatever it ran into, whatever was pushed into its path, that was the mouth, the jaws, the teeth.

The giant fans for separating the light organics were the breath of the Fork.

The spectrophotometers that separated the glass from the plastic from the ice, and the plastics from one another, and the colors of glass from one another, those were the machine's eyes.

The magnets that pulled the metals from the mess were the

machine's biceps, drawing some things away and up and out from the rest of the machine's food.

The electromagnetic scales that figured out when a cast-iron bin was full, those were the palms, hefting the weight of objects in the hands.

The ceramic gratings that held metals and non-metals separate in the slagging chamber were the fingers.

The furnaces were the machine's hearts, the machine so long and huge that it needed four furnaces, four kilns, four steam generators, to keep it all moving.

The grinders, the mills that would grind everything finely, down to a powder, that was the churning of the stomach, the acid that broke the food down to smaller, digestible pieces.

The intricate gearing system that sent power to the wheels were the legs.

The iron wheels the machine rode were its feet.

The drops at the end of the machine was the anus, dumping out what it no longer needed. Its fuel was reduced to less than ash, but the raw materials that were spat out from the machine were, as far as the machine knew, rubbish.

And the Fork's brain was the Fork itself. Drake, Scotto, Freeman, even Joyce now driving it at its top speed of less than a foot per second, they was the brain of the machine.

Could a machine so large, so overpowering, so complex, could such a machine be said to not make choices? And if such a complex machine did not make choices, but only distinguished between what was in front of it, could Freeman be said to make choices?

From up and down the Delaware, from the farms of South Jersey, from Philadelphia and the rest of Pennsylvania, people came. From everywhere around, on a daily basis, singly, in pairs, in families, people walked and rode and sailed into Camden to join the Fork.

It was rather amazing how many people came to join the resurgence of Camden. Most everyone Freeman knew stayed with one group, living in one place, for most of their lives. The lifestyle of the world was required to be landbound, tied to one place—or in the case of traders, one route—and so much movement was unlikely at best.

Each had their own reasons. Sometimes, men joined up because they were youngest sons and their parents refused to split the family farm. Sometimes localized famine or drought would drive people from their homes, sometimes raiders took everything and left only one remaining to find her way to the Fork. Sometimes, mostly in the case of the Philadelphians who joined up, they were sick of living in the crumpled tenements they'd lived in their entire life, and wanted to live where roofs were repaired, walls were patched, where new housing was being produced and there was maybe electric light. Some women came to the Fork because they had the men. The Fork took them all in.

Freeman was constantly amazed at this. The processes for joining the Gleaners, the Collective, even Fishtown, were complex. The Fork had none of that. They wanted every warm body around, and put the new citizens to work immediately. Somehow the Fork never ran out of jobs for the new citizens. Some were moved to the fields, some to the gendarme training grounds, some to construction.

Sometimes whole groups of people were moved by wagon train to the other Fork locations in the north, uprooted wholesale, and moved to a new place to live and work. Which wasn't to say that the Fork kept everyone. A place would be found for you to work, to sleep, food would be found for you to eat. At first. As long as you worked, you'd keep your place at the Fork. But if you fell asleep on guard duty, or showed up with too much 'shine in your system, or simply didn't report, well, the bridge was right there and the road went in both directions.

Sometimes people left the Fork. The Fork watched them go. Sometimes they came back, only to find themselves at the bottom rung of the housing ladder, back in the shanties. Why would people leave? Everyone thought that the most successful people in the world worked their own farms, that you were only rich if you had your own place and could defend it. Those who could were deified by anyone living in the housing complexes; one of the few places where the Collective and the Fork overlapped was the sense of superiority that the landowners around them felt. It wasn't always the case—Lydia and Matt, for example—but often, settling down to a small farm was the goal.

It was easy to see that those small farms weren't so different from the collective living arrangements that the Fork and the Collective shared. The town Freeman had grown up in was a fine example; the farmhouses were built around an old circular road, with the farmhouses on the outside ring and the farms expanding out from it like spokes. In the center of the ring, the town built a watchtower; citizens took turns standing watch to ensure that no raiders were able to find their way into the farms and steal grain or tomatoes. And, of course, Freeman's family owned the wagon that took the town's goods to market.

Every living arrangement around shared one thing: a family. A man or woman couldn't make it alone.

"You asleep?"

"No, you?"

"No. Keep your voice down. You-and-I have to talk, and talk quiet."

"Alright. What's going on, Molly?"

"Listen, oh good, hear that wind. I don't want anyone to hear us."

"What's up, Molly? What don't you want anyone to hear?"

"Freeman, look, you're doing too good here."

"What do you mean, doing too good?"

"Jase is worried. About you. I overheard him and Crissa talking. You're dumping too much on the group, too fast."

"How so?"

"Freeman, look, how do I say this? The things that you've brought us, they're incredible. We're doing so much better since you've been here. But, but Jase is worried that people are starting to look to you as some sort of leader."

"But Jase is the leader. I'm no leader."

"Right. But Jase, well, Jase is paranoid. He's kicked people out before who get too much influence with other people. You're starting to have a, a patina of power; people are so impressed with what you've brought us that they're starting to look to you as a leader. Even though you're younger than all of them. You've brought, what, scurvy cures, vegetable and fruit canning, those new drill bits, the foot lathe, the mordants, the reading, the pine pitch..."

"They're all things that help the group."

"Right. But it's all been in a year and a half. If you keep going at this rate, you're going to run out of stuff to teach us. And when you do, Jase will give you the boot. You'll be out on the street."

"Why would he do that?"

"Because he likes his little bit of power. He likes being able to lord over us all. And if you erode that, even through teaching us things that help us out, then he'll put you out on the street faster than you can blink."

"...so what should I do? You know him better than I do."

"You should slow down. Keep with the reading lessons, we all need that, and he won't let you stay if you don't keep those up. But see if you can slow down people's progress. And slow down the new skills you're bringing in. Start like, I don't know, bringing out one or two a year."

"What do I say if it's something I've always known how to do? I mean, I was going to show people how to make dowels. They're like nails, but cheaper and made of wood. And gluemaking. How do I say, oh yeah, I've always known how to do this, but just decided to not tell you about it?"

"I'll get you some more books. Slow it down, 'experiment,' say you learned things out of books. It'll work, I don't think Jase will go back and check up on you. He hasn't been keeping up with the reading lessons as well as anyone else. You need, now, to keep bringing in new stuff, but you need to slow it down so Jase stops noticing that you're eroding his power."

"I'm not eroding anything. I'm just trying to help."

"I know that, Freeman. But Jase doesn't bring us anything new. Except food. And, frankly, while food is the first thing that we need, you're bringing us what we want."

"Ah, Freeman, it's good to see you."

"Drake. What a surprise! It's good to see you too. What are you doing here? Usually Scotto or one of your other managers comes down for each week's shipments. I'm surprised to see you."

"I wanted to propose something to you. Would you mind leaving the mule and wagon here with Infidel to unload and heading upstairs with me for a few words, and perhaps some tea?"

"Infidel?"

"The-Infidel-Shall-Burn-In-The-Righteous-Fire-Of-The-Lord. My name, sir."

"Ah. Do you mind taking care of the mule? Sal's a little fussy with people he doesn't know."

"That's why I'm here, sir."

"Then sure, Drake, I'll come up with you."

"Good. Now, Freeman, do you remember the plans that I showed you the first time you brought your batteries here?"

"I remember them well."

"Freeman, our plans are maturing slowly, slowly. Camden is beginning to come together. I'm sure you remember what it used to be like. That morass of brown fields is slowly becoming a city again, and the heart of the new city of Camden is going to be this building that's being filled with machinery. Your machines, and your ability to fix the few machines that we have here, have been invaluable to us. But our plans cannot go forward as quickly as we'd like without you around."

"But sir, I am around. I bring batteries, and any machines you request that I have or can make or repair, every week."

"That's not enough, Freeman. How much of the week do you spend gardening, or making preserves, or picking berries?"

"Enough."

"Come work for us full time, instead of for the Collective full time. Work with the machines, don't waste your time with gathering foodstuffs, or preserving food. Your skills are too valuable to have your time spent doing mere survivalist drudgery."

"Drake, respectfully, the Collective is my home, my heart, my family. I will not leave them."

"Then live there, but work for us during the week. You might not do as well on any given week as you would on your best week of trading, but I promise that you'll bring more food to your family by working for us, working with machines at all times, than you will by trading your machines to others, and by spending the daylight hours gathering food."

"I can't just leave the Collective. It's a tempting offer, but we make our decisions together. How many hours, and what's the pay you're offering? I have to bring this up with them."

"This is your life, Freeman? Are you going to let them tell you what to do?"

"Respectfully, again, Drake, yes I am. We are a family."

"Good. I like a man of convictions. Forty hours a week, and six bushels of grain."

"I'll talk to the family, and bring you our decision next week."

"Argue well, Freeman. We need you here more than they need mulberries."

As Freeman pounded through the subway tunnel, he knew what was happening behind him. The rats underground were always looking for food, and there were quite a few of them around here, lean and hungry and ready to fight for a next meal. Behind him, he had dropped more food than showed up in one place in a week. As soon as he pounded past, he could see—even without his eyes—the causal chain that would develop.

Rats would swarm from the walls and tracks and converge on the grain. They would carpet the floor in a squirming mesh, squeaking and fighting over the tidbits on the ground. Then the cats, never too far away, would drop in to see what their favorite food supply was doing. Claws, teeth, fur and fur, grain. Into that maelstrom would wander Scotto and whoever he had with him. And the rats never ran from humans. The rats would hold them up just fine. You never ran into a rat swarm; the rats would attack, and if you fell, a struggling or prone human was the same to them: a fine dinner.

Freeman pounded along. He could begin to see light streaming down from the upstairs entry gallery. Not enough light to see by, but enough to cast the darkness into a bluish haze.

He triggered the flashlight again, and not a moment too soon. The rusted hulk of some huge piece of equipment rose out of the shadows at him. This wasn't a train, but looked instead like some sort of repair vehicle, whether for the walls or the tracks he didn't know. He slowed as he passed, inspecting the front; could he use the blade to augment the Fork?

He stopped abruptly. Could he use the blade for the Fork.

Could he use the blade to augment the Fork.

The Fork was burning, ripped into a thousand pieces. Holes were blown through both its outer skin and the power plants; the drive train was wrecked; the kilns were spewing hot lime across the surface of the bridge. The Fork would never run again, let alone be augmented.

And whose fault was it that the Fork was wrecked beyond repair?

For the first time since he set off towards Camden from the Walt Whitman Bridge on that fatal night, he knew what he had done.

Life with the Collective had been good; he had chosen to wreck that.

Life as the Gleaners had been good; they had all chosen to end that.

And life with the Fork had also been good.

Could it be that life was simply a process of building up something good and then watching as some part of you that you couldn't understand wrecked it?

A beam of light skittered across the ceiling. Time to run.

Freeman's fitful flashlight beam scritched across white wall tiles, scattering light as steel scatters sparks from a flint. The station was nearby. There—concrete steps leading off the tracks onto the platform. He took them two at a time.

Finally, he could see light from above. He made his way down the platform to the rude mechanical steps rising from the tunnel, steps frozen into place by time and rust and lack of electricity. He hadn't plundered these for parts, though he well might have if they'd been needed. Good.

He ran up the frozen escalator and into the light.

"C'mon now. Grab each cherry—like this—and squeeze over the strainer. The pit pops out—like that—and the juice drips through. Drop the cherry skin and pulp into the bowl. Then grab the next one and do it again."

"Why do I have to learn this gramma?"

"Because you have to, Free."

"But daddy says it's women's work."

"Your daddy's both right and wrong about that. Yes, it's women's work—c'mon, start squeezing—but you need to know how to do this. I'm not going to be around to do this for you—your mommy and dad might not be either. We never know when we'll be called home, so you need to know how to feed yourself."

"I know how to do that."

"Then you need to know how to feed yourself over the winters. I know that you know how to fish, and soon enough you'll be able to shoot a bow and take down birds and deer, but meat only takes you so far. You need vegetables too, and preserving fruit as jam is as important. Meat only goes so far."

"But we make tomato sauce, and pickles. Why this too?"

"Because it's there, Free. You just trust your gramma and keep the work going.

"There, now the whole batch of cherries is done. That wasn't too hard once we got going, was it?"

"Why can't we boil it with the seeds in?"

"Because some cherry seeds are poisonous, even though the flesh is good for you —full of vitamins. First, take that pot of water off the fire. Good. Now, put a little water on the fire, good, and put the cherries in with it. Add the honey, a little more, a little more, good. And finally, the jelly stock from yesterday. This is from the apples we culled yesterday, it'll make the jelly set up nice and firm. Now let it come to a boil. While it boils, take these jars and put them in that pot of hot water. Careful, you don't want to burn yourself. Now we need to set the wax pot on the fire. Good, and add a little more wax to it. That's to seal the jars."

"What's the wax do?"

"It keeps insects out, and it keeps the jelly from going bad. You know when you leave the jelly out too long without eating it, it gets nasty? The wax keeps that from happening, it keeps the little insects from getting in and spoiling it."

"Okay, gramma."

"Yes it is. Now, look at the jelly. You see where that white foam is coming up? That's from the honey, and we don't want that. Take your spoon and skim it off the top, careful to not take too much of the jelly with it, we don't want to waste our work. Good, good, yes, just drop it onto the ground like you're doing. The grass will soak it up."

"What if we leave the foam on?"

"Don't know, never tried. My gramma wouldn't let me, and by the time I was doing it by myself, it was habit. And I'm not going to let you. Now take the first jar out of the hot water, with the tongs, good, and pour the jelly into it, leave about your little finger's nail of space. And pour the wax on top, all the way up, good, and you've preserved jam, Free! Wasn't that fun?"

"Yes, gramma."

"What's this?"

"This is a bicycle."

"A bicycle?"

"Yep. Two wheels. This one's just about ready, and best of all I think I can train other people to repair them – it was pretty easy."

"Really now."

"Yep."

"What are the wheels made of?"

"You remember when Molly picked up that huge pile of gutta percha on the cheap from that trading boat who'd lost their captain and were out of food and we'd had a good year?"

"Yeah."

"And we didn't know what to do with it? Behold."

"So, um, what do you do with it?"

"Travel long distances fast and easily. Like so."

"Oh my. Oh. Oh my. So that's why there's so many of these things around."

"Wanna try to catch me? Bet you can't."

"How are the wheels staying all swollen like that?"

"There's an inflated piece of intestine inside the gutta percha tire. I don't know if we can get more blocks of the stuff, but we've got enough now for forty or fifty bikes. And there's prolly some of the actual tires around intact that we can glean."

"Do you know what this does for fruit collection?"

"Dust yes. We can range farther than we ever could before. It took four bikes to get this one together because they're all a little different but I bet if we could get two or three people out collecting bikes in Sal's wagon we could easily get four of these together for next year. I mean, it's only January. Food starts in April. The worst part about repairing these things is the chains."

"What about them?"

"They rust bad and they have to move freely. I had to leave this one soaking in oil for weeks before I ran it through a sand barrel. And then two more weeks of soaking before I could get it moving. If we're going to try to get a bunch of these working for the spring we're going to have to get out gleaning like *ligne nu*."

"You want me to get everyone together for a demo and we can run it past the house at the meeting tonight?"

"Reckon that's a good plan."

"Anything else you can do with them?"

"The bikes? I bet you could run generators on them, or sewing machines, or... Anything that turns. If we wanted to we could turn any downtime into production of some sort if we wanted to."

"Huh."

"Yeah. I've got an idea for a water pump already. I bet we double the water pressure for irrigation about as easily as you care to without having to waste battery power for it."

"Alright. Let me go get people together. Good job, Freeman."

"Thanks, Steve. Any time."

Jamie had just finished chasing Rusalka and her brood into a barrel as Freeman came back from Matt and Lydia's place. The cats mewled miserably from the barrel; their cries would get no softer during the trip to the new compound at Chestnut Street. Rusalka was half-feral anyway; she'd wandered into the gardens as a kitten and stayed, the only cat in the city that the Gleaners didn't see as a food source and who didn't see the Gleaners as hunters. Now, they'd have to find a place for her to stay until they got the compound sealed up properly.

Jamie hefted the barrel and hauled it out to the waiting cart. It went next to the barrel of chickens, which only made her angrier. Freeman helped move the grain stores from the room Rusalka lived in – she helped keep the mice down – until the cart was full, then snagged some spare boxes to pack up the workshop.

Most everyone in the Gleaners stayed out of the basement workshop, except for dropping in for prosaic purposes like sharpening knives or shaving down new handles for axes. Those tools had already been packed up; Freeman started getting the workshop together by disassembling Crissa's wall.

No one knew why, and Crissa never explained, but she'd been gathering aluminum and steel signs from around the city since Freeman taught her to read. When the workshop needed a new wall, Crissa donated her sign collection; rotting studs had been covered in a plate-mail assembly: Bainbridge Avenue, Exit Only, Stop, Handicapped Parking, Official Inspection Station, Broad Street. Yield. One Way.

Freeman took them all down and carted them upstairs in as few trips as he could, stuffing them in the cart wherever they would fit.

The workshop itself was a more difficult proposition. The workbench was scattered with metal shavings, powders, sawdust, and plaster; this detritus was itself covered with a layer of screws, shims, tools, and whatnot. The twin problems of too little space and too many projects had turned Freeman's shop into a cyclone of material.

He set down the oil lamp he'd brought down from upstairs and plugged a light into a charged battery. The fluorescent bulb flickered dimly to life; it wasn't enough to work by, but it would be enough to see by. He blew out the oil lamp; with the moving going down, oil was likely to be in short supply soon, at least, here on South Street. Then again, who knew when he'd get new generators up at Chestnut...

Little enough time to worry about that. The metal bins of parts would go up first. He swept useful materials from the workbench into the wooden box he'd brought downstairs, swept the dust and detritus onto the floor. Once there was enough clear space on the workbench, he started unstacking the metal drawers and putting the drawer sets onto the workbench. These were what he made his magic with; bins of resistors, screws, spools of wire, solder, capacitors, magnets, motors... all the parts he could scrounge, repair, or strip from non-functional machinery. These could not be lost on the trip.

The bins were heavy, but he brought them up the stairs one by one. The second, hand-drawn cart was back by now, and the bins went into the back of it, stacked next to hay bales and the shaking barrel of cats, who had been moved off the last cart for the sake of the chickens.

Once the bins of parts were into the wagon, it was time to get the tools, the batteries, the alternators, the... he hadn't realized how much he'd collected. But the more he collected, the more he'd be able to fix. He squared his shoulders and went down the steps for the next load.

"And thus the greater consensus stands for Angie's plan to add another pump to the lower level. Are there any other matters to bring before the group?"

"Yes."

"Ah, Freeman. What do you wish to bring?"

"I have been offered a... an unprecedented opportunity. An opportunity that will aid both myself and the Collective. I fear, however, that it is something that the group will find disconcerting."

"Just spit it out, Freeman."

"The Fork wishes that I work for them, and solely for them."

"..."

"..."

A breath against his ear. "Couldn't you have brought this up to me in private?"

"No. It needed to go before the group, and you know that."

"..."

"..."

"They're trying to take over!"

"What are they offering us?"

"Are you going to have to move there?"

"They're bastards!"

"Does solely for them mean we have to give up our batteries?"

"What about our pumps?"

"Why do they want you to work solely for them?"

"I told you we shouldn't trade with them!"

"What does this mean for us?"

"Do you want to do it?"

"Do we want him to do it?"

"I am afraid, people, that Angie has hit upon the crux of the matter. Freeman brought it before us in good faith, and now we must decide if we want him to do it. But first—QUIET DOWN—we must ask Freeman: do you want to do it?"

"If it will benefit the group, and not divide us."

"What do they want you to do?"

"They want me to provide designs, they want me to find and repair equipment for them. They've got some pretty impressive machines, but there are no people to maintain them. And they want more machines. They have a plan for Camden—like we knew—and want to drive it forward, and they want my help."

"..."

"..."

"This is a complex question, Freeman. Why did you wait until the end of the meeting?"

"I told Drake that we likely would not decide what to do tonight. I told Drake that I would continue to live here, if I were to work for them, and that I could not make the decision myself, but that we would come to it together."

"Well, that's one thing right, at least."

"So? What questions do you have for me?"

Everything here is delicately, carefully balanced, even when the original source of the balance is unknown. The perfect example of this is the fruit trees.

No one group in Philadelphia can own the orchards. It is a simple impossibility. The orchards are too widespread, too random, and productive for too short a time each year. Yet, the food that comes from the trees is too important to the survival of the city as a whole for them not to exist. So the question was how to keep the orchards thriving.

The main problem is firewood. It needs to come from somewhere for the winters to be survivable, and windfall only works so far. There are Trees-of-Heaven and ash and red oaks aplenty growing through the streets, and from homes and businesses, but even with these trees, cherries and peaches and apples could be cut down and hacked up by lazy or weak or ignorant or just plain cold groups of people.

The solution evolved gradually. At some point in the past, some unknown potter started firing small clay tablets with a nailhole and fruit carved into them. This potter nailed a tablet into each fruit tree with its appropriate fruit on it. While no one knows who started it, everyone keeps the tradition up.

Potters in the market sell the tablets cheaper than anything else they make. Harvesters take the tablets with them while harvesting, and mark each useful tree with the correct tablet. The mental maps of the city's denizens include the locations of the trees, the time they fruit, when they can harvest; there are often runs on trees that have ripening fruit, and small children watch certain segments of the orchards for incoming harvesters so they can get their parents if it looks likely that a tree will be stripped. It is understood, of course, that each person or family is looking out only for themselves, but there are rarely fights over the fruit from any particular tree.

Most trees supply more fruit than even the hungriest of families can eat before the fruit rots, and few enough know how to properly preserve the fruit. And besides, if one tree in a particular spot is fruiting, the chances are that any number of others nearby are also.

Any unmarked tree is fair game for firewood. Any tree which falls is fair game for firewood. People who cut down marked trees rarely last the summer, let alone the winter. There are no police to stop them, but here, someone sees everything, and the community's enlightened self-interest leads to people who would hurt the community disappearing in one way or another. If these people are ever spoken of, well, they deserved what was coming to them. New residents are gently informed of the way things work; old residents have always done it this way.

So the parks and streets of Philadelphia have slowly been turned not into forests, but into orchards. Careful husbandry, completely disorganized yet agreed-upon by history and community, and the culling of unproductive species from the streets, has led to the city becoming a vast orchard. Some parts, of course, remain clear and are not choked by the fruit-bearing trees; other sections are covered in sun-ripened cherries during midsummer and choked with windfall apples in autumn.

The trees also keep the birds around, and keep the rats fat, and the rats keep the cats and dogs fat. The roving herds of cattle and zebra rarely come into the city, so the local food source is kept by both the trees, and what the trees help provide. The trees, and the culture that has grown up to protect them, are part of the true wealth of Philadelphia – even more than what can be gleaned from her buildings.

"What's so important that you needed to see me right away?"

"I made it work!"

"Made what work?"

"The alternator that I've been trying to fix. I finally got it working. You're gonna be impressed."

"Okay, I'll bite. Let me see."

"It isn't quite what it will be, but look, just watch the bulb on the workbench."

"Bulb?"

"The glass sphere with the wires coming from it."

"Okay."

"I can't turn it fast enough by hand to get a bright light from it, so we're gonna have to figure out how to make it turn faster, or store the power, or something, but watch the bulb as I hand-crank the alternator."

"Oh, it's glowing? Glowing? But there's no smoke!"

"No smoke. Nothing burns. Little heat. Problem is, I don't know how long the bulbs will last, and we can't make new ones. In truth, this is great, but it makes a whole new host of problems for us."

"Stop talking about problems, Freeman. This is amazing. Does anyone else in the city have this?"

"We know that neither Haddon nor Fishtown do. If they don't, I can't see anyone else having it."

"We're gonna have to keep this quiet."

"Real quiet. Everyone's gonna want it, but not know how to get it. I worry about more raids if we don't keep it under wraps."

"Agreed. But we've got to tell everyone else in the house."

"Of course we do."

"Turn the handle again, I want to see it more."

"Sure. As much as you want."

"How bright does it get?"

"I have to assume they get as bright as a fire. Most every house in the city has bulbs, or fixtures. They look like something that everyone had before the Hemorrhage. I think that they get really bright."

"How many can we have?"

"I don't know. It depends on the number of alternators I can get working, and whether we can store the power or not, and if we can come up with better things to use the electricity for."

"Better than light?"

"Pumps. Defense. Heat. The list of things that we can do with it is almost endless."

"This is amazing."

"This is only the start. But we have to see how we can generate the power without having to hand crank the alternator. And we have to get more alternators up and running."

"When do we tell everyone?"

"Now?"

"Why don't you-and-I bring this assembly upstairs?"

"Alright, the girls should be done. Make sure you don't pick up anyone else's sheep. Remember, we've got eight here today."

"How do we do that?"

"Check their ears, dummy."

"Oh yeah."

"Hey Matt, you've got one of ours."

"How so?"

"Well, we've got one of yours anyhow."

"And so you do. Looks like I've got the right count here so c'mon over and get yours back."

"Freeman, you go get the right sheep. I'll keep loading these guys up."

"Fair 'nuff. We're missing a black one, right?"

"Right."

"What's your mark, Matt? We use a SS for South Street."

"We use a quartered circle."

"They really don't like it when you mess with their ears."

"You wouldn't either, would you? Where else would we mark them though? Can't ruin the fleece."

"No. Just—stop that—wish we didn't have to brand them."

"You'll get over that soon enough. It's the only real way to do it. Well, Fishtown does use a stamp for a hole pattern in their ears."

"Yeah, so, branding, huh?"

"Pretty much. Here's your sheep. Steve's looking ready, better get back. Good to meet you, kid."

"Good to meet you too."

"Got the last straggler?"

"Yep. Trying to hide out with Matt's bunch. She didn't much want to leave."

"They do that. They don't like the wagon much."

"Everyone just uses the commons? Even people who don't like each other?"

"There's commons-peace just like there's market-peace. Sometimes you'll get fistfights over grazing time, like you saw today, but more often everyone comes when they're supposed to, and if people really do have problems with other people, they just shift their time to bring their animals. The number one rule is play nice. You can't have the commons without it."

"Or the market."

"We live by trade. No one stead can grow or make everything we need. We need the farmers from outside the city who come in to trade, and they need us. We can't exist without market-peace, and we can't exist without commons-peace. It's just like the fruit trees: we may not like everyone but we have to recognize what there is in the common lands that everyone needs for survival."

"But people disappear."

"Of course. And sometimes other people do it. But that's why we're mostly in groups. Anyone who will obviously be avenged is unlikely to be killed by a rival. It's just one more form of making it through the winter."

The pull string to the attic door had long since rotted away. Freeman had to drag a chair frame over to the door and reach up to where the flimsy door had unsquared from the building's sinking to haul the attic door down. The door and attached steps squealed and screamed at this unused-to violence; halfway down they got stuck and Freeman had to hang from them to pull them the rest of the way. But they eventually did come down, and Freeman was able to pull the stepladder out and set it onto the floor.

This was beyond surprising—it was shocking. When concrete has collapsed and stonework has fallen apart, for mere wood and metal hinges to still be intact after this much time... Freeman leaned in close to inspect the ladder. The metal hinges of the ladder were covered in a thick black crust that had flaked away as the door came down, and was now flaking away as Freeman brushed it; the wood of the ladder was a queer greyish-green under the thick layer of dust and smelled slightly of turpentine, slightly like the way the metal wires from a record player had smelled when he put one of them into a candleflame.

After marveling at the still-intact ladder, Freeman gingerly put one foot onto it and gently shifted his weight to it. The ladder groaned and bucked down, but remained anchored to the ceiling. He slowly made his way up the steps and into the attic.

The attic was covered in the same dust everything else was; there was a pile of shreds of wool-like material against one of the walls and squirrel tracks in the dust. The tracks looked old, their edges faded with dust. Freeman looked up then to see a pile of cubes, perhaps two forearms long on each side, packed against the side of the room, covered in the same dust as the rest of the attic. There was a window in the wall facing the street, which let in a dull, hazy, muted light.

The first order of business, then, was the window. Freeman carefully and slowly walked across the stringers to the window and gently tugged the frame. The rotted wood came apart in his hands. That was fine; he was going to strip the place of everything useful – including this pane of glass. He pulled out his belt knife and cut the mottled wood away from around the pane on both sides, then tugged upwards to pull the glass away from the wood.

After setting the glass against the wall, he cleared the rest of the scrap from the windowframe in the now-bright sunlight. There still wasn't enough light so he performed the same operation on the unfortunately-cracked upper pane; he still got this pane out in two pieces, so he was still in good shape. With light and air now flooding into the abandoned attic, he walked slowly across the beams—ducking his head to avoid roof-support struts—to the cubes against the wall. He ran his hand across the top of the cubes and swept away the dust.

Under the layer of dust was a relatively fine metal mesh that was covered in the same flaky crust that coated the hinges on the stairs. The flaky crust fell into the mesh, settling onto a layer of dust that was clogging the inside of the cubes. He shifted the box around, stirring up dust and trying not to sneeze. The boxes were entirely made of metal rods, about an arms' length on each side, like a dovecote made only of metal. On one side of the cube was a door made of the same metal mesh. The latch needed to be worked before it would move, but eventually he managed to pop the lock off the door and swing it away, and then work the ancient hinges until they allowed the door to be swung open. What he found inside the cage changed everything.

"People of Penn Medical! You have just felt the first ram of our machine against your building! We are the Fork, and we have come and told you that your building was to be demolished time and again, and that today, the day after the new moon, was the day by which you had to leave. Those of you who have not left—and believe you us, we can see you up there—if you are not out within twenty minutes, we will ram your building again.

"We are taking your building and there is nothing—nothing—that you can do about it. People of Penn Medical, it is time for you to move. Our crews are coming in now to help you gather what you need and to help you leave. We do not know how many strikes it will take to crumble your building but, I repeat, we are taking your building. It comes down today."

"Are we sure we should be doing this?"

"Freeman, don't get cold feet now. This wondrous machine is your doing. We could never have gotten here without you. Don't worry—this is the right thing to be doing."

"But these people live here."

"And we offered them relocation services, which some of them took us up on, and some of them refused. This is what happens when you refuse the Fork, Freeman."

"I'm going to go help the evacuation crews."

"Freeman—"

"Drake, you can't tell me what to do here. Don't crush the building until I'm out; if something goes wrong with the Fork, I am still the only one who can repair it."

Even now, even here, the Penn Medical building could only be described as a slum.

"Come, little Mother, let me help you.""You bastard, you're letting them do this! How can you help them?"

"I'm sorry, Mother, it is all I can do. We must do something. Forgive me if you can, curse me if you must, but in the meantime, let me help you get your food into this wheelbarrow."

"You were our hero! We called you the Lightbearer, do you remember that? Do you remember giving us music? How can you do this to us now?"

"Little Mother, all I can do now is help you load this wheelbarrow. Do you have more food that I can load in? You are not the only ones I can help; I need to help the world at large. The best way to help everything, everyone, everywhere, is to help the Fork rebuild their city. I know it hurts you now, and I wish it didn't. But it helps the world recover, little Mother. Is this your food store?"

"Yes it is, you bastard. Load it up—and I hope that the fancy food that the Fork feeds you causes you to choke, you tame lapdog, you stupid henchman. Tomorrow the people will rise up to your horror."

"Alright, Drake, is everyone out?"

"You were the last, Freeman. You were the last. I'm disappointed in you."

"Save it, Drake. Keeping these people alive is the least we can do."

"Can the building come down now, O Engineer?"

"Give your signal, Drake. Whenever you like. Whenever you like."

The room was swept clean, and appeared to have actually been mopped. Each windowframe had a clear, clean pane of glass in it; the room was bright without being breezy. The walls of the room were freshly plastered and smelled of drying plaster and whitewash. There was no hint of mildew, or mold, or smoke, or old dust; only new construction and chemicals.

Freeman leaned against the kitchen countertop and let his bag slide to the floor. The Fork took care of you when you were doing what they wanted you to, that was certain. This apartment at Fourth Street and Spring Garden was more than he could have ever asked for at the Collective; they certainly didn't have the time to mix up plaster to fix walls or wood to waste on new lath.

He stood to the side as some of the Fork's employees carried chairs, dressers, and his bed from the cart out on the street up the steps to the apartment. He knew that this wasn't what the Fork actually wanted, that they would prefer that he live in the complex in Camden. While he was willing to do some of what they wanted, now, he wasn't willing to give in completely; Philadelphia was still his home, even if he wasn't living with the Collective.

He had taken very little from the Collective when he left. Most of the furniture he'd used was too infused with Molly for him to want it here. Most of the technology that he'd rebuilt was either too bulky for him to bring or he had better, more newly built versions at the Fork headquarters in Camden. And the Fork was more than willing to stock his kitchen for him, he'd only taken a few jars of his favorite batch of white cherry jam from the stores at the Collective. He didn't think they'd miss it.

He hoped they wouldn't miss it. They sure wouldn't miss him.

Everyone at the Collective had turned out when he left, everyone dropping their tools and work and laying their baskets on the ground to turn and watch as he led the mule-drawn cart from the compound. He met no one's eyes; he could not stand to see the accusations that would stab into him if he dared to meet anyone's eyes.

He knew what they had lost in the last few months.

He just couldn't bring himself to fix what had happened. Too many words, too much pain. If only the Betsy Ross house hadn't burned, and burned when it did, if only Molly hadn't...

No more "if onlys." They weren't going to help now. They had all made their choices. And no child whom he'd helped rear with tears in her eyes would make him change his mind now.

It seemed that no birds were singing, that no crickets were chirping, that no wind was stirring; as if what was coming out of the eyes of his former friends and family was enough to stop even the great machine of the world. The only thing moving was Freeman and Scotto and the mule. And slowly, slowly, they drew away from the compound, despite the ranks of people watching him go with pain in their eyes.

The workers banged up the steps, careful of the new plaster. He wondered which of them would be moving into the abandoned café downstairs, to act as both a guard for him and a watcher for the Fork.

He found himself not caring that much. It wasn't important. They had no vision.

Even with all their noise, the building was empty.

"This is Sprawler business. What are you doing here?"

"Look, we saw the smoke from the Penn's Landing market and we're here to help. What do you need?"

"You to get out of here."

"Let's not argue about this? The Spectra is our favorite bar and we want to help. What's happening? Was there anyone in there when it started?"

"Yeah."

"Do you have any pumps?"

"No."

"Crap. We brought buckets. It ain't much but we can do what we can. Where's the nearest spring?"

"There's not much to do."

"Someone might have gotten around back of the bar. Let's try."

"'bout two blocks that way."

"Alright, Jamie, Molly, Steve, you two, come with me and lets get these buckets filled. Rest of you, pull down the houses closest the flames."

"What?"

"If we sacrifice the houses closest we might be able to keep the fire contained. Move it!"

"Molly, you and the Sprawlers stay at the spring and keep filling buckets. We'll start ferrying water over in the carts."

"Alright. Luck."

"Freeman, there's burning houses between us and the bar."

"Anyone in the houses?"

"No."

"Alright. Shove as much of the burning crap as you can off the bridge. Anything not burning get it out of the path of the fire. The wind is heading north so be careful, start on the south edge of the bridge. You four, uh, you four try to clear a path down the lane. Put these wet rags over your mouths to keep the smoke out of your lungs."

"Let's keep ferrying people! Come on we need more water."

"Freeman, this is the seventh load of water and the fire's still going. Are we even doing anything?"

"We've got a few of the houses put out and they're wrecked but we got some stuff out of 'em. People may not starve this winter. And we're almost to the bar. Let's keep going."

"Alright. We're not gonna be able to put the bar out, though. Look how it's burning."

"If we can get to it, we can see if anyone's huddled around the back, or if anyone's... well, we can get the bodies out."

"Is it worth it?"

"Maybe someone's been hiding somehow. There's enough holes in the bridge deck that they might be able to get clean air. You take my bike, I'll stay here and help deal with the fire."

"Sure thing. Sure do wish we had a better source of water though."

"Me too."

"Okay people. Good job getting the stuff together, but we need to move faster. Mary, we need you and your prowess with the broom over at Chestnut Street more than we need you here packing. Kevin, get a group of men together, we're going to need extra guards, especially tonight. Dave's there already, Steve will get there with the next load, who's a good candidate that we can get over tonight who can help guard?"

"What about Matt and Lydia from Bainbridge?"

"Will they leave their farm?"

"If they're smart they will. They got hit hard by that storm this summer, lost most of their wheat harvest. We can bring them in and they'll be a good addition, if we can convince them that whatever they can't bring over in their cart in one load they won't miss if they lose it."

"Good. Go get them, and like *ligne nu*."

"On my way."

"Freeman?"

"Molly."

"How's the packing of your machinery going?"

"I'm getting it together. I need someone to help me in the sewers to keep the rats away, they're going to be hungry at this time of year and will likely look to me as food. Can we spare Lana, she's good with the sling, to help me out?"

"Take her and go."

"Excellent. Lana, do you know the sewers at all?"

"I've been down once. I don't know the layout if that's what you're asking."

"No, I'm making sure that you've been down there so I don't have to explain what to do. I'm going to have my hands full with unhooking the generators and I need you to keep the rats down without guidance. Think you can do it?"

"Sure thing, Freeman. You can count on me."

"Good."

"Who's taking care of moving the looms and bolts of cloth?"

"I was taking care of that until you asked me to sweep."

"Sweeping is more important. Freeman's working on the powered looms, we might not need the hand looms once he's done with them, so long as we've got enough cloth for the winter."

"What if we need to hang cloth on the walls to keep the cold out? We don't know enough about the Chestnut Street compound yet."

"True enough. Get the cloth together into this wagon load and then get ready to head over. You can come by tomorrow to pick up your personals."

"Done."

"Let's head down to the sewers. We've got to get the functional alternators and the paddlewheels. They're the most important thing for me now, especially now that the workshop is packed and just needs to be carried upstairs."

"Okay. Torches?"

"The smoke will keep disease away. We'll definitely want torches. Grab some and I'll go get the sewer plate off the roadway. Meet me out at Fifth and South and we'll get it done."

He pounded his way up the subway steps, out of the underground and into the light. Fortunately, there was no one waiting for him here; the shock of finding himself in sunlight after what had seemed so long underground made him stop for a second to get his bearings and to let his eyes recover. He was standing on what used to be Broad Street; what once was a huge thoroughfare for passing cars like ice down the Schuylkill in early spring was now one of the best sources of firewood in Philadelphia. He had half expected some of the Fork's men to meet him here; if they had, he would be dead. Instead, he found himself alone in a circle of cut stumps, taking a moment to figure out where to go.

One of the stumps had a ceramic marker on it with a cherry carved into it. He remembered placing that marker with Molly, in another life.

He turned to the west, and started jogging. To the west was St. James Street, a narrow orchard of dwarf street trees between two huge, mouldering buildings. Once down St. James it was into the maze of streets, the old financial district, that led to the First Unitarian Church. People used to go to churches for salvation, and for the first time in his life Freeman found himself heading there for that reason. He had cached the belongings he needed in the ruins of the church.

The sections of Philadelphia west of Broad Street were dangerous, more dangerous than the rest of Center City. Market Street and Chestnut Street—the two surviving bridges over the Schuylkill—were exceptions to the rule; a truce reigned between the people of the city and the savage dwellers in the high-rises on the two main streets. He could only hope that he was dirty, dingy, and disgusting enough for them to decide he wasn't worth chasing, and that Scotto and the rest of the Fork's dogs were clean enough to be targets.

His side ached from whatever piece of ammunition or glass had grazed him.

Raspberry canes and nettle vines choked the narrow St. James, but it was the only way to go. Market Street was too open, too obvious. Silently cursing the thorns that gnawed at his sleeves and pants, Freeman slowly trod his way through the bramble. He narrowly dodged a rusted-out manhole cover, a pit yawning down into the darkness. One foot on a piece of concrete discarded from the building facing the street, one hand on a shard of glass covered in vines, the next foot down onto the shattered asphalt. He made his slow path down the street until he reached the shaded glade at the corner of Fifteenth Street. Here, a turn to the north would be the best way to go, but a nightmare of rebar and concrete from a building that hadn't survived blocked his path. As so often happened in this city, the path preferred was blocked by the ruins of the old world; he had to turn south instead, even though the First Unitarian Church, where he'd hidden his cache, was to the north.

South it was, down through more breaks and canes to an unnamed alleyway. The alley was too shaded to grow anything other than the Trees-of-Heaven that were so desired for firewood and nothing else; apparently the way through here was too rough for people to bother harvesting this wood – easier to take out the cherries on Broad Street and hope no one found you.

After squeezing through the narrow trunks and ignoring the birds yelling at his invasion of their homes, he came to the end of the alley and spilled out into the valley at Sixteenth Street. He peered carefully around both corners; no one was in sight in either direction. He headed north at an easy lope, each footfall a minor victory, a minor survival.

"Do you think that this is all there is?"

"What do you mean? Us? I like what we just did. Are you unhappy with it?"

"No, no, that's not what I mean, Freeman. Sorry, that's not at all what I meant. I meant, us, here, the Gleaners."

"Of course not. We'll be much bigger once I start getting some machines made, and we're spending less time working and can do other projects, maybe start trading machines..."

"That's not what I mean, Freeman. I mean the Gleaners themselves, ourselves. Do you think of us as a group?"

"I do, but, no, I don't know what you mean."

"Do you know how I grew up?"

"You don't talk much about it."

"I grew up in a Quaker village. And each household did their own thing, but when it came down to village decisions, we'd all come together and decide as a group, and nothing would happen unless everyone was happy with it. We'd make decisions as a collective group. It made for much slower decisions, but when we did something everyone threw their all into it. It wasn't like here, where everything is catch-as-catch-can unless Jase wants it, and then we don't get any input."

"What do you mean?"

"I mean, I wish, it would be wonderful if there was some way for us to make decisions where it wasn't Jase's will all the time, where we could come together, all of us, and decide what was best for the group. Some way that we could all decide what our future was going to hold, rather than being told by Jase."

"I thought you liked Jase."

"I do, Freeman, this has nothing to do with liking him. What it has to do with is that he tells us what to do, all the time. I don't think anyone's happy with it. Especially Crissa. But there's nothing any of us can do."

"But Molly, this is a lot you're asking of us. We've all been told for our whole lives what to do. You're asking people to break that. Maybe you, can, but I don't know about everyone else. And how much do you want us to decide? Do we tell Crissa as a group what pattern to weave? Do you tell me what to make? What to farm?"

"Fair enough, Freeman. I don't know. Not that it even matters. Jase likes holding on to his tiny bit of power too much. He'd never let it work. Ah, it's just a dream."

"Stop being so ambitious. Work with a little bit of the project at once. What about the Full Moon Parties? How are they planned?"

"The word goes out, and then people show up."

"What if you started asking around, just our group, say a moon or two in advance, and planning it out with everybody. Then maybe get a few other people involved. Don't do it as a, you know, a big, overwhelming thing. Start it with something small, and work from there."

"That's not a bad idea, Freeman. That might work. What other places could we try, to get people used to the idea?"

"Let me think about it. But for now, come here you."

"Freeman—"

"I don't like what's happening, Freeman."

"What's happening where?"

"With the Fork. With what you're doing for the Fork. I don't trust them."

"Oh, Molly, enough about the Fork."

"No Freeman. You're giving them power. Your machines, your skills fixing their machines, your... you're going to let them kill us. They're going to, and it's going to be your fault as much as it's theirs."

"What are you talking about?"

"Freeman, they're moving faster than before on whatever they're planning, right?"

"I think so. They're not telling me much about their long-term plans but, yes, they seem to be moving faster."

"Then what you're doing is making them so much more powerful. They already outstrip us in power. Don't you remember about Rosa?"

"What do you mean?"

"Captive selling? They're not beholden to us as a producer's community anymore. They're just beholden to you."

"But I'm here, I live here, they need all of us."

"No. They need you. And you're only keeping them dependent on you, not on us."

"And I need the Collective, so I'm not going anywhere."

"Something's going to happen, Freeman. Something's going to happen to break us up. The whole group. And they're going to do it. And it's going to be your fault."

"How?"

"Your machines, Freeman. You are responsible for how your tools are used. And you're not paying attention to that any more. You're just looking on to the next machine with never a thought to their use."

"But I'm not giving them their weapons. They have muskets and gunpowder, things we don't have."

"And you're not improving the process?"

"I did improve their mill."

"Then their gunpowder is your fault."

"No! Molly, they already had it."

"But you rebuilt their mill. The builder and the user, Freeman, they share responsibility. You share responsibility in what the Fork does with the tools you give them. But you've never really seen that, have you?"

"I know that I share in the responsibility for how fast the Collective has grown."

"Sure you do. We'd be a little tiny nothing without you, Freeman. That's right."

"Well? Not tiny, but you can't say that the extra food from the Fork hasn't helped."

"It sure has. And the extra food I throw to the curs on the street keeps them strong too."

"The Fork doesn't think of us like that."

"Sure they do, Freeman. They can't tolerate any other power structure nearby but their own. They need us gone. But you won't see that. And you won't ever see that until it's way, way too late. Now get the lamp, and I'll see you in the morning."

"Good night."

"..."

"Hold. What business do ye have with the Collective?"

"Whoa, Tiger. Hold? Ye? Spears? This is an awfully formal meeting to be having at the gates of our old homestead."

"Your old homestead? Then you are with the Fishtowners."

"We are with Fishtown, truly said. Things need not always remain in the present tense."

"Why are you here?"

"Things in Fishtown are ugly. Have you heard any of the news?"

"We have heard a little news, yes. Rumors of another poisoning, news of a fire in the hall. We of course know of the succession crisis that prompted your evacuation from this compound here at Chestnut Street."

"And that was an evacuation which we are paying for dearly. You have not heard, then, that our fields were salted over the winter past."

"How many of your fields?"

"Half of our acreage is ruined. We are growing grass that was brought up from the ocean's shores, and keeping it wet, and dumping the clippings into the river, but there is likely to be too little food for all of us this winter. We three are looking for a place to come to. We know this compound well. Will you have us?"

"It is quite too soon for that. Is it only the three of you?"

"No. We are all three of us married, and Mote and Forever both have one son apiece. My wife is heavy with child and is likely to bear our first before the autumn is done. There will not be enough food for us at Fishtown, and we need new homes. We hoped that the compound here would still be empty, though we also heard strange tales of the demon-worshippers that live here."

"Not just demon-worshippers, mind. Touch the bars which run across the gate."

"Ouch! What sort of—"

"No, not just demon worshippers. We also command the demons. Are you certain you wish to join us here, here where the demons obey our beck, call, and command?"

"If you can feed us, and our children and wives, over the winter, then yes. Yes. We will gladly stand with you who command the demons."

"What will you bring us?"

"Three fast stallions, the ones that my company and I ride here today. Six fine mares, who are well used to living in the compound. Fifty straight ash spears. Ten bows and one hundred arrows. Five barrels of salt fish, caught and smoked this year."

"What do you do?"

"I am a hunter, Mote and Forever are farmers and guards. My wife is a weaver, and makes the tightest cloth you have ever seen. Forever's wife is an embroiderer who decorated Duke Fishtown's cape. Mote's wife is the finest baker in Fishtown."

"And what else do you do? We will not accept people into the Collective who can only do one thing."

"I train horses."

"I sing the story of the town."

"I am a carpenter."

"I will bring your offer before the Collective. Come back in three days."

Each of the giant freight containers that had become a section of the Fork rode on two axles stolen from tankers, from tractors, from the shoddily-built trailers that used to move freight around the city and state. Those containers were far too fragile to have survived the years since the Hemorrhage, but their axles and wheels—tires stripped for fuel, of course—were still to be found almost everywhere. Especially in Camden; throughout and surrounding the city were areas surrounded with rotted, rusted chain-link fence that were full of wrecked trailers; these became fodder for the Fork.

Teams of men went out with hacksaws and mule-drawn carts and came back bearing one or two axles apiece. These axles, if they were in good enough shape, were disassembled by one team of men. Another team built wooden tires with steel crowns for the removed rims. Yet another team scoured the rust from the axles and greased them with animal and vegetable fats to help weatherproof them.

Then the skilled labor came along. Freeman had devised a system to keep the axles and wheels moving properly; a series of harnesses attached to the underside of the freight containers by leaf springs stolen from the same trailers both supported the freight containers and acted as a suspension system to keep the fragile machinery inside the Fork-to-be safe. Then the tires were reattached and the monstrosities were attached to the bottoms of the new Fork segments.

This was just for the unpowered sections of the Fork.

Each of the boilers inside the Fork was to serve a multitude of purposes. Each fed a furnace: one was to slump thermoform plastics, one to push out Bessemer steel I-beams, one to slump shattered glass into bricks, and one to bake the new concrete into cinderblocks.

They would all eat the raw materials, the tires, the paper, the non-thermoform plastics, the trees, the rubbish; what the Fork ate would keep the Fork moving and producing. Each had a power plant attached to generate enough electricity to keep the interior conveyor belts working, to keep the spectrometers alive, to keep the fans that were blowing the loose organics into the furnaces moving. And each would power two of the eight powered segments of the Fork.

The eight powered segments of the Fork each had four axles; each of the four axles bit into part of a tread removed from giant, abandoned, earth-moving machines. These segments were evenly distributed throughout the Fork: two at the head, two at the tail, and two each a third of the way down the giant machine. There was a boiler close to each of these powered segments.

When the drive train of the Fork was engaged, these segments would alternately push and pull the machine, slowly, inexorably forward, ramming its huge head into whatever was in its way. Trees, buildings, shacks, road embankments; what the Fork ate at its head would not matter to its mouth. It was all to be grist for the mill.

The drive train would be controlled from the operator's cabin on the third segment. Only the front segment, near the mouth, would turn; the rest of the segments would follow like baby ducks following their mother into the pen. The Fork was to have three speeds: forward, reverse, and neutral. Either going forward, going back to build up momentum, or still; it was far too big and would eat far too omnivorous a diet to have any sort of speed control on it.

Freeman could already see it moving, and it was good.

"Have you ever seen the ocean?"

"You know I haven't. I haven't left Philadelphia since I came here from Germantown. The closest I've come to the ocean is this river here, the river that the bridges cross."

"It's called the Delaware, you know."

"I know. What's the ocean like?"

"The ocean... you can't really describe it."

"Thanks."

"No, really, I'm trying. Look, you see how there are the little waves on the surface of the river here? And how there are little white crests on top of each wave?"

"Yeah."

"Well, the waves on the ocean are two-three forearms high, when it's calm, and the waves come into the shore with crests almost as big as the waves themselves. They crash repeatedly against the shore, so as you sit and dig for clams, or crab, or fish, you hear the constant sound of the waves striking the beach."

"What's the sound like?"

"A roar, a crash, a wet thing; like a cross between dropping a barrel of water and a thunderstrike. When it's storming the crashes of the waves are loud enough you can't hardly hear anything else. And that's just the waves... When you look out across the ocean, there is nothing but water, all the way to the horizon. No islands rising out of the clouds, no city far past the breakers. If there are derelict boats, they're close in where the water is shallow. Once you look past a few hundred feet out, there is nothing, not like here where the bridge pilings stick out of the water, where you see wrecked boats just below the surface of the water, sometimes breaking it. Just miles and miles of empty water."

"It sounds lonely."

"It is, in a way. And even though we went to mostly the same beach every year, the beach itself is never the same. The beach is a pile of white sand—nothing much grows in it, only a few grasses and some rose bushes high in the dunes—strewn about with logs, with branches, with chunks of timber ripped from some seaside ruin and deposited far, far from its source. There are shells of animals I've never seen alive and shells of the animals you eat, piles of seaweed, bladderwrack and sea lettuce and these brown hairy things. Jellyfish in the summer and horseshoe crabs in the autumn, fish bones, plastic bottles, rope... Of everything that the ocean eats, some gets washed back up.

"When you're fishing on the beach, the gulls will come for miles—not one or two gulls like we get here, but hundreds of them—surrounding you, cawing mercilessly for handouts. My grandpa said—"

"You okay?"

"Yeah. Sorry. My grandpa always said that they were bad luck to kill, and not tasty enough to risk the luck. We'd throw stones or shells at them, but they always just dodged what we tossed and kept hanging around for more.

"And that's not even the smell of the ocean. You know how sometimes, when the wind is right up from the south and the summer's been dry, you'll get the breezes that smell of salt and fish? That's what the ocean smells like all the time."

"It sounds amazing."

"It is. I miss it, miss it more than almost anything else, living here in this city."

"...producer's cooperative can survive within capitalist economy only if they manage to suppress, by means of some detour, the capitalist contradiction between the mode of production and the mode of exchange. And they can accomplish this only by removing themselves artificially from the influence of the laws of free competition."

"Freeman, what is Rosa talking about this time? I don't understand so much of this."

"Which words? Dictionary time!"

"Stop that. Um, artificial."

"Um, let's see. In this case? Probably um feigned, fictitious, not genuine or natural."

"So what is she saying?"

"She's saying that a group of people in one of those socialist groups, in one of those capitalist societies, can't exist unless there's a false break between the method of production —like farming—and what's sold. That a worker's cooperative can't outperform a normal, non-exploitative group, because there's no way non-exploitative groups can produce goods as cheaply as exploitative ones."

"Alright, so what I'm dreaming of is a 'producer's cooperative,' right?"

"I think so."

"And she's saying not only that doing it one piece at a time, like we're trying to, is not going to work, because it has to fall into place all at once, but that also if we do it on a small scale here, we have to find some way of making a false distinction between what we do and what they do if we want to expand."

"Because expansion will always be easier if you can keep people beaten down."

"What does she say next?"

"And they can succeed in doing the last only when they assure themselves beforehand of a constant circle of customers, that is, when they assure themselves of a constant market."

"So, it can only work if we can make sure people buy from us and only us."

"I don't necessarily think so. There's not much expansion in the city. Most of the power groups that do exist are, you know, either stable or shrinking. Fishtown, the Sprawlers, they haven't expanded much since I've been here; in fact, the Sprawlers have been shrinking a good deal. We see them around a lot less than we used to. And the family groups already function like these producer's cooperatives, I think. You're looking to take how family groups work and expand on it."

"I have seen family groups that are run like Fishtown."

"Good family groups, then. Good ones. But still."

"Yes. That's what I want."

"But the markets around here are inconstant. We never know who we're going to see on any particular market day, who's going to be in the city, what they're going to have to trade. Do you remember the drought two years ago? We hardly saw anyone come in the city that year."

"I remember."

"So how do we make a constant circle of customers?"

"I don't know. I don't know that any more than I know how we make everything happen all at once."

They never let dry leaves get into the house while they lived here. Now, withered leaves whispered across the floor, their dry skritching underscoring the emptiness of the house.

Freeman couldn't remember the details of the house he, his parents, grandparents, aunts, and uncles lived in, out in the sticks in New Jersey. Now he walked the compound at South Street, trying to fix in his head the details that he knew he would later forget.

All the windows were missing, removed from the panes and packed in hay and straw, carted over to replace the missing windows at the Chestnut Street compound. The smells of bread and cooking and people and cats were starting to fade from the house; now there was only a faint hint of woodsmoke and the cold, metallic smell of the city in winter overlaying the always-there smell of mildew and mold in the air.

He started down in the basement. Even here, details were missing that he would forget; the wall of signs, their exact order no longer in his head. The workshop: yes, the resistors were here, the caps here, the motors here, screws, bolts, nuts, washers here and here and here and here. The grain store, amaranth in bins here, wheat in bins here, barley in bins here. Mike's homebrew carboys here. Potatoes, leeks, onions, coal here, here, here, and here. Radishes here. Apples here. The bins that they once sat in had been torn roughly from the walls for future reassembly at Chesnut Street.

He made his way up the rickety steps for the last time. Here was the kitchen, here where the dried vegetables were kept, here the game larder—door missing—this cabinet kept the dishes, the drawer once here kept the spoons and forks and knives. The knife block once against the counter here. If he closed his eyes, he saw it lit by fire and candle and lamp, warm with cooking and family; when he opened his eyes it was stripped bare, grey in the cold, unfiltered light of the winter sun.

Here was where Steve would sit, playing guitar, here where Allan would drop to the floor by the fire and play the banjo, his body shielding the strings from the heat. Here was the bookshelf, their king's ransom of books doubling as insulation against the cold wall. Here was where Sally's tapestry hung, here where the new one, unfinished, was being woven for. That carefully charred wall was where the map was drawn.

Upstairs, then, with eyes closed, feeling every whorl and knot in the banister in a futile attempt to remember their exact pattern in the age-polished wood. Up to the fourth floor, where he and Molly had their room. He'd never remember the setup of anyone else's rooms, but his and Molly's he'd keep forever, their first room together in their first house together; the first room that was even partially his. His haven after Camden. *—hoofbeats sundering the world—*

No, up the steps. Here, in the hallway, the door that led outside, over the steel skyway to the house next door where Sally and Mary made their rooms, up on the fourth floor of the otherwise uninhabitable house. The skyway, where they would put out their seedlings during the spring before bringing them inside again for the chilly nights.

He stepped through the empty doorway and looked into the room where he and Molly had lived, then turned away again quickly. Without her presence, the room was emptiness itself. He'd have to remember it with the last quick glance he'd given it while quickly packing. And, and she was waiting for him at the Chestnut Street compound.

Time to stop remembering and start unpacking.

"Who's going up, then?"

"Eh, you are. You're smaller than I am, and this tree isn't old enough to be too sturdy. Even you'll be enough that I can get the lower fruit while you pick the higher."

"Alrighty. You got the rope so I can pass the bag down?"

"Here you are.

"Hey, you're not bad at the tree-climbing."

"I used to do it a lot—*hoofbeats sundering the world*—back at home."

"You okay there?"

"Yeah, I'm fine. Just remembering."

"Remembering is a bad plan in this world. You don't want to be doing that. As my pops used to say, 'Steve, memory is a slippery slope, and its paths are neither straight nor safe.' It's best to just live in the moment, you know?"

"Why Steve, that was almost eloquent."

"What did you just call me?"

"Well spoken."

"Oh. Well, I ain't that. My pops was the well spoken one in the family. I can't dustin' talk for nothing."

"Maybe if you just quote your father more often."

"You almost got that bag full, or is your mouth just filling up?"

"Eh, here you are."

"Alright. Here's an empty one, just pull it up."

"You don't want me to fill it from down there?"

"Yeah, yeah, ain't you the smart one, Freeman."

"Hold up with the chatting while I get higher in the tree. There's more apples up higher. It looks like someone's already picked over these lower ones."

"Well, if we get the higher ones that they didn't, then bully for us."

"Exactly. Hey, these look great."

"Not too surprising. You get really good trees around here, with good fruit. I'm not sure why, but I do know that this is one of the best sections of the city for fruit."

"I'll bet that store over there used to be a grocery."

"What would that have to do with anything?"

"More seeds in the fruit at the store would mean better hybrids growing around here, and as they naturally hybridized together you'd get really strong fruits. They used to seriously select for fruit, you know."

"How do you know all this shit, Freeman?"

"My dad wasn't as eloquent as yours but he knew a lot about fruit. It was passed down from parent to parent. My grandpa knew more about fruit than I think I ever will. My gramma too."

"You all must have eaten well, then."

"We had an orchard, an orchard of our own. Dogs to keep the few travelers or gleaners who'd come around out. But we didn't have to worry too much about them. They used to keep me in the orchard one year, then take me to the ocean for fishing and clamming the next."

"Sounds nice."

"You have no idea. It was paradise, that I know now."

Even though a part of it was marked up by him, Freeman could never stifle the small thrill of awe that ran through him when he looked at the map of the city. It took up an entire wall in the family room of the South Street compound. He saw it daily, twice daily, sometimes all day long. Still and all, the map was somehow magical.

Chris, before Jase drove him out, started the map. He found a place where a poorly laid street had oozed asphalt, gathered it in an old jar, and brought it home, thinned it out with homemade turpentine, and sketched the streets, out of scale and not entirely straight, on the wall in homemade, thick, black ink. Then the marking up started.

Crosshatching in pencil meant "don't go there." Those streets that were off limits to the Gleaners were drawn in, but dimmed into nothingness where distant visual inspection would no longer allow detail; some streets ran straight from river to river, others died out and picked up, others came out of nothing and turned into nothing.

Buildings that were known to be inhabited were marked with stars. Buildings that were unsafe were marked with X's, X's drawn in shrub honeysuckle berry ink, refreshed in red every year that faded to brown, then nothing, by the next autumn that ran around.

And that was the least interesting part of the map.

Where fruit that was gleanable grew, there was placed a mark. There were checkmarks, circles, boxes, dots, triangles, boxes with one strike through, lightning bolts, snakes, ovals, all drawn in a riot of colors.

The dyes used on cloth were thickened with heat and flour and then applied with the trimmed point of a feather. There were colors for different seasons; the colored symbols were memorized until Freeman started writing the legend across the room on the wall next to the south-facing window told what each mark, in each color, meant. Indigo was used for spring, blueberry for early summer, tomato for late summer, and pumpkin for fall. Each marking was carefully scrubbed off the wall when the tree was picked over; if the tree looked to be viable for next year, the mark was carefully reapplied.

And reading the map took some doing, it did. The Gleaners scavenged every fruit that was edible, every fruit that would make a dye that held, every fruit that grew in the city. Honeysuckle made an acceptable dye, holly berries were good for traps to keep the rats out. Serviceberries were marked twice, once for the early spring, to know when it was time to start digging, and once for the midsummer, when their blueberry-like fruits were ready to harvest. Blueberries marked once, a tomato circle on the map. Black cherries in blueberry checks, white cherries in blueberry circles, red cherries in blueberry boxes. Chokecherries in tomato snakes. Persimmon in pumpkin boxes, aronia in pumpkin circles. Raspberries were marked in blueberry triangles, blackberries in blueberry lightning bolts. White oaks were marked with pumpkin boxes with a line through—they were only every other year—and if the line ran left, it was one year; if the line ran right, it was the next year. Unless you spent time, good time, memorizing how the map was drawn, the map would not yield you any information.

From close up, you could tell what the map was, even if you couldn't read it. From far off, the various markings inscribed year after year on the map turned it into a tangle of colored shapes; your eyes turned it into a shapeless mash of arguing colors, all inscribed between detailed lines. The map was what told them what they were doing on any particular day. The map was what they needed to navigate the city.

"So, Molly, I'm just wondering, how is it that people don't bother you about going to church?"

"I told you I was raised as a Quaker. That's been enough for most people."

"I... I don't see. Sorry."

"Oh. Do you know anything about Quakers?"

"Nope."

"What's bringing on the interest in religion? You've never seemed to really care before."

"Oh, just, you know. Want people to stop bothering me."

"Ah. And they ignore me?"

"Um, yeah."

"Ah."

"..."

"..."

"Is, Quaker, um, ness important to you?"

"My faith is, yes."

"Oh, I didn't really know that. Can you tell me about it then?"

"Sure. Quakers are Christian, but we don't believe that we need a priest between us and God. In a way, every Quaker is her own priest."

"How does that work? Who gives the sermons?"

"No one does. If you're interested we can head out some quarter-moon to one of the Meetings outside Philadelphia; no one in the city is really calm enough, ready to be still enough for a Quaker meeting. I've tried to start one but it's easiest to just do it myself.

"But anyway. Basically, no one really speaks. Everyone just contemplates quietly on the nature of God, and God's love, and we sit like that for a long time, or as long as we're moved to. Anyone is allowed to speak, if their remarks are brief, and they're moved by the Holy Spirit to do so, but in practice no one really does. It's thought best if you don't put too much of your own worship onto the other people."

"How do weddings work?"

"Well, there's a group of people who make sure the match is good, and that it's thought through, but during a wedding the whole meeting just meditates on love. Usually there's more speaking at one of those than a normal meeting. But there's no priest who does it. Only God can marry two people."

"Huh. So, why don't people bother you then?"

"I still know my Bible, as well I should, I had to memorize lots of it at home. So people argue with me and I argue back ,and when I talk to them they usually walk away more confused than they started. Enough of that and now people tend to leave me alone."

"When do you worship?"

"The same time everyone else does. I just lock myself in a room and do it all alone. Didn't you ever wonder where I went on those quarter-moon mornings?"

"Ah... I... yes?"

"So no."

"Sorry. Can I try it with you sometime? It actually sounds, um, interesting."

"Why not? But only if you promise to sit still."

"What are we going to do with these guys?"

"What do you think we're going to do with them?"

"Any of you all have the stomach to do this?"

"Looks like it's your job, then, Steve. Do you mind?"

"Nah, if it's what I've gotta do. Someone load the wagon up with hay, it'll keep the wagon cleaner. These guys look like they're going to leak."

"What are you going to do with us?"

"We're going to take you someplace quiet, like probably Broad Street, cut your throats, and drop you into the underground river. Is that a problem?"

"Well, on the whole, I'd prefer it if you didn't."

"Of course you would. But I'm going to."

"Look, this wasn't even my idea. You can't do this to me, I have a wife and children! Do you know what Haddon will do to her if I don't come home? You've already killed half of us, you've taken our weapons, you've taken our horses, what more do you want from us?"

"What do you expect from us? You came over our fence, you killed our leader, you killed our dogs, we stopped you, but what was your plan? Take our women? Kill our men? Take our food? What were you planning on doing? And what did you expect us to do to you if you failed? You had to know there was a chance of failure. There were four of you and twelve of us. This was not a great plan."

"Listen, this raid wasn't even my idea. The King of Haddon thinks you have something magical in here, and he wanted us to raid you and try to take it."

"The King of Haddon isn't very smart, is he? Magic? We have no magic here. What even gave you that idea? And if we did have magic, again, four of you? You've done your damage to us, but what did you expect coming after twelve people who have magic or demons or whatever on their side? Whatever. What you got is you two are captured, and your two friends are dead. With our leader."

"Not friends. One was our commander, and he's better off dead. I'm not upset about him. Look, you can ransom us to Haddon, you don't have to do this."

"We'll talk, maybe. Or rather, you'll talk, and I'll listen. Why did you think we had this 'magic' here?"

"There's talk around the city of people who have control over demons. After hitting up the rumor mills we found out that it almost had to be your compound. But I see nothing demonic here. Obviously we made a mistake."

"Obviously. We do not summon up demons or anything like that. We have no witchy ways at all."

"Good! No reason for another raid."

"I can't believe that, in the position you're in, you're ready to talk about another raid. Look over there. You see the weeping girl in the corner? That's Crissa. She was Jase's mate. Jase was our leader. You want to talk about more raids when we've got a weeping girl, ignoring the people trying to calm her, rocking back and forth? You've got some nerve."

"I'm saying we won't."

"And we're saying you won't, because we're not going to let you. Steve, Byron, we have to do this. You two, say your final respects to whoever you say such things to."

Just as the sun was poking its red face above the horizon, Freeman and Byron pulled Sal out of the Gleaners' compound with a cart full of produce and repaired salvage to head to the City Hall Market.

Appropriately, the market was at the terminus of Market Street east, at its intersection with Broad Street, at the old City Hall in the center of the city. The building itself is a charred hulk, burned long before, some said, in Fishtown's rise.

Even though the building itself burned, the courtyard in the center of City Hall is still as it was, a stone-paved, uneven plot of land whose foundation reaches low enough into the earth that it is still remarkably clear of weeds and trees.

Passing through the burned-out arches, past the stone stairwells that disappear blackly into the darkness beyond is a little creepy, but it is the most accessible market in the city for both the denizens of the city and the traders who come in from outside, and therefore where you get the best prices.

The best market used to be on Vine Street, before Freeman was born, but the concrete walls collapsed onto the westbound lanes of the underground roadway in a flash flood, and since then Vine has been a river, and the major market has been at the recent–at least, compared to the rest of the city–ruins of City Hall.

They pulled into the market early enough to get a spot inside the courtyard itself. There was a spillover market out to the west of the building, where the front steps and the stairs down to the cellars are, but the area inside the courtyard was where you wanted to be. Since the north and south entryways collapsed, there was little wind inside the shelter of the building, and the high walls gave shelter from the intense sun even while the huge open roof allowed enough light in that your wares could be inspected – later in the day, at least. Now, the courtyard was still in shadows; the other merchants were setting up by lamplight.

They tied up Sal and left a pile of hay for him to munch on, then started setting up the tables and pavilion. The pavilion went up quickly; there were pitons in the ground for tying off the support ropes, and Freeman and Byron had plenty of experience getting the poles up quickly. Then they started setting out their wares: jars of jam, of tomato sauce, of pickled cabbage and cucumbers; fresh greens, broccoli, carrots, apples, and pumpkins; a bin of pins and needles that Molly had found in the ruins and that they had all painstakingly straightened and polished; a few chairs that were repaired by Steve and reupholstered by Crissa; ceramic plates and assorted glassware – in short, the sort of vaguely-junky setup that almost everyone else had.

And this was likely to be a big day at the market, just like it always was near the full moon. The center of the Hall was already full, and the noise of setup was becoming deafening; a quick peek through the northern archway showed a pile of people setting up tables in the courtyard. Already, early risers were picking through the piles of vegetables, clothes, and detritus scattered about while the merchants were getting their acts together. Byron was helping a customer who wanted some jam. That was good; the Gleaners were quickly making a name for themselves with their jams, jams that were well-preserved and botulism-free. Freeman smiled, then kept looking around the market.

More jam sold meant more wheat, and the more wheat they traded for the less they'd have to grow. And since they'd grown little wheat this year, good sales were essential.

"What was Jase talking about earlier with the tea and stuff?"

"He was talking about the Pennyroyal Lottery. Usually we, well, there's four girls here, right? They mix up two black beans and two white beans and whoever gets the white beans drinks the tea. We do it on the night of the new moon."

"Um, why?"

"Oh. Ha. Pennyroyal makes people lose babies. Since we can't really afford to have any kids around we, well, deal with it that way."

"Oh. Um. Why don't you all drink pennyroyal tea all the time?"

"Because, well, you saw Crissa tonight. If it's a lottery, it's okay, you know? I mean, I drink the tea anyway if I've been with a man, because, well, I don't want a kid anytime soon. But Crissa, I mean, she and Jase are all paired off, they're gonna get married, and Crissa wants kids around. She's not going to take it if he's telling her to drink the tea all the time. But if it's chance..."

"How, um, often, um..."

"A few times here and there. I drink the tea."

"What happens if someone's showing that they're pregnant?"

"Then the lottery's off for that person. Lara lost a child about six months back; she missed the lottery three months in a row and well, she was very pregnant. She was taken out of the rotation. If someone's pregnant then they don't need to do it if the baby's far enough along, and we'd deal with the child."

"I guess you've got something of a chance to keep the kid, huh? One in eight to dodge the pennyroyal."

"What do you mean?"

"If there's four of you and two drink the tea, it's one-in-two for the first month that you'd not drink the tea, right?"

"Yes..."

"So then the second month it's the same chances. Still one-in-two. But over the two months it's a one-in-four chance total that you didn't get the tea. By the third month, it's only one in eight. Your chances of drinking the tea are very, very good. How many times have you gone three months without drawing the black bean?"

"Never."

"Right. So."

"So what?"

"So... there's a really good possibility that there will never be kids in this group."

"I don't know if that's a bad thing, really."

"Why not? I know I was useful around the farm and I bet you were too."

"Ha. Right."

"What do you mean?"

"I mean I don't want to talk about growing up."

"Okay. What does the tea taste like? Is it any good?"

"It's a... a very bitter mint. With a bit of thyme, maybe? It's nice but I definitely wouldn't want to drink it all the time."

"My grandmother used to drink it to settle her stomach. I didn't realize it had so many uses."

"Oh, it does. And thank God we have it. I don't know how we could expand to take care of children here."

"What are you talking about?"

"I'm sure you know what I mean."

Molly leaned in closer to him. "Actually, I'm sure that I don't. However, I'm positive that this isn't the place to be talking about this."

"What are you talking about? First of all, no one is even looking at us – they're all focused on the music and the food and the party. Second, I'm pretty sure that this is the perfect place to be doing this. You're the one who claims to want everyone to be happy with everything, shouldn't then we talk about things like this, particularly this, out in the open, where everyone can hear both the accusations and the refutations?"

"Have you been practicing this?"

"No. So. Here are you-and-I. I say, for all our fancy words, that you run the Collective. Do you have a response?"

"I'd rather hear why you think that 'I run the Collective.'"

"Isn't it obvious? Any development of import to the Collective is one that you suggest, or that you support. Yes, the voting is supposed to be on everyone's own conscience, but look at the way that people look at you before they vote. If you argue against something strenuously enough, people take their cue from you and vote the way you want. If you argue for something strong enough, people take their cue from you and vote your way. Dust, I've watched people look at you before voting on motions that you don't even speak out on – everyone always looks at you before they vote to see how you're sitting, to see the expression on your face. Anything important that happens in the Collective is due to you, and goes the way you want it to, no matter what."

"That's not true."

"Give me a counter-example, please."

"You work for the Fork. I didn't want you doing that."

"Don't you remember how hard we argued over it? How it was pretty much an even split vote, even though everyone knew we needed the food? Don't you remember how the trading that year hadn't been enough to get us enough wheat to survive—especially after the rust—and how the excessively temporal, yet most important, question of how we were going to survive the winter almost left people's minds when the alternative was voting against you?"

"Why are you doing this? Why are you-and-I even having this conversation?"

"Because it needs to be had."

"People are staring at us."

"No one is looking at us. You-and-I're being ignored, we aren't quite enough of a dog-and-pony show to draw people away from free food and free dancing. Don't worry, we may as well be alone here. Now, answer me: do you run the Collective or not? And if not, tell me how."

"What do you want me to say, Freeman? You've already made up your mind, it sounds like. Do you just want me to admit it? Fine. Fine. You're right, I run the Collective, and your life, and everyone's life. I want to rule over the city of Philadelphia and resent that the Fork is here. Fine. Have it your way. What do you want to do with this information now that you have it?"

"I'd rather that you weren't being sarcastic."

"And I'd rather this not be happening. We can't always get what we want."

Freeman hooked left on Walnut Street and moved through the heavy tree cover eastwards. His goal was the First Unitarian on Twenty-First and Chestnut—always Chestnut—but Chestnut was too clear down here for him to be able to move carefully and out of sight down the roadway. Instead of running quickly, he carefully slalomed through the trees and thistles, which were at their height this late in the summer. The jagged teeth of ruined buildings rose on either side of him, and as he ran, he carefully gathered his final imagery of his city, his Philadelphia, in his mind. This was his town, where he had spent most, if not all, of the most important moments of his life, and now he fixed it carefully in his head, like a leaf in the horticulturary or a scrap of drawing to a book. Here, a parking garage, filled with lowing sheep and the rusted hulks of cars; here, a wreck of a car covered in canes and briars; here, a bus, windows missing but remarkably free of weeds, with a Tree-of-Heaven growing straight out of its roof—*Steve and he pulling the battery and alternator from it in a different life*—its engine compartment cover damaged.

Freeman fixed this city to his mind; on his path, details may be the same, but this, this was his city.

He passed Rittenhouse Square on his left, glanced at it once to fix it in his head—*he and Molly touching, kissing as they lay down in the bowl of the fountain*—and kept running past it, giving it hardly a second glance. He vaulted a knocked-down traffic signal at Nineteenth Street, cleared his way through the intersection quickly. He had to get to the First Unitarian and get his cache quickly; there were three routes out from the Old City to University City, one underground and two intact bridges, and the Fork was likely watching them all. Of course, they'd probably split part of their of their force down to the bridge on Vine Street, and possibly sent some down to Fairmount Park...

No matter. To his left was an orchard—*gathering cherries in the middle of summer, Molly below and he high up in the tree*—which at this time of year was empty. At the intersection with Twentieth Street he skirted right, around a pile of crashed cars—*no intact alternators to be found, even though he and Steve levered open every hood to be sure*—and ran down Twentieth to Sansom, where he made a quick turn to the west. He was getting close to the First Unitarian now, and ever closer to the bridges, where the Fork could lay in an ambush and probably get him if they really wanted to.

Sansom Street was full of peach trees, trees that they used to harvest—*Memory is a slippery slope, and its paths are neither straight nor safe*—for the summer's canning of peach butter. This final, lonely, and rushed trip through the city environs he had not been through in years was registering as a series of flashes, of images caught forever in amber, not as a continuous trip, but as a discontinuous function, full of singularity after singularity. His heart felt almost as heavy as his knees, now screaming after unaccustomed-to abuse. But he could not slow down. Now he was out from the peach trees and among the beeches—*gathering triangular nuts that crunched sweetly between your teeth*—and just as quickly past them.

And then he was at Twenty-First Street, and it was a right turn, and one short block to Chestnut Street and the First Unitarian, where he would pick up what he needed for the journey and what he needed for his life. Then he would rush through the city and finally outrun the Fork and its dogs and their chase.

"The ocean is so beautiful."

"You'll have time to look at that later. Look at this, now."

"But I have all the maths that I need, you told me that."

"I told you that you have all the maths that you need for your daily life. Now you need to know the rest that I can teach you. Look where I'm pointing with the stick, and tell me what's different about it."

"There's an 'X' in the equation."

"Good. What else? There's something else that you need to see."

"Um. You've given me the answer."

"Not the answer. What the equation equals, yes. But not the answer. The answer is what that 'X' is. When you can tell me what X is, then you've got the answer. Can you see how you'll go about it?"

"Why am I going to need this?"

"My father, who you never met, taught me this. It has been handed down in the family, and you need to know it. Not for your daily life, but if we want to fix anything. You must know this math so that if the time comes that you are the one called to help put the world back together you'll know how to do it. I was not called to help put the world back together, but you might be. And if you aren't, then your son may be the one, and you must pass this on to him. Too much has been lost, Freeman, and you may be the one to find again. But before you can do that, you must tell me how to solve this equation."

"Well. You're saying that 'X' plus six equals ten. So 'X' has to equal four."

"That is the answer, indeed. How did you find it?"

"It makes sense."

"That's not good enough. How did you find it?"

"Um. Well, four plus six equals ten. So 'X' has to equal four."

"Because..."

"Ten minus six equals four."

"Right. How about this equation."

"In that equation, 'X' has to equal six. But 'X' already equals four."

"'X' is different in each equation. 'X' is not always going to equal one number. 'X' is just the unknown, that which we don't know and want to find."

"Oh."

"Oh indeed. How about this equation."

"Um. Well, if 'X' minus four is eighteen, then 'X' equals twenty-two, doesn't it?"

"Right. Why?"

"Well, you add four to both sides and get twenty-two."

"Well done. I wish we had paper so we didn't have to do this in the sand. But, at least sand is easy to erase. How about now?"

"'X' divided by three equals one. So 'X' has to equal three too, right?"

"Right. Why?"

"Um. Because it makes sense? No, that's not good enough, right? Multiply both sides by three, and you get 'X' equal to three."

"You're getting there. Now, how about this one..."

Leaves swirled around Freeman's feet where they'd been blown into the building through the broken second story windows. Rain and snow had ruined the machines on the first of the three long, black benches that stretched across the room, but the rusted cabinetry still contained intact glassware covered in ancient brands and markings: Kimex, Pyrex, L, mL, and a host of numbers. His two aides were busy packing the intact glassware from the benches into hay-filled cartons as he inspected the machines on the other benches.

He ran his fingers through the inch-thick dust on the long black table. These would have to be carried down the steps, he decided, the tables were hardly damaged even after all their seasons abandoned, as if they had shrugged off not only the elements but time itself.

The machines that he had come for were different. This was not the first lab like this that he had come to glean, but it did show more promise than the other labs, labs filled with broken glassware and piles of rust that were once carefully assembled machines. He had come for specific machines, machines that here at Rutgers Camden might not be simple piles of rust.

Some of the books that he had taken from the attic that he still referred to as The Bookstore referred to the ancient arts of spectroscopy and spectrometry, in addition to other arcane sciences such as NMR, PCR, HPLC... chemistry textbooks, they called themselves, though there were other terms often attached: physical, organic, inorganic, bio-, quantum. He had scanned the chemistry, glanced over the math, but put most of it aside, knowing that reliable sources of these pure chemicals that the books talked about were quite beyond his reach, let alone functional electron microscopes or electron densitometers. But other machines might be useful...

He stopped thinking and pulled a duster from his belt and started clearing off machines. Any of them might be useful, even if not for the purposes he was specifically looking for. This appeared to be a water bath of some kind, and not too rusted; this would go into the cart. This next machine, with all the holes in it, he thought he recognized as a heating block. Again, possibly useful, possibly not. Into the cart!

He coughed in the dust that he was stirring up. This next machine, with the digital display and the hinged cover... this one might be a spectrograph. Good. What other machines in the lab were roughly the same shape? That one, and that one. He dusted them off one after the other, and indeed, they were the same machine. And glory be, none of them were overly rusty. Not that a lack of rust meant that the machine would work.

The dust motes hung gold in the sunlight as he stared at this treasure trove. He'd been searching the texts that had been preserved for some way of mechanically sorting glass and plastic from rocks and metal, and from each other, and now he might have found that way. According to the books, all clear materials had different transmissibilities to light, and that property could be measured with a spectrograph. The materials would have to be washed carefully, of course, but still, but still.

The giant machine was taking shape in his mind, the machine he had not yet pitched to the Fork, to Drake, but the machine he was planning on pitching soon. The most impressive parts were easy, but the smaller parts were harder to figure out how to assemble. And now, now, he had found its eyes.

"Oh, Rusalka, what happened girl? Who could have done this?"

"Rusalka's a problem but this is worse."

"What could be worse than this? I don't know if she's going to survive this?"

"Look at the seed stock."

"..."

"..."

"Starvation."

"What happened to the stock?"

"The same thing that happened to Rusalka, I'd guess."

"What was that?"

"Nice shot."

"Thanks. It... oh crap. Nutria. Beaverrat."

"Bloody Fishtown must have not kept the basement sealed from the sewers."

"And we didn't check because who would do that? Oh this is serious."

"This is past serious."

"You go get Molly and Byron, I'll see if I can see where they came in. They need to see this immediately. They've got the best idea of what we have, and what we need to survive the winter. Especially since the inventory sheets are still packed away, Lord, somewhere."

"What's going... Oh, Rusalka."

"She's not going to make it. It gets worse. Look over here."

"Oh dust."

"How are we set on food, Molly? You know better than any of us."

"Well, we caught them early, but with the move and the expansion... Christ. I don't know. What do you think, Byron?"

"We're going to have to ration, or we're going to have to get new seed stock from somewhere next year. Maybe both. I don't know if we're going to be able to ration based on the expansion plans this year."

"Can we hunt more?"

"We can try, but there's a limit to how much game we can even bring back on each load. If we have the hunters out every day... maybe. But this is not good. We measured down to the cup how much grain we'd need for the new fields and for the expansion. This is ugly."

"We could not plant as much new land next year."

"We could, but what about your plan?"

"We'll have to stall the expansion significantly."

"Molly, there's another way."

"Freeman, I know what you're about to say. Let's discuss it alone."

"Something we should be concerned about?"

"Nope. But we do need to go through and fill up every blessed hole in this place any way it slices. How many of Rusalka's brood do we still have around?"

"There's still a couple of them. If we can keep the Nutria out they should be able to keep the rats down."

"Alright. Freeman, go mix up some concrete please? I'll find all the holes in the basement."

"And Freeman, you-and-I'll talk tonight."

"Why are there so many cherry trees here? I've never seen so many fruit trees in one place before."

"This is one of the orchards, silly. This is the old Benjamin Franklin Parkway, and it's the biggest orchard in the city."

"But no one plants it, or owns it, why don't the trees just get chopped down for firewood like that stump over there?"

"That tree died and needed to be taken down, so it was. You don't cut down trees that bear fruit if you know what is good for you. And dead trees have to stand for a season so that everyone knows they're dead."

"Oh."

"But this isn't why you-and-I're here, these cherries and peaches and apples. Though the apples are tasty, huh? You-and-I're here for these steps."

"Oh my. I didn't even see the building. It's..."

"Stunning, isn't it? Come on, the doors are open."

"I've never seen steps like this before. What are they made of?"

"Stone of some kind."

"The roof is so intact for something that burned, though, how is it still so intact?"

"Only parts of the building burned. It's so well built, and there was so little in it to burn, that even though parts of it burned the fire didn't spread so far."

"It's amazing."

"And this is just the outside. Wait 'til you see the inside of the building. Watch your step through the doors, it's all glassy and there's broken metal all around."

"Who could build a staircase like this?"

"This is how they built back before the Hemorrhage. The Customs House down on Second is the same way, but not as pretty. Look above you."

"How is it still twirling? It's so heavy looking, it should have fallen a long time ago."

"My father usedta say that it was built to be balanced, not all jumbly like it is now. Some of it has rotted away over the years, but not all. Come to the top of the stairway with me, I want to try to show you something."

"These steps are..."

"Yes. C'mon.

"Okay, you see the jumbly metal thing? And that fountain that we were at?"

"Yeah."

"And the statue up on top of the Market at City Hall?"

"Yeah."

"Each was built by one generation of a family of artists. The great-grandfather built the statue, the grandfather built the fountain, and the grandson built the jumbly thing."

"What were their names?"

"I don't know that. But they were all built by the same family. Isn't that just the best thing ever? That a family could actually put a fingerprint down on Philadelphia in such a way that it would last this long?"

"It's amazing."

"Come on, there's more I want to show you."

Freeman hooted as the cold air hit his body. Winter was the least pleasant season, even with the lighter workload, but even now there was work to be done. He reached for the broom from beside the window, groping blindly under the blanket hanging across the frame for the handle. Finding it, he leaned out the window with the broom and began sweeping the snow off the greenhouse down onto the farm surrounding. While the snow would provide another layer of insulation for the greenhouse, if too much built up on the frames the windows would shatter, and then they'd be in far worse shape.

During the winter they grew very little food, but what they grew was important enough. Kale and lettuce, onions and leeks, the remains of the fall squash plants; this was the only source of fresh vegetables during the winter. Of course, there were apples and butternut, acorns and pumpkins, acorn squash and onions, carrots and potatoes, all piled carefully in the basement cellars, but the greenhouse was still an important food source – even if it was a relatively minor one.

The greenhouse was constructed of whatever intact windowframes they were able to find around the city. Single- or double-paned, it didn't matter so much here; they were carefully fitted in a single layer around a wooden frame, then there was a layer of plastic over that, and another layer of panes on top of that, with the cracks between the frames sealed with pine sap and seepings from the asphalt streets around the city.

Freeman leaned farther down to finish his sweeping with the extra-long broom they kept just for this purpose, then pounded it off against the concrete side of the Gleaners' home on South Street and went back inside, shutting the window against the cold. This window, while different from the rest in the house in that it would readily open and and close, was no different in the quality of its construction. The pane of glass across it was cracked, and a chunk of the original glass missing; overlapping pieces of broken glass that they'd found around the city were patchworked on top of it, glued down in place with the same pine sap that they used to hold so much down.

Freeman pulled off his gloves and ran his hands across the glass, careful not to run his fingers directly along the deceptively sharp edges, feeling for drafts in the glass. The window frame itself leaked, of course; but every leak that was easily fixable would be repaired as soon as possible. This window was fine.

He slipped out past the double-layer of blankets that were nailed up over the window. Ironically, this room, with the only openable window in the compound, was the darkest; the other rooms had sheets of plastic either nailed or glued around the frames, depending on the thickness of the plastic they'd been able to find. Every window looked more-or-less the same, each made of the same sort of patchwork glass; here a piece gleaned from an old subway train, here a piece taken from a car's door, here a chunk from the screen of one of the innumerable glass-fronted boxes that could be found in almost every dwelling in the city.

The room was warm after the chill of the outside air. The smell of the fire was freshening up; Lana must have started the cooking. Had it been that long? Freeman had spent part of the morning with his books, and part of it with his machines, but didn't think that so much of the day had gone by; especially with him still having to collect wood and water for the night. Time to keep moving. Always more to be done than he thought there was.

"What do you guys want?"

"Yeah, what was so important that you dragged us away from what we were doing? That cloth isn't going to weave itself."

"Where's Jase?"

"He was busy. He said he couldn't be disturbed."

"He should really see this."

"He was busy."

"Alright, fine. So. You all remember that pile of books that we recovered from the attic of the house on Second Street? And that the books were full of words that we didn't know, and full of diagrams, and strange equations? And you all know, of course, that I've been spending the last year working with little else in my free time. Well, I have something to show for it. This small device here is called an alternator, and it was taken from under the hood of one of the myriad cars that are lying dead in parking garages throughout the city. With a few other alternators that were taken from similar cars, I was able to repair this alternator."

"What does this have to do with anything?"

"Thank you, Byron, what this has to do with is what alternators do. Alternators are electrical generation units for cars. When the cam inside the alternator is rotated, electricity is generated. What is electricity, you may ask? I don't know yet, but I hope to find the answer in the books that I have not yet been able to understand. This doesn't matter. For us, now, that's not important. What is important is what electricity can do.

"Now, you all know that these small glass spheres with screw-mount metal bases are found in nearly every building in the city, some intact, some not. Please watch what happens as I hook the bulb up to the alternator—like so—and then turn the crank."

"..."

"..."

"..."

"But, it's glowing!"

"Yes. And with little heat, and no smoke."

"But it goes out when you stop turning the crank, why does it do that?"

"It goes out because the alternator only generates electricity when its turning. The books talk about things called batteries that store electricity, and I have not yet been able to learn how to make batteries. But I will, and then we can store electricity."

"Turn it on again!"

"Okay. Now that we have this, we need to decide what to do with it. Byron, you said that what you were doing was too important to interrupt, so, do you have any questions before you run off?"

"I'm not sure, um, I may stick around. How did you do this?"

"I repaired a generator. We can make more generators, and turn them with things that aren't hand power. We can use animals, or water, or wind to turn them. But Byron, you needed to do something? You can go."

"I don't quite remember what I, oh. Um."

"Freeman, can I go get Jase? You're right. He does have to see this."

"Go for him. *Devai.*"

How's a cinderblock made? Take lime and water, and mix it with crushed stone. Mix them well, and then pour into forms. Let dry, turn out of the forms. Refill the forms. Continue as necessary.

Lime came from the lime beds of South Jersey, mined by hard labor. Water came from the Delaware, pumped out by repaired machines.

The crushed rock came from the fourth strike of the Fork. The first, as gentle a tap as the several-hundred-ton machine could give, served as an alarm bell to the people of Penn Medical that their building was coming down. The second strike, after the Fork had been rolled back and allowed to gain some momentum before striking, made the now-empty building ring like a bell. The third strike, with the Fork's ram down, shattered what few windows were still intact. The third strike, with the Fork's giant jaw closed, spread cracks throughout the semi-circular stone building. The third strike, with smoke and steam pouring from the Fork's four boilers, caused the many-story building to list slightly in the direction of the river. As dust and glass shards rained down around the building, the Fork pulled back and struck Penn Medical for the fourth time, and was then obstructed by dust and stone as the building crumbled beneath the iron fist. Drake sucked in his breath as Freeman watched, arms folded, waiting for the dust to clear, to see the Fork eating its first huge meal.

This wasn't the first structure the Fork had taken down, of course. There was a highway overpass that the Fork struck down, right off the bridge, and the rusted pile of metal that had once been a statue at the foot of the bridge. The trees growing out of the roads, and the park, and all the rubble swept into its hungry mouth – these things the Fork had already eaten, and proved that it functioned properly. But Penn Medical was the first building that was significantly larger than the Fork, so Penn Medical was the Fork's first real test.

Freeman listened closely. Out from the plumes of dust came the sounds of grinding, chewing; the Fork was eating, that was for certain. What was uncertain was whether or not the Fork was badly-enough damaged that its meal would slip through an unintentional tracheotomy, spilling the rock and glass and organics out from its throat into the street.

But then the breeze was picking up, and as the dust cloud was swept to the north, Drake sighed in relief, Freeman nodded with satisfaction, and the workers cheered; there were new dents, that was for certain, and the paint job was no longer the bright-reflecting black that it had originally been, but the Fork was doing its job, scooping up rubble and passing it into its entropy-reversing body.

Freeman nodded, and kept nodding. This machine was doing what he wanted. And he could keep being proud of it if he ignored the weeping, shocked faces on the other side of Eighth Street, who watched as their former home was quickly turned into dust, scrap, and the future.

"You could have told me about it."

"What are you talking about?"

"The offer from the Fork."

"You-and-I've talked against the day it would come. You-and-I both know where we stand on it."

"You should have told me when it came."

"Molly, I told you when I told everyone else, like you-and-I agreed."

"Dust it, Freeman—"

"Molly, we don't have that many glasses! What are you—"

"Freeman, do you know how I felt when I stood there and heard with the rest of them, and everyone looking at you-and-I to see how we stood on it? They know about you-and-I, Freeman, and there is an us. Do you understand that?"

"I brought it before the consensus like we do everything, Molly, as we decided to do with everything. Why are you coming at me now and telling me that—"

"Keep your voice down."

"My voice? You're the one yelling and throwing glasses."

"Freeman—"

"Of course they know about us, Molly. You-and-I live in the same room, they've seen us kissing, you-and-I live in the same compound with them and of course they know about us. They've known of us as 'Freeman 'n Molly' the whole time most of them have known us."

"Do you think of us as 'Freeman 'n Molly' then?"

"Of course I do."

"Of course you don't. If you thought of us as a collective within the Collective, you would have told me before you told the group. Do you think I like to look a fool, standing there poleaxed with the news that yes, now the time has come to make a choice?"

"You're the one who tells me at every chance that you-and-I have to bring everything before the group and that you-and-I can't make decisions between ourselves. That everything that you-and-I do affects the collective and that you-and-I have to bring things that affect us more than the rest of the group before the group rather than deciding between ourselves. I just did what you say we must do."

"Freeman—"

"No. You're the one who makes sure that you draw the black bean at the pennyroyal lottery every moon. You're the one who doesn't want to be cemented into the group, to be cemented into place, and you're the one who founded it."

"I didn't found the group."

"You were the one who put forth our decision making process, the one who makes sure that people who don't bring choices before the Collective before making up their mind what to do get reprimanded, even lashed. Or driven out. This is your plan, and now when you're at the sticky end of it you're balking?"

"How dare you bring up the pennyroyal lottery. What are you trying to do here?"

"I could ask you the same thing. What are you trying to do here? And what are you trying to do to us?"

"What am I trying to do to us? Better yet, what are you trying to do to us?"

Despite the cool air, Freeman was sweating. The nails were getting progressively harder to pull as the day went by; the windows that were light by themselves were getting heavier by the frame. And there was more and more work to do; though half of the windows were down from the greenhouse frame, the windows that made the roof that leaned towards the house were going to be far harder to remove, and the light was failing. Steve was already up on a ladder, pulling windows down from the roof, but there was only so much longer that they'd be able to work with the sun setting as quickly as it was.

Sal's wagon was full of the Gleaners' most important, and most fragile, possessions. At this time in the year, if they had to be moved, they had to be moved quickly, and in heavy packing, from the building on South Street to their new home on Chestnut. Once at Chestnut Street, they had to be quickly hauled indoors, to the place in the compound safest from the winds of the autumn. And they all had to be moved fast, because once the move started, they all had to be moved quickly so their old home could be disassembled and moved to Chestnut Street as soon as they could be.

The Gleaners' most important possessions were, of course, perennial plants. The fig trees, heavy though they were, had to be dug up from the greenhouse, wrapped in fabric and leaves, and carted across the city to the compound. It was the same with the few citrus trees that they had, the hazelnut and cherry saplings, and the herbs. The trays of lettuce had to be moved in their coldframes, with four people carrying each of them, and placed carefully in the cart; the winter tomatoes had to be hauled in their containers and loaded quickly into the wagon, which was then covered in hay and heavy cloth. Other winter crops, the kale and beets, the turnips, radishes, and carrots, the cabbage and squash; all were quickly harvested to the ground and bagged and dropped into the cart. It made trip after trip from and to Chestnut Street, carting this winter's food from South Street over to Chestnut. No one knew how well it would work; never before had they tried to move so many vegetable plants so late in the year.

But they were not prepared to leave the plants behind. Every plant must be moved to Chestnut Street, lest the winter be too lean.

Once the plants were moved, they began disassembling the greenhouse. The greenhouse was built of windowframes filled with cracked glass, two-three layers thick, all bolted to giant pillars of wood sticking out of the earth. The windowframes also had to be moved carefully; the stores of pitch pine sap to seal cracks in the glass were running low, and more of it was earmarked to quickly fill gaps in the stone walls at Chestnut Street. Freeman worked with a claw hammer, pulling nails from the windowframes and carefully carrying the windows over to the cart, where they were being packed in hay.

The next transits by the cart would be slow ones, over paths that Sal had already worn flat; too much breakage of the windows was not something that their group could survive.

There were still some sources of glass in the city, but there was no time to go and glean it before the greenhouse had to be rebuilt.

Freeman loaded the last frame that would fit into Sal's wagon, then threw the lashes across and tied them down quickly. There was just enough light for Kevin to cross the city with the windows, but probably not enough light for them to be unloaded tonight. The plants would have to live through the night in the kitchen of Chestnut Street.

"Alright, Crissa, what's behind that door?"

"I don't know. Jase would never open it with me around."

"Locked."

"I'm sure."

"He had a key for it. He kept it around his neck."

"Oh crap, that one that was still on him when we buried him?"

"That was probably it."

"Well, the ground's frozen now. We're not going to be getting it out."

"You guys can't go through his stuff like this!"

"Crissa, what else are we going to do? We voted, you gathered your things up, what would you ever do with all this stuff? And why do you want a locked closet? What if what's in there will help us, I don't know, survive the winter?"

"Right, right. I know. I voted for it too. It's just... weird. Intrusive. I'm sorry. I don't even sleep in here anymore. Can, can I, just, like not be here?"

"Go. Don't even worry about it."

"Alright. The pins are on the outside. We can try to get it open that way or we can axe it."

"I say we axe it. We don't need locks here."

"Go for it. You've got your axe and I'd have to go get a hammer and screwdriver anyhow."

"Well that was easy."

"Yeah. Oh dust."

"Oh dust indeed."

"..."

"..."

"Starvation!"

"Why would he hoard all this food here? And these tools? What was he thinking?"

"He was thinking that he'd stay strong while all of us weakened if a year went bad. He wanted to keep his little sliver of power no matter what it cost the rest of us."

"Unbelievable. This sack... there's got to be seventy pounds of jerky in here."

"And there's... Jesus. Gallons and gallons of preserves. This is weeks of food for all of us in here."

"Alright. We've got to get this inventoried. Is anyone else hoarding? We should know now. This is not good."

"Not me."

"Not me."

"Alright. Should we search? I don't know."

"No. If we're going to search we have to decide as a group, but I don't think we should. I think we should trust each other, and trust that Jason kept the inventory of everything we had, and that if he found any of us hoarding he'd have kicked us out at minimum. He had to keep himself together, and that's why this is like this. But this is why we have to put some sort of double-triple check inventory system in place. We can't let one person control our food and our future like this. This is... I mean this bag of dried cherries alone could mean the difference between scurvy and not."

"Freeman's right. But we'll have a vote anyhow, right?"

"Where in the city is the Fork?"

"The intake of the Fork is here, at the old Lit Brothers building, at the intersection of Eighth and Arch. We have a few choices here. We can try to back up a little bit, and go straight west through Chinatown, or we can head through the Lit Brothers building and towards South Philly."

"If the intake of the Fork—hey, why don't we have a better name for it than that? Can't we call it the mouth, or the maw, or the teeth or something?"

"I prefer a more technical name, Drake, to something fanciful like that."

"Fine. So, the mouth is here at Eighth Street. There's a large building here, on a direct line southwest from the current path of the Fork—that's where its pointed. Can't we just head that way?"

"There is a large underground mall to the southwest called the Galleria. We surveyed that path and we're certain that the Galleria is too deep for the collapsing building to fill, and that the surrounding architecture isn't strong enough to support the rather immense weight of the Fork."

"You're saying we could lose the Fork if we go the southwest."

"Yes. We can head straight west, or directly south."

"Where are the better buildings to take down?"

"Lit Brothers is an excellent building for us, it is large and stone and we will get more out of that than we will if we head directly west. However, while the buildings directly to the west are smaller, there are a number of large buildings a few blocks from the Fork's intake's current position. The stone harvesting has been going well for now, and there are currently more raw materials ready for the workmen than they will need in the next week. Now, the Fork will take about five days to properly harvest the buildings to the west before reaching the convention center. If we head through Chinatown we'll pick up quite a large amount of stone, glass, and metal before hitting a large store of just stone. If we head straight at Lit Brothers we're going to have to step up the shifts at the egress of the Fork; more materials will be coming out than we can process right away. I recommend going west."

"There's no other reason for your recommendation?"

"What other reason might there be?"

"I notice that going south takes us to Chestnut Street, and close to your precious Collective."

"The Collective are just a group of farmers, Drake. I don't much care what happens to them. I'm worried that we're going to have to slow down building in Camden if we take down Lit Brothers next."

"I've surveyed our production and our hauling teams, and I disagree with your estimates. Heading south is going to be easier on the Fork. Direct the driver teams to take down Lit Brothers first."

"I don't know that that's the best idea, Drake—"

"Don't question me, Freeman. I value your input, but my mind is made up and you will not question me. We will take down Lit Brothers, and then once the Fork is on Market we will decide the next place for the Fork to demolish—or harvest, if your farmer stock prefers."

The First Unitarian was lit by the late morning sun shining in through the huge gaps in its roof and walls. The central hall was covered in litter, with a central area swept out; the stone-paved floor there was soot-stained where bonfires used to be lit, back in the days when a small consensus in Philadelphia held Full Moon parties here. The first party that Freeman attended had been here, the first party after that terrible night, on the first night of his life in Philadelphia—*Molly's surprised face turning to him as he collapsed weeping in her arms*—and he could never stand coming here after that night. As silently as he could he walked past the swept area to the apse. Here, a jumble of masonry, studs, and shingles had spilled onto the altar, undisturbed until last night, when Freeman stashed his frame backpack full of supplies, books, and the most irreplacable of his tools here.

Freeman quickly dug the frame backpack out of the rubble and dumped the contents of his smaller backpack into it, wincing as the scars on his side screamed. He hoisted the backpack up onto his body, cinched the straps tight, and set out for the rotten main doors of the church. The backpack rode heavily on his torn side.

He paused at the archway, scanned the street in front of him, and was instantly glad that he had. Through the trees that had sprung up through the street, he could see a person, tall, clad in dyed leather, and clutching a bow, peering down Chestnut Street, partially concealed behind a rusted-out car. Freeman stopped still, keeping his breathing slow and shallow, waiting to see what the tribal was looking for. It could be a deer, or a zebra, or one of the wild Holsteins that had spread throughout the area, or even something more exotic, but Freeman didn't think so. Had the tribal seen him enter the church? Possibly, but probably not; if the armed man had any interest in killing Freeman he could have done it easily while Freeman was repacking his backpack.

Freeman stood and watched and waited for an answer.

It came as the tribal quickly raised and drew his bow, arrow nocked, just before the explosion of a musket echoed off the buildings around the church. The tribal spun, blood gushing from his side, the arrow loosed and thudding into a nearby tree. It had to be the Fork's dogs, mostly no one else had gunpowder. Another arrow whistled down Chestnut Street from somewhere that Freeman couldn't see. There was no time to worry about that: Freeman bolted from the doors of the church, dodging branches and underbrush. The trap was laid at the intersection of Twenty-third and Cherry, and he had to get there before the Fork or the tribals could get a lead on him. Freeman ran, another arrow thudding into a tree as he passed it, dodging through vines and jumping bushes and detritus, running for the shelter of the cliff-like buildings of Cherry Street.

Shouts went up behind him. He wished, not for the first time, that the frame backpack was a different color than red. Another shot rang out, hopefully aimed at the tribals... and then he was in the alley. There was a small path here, and he ran the block to the intersection. The buildings here were in horrible shape. The shouts rose up louder behind him. Yesterday he had wedged a log into the wall of this camera shop, and as Freeman turned the corner he ran straight into the log as fast as he could. His breath exploded out but the log moved, twisting the steel beam holding the remnants of the building together. The Fork's dogs' shouts were instantly drowned out by the waterfall of collapsing bricks. Freeman got his arms up and bolted away from the pelting rubble.

"What's that in the road up there?"

"Hmm?"

"Son, get your head out of that book and get on the lookout. Last time I'm gonna tell you. Drop the book and hold the reins."

"What are you doing?"

"If you wrap two of these lenses you and that Molly found in a tube of leather you can use them to see farther. Potter showed me. Eh. That doesn't look good."

"What doesn't?"

"Since we came down this way last there's a barricade looking thing across the road. Either that or a tree fell, it's hard to tell from here. These damnable lenses aren't worth a thing. Dust. Could be trouble."

"Mom doesn't like you using those words."

"That's just fine. Get my bow, and get the spears out."

"What are we going to do?"

"There ain't much by way of other routes to take, and if its something that someone erected they've seen us by now. They'll have horses, and won't have a cart behind them, they'll be able to chase us down if they see us. We go forward."

"Um, Dad? What do you think they want?"

"Some petty lordling who wants to scare the peons. They're easily enough dealt with. They'll probably want a tax of what we have in the cart. We should be able to scare them off, we've got bows and no one likes getting shot. Unless there's a lot of them. Or maybe it's a tree, but I'm not betting on it. Wake your mother up, she needs to come out here. When we get closer to the—whatever it is, you'll go down and hide in the wagon with your spear. Pay close attention. If anything does happen to your mother and I you are not to protect the cart, you are to run. Do you hear me? Staying and fighting if something happens to us is not worth your life. Do not try to avenge us. And don't cry, it could still be nothing. We all knew this day could come. Remember those bandits we fought off last year? It's okay. Nothing will happen. But if anything does, run. Try to get to the village, or if you can't go back to the city. But do not stay and fight."

"What if—"

"Nothing's going to happen. But we're taking precautions anyway. Go."

"Mom? Dad says you have to get up. There's something in the road."

"What is it?"

"We don't know. It's either a fallen tree or a roadblock, we're not close enough to tell."

"Alright. I'm gonna take care of some business here, and be out in two minutes."

"Faster, love, we're coming up on it pretty quick."

"I'll do my best."

"What is it, Dad?"

"There looks to be a horse near it. It ain't natural. Some little bastard wants a tax of our goods from the city. Well, they'll get their tax if they need it, and if they're looking for more, they'll get a fight out of us. We've dealt with this sorta thing before and it's fine."

"But Uncle Earl was with us last time, and he...

"It'll be fine, Freeman. Trust me."

Freeman rocks back and forth on the soles of his leather moccasins, eyes closed, feeling the new bricks under his feet and smelling the soot of the coal and tire fires in his nose. He stands facing away from the setting sun, but sweeps his head back and forth across the street in front of him; even through the red filter of his closed eyelids he can see where the sun reflects off of new glass, and it fills him with the satisfaction of a job well done.

Camden is not now what it used to be. The piles of rubble that—*hoofbeats sundering the world*—used to litter the roadways, that one had to duck and weave through to cross, are now gone. Crumbling buildings have been recycled, their concrete smashed down to gravel and reused, broken bricks used for fill or foundations and whole bricks used for facades; steel has been reforged into new shapes, new tools, new structures. Glass bottles are now windows, the trees that grew through the streets are now chairs and bars and tables and frames.

The sounds of sawing, of hammering, of demolition and construction rage through Freeman's ears. The people of Camden, and some of the Philadelphians, have cast off their tribal roots, and are now enlisted soldiers in the Fork's war against decay. Whether navvies digging irrigation trenches or farmers using the new water to raise more corn than they could before, whether masons or welders, or even engineers and architects studying under Freeman and picking up the skills to keep this grand new machine working, all are enlisted in the war against entropy and fight it with almost every breath they take, with almost every powerful push of their muscles against the ground.

Freeman opens his eyes, glad to know that for today, at least, work on the Fork has stopped and all of the machines are running smoothly, that his machinists are keeping the machines oiled, the furnaces stoked, ensuring that each of the little things that can go wrong with any of the machines are being kept at bay as best as they can.

And instead of looking to see what can be done, what needs to be changed, he instead looks over the newly paved street, looks at the horses tied up against the tavern blowing breath and snorting, chewing at their feed, looks at the wives and merchants haggling over vegetables without constantly looking over their shoulders, looks at children playing in new clothes outside the gleaming apartment homes, and nods to himself in satisfaction. The brown fields of the Camden waterfront have been transformed into a place worth living, a place where all the goods of all the local villages and towns come in to be sold in safety. A place where boats from Wilmington and Trenton and even far Washington can dock in safety, a place where enough other traders gather to make the journey worthwhile for the new generation of larger ships that are slowly being built. A place where the flat-bottomed coal barges from Scranton and Allentown are now coming in with regularity, where the river raiders have learned that you do not raid and burn ships with the angled cruciform sigil of the Fork on the prow, lest the gendarmes of the Fork come down upon you.

Freeman turns and looks out, now, across the rest of Camden, the parts of the city that are still ridden with entropy and disease, the parts unprotected by armed gendarmes. Only parts of Camden look as they should, after all the work and sweat and tears; past the local farms and areas earmarked for new building, a sea of rubble that is no higher than ten feet, but immeasurably dense swarms out before the eyes. There is work to do, and there is, but the future, in Camden, is taking shape.

"I still can't believe none of you know how to preserve fruit for the winter."

"Oh, shut up. None of us are from farms. There are plenty of vegetables that keep, winter squash and apples and potatoes and such, and we hunt. It's enough."

"Fair enough, I suppose. That water at a good boil yet?"

"Sure thing."

"Alright. The bottles that we're going to use get put into the water bath and left to boil for as long as this takes."

"But we already scrubbed them a lot cleaner than we ever do."

"If you don't boil them you get sick, according to my gramma. And this is according to her gramma and who knows how far back."

"Alright. Bottles in the water. Damn, that's hot."

"Yep. Now we're using three pots, right? One is the water bath, one for the jelly, and one for the wax. We've got this pot full of mulberries and water, and it's at the boil. We're going to work it through the food mill. Again, I can't believe you guys have a mill and don't know how to use it."

"Keep it up and you're out on the street."

"Fine, fine. Alright, pour out this pot into the bowl over here, then take the pot off the fire. Mill goes over top, and we're going to spoon the berries and juice into the mill. Running the handle of the mill pushes the pulp of the fruit through and keeps about half of the seeds out, and all of the stems. Keep spooning."

"This is a lot of fruit. How are we going to eat it all?"

"We're gonna keep it for the winter. This will keep until fruit starts coming in next spring."

"I don't quite believe you."

"Oh, believe me. It will. Now we dump a bunch of the honey into the pot."

"Why?"

"It helps keep it from going bad."

"I'm not sure how, though."

"Me either. But it's gotta be really sweet or you get sick when you eat it."

"If you say so. That's a lot of honey."

"Sure is. Now that it's all milled, we put it back on the boil, and add the jelly stock—the pectin—that we made yesterday. This makes it set up real nice, and besides, if apples grow too close to one another on the branches, they're more attractive to insects, and then you lose more of your harvest to bugs than you do to pectin making. You'll see when we get tons of apples off those trees in the fall."

"You're repeating yourself, you said that yesterday."

"Alright. Now that the jelly is boiling, we get some wax on to melt. Fish out one of the jars with a stick."

"Ow! It's hot! You're sure we need to boil them?"

"Positive. Now, dunk the funnel in the hot water and put it over the jar. I'm going to ladle the jelly into the jar, like this, and once it's about half an inch from the top—like so—we pour the melted wax over it. That's one jar stored for the winter. Fish me another jar out of the water —and don't disturb the jar we just finished."

Freeman bent and scritched Rusalka on the head; Rusalka, busy stalking something in the basement, jumped, gave Freeman a look of utter annoyance, and padded off towards the grain bins to start over. Freeman shook his head and went off to gather what Lana had asked him to bring up from the storage bins.

The bins were in the corner of the basement, and each was filled with what the Gleaners had spent the better part of the summer growing and harvesting. There were thrown-together bins of winter squash, of beets, of onions, potatoes, and apples. This year's harvest had been a good one, good enough that they were still busy canning what they wouldn't be able to eat before it spoiled. Lana had sent Freeman down for apples, apples that were going to become canned sauce before the day was out.

While filling his bag, Freeman looked longingly over the half-wall to his workshop in the dank corner of the basement, the piles of books and machines and parts still scattered haphazardly over makeshift tables. There was still too much to do today to work on getting it together just yet, but maybe after sundown...

Freeman finished gathering the apples and clambered up the steps, blowing the candle out on his way up. The basement gloom was now only cut by the cold light flooding from the upstairs of the house. There was a scrabble from the corner as Rusalka went after whatever it was she was stalking; good for her, she'd be able to eat tonight.

Freeman deposited the bag of apples next to Lana, grabbed a quick kiss from Molly, and headed out into the streets of Philadelphia, dragging a sledge behind him.

What they were worried about today was firewood. While it was likely that they'd have enough for the winter, especially with the coal that they'd bargained for from the tramp captains down from Allentown, the winter had so far been colder than they'd been expecting. With Candlemas right around the corner, they'd burned through about half the wood they'd stored away; any sort of problem—thievery, a flood, or a quick freeze—and they'd either lose their wood or burn through the entire supply.

Freeman walked through the streets, casting his eyes about for a limb shattered and fallen in the blizzards, or a non-fruiting tree that was somehow missed by one of the other, equally desperate, communities around the city. He was struck, again and often, by how deserted the city was, and how crowded it must have once been. He would walk past entire blocks, crumbling and abandoned, before passing a house where a candle burned in the window and smoke billowed from the chimney, and then just as quickly as he passed it he would be back in the empty streets.

There: a cherry tree had a limb snap under the weight of the snow. He jumped up onto the limb and let his weight rip it from the tree, then unslung his axe and started chopping. His blows and breath echoed off the walls of the cold, empty tenements. In the cold, it was hard work, but as he chopped his muscles loosened up, and the blows came faster and faster. Eventually it was done, chopped up, and he threw the two-foot long logs onto the sledge, tying them down with deerhide straps.

And then it was back on the road. Now that he had a load, he had to move more quickly; he knew most of the people in the city, but he was out alone with a load of firewood, and one never knew who was watching.

"Reform and revolution are not different methods of historic development that can be picked out at pleasure from the counter of history, just as one chooses hot or cold sausages. Legislative reform and revolution are different factors in the development of class society. They condition and complement each other, and are at the same time reciprocally exclusive, as are the north and south poles, the bourgeoisie and the proletariat."

"I like this Rosa woman."

"Me too."

"Alright. So. What she's getting to here is that what you-and-I've done with the Full Moon Parties is good, but it's not enough to get ourselves moving."

"Well, it's a start I think. But she's saying we need some sort of, of, seasonal change almost. We need a winter-to-spring, not just changing things little by little. I think, honestly, she's used to talking to larger groups of people than we've ever seen. I don't know that we could spark a full revolution in Philadelphia. I doubt we could even spark anything in the house here the way everything currently lies."

"Because Jase controls us all."

"Exactly."

"..."

"..."

"But I like Jase."

"Sometimes. When he's not threatening me."

"We all owe him so much."

"He'd be really angry if he overheard this conversation. You should read more quietly if you can."

"I've been reading pretty quiet. Besides, he doesn't like to come upstairs unless he has to and we'd hear him on the steps."

"Still and all."

"Is Jase really bourgeoisie, do you think?"

"I don't think that the labels she uses are really, um, accurate to our times. I think they worked well for her when she was writing. I'm sure that when Philadelphia was full and alive and, you know, back in the day, that they had less faces for their labels than we do. But I think, still, that you can, at least in the house, look at Jase as the bourgeoisie and the rest of us as the proletariat and get an idea what she's saying."

"But... I mean, revolt against Jase? That's not who we are. How could you-and-I get everyone else on board?"

"I don't know."

"Keep reading."

"'Every legal constitution is the product of a revolution. In the history of classes, revolution is the act of political creation, which legislation is the political expression of the life of a society that has already come into being. Work for reform does not contain its own force, independent from revolution."

"So wait, this, and what she said before, means that we have to because Jase will never ever let us reform his system."

"I think that's what she's saying."

"I don't know how we're going to do this."

"Is that all of them?"

"Not sure. Keep quiet."

"I don't... Oh! Nice shot."

"Thanks. I'm sure they'll be back, but damn! Six rats. We're eating good tonight. Why haven't we come down here for them before?"

"Because none of us really like the way that they taste, and you're the only one who's a good enough shot to hit them regularly. Also, you can go out and get a deer by yourself. We don't go down into the sewers unless there's more than one of us."

"True enough, true enough. What did Lara say she was making for us tonight, did you hear? I hope it's stew. Oooh, I love her rat stew."

"No you don't."

"Alright, alright. True, true. It's better than anything else we can make with rat."

"I'll give you that one."

"What did you want to come down here for?"

"Ugh, this one's gross. Hold out that bag. I got that hole through the wall, and I want to see if it comes out where I think it does."

"How are you going to see a hole in the wall from here?"

"I stuck an orange wire through it. We should notice something orange sticking through the wall."

"Fair, fair. In fact, is that it?"

"Yes it is. Hot damn! It is close enough to the running water for this to work."

"I still don't understand what you're doing."

"Okay, look, I fixed up one of those alternators to make electricity. Do you remember how I could turn it and have the light come on?"

"Yeah, that was really amazing."

"Okay. You see how the stream is moving? If we put the alternator near the stream and attach it to a waterwheel, the stream will turn the alternator and we'll get power out of it. Then we use a longer wire than I used during the demonstration and we'll get electricity without anyone having to turn the crank."

"Oh. I get it. That's... That's a great idea."

"Thank you. And the great thing about it being in the sewers is that we don't have to either defend it or advertise its presence. No one will know that it's down here, so we won't have to keep anyone away from it. And no one that we don't tell will know that we have it, because they won't see it, and so we won't have to worry about any incursions to steal it. There will be no more defense than there was before. Here, help me set it up."

"What do I do?"

"We just set it here, and bolt it down like this. These bolts should go into this crack here well enough to keep it in place. Then, we attach the wires, hold the cable, I'll strip the ends... Good. Now we attach these wires to the leads on the alternator, and screw them down with wire nuts, then attach the wheel. I'm going to have to get in the water to attach it. Can you hold the wheel steady?"

"Sure."

"Good. A few turns, and... the wheel is attached. Now let go."

"Hey, it's spinning on its own!"

There is a hole in the roadway of the Ben Franklin Bridge, a gash in the tarmac where the rusted, fraying edge of the laminate roadway suddenly ends in a drop of dizzying proportions. It is just over halfway across the bridge, and from this height, where Freeman gazes down, chewing a fingernail and thinking, he can just barely make out the rusted skeletons of boats that wrecked and sank in the center of the mighty Delaware. Giant, floating machines, machines that once moved the world, machines that were, in their own way, his inspiration.

He hears a metallic cough from before him, and looks up. The morning has been one of last-minute tests, last-second adjustments, inspections; work crews to organize, management to deal with, coal and tiresuppliers to argue with. But on this morning, the fuel has been shoveled into the boilers, the water lines have been established, the pumps are moving, and the Fork is bringing itself up to heat. The Fork is preparing to move.

Freeman retreated from the brink of the hole, the sunlight still making him blink. For the last few weeks, he'd been inside the body of the Fork from sunup to sundown, leaving only to sleep, and sometimes not even then. Even today, he'd only emerged to watch the Fork begin to wake after a last-minute lubrication of the drive train.

As he backed away from the hole, a hole that the Fork was built to drive over, he heard the whistles begin to squeal one-two-three-four. The white vapor pouring from the whistles blew high and fast, steaming into the black soot-filled clouds that the boilers dumped into the sky.

He turned, looked up at the ceremonial dais on the bridge's walkway where Drake stood and watched, and nodded his head to Drake. Drake raised his hand, then swung his arm to point at

Philadelphia. Joyce, the driver, a mustachioed man in stained overalls and dark goggles, nodded at Drake, then at Freeman, and slowly engaged the Fork's drive train, slowly pushing the giant machine forward.

Even then, it wasn't an instant affair. There was a knocking as the four boiler cars jammed against the cars in front of them, which pushed the cars in front of them, slow, giant dominoes beginning to fall...

And then it moved. Creepingly slowly at first, but movement still. The Fork began to crawl down the roadway, far slower than a person might walk, pushing on ahead towards Philadelphia.

The crews around it cheered. Drake shouted in triumph. Freeman merely nodded.

The Fork's movement was but the first test. The next test was coming up in front of it, a pile of tangled steel formed from a pile-up of the ubiquitous automobiles, wrapped around the concrete Jersey Barrier that ran between the lanes of the roadway. Joyce aimed the Fork, and slowly dropped the blade of its intake down so it was just brushing the road surface.

The Fork bore down on the tangle of steel, unwilling to stop simply because some pile of wreckage dared cross its path. The scoop met the tangle in a squeal of metal on metal, and slowly began to take the metal and draw it into the body of the vehicle. As the raw materials reached the crushers, Joyce engaged them, and the bass hum of the boilers was joined by a rhythmic percussion as the press began to crush the wrecked cars into chunks that could be dealt with.

Freeman nodded again with satisfaction. The wrecks would go, and the future was coming.

"You're not serious about this, are you? God, dust, stop, we can be ransomed, you can get food out of Haddon for us—"

"Alright, he's gagged, the other one is still out cold. What do we do?"

"We vote. We have no leader so we all decide. Everyone take a white and a black bean. If you want them to die, drop the black bean in. Ransom, the white bean. That's what we're going to do."

"One of us should decide."

"No. We all decide. Do it."

"The count is four in favor of ransom."

"Don't look at us like that, you knew this was a possibility when you decided to raid anyone, let alone us."

"Ungag him. Any last requests?"

"Don't kill us?"

"I don't think that one works. How do you want to be returned to the earth?"

"Can you leave us on the bridge? I can't speak for Davey, but I'd prefer that after we're killed our souls can be shriven by the pastor back in Haddon, not sacrificed and dedicated to dark demons."

"Look, if we could control demons, don't you think this would have gone even more poorly for you? Your request is fair. Anyone have objections to leaving their bodies on the bridge? None? Alright. Byron, you come with me, the rest of you, it's getting near dawn, start cleaning up the mess they left behind."

"Are you sure you're okay with this, Steve?"

"Absolutely. I didn't even want to leave this up to a vote. I'm glad it went the way that it did and I'm happy to do this. You, Haddon-boy, you want some 'shine before we take you out?"

"Offering the condemned a last drink?"

"Seems only fair. We'll let you get liquored up so you don't notice."

"Thank you. This is an unexpected kindness."

"Alright. Freeman, Byron, throw them face first in the cart, I'll drive, Byron, you keep your eyes on them and make sure they're not trying to slip their bonds. We'll be back before sunup."

"..."

"..."

"Is this my fault?"

"How so?"

"They said that they wouldn't have come in here except that they heard about the demons. That's the cover we've been spreading."

"Not your fault. Haddon's been raiding more firecely than normal this year. This is not the first attack by them I've heard of. Though we came out better than most. We only lost one, and our dogs. That's not as bad as others. Cherry Street was burned to the ground."

"Still. What are we going to do without Jase?"

"We'll figure something out. There's got to be a way for us to make this group work, even without Jase. But dust. Jase. I don't know if it's sunk in yet."

"We've got to check on the garden. Let's see if you-and-I can salvage anything. We're probably going to need it."

"Hello, Freeman."

"Hi Drake. I wasn't expecting you down here. What's happening? What do you need?"

"Nothing, nothing, don't you worry about that. I'm just down here to congratulate you."

"Oh? On what?"

"Well, we've finished compiling our data on the Rowan raid, and I have to tell you, we've never seen such excellent statistics. Fewer misfires, fewer jams, less smoking of the powder... On and on. Your machines have improved our capabilities so far. I just wanted to tell you to keep up the good work."

"Great, thanks Drake."

"The success is truly your responsibility."

– The builder and the user share responsibility –

"That's great to hear."

"Are you okay? That didn't look like something you were happy about."

"Oh, I was just remembering something someone said to me once. Nothing to worry about."

"Good to hear, good to hear. Did you get all the parts you needed?"

"I sure did. I had no idea that there would be so much at Rowan that we could use. It's really an exciting time for me."

"An exciting time for you, Freeman, is an exciting time for all of us here at the Fork. Look, son, you've been working so hard recently. Do you need a little time off?"

"No, Drake. I'm fine."

"Are you sure? Some of the men said that you seemed a little... unfocused, preoccupied during the raid. Maybe you want to take a few days? Just relax, get some stress out? The men on the assembly teams don't need you right now, they know well what they're doing."

"And risk having something get screwed up while I'm not there? No thanks, Drake. I'd rather make sure my eyes are on the assembly teams at all times."

"Alright. Well, if you change your mind, you make sure you let me know. We need you, but we need you focused too."

"Thanks very much, Drake."

"Oh, and just so you know, we've been talking back and forth with our home base a lot, and they're really interested in meeting you. Do you think you might be up for a trip north sometime soon?"

"I have too much work to do, Drake. If I can't take time off to relax how could I take a trip north? It's a long trip, isn't it?"

"At least two weeks."

"We have nothing like that kind of time. We're running behind schedule and I really want the assembly teams to have all the materials they need. That's why we're doing this, right?"

"True enough, true enough. Well, maybe if someone comes down, they can meet you here. Once the machine is running you may well have to take a trip up there, though."

"So long as there's no bugs to work out."

"Good man. Thanks for your hard work, Freeman."

Freeman's hands shook as he pulled the plastic bag open. Like each of the bags before it, a sharp smell, not one that he had ever before smelled, nor one that he thought smelled like paper ought to, tumbled forth from the bag. The smell was unpleasant, and sharp, and more like the smells of dying cloth or alcohol than anything else, but despite its unpleasantness, the smell was ignorable. Because what the bags yielded...

The Way Things Work. Physics. Chemistry. The Complete Works of Shakespeare. Starting Electronics. Each of the unfamiliar titles assaulted him, each of the books filled with crawling words and dark sketches seemed to present vistas before him that he had not previously known how to see. *The Calculus. Foxfire.* Words he had never seen before, but books filled with the numbers that he'd been able to make dance since he was a child.

He had to stop looking. As soon as he'd realized what he found, he'd carefully put the first book back in its plastic wrapper, pinched it shut, and somehow made himself walk calmly back to the Gleaners' compound on South Street, walk as if he had found nothing worthwhile. Once at the compound, he'd quickly gotten Jase and Molly to head back to the building with him, Molly to go through the apartment on the fourth floor and sort out what they needed, what they could use, and what they could trade, and Jase to stay below with Sal and the wagon. Then he'd left Molly wide-eyed at the storehouse he'd found, and started packing the books.

A piece of rooftop and a brace had let him quickly construct a platform, which he tied a rope around and put out the window to where Jase was waiting below. Over and again, he carefully loaded the books onto the platform, then lowered it out of the window, letting the thick sisal rope score an etch in the rotting windowsill. Between each load of books, he carefully raised the platform to the third level to let Molly load it up with what she was finding in the apartment. And what she was finding was more immediately important than what he was: she was loading silverware, bottles, jars, pots, pans... all the things a growing group of people needed to help survive the winter. Some would be traded, some would be used; the bottles she was passing down were in miraculously good shape, and could easily be scrubbed out for storage.

But what she was finding was only important for the winter. What Freeman was finding was the key to restoring the city. He knew it, deep in his heart, he knew that the books he was finding, that the long-dead former owner of this apartment preserved for this very reason, he knew that these books would allow him to start fixing the machines that lay scattered, rusting and decomposing, all around the city. He knew, with only having skimmed several of them, that these books would answer the questions he'd been asking himself for so long, answer the questions that the rusting piles of machinery asked him every day.

He pulled the platform back up to the window, tied off the rope against a stud, and leaned out, carefully depositing books on the platform, checking its balance, making sure that the books wouldn't tip the platform over and fall to the ground, their ancient bindings splitting as they hit the concrete.

He took the knot out of the rope, sent the platform slowly down to the ground. There was still another crate of books, but Molly was shouting for a rest, and Jase was agreeing, and there were other piles of wonder jutting out of the darkness at him.

"Now that we've taken care of division of duties with rehabbing the inside of this compound, we need to discuss what we're going to do about new membership. We've got a lot more arable land here than we had at the old place, and there aren't enough of us to farm it all and still do the other work that we do for trade. We need to discuss how we're going to expand. Does anyone have any commentary? Yes, Molly?"

"Alright people, let's look at this. We've got enough space in this place for at least forty people, and that's without stretching or expanding our space resources. If we have more people, we can farm more land, we can gather more fruit, we can fish and hunt more animals. None of us have to work as hard, and we can have other projects go forward, specifically the work that Freeman has been doing with everyone's help, and the work that Crissa's been leading in increasing our cloth production. We all agree that Crissa and Freeman's work is important, and that they need to continue, right? Right.

"Crissa's work in increasing our cloth production well past our current stock of raw materials has meant that we can increase our stocks of coal, which has aided our winter survival. We don't need to harvest as much wood, which means more time can be spent in the fields come the end of the year, and we're getting more food in as a result. If Freeman's work with electricity can continue, we're going to be able to learn more music, spin more wool into yarn, make better cloth, better clothing and sails, and increase our trade that way. Crissa and Freeman have been talking about electrifying or at least machining looms, which would massively increase our cloth output, allowing us to trade on a level with Fishtown come next year when the traders' sloops come in August. The more trade we have, the more people we can support, the more workers we have to increase our trade, and, importantly, the more people we have who we are taking away from the dangers of life under kingdoms and duchies and instead living free, here and at the other outposts we can begin to support.

"How do we do this? Here is what I propose. We should have enough food to support nineteen people through when the harvest begins, especially since those people should be able to bring some food with them. They'll want to join us because this compound is extremely secure, and we've got great heat thanks to the coal burners. We've had Matt and Lydia and Peter and Gwyneth join us already, and we're glad to have you here, but we need three more people this winter. Because we have to expand this compound.

"I see that you're all surprised at what I say. Listen. There are two more things that we need to do here. We need to incorporate the parking garage that's on the Delaware River side of Eighth Street, and we need to incorporate the empty lots—and make a new empty lot—off the side of Walnut.

"We're mainly bound in our cloth production by not having enough sheep, and we're bound there by not having enough land. There are structurally-sound gaps across all four exterior walls of the garage across Eighth Street, and the bottom floor is already protected by walls. If we can enclose the one access path to that building we can increase our grazing area by twice the size of the building – it's a four floor building, and there's enough soil buildup on the outside floors to support a layer of sod. Sheep go up, sheep go down, it's perfect for us to increase our herds without straining the commons. And if we can increase our wool production, we can increase our trade balance."

Freeman scrambled off of the ground, furiously pushing himself away from the waterfall of the collapsing building behind him as quickly as he could. After getting himself out of danger, he leaned his back against a pitch pine and allowed himself a few seconds to get his breath back. He knew he didn't have time to rest, but the last sprint, away from the firearms and arrows of the gendarmes had torn the breath from his chest, out of shape as he was.

Three heavy pants in, and he lifted himself from the ground and started towards the Schuylkill. The frame pack on his back jounced heavily, but he jogged anyway, keeping to the walls of the buildings, ducking behind trees at any chance he got. There were two bridges he could take to get across the river: the bridge at Market Street, or the bridge at Chestnut. Of these, the Market Street bridge was the least safe; stones had been falling into the Schuylkill every winter, and the steel girders that ran the length of the bridge had been failing for the last lord-knew-how-many years. It had been enough time since Freeman had crossed the bridge that it was unsafe.

The train bridge had split at some point in the past, its girders splayed out in a ragged rusty chrysanthemum. No crossing there.

Then there was the bridge at Chestnut Street.

The bridge at Chestnut Street was in the best condition of any of his routes out of Center City. But even aside from the backtracking he'd have to do, it had its own problems. The first, and most obvious, was that he'd had more than enough to do with Chestnut Street today already. He kept trying to put the street from his mind, but simply kept coming back to it. The second problem with it was that the bridge led straight into Upenner territory. And even if he could deal with them, after dealing with them, he'd have to deal with whoever was left of Drexel. The third problem was that since the Chestnut Street bridge was in the best shape, it was the bridge that he'd be most exposed while crossing. Nothing grew from the tarmac of the Chestnut Street bridge.

The Schuylkill didn't need to be crossed, of course, but the Art Museum area of the city had long ago been taken over by the Fork for supplemental farmland. If he would be ambushed anywhere, it would be there. Freeman was certain that all of the Fork's spare manpower was chasing him, but if he was wrong...

This was the part of the journey that wasn't as planned out as the part up until now. He had known this morning that he would lead the Fork through the glass labyrinth, that he would take the subways, and that he would pick up his cache at the First Unitarian, but from here, he wasn't sure what path to take to his destination. All was a gamble.

Freeman kept running west as he tried to decide between the bridges until he reached Twenty-Eighth Street, which ran along the riverside. He looked right, then left; the Market Street and Chestnut Street bridges were equidistant; the Market Street bridge was as holed as the cheese the Trenton farmers used to bring down to the markets.

Two more quick looks, and he started for the Chestnut Street bridge. Once he was over the Schuylkill, he was out of both his territory and the Fork's territory, so he stepped up his running. The noise of the collapsing building had finally ended, and he could hear shouts over it. Hopefully the Fork was busy with the tribals. And hopefully the Dean of Upenn had forgotten his promise. He came to the foot of the bridge and hardly paused. A quick turn to the left, and he was running across the surface of the bridge, and deep into enemy territory.

"What do you think, love?"

"It's a roadblock. That's no tree. It's gotta be a 'tax collection' scam. Dust it woman, I told you that we should have taken 130 to 30 and not have followed 70."

"Love, we ain't at the intersection yet. They've set up in a place to catch people who try that. Looks like they ain't stupid."

"What are we going to do? We can't afford to pass them any of the food that we have. We didn't do that well trading this year."

"We're gonna do what we can. The family is depending on us to bring these tools back. I don't know how they'd survive without us, or without any of the food that we're bringing back. It's too cold, the game has been scarce by the ocean. If we don't get anything back, after bringing so much salt, and so many tomatoes..."

"Right. Well, right. Dust. They're mounting up."

"Dammnit. You've got your bow, and your spear?"

"Yep. Freeman? You have your javelin?"

"Yes, mom."

"Don't worry. Nothing's gonna happen. These men are probably going to try to take some of our goods, but they can't do anything to us. We're a family, and we're staying a family no matter what. There will always be a family to take care of you, and for you to take care of. Remember that, and that I love you Freeman."

"Yes, mom. I love you, mom."

"Don't be concerned, but remember! If anything does happen to your father and I, get back to the village if you can. If you can't, go to the city. We don't know where these people are camped. If their base is between the village and the city, you're better served going to the city. The village knows that we might not come back. They'll assume that we're all dead if we don't come back, but remember! Your brother and sister are still there with your grandmother, they will grieve and move on. Do you remember when your older brother was gored by the hog?"

"Yes, mom, I do remember."

"We were sad, but it's a fact of where we are. We may not survive. The family will continue at the village, that's something that we're sure of. If you can't get back to the village, bring the village to the city. Teach people there what you know and you're guaranteed a place to live. Teach them reading, or math, or canning, or any of what you've been taught. You can live. Be safe, and remember that your father and I love you."

"They're coming, love. Hold your bow, make sure they know that we mean what we say."

"Of course. I hope they're just looking for a tax. We can't afford it, but I don't want any bloodshed, especially any of ours."

"Nor do I, love, nor do I. Does it seem to you that there's more of this recently?"

"Last year's was the first I remember, but, you're right. I do wonder what's happening that there are more brigands every year..."

"Maybe just more people. Look, if this all goes south? I love you. I've had a good life."

"Me too, love, me too. Luck. Freeman? Be ready to run."

The head bone's connected to the neck bone. The neck bone's connected to the arm bone. The hand bone's connected to the arm bone. The arm bone's connected to the shoulder bone. The shoulder bone's...

The idiotic children's song ran repeatedly though Freeman's head as he dissected the Singer. It wouldn't stop, not matter what he did, nor how idiotic it was; anyone who'd ever looked at a skull knew the head was made of multiple bones. Let alone the neck or the arm. Even still, the analogy was apt.

He longed to be working on the record players, but knew that this was more important. He'd set Crissa up with two powered spinners, but they weren't enough for her. She'd improved the looms they used slightly herself, but still wanted electrical looms and electrical sewing machines. And he understood; the songs they could learn off the record players gave them a cultural one up in the continual ebb-and-flow of Philadelphia politics, but the real meat of polity was trade. Crissa and Shell were producing wool as fast as their teams of workers could card it; with the electrical spinning wheels they were putting out finer thread and yarn then Philadelphia had seen since, well, the Hemorrhage. But they were still hand-producing clothes and fabric, and Crissa had developed a demon behind her farmhand's face. She wanted them electrified, and now.

Freeman had some ideas on how to power a loom with electricity, but what he really liked was working with finer things, things he and Davey couldn't smith. They were getting better, but machined work like the this armature, so delicate yet strong, was still beyond their skills.

Freeman delicately tweezered the connecting pin, and gently

removed it from the joint. The joint popped apart, and he could finally pull the broken spring from the join. The metal rods, connected together like, yes, arm and shoulder bones, were rusted, and needed to be cleaned before they could be reassembled with an intact spring. He thought he had one that he could replace it with in one of his drawers of parts, but first...

He took a rag and dipped it in the small pool of oil that he allowed himself for things like this, a small drizzle of what they'd managed to scavenge from the engine of a car in the basement of the garage. He was always low on oil. He rubbed the thin metal rod carefully in the oil-soaked scrap, felt the rust of years flake off. After polishing the roughest parts with the rag, he inspected it under a lens. It looked intact.

Part of his workbench here at the Collective had a depression in it. He scooped a handful of fine white sand from a barrel at his feet and dumped it in the depression; smoothed out the sand on the tabletop and collected the excess to the side, then held the rod in his calloused fingers and ran it through the sand, applying gentle pressure, watching the rust scrape off and turn the sand red. Once the one side was clean, he swept the sand into a side bin for Jack, who would turn it into red glass in his kiln, pushed some new sand into place, and polished out the other side of the rod. A few times of this, and the rod was metallic silver again; Freeman again oiled it and placed it on a chalk line on the other side of the workbench, a chalk line that described its place in the puzzle of the construction of the sewing machine.

Freeman sighed, took up the next piece of metal, and started the process over. With any luck, this machine would be repaired in a few more days.

"This is... this is a problem."

"Dustin' fuckin' hell it is."

"Oh Rosa."

"Rosa's not who I'm concerned about. I don't know...

"I don't think you all should be here right now."

"Yeah. Yeah, we'll get going. Is there anything else you guys need from us."

"No, no. Um. Look, thank you. Thank you for trying. We've never much gotten on, the Sprawlers and the Collective, but..."

"We liked your bar. And we liked Rosa. We were happy to help and are terribly sorry that it's come to this. Look, if y'all need anything for the winter, if there's any more help the Collective can give, we'll do all we can. Just come by and talk to us. We can work something out."

"We're not going to accept handouts. We never have before and even now we can't."

"Not offering handouts. We'll give you credit. And not the Sprawlers, whoever it is who comes to us we will work out credit with them alone. What are you going to do with Rosa's kids?"

"Don't know."

"I... let us talk. Hold on."

"Can we take them in? They're good kids."

"We don't have enough people here to decide."

"Well... We're more than a third of the group. If we all decide unanimously they can at least come home with us tonight. And a third of the group, that's no small shakes. We'd probably be okay to assume enough others in the Collective would say yes that we can take them home with us."

"What if we can't bring them back?"

"Well... Matt and Lydia's farmstead is fallow. They could live there. We could help support them."

"We can take them in provisionally for the winter probably. I think the group of us could sway the rest."

"Alright, let's vote. Rog can count for us. Hey Rog! We're all gonna close our eyes and some of us will raise our hands. Can you tell us how many hands are raised?"

"Um, sure?"

"Alright, thanks. People, close your eyes, and raise your hand if you want to bring Rosa's kids back with us. It's only two of them remember.

"How many, Rog?"

"All of you."

"Rog, we can possibly offer Rosa's children a place in the Collective for the winter if you want. Can't make any promises until after we talk to the rest of the group, but if they'll work for their place they can come with us tonight."

"Hold on."

"Alright, they're going with you. Thanks again for your help. And this will be a definite help to us too."

"No problem. Good luck and Gods bless."

"Hah. Gods. Right."

"What happens to our pumps, our looms, our sewing machines?"

"What I do in my own time will remain ours. What I have done up until now will remain ours. The Fork understands that we have our machines and that we have our need for them. They understand that people who bought our machines will need repairs. Dust, I can still make machines for us to sell. The difference is that I will be working for them during the time that I would be either farming or making machines for us to sell to the people of the city."

"And how much do they want to pay, again?"

"The Fork wishes to pay the Collective four bushels of grain per quarter, or sixteen bushels per moon. You all know that no one of us here can pull in that kind of grain by ourselves."

"That's not the point, Freeman, and you know it. We operate as a Collective here. What one of us can bring in doesn't matter, even if it is shared. What matters is the amount that we can bring in together. Your machines, yes, they are useful, but only useful because we have people to operate them, people to make sure the batteries stay charged, people to sell them to the city at large. We say that the machines are yours, but they are no more yours than the looms and the fabric are Crissa's. Crissa works very hard, but she could no more produce all the fabric that we sell by herself than you could make these miracle machines that you do without, say, Lana to do the cooking, or Peter forging parts for you."

"Yes. Yes, you're correct, Molly. Absolutely correct. Nonetheless... Steve, how many acres of wheat would we need to produce two hundred and eight bushels per year?"

"More than we have under cultivation now."

"Right. How much of our grain comes through trade?"

"Almost all of it. We mainly, as you well know, grow vegetables and fruit, as their products tend to be more expensive than grain itself."

"Right. Without trade, we would have no grain. This is a permanent sort of trade, one that is not based on how much grain people grow each year, not based on the price of grain, but rather a solid trade, my time for grain. Yes, it is true, we will have fewer machines to share with Philadelphia. I won't have as much time to make machines to sell.

"On good weeks, we will bring in more than four bushels of grain through trade in the machines. But most of where we make our trade is through the electricity. If you take the electricity out of the equation, any good week we only sell about two bushels worth of equipment. And we will keep selling electricity to those people in the city who bought our machines; I have no wish to drag the name of the Collective through the mud. Any of you can hook the batteries up to the turbines; if more turbines are needed, I will still be able to fix and install the generators, either in the sewers or in the wind tunnel between the streets."

"How many days per quarter would you work for the Fork?"

"I will work five and a half days per quarter. The remaining six days per moon I will spend here."

"How are you going to get to Camden?"

"By bicycle. I would not ask the Collective to give up Sal for any time."

It was a rare day at the Fork that a machine did not have to be repaired, that some new piece of refurbished equipment did not have to be supervised, that all the weekly maintenance that could be and needed to be done was complete, but these days did come, and these were among Freeman's favorites, because these were the days that he could work on the Project. It did deserve the capital that he always gave it in his thoughts, because if he could convince Drake to build it, and if he could get all the parts together, it would be the most impressive machine built in the world since the Hemorrhage.

Among the benefits that Freeman didn't know about before accepting the Fork's job offer was the large pile of incomplete texts that the Fork had managed to assemble. While Freeman's library of complete texts was larger than the library of texts that the Fork had assembled, the Fork's archive of portions dwarfed Freeman's paltry pile of books. Another reason that the Fork needed Freeman is that no one had been able to dig though the piles to determine what was important and what wasn't, what was immediately useful and what wasn't. One of Freeman's jobs was digging through the archive of blueprints and texts and random sheets and turning the pile of text into an archive. It was on a day of listless digging that he had found plans for a train engine.

After poring over one plat he'd found for hours, he realized that the locomotive engine fit into the general shape of the idea he'd had a few moons back. He grabbed a sheet of blank paper—something else missing at the Collective—and started sketching, labeling the rough pencil sketch with short labels.

Since he'd roughed out the idea the night of the Betsy Ross party, he'd been shepherding the idea along, keeping small sketches of ideas, writing out pages of notes in his engineer's shorthand, and every now and again he could roughly connect a few of the sketches, then a few more. For the last year he had been steadily turning that rough sketch into a plan, and he thought he had the tools to do it.

He flipped though the sheaf of sheets in front of him, each sheet containing a blueprint of a piece of the whole. Here a sketch for a boiler, here a sketch for a part of the drive train, here a sketch for the device to transmit power from the boiler to the conveyor belts. Here a sketch for an electrical generator. Here a partial sketch for a sorting device.

The Fork occasionally foraged inside Philadelphia for raw materials. More and more often, as the scouring teams went deeper into the ruins, the teams were hassled by bands of foragers, bands of gleaners. Not the Collective, he was sure, but other, smaller groups of people. He was sure he knew some of the raiders but went on very few of the scouring trips. The machine that he would build would end all that.

He saw it in his head, stretching across the bridge to the city, a giant train of cars, each car an integral part of the factory. Shipping materials took too long, and was too difficult with the Fork's small wagons. The barges on the river were faster, but had limited use—the docks were just too far from the apartments. Here, the materials would be turned from rubble into raw material as they were carried in the belly of the machine, a long, moving factory, transporting the bulky materials of civilization from source to sink. Would it take a team of people to run this machine? Probably. That was okay. A team of people would run the machine, and it would produce an output of materials larger than any other. The Fork may be sparking civilization, but this machine would be what fanned the small flames into a fire that would light the world.

"Farmer Rick."

"Well hello there Molly. This is a great party, isn't it? I haven't eaten this well in the last few months, I'll tell you."

"That leads me into what I wanted to talk about, Rick."

"What's that?"

"I heard around and about you had problems with a raid a few moons back."

"If you're talking about those Haddon bastards, then you're right. I heard you had problems too. I also heard it was Steve who strung up those bastards up on the bridge."

"You're right."

"They're unlikely to be pleased with you Gleaners, you know."

"We've been keeping to groups of three when we leave the house."

"That's a better plan."

"We thought. Anyhow. Word seems to be that they hit eight or nine houses in the city before they got to ours."

"More like eleven."

"How many of the people hit do you know?"

"Most."

"Us too. We've all lost a lot to Haddon. And Freeman here and I are thinking that it's time we try to take something back from them."

"What did you have in mind?"

"We've got some ideas. But we were thinking we should get together to do it."

"All of us?"

"Everyone hurt by the raids. Any relatives of people hurt by the raids. Anyone who wants to make sure that Haddon doesn't come back here."

"Freeman, is it? How do you expect to do this?"

"We're hoping we can get everyone together to talk about it. There's a big space down Second and Chestnut, the old Customs House. We had a Full Moon party there last summer, remember?"

"Sure do."

"Two new moons from now it should be warmer than it is now, warm enough to meet there without having to have too big a fire. We're going to get some torches together and have a meeting there on the night of the new moon. Let everyone get together, and see if we can't figure out a plan to strike back at them."

"Count me out."

"Rick, wait. You... We know you lost more than most everyone in the city. The only other person who lost as much is Crissa, in our compound. We can't bring Diane back, but... you could help strike back against them. It won't bring her back, but if they think that we're just a group of farmers in this city then they'll send squads in again, skirt the Fishtown and Southie territories, and take more from this city than we're prepared to give. This is a chance to make them think twice before coming back here."

"What do you want me to do?"

"Just spread the word about the meeting. Anyone who lost anything to Haddon, anyone whose relatives were caught up in it. You can tell them. They'll listen to you."

"And you don't want me to go with on your... vengeance?"

"Not if you don't want in on it."

"Aye, I can spread the word. That I can do. Count me in."

"And you're going to ask me, Molly, why do you want to increase our arable land? Don't we have enough here already? And the answer is, no, no we don't. While yes, we have more arable land than we did at South Street, it's still not enough. The land here will not support the forty or so people that we can easily fit in the house. A compound of forty people is strong enough to become a power in this city, don't you all realize? We showed the groups around that we were strong enough to take this. Now we have to be strong enough to keep it. We're going to be faced with challenges a-plenty this year, but if we start off by expanding the grounds that we're farming, we're going to be able to show the people who want what we have—you all remember Haddon, I'm sure I don't have to remind you that people want what we have—that we're ready to bring even more into our consensus.

"Freeman and I have checked the buildings off Walnut Street, and we agree: they are not structurally sound. But. But. The raw materials from those buildings can be used to expand the walls of the compound. While I don't love the idea of walling ourselves off from the city, we must expand the walls now because that's the only way for us to make sure we stay safe, to make sure we can hold what we have.

"If we work hard this winter, we can take down the buildings around us and expand the walls with the stone of their construction. There's a store of lime in the basement, and we've got sand aplenty, we can make new concrete. Come March, we can fill the foundations of the buildings with ash from our firepits and dirt from the riverbanks and from South Street and from Fairmount Park, and even from the streets themselves. We can increase the land that we can have under production by a third, and we can do it easily.

"With more land, we'll be able to bring in new people during the spring to work it, people who will want to come, people who will be made safe by the strong walls around them. People who will be included and made safe by our ways of making decisions, by our ways of arguing, by our ways of not letting the strongest tell us what to do.

"These people will help us support Freeman and Crissa as they make our Collective into a trading power that the rivermen will have to sit up and notice. They will, of course, not pay for themselves until August, when trading season is in, but come August they will ensure that we survive the next winter in a style that few can achieve. A trading power that will allow us to make even more people in this city safe.

"But who shall we bring in? Lydia and Matt claim to know a couple who can join us, Davy and Mary. They are farmers, Davy is a woodworker, Mary a beekeeper. Independent people who we need to bring to us. While we have woodworkers and beekeepers we need more. While we do have requests from former Fishtowners to join us, I feel we should be careful with those requests. We want independent people, people like us all, not people easily cowed and used to listening to the selfish demands of a single ruler. We need people who will argue, people who will fight, people who will make demands of themselves and others, people who will take responsibility for the direction of their lives, of this house, and of this city. People like us, and people like Lydia and Matt. I say we bring in Davy and Mary, and that we look for three more people, or, if they can bring enough food, four more people, to round out the house. I say we expand, and I say we start work in bringing this city back to what it once was.

"What say ye? Who is with me?"

There were any number of things that could have happened to make the parking garage at Eighth and Vine easier. Perhaps the loose confederation of tribals that had lived there had seen what short work the Fork made of Penn Medical, and had used their innate hunters' geometry to determine the next building in the Fork's path. Perhaps word had spread down the twisting paths of rumor, and through family or friend or trading partner the tribals who lived there had heard that the Fork was coming, and that if they valued what few possessions they owned those who lived there had best pick up and move, and move quickly. Perhaps the hunter-gatherer-ranchers who lived in the garage with their small herds of sheep had simply done the math and realized that the Fork was coming.

Or perhaps it was the voice of Smite-Them-Mightily, promoted from gate duty to megaphone duty on account of his absurdly deep voice, informing them in no uncertain terms the night before that today their home was coming down, and that they were to leave that made them finally pick up.

Whichever of these it was, the sunrise found Freeman and the rest of the Fork listlessly waiting for the Fork to begin moving and to begin turning the parking garage to rubble. Freeman kicked the dust of the years and Penn Medical with his feet. Despite the iron plates of the Fork's head and sides, it had taken more dents and dings in the felling of the building on the east side of Eighth and Vine than he'd expected, and he was anxious to see how the Fork would perform against the concrete, rebar, and steel of the parking garage.

This was a garage that he had never been able to glean for batteries or metal; the tribals who owned it guarded it jealously.

Freeman remembered nights, years in the past, when the parties thrown here that he'd never been invited to—nor particularly wanted to go to, mind—would fill the street with light and sound, competing bands fighting to outplay the clumps of shouting partygoers, all drunk on life and moonshine.

Now, silence. A few tribals crouched on the half-walls, occasionally firing fitful arrows at the steel-sheeted platform where the principals of the Fork stood, everyone waiting for the movement of the giant device.

As Freeman waited, the Fork began to whistle, the sign that the fans and belts had been disconnected, that enough of power had been diverted to the drive train to bring it up to ramming speed. He watched, noting how the Fork began to move; it seemed to be moving properly, though there was a vibration in the fourth car that bore watching.

As soon as the Fork began to pick up speed, the tribals began shooting arrows in earnest. They shouldn't have bothered. The arrows glanced off the iron plate, off the thick windows already starred with cracks, bouncing into the jaws of the ram; Freeman watched a spearman toss his javelin at the window only to star the window further, to have the javelin fall beneath the tracks and be crushed. He went to stand, to tell them to run for what of their lives were left, but he was stilled silently by the firm pressure of Drake's hand on his shoulder.

When the Fork hit, it was nothing like Penn Medical. Maybe the parking garage's concrete was older, maybe the steel frame was rustier; whichever, it didn't matter. The building crumpled immediately under the force of the Fork. Freeman watched as the facade of the building fell, concrete and steel and cars and bodies, and as the tribals fell, Freeman fell to his knees and gagged.

"Dammit Molly, if you don't want everyone to think of us as Freeman n' Molly, and you don't want everyone to hear the argument we're having, going out into the hallway is not going to forestall any of it."

"Freeman, I don't want to fight with you."

"And I don't really want to fight with you. But you're flinging glasses so it sure seems like that's where we're at."

"Why couldn't you have told me what the Fork offered, Freeman?"

"Do you remember when you kicked Sarah and Lloyd out of the Collective?"

"We kicked them out."

"No, Molly, you booted them. You led the vote and you argued for it and everyone followed you despite Sarah's tears. You booted them because Sarah hadn't drank her pennyroyal even though she'd come up in the lottery and was going to have a child. And you kicked them out, and then we found out that she'd lost her child, and you led the vote to deny them reentrance. That's why."

"That makes no sense, Freeman."

"You said during your argument that they'd ignored the will of the Collective and that they should pay their price for ignoring the will of the group. That they should have discussed it with the group first. And everyone agreed with you, including me."

"What do they have to do with this?"

"Everything, Molly. They contradicted the will of the group, the will to only have a certain amount of children per year, when we're all about increasing our numbers. You put the pennyroyal lottery in place—"

"Dammit Freeman!"

"Stop throwing things at me!

"Molly, if you'd asked me I would have said we should have the child!"

"We kept what Jase started because it was the will—"

"Of you, Molly! If I wasn't with you, if I was with someone else, you would decide whether or not I take the job. The decision being up to the will of the group would be an illusion at best. You run this place, and I'm some figurehead or something that you dare the group with. You can't run the place without me, and I back you up, and this is the first time that I've defied your little plan."

"Freeman—"

"Don't Freeman me."

"..."

"..."

"So what are we going to do then."

"You're asking me as if you know the answer already."

"You're not going to take the job."

"Of course I'm going to take the job, if it is the will of the group. I like what we have, but that's not the point. The point is that the Fork is not going to damage what we have here."

"Of course they are, Freeman. The Fork destabilizes every group that opposes them, whether they oppose them directly or just through their existence. The future is here, Freeman—"

"The future isn't here. The future is with the Fork."

Freeman and Scotto had finally finished loading the last crate of books into the cart. The Collective was surprisingly quiet. On a normal day off, Freeman would have had to brush any number of children away from him, fend off any number of queries about the state of the generators, answer any number of questions from eager students who wanted to learn the forces that Freeman controlled. On any normal day, Freeman would have been glad to do any of these things. Today, it would have made him ecstatic.

As it was, even Rusalka's mongrel brood had stayed away from him. The workshop was quiet, the Collective was quiet, nothing seemed to be happening. The only noise was his and Scotto's movements, a low rumble of loading and questions about what to pack and how to pack it. And now, the cart was loaded, and Freeman was ready to leave this place he had called home until so very recently.

Scotto began to drive the cart forward, the nameless mule straining under the load. The sound of the wheels was sharp and echoing against the empty concrete loading dock.

They exited the rusted hole in the loading dock doors into bright sunlight, and though Freeman was far too used to this to have to blink, he did anyway, tears welling in his eyes from the sun, or perhaps the day. He hadn't realized why it was so quiet. On a normal day in the Collective, everyone would have been planting or weeding, hunting or gleaning, scouring fruit or canning, weaving or spinning. Today all was still, as the entire remaining Collective stopped to watch him leave.

The remnants of the Collective stood on the sides of the stone path, a stone path that Freeman remembered building from the rocks of the buildings they'd demolished, they stood, lined up, two deep, along the short path that led from the loading dock to the gate on Ninth Street. Everyone was silent, no one was smiling.

After everything that had happened, he had assumed they'd be happy to see him go. After Molly, after Crissa, after Byron... But no one seemed to be. He'd decided to leave, to break the consensus, without letting anyone know; even still, when he announced it in the house meeting, they'd seemed to know it was coming. Perhaps if the other group hadn't left right after the funerals, they wouldn't have seen his betrayal for what it was. But they saw it, and stood silent in the sun, watching him leave. Little Bessie had tears on her face. Susan looked ready to cry. Ross looked lost. The children were the hardest part, as they stood, their parents' faces stony, eyes following him as he sat in the back of the mule-drawn cart, leaving for his new life.

No one even began one of the laments that the group was so fond of singing, no one began a song to share the sorrow. It was as if his leaving was the final match laid to the pyre of the consensus; as if his leaving was the final sundering of the family that had been so strong.

The cart seemed slower than it actually was. He knew he was leaving them in capable hands. So, no Molly or Steve or Crissa or Byron; still, still, still, there was a surplus of food, and enough grain sown—especially now—that they'd make it through the winter, and if they followed what they'd done for the last years, they'd be fine.

He'd passed this way more slowly before, but today it seemed he was moving through frozen molasses. No one waved, no one smiled, there were no yells of goodbye; the entire Collective as it stood just watched, hands at their sides, as Scotto drove the cart out of the yard, and Freeman followed under something else's power.

"Alright, people. We started out a year ago, almost to the day, on a six-month trial of working together as a group, with no leaders. Then we extended the trial by six months; it worked during the winter, we said, but who knew about the summer? Well, the summer's over now, just about, and if we're going to break up the house we want to do it now because, frankly, my original argument stands. If the Gleaners break up, we're going to need to find places to go and no one likes taking people in during the winter. At the same time... I don't think we should bother with these extensions of the trial anymore. It's been a year—either our little family is working or not, but there seems to me to be very little point in pretending that we want to keep testing it. Any thoughts?"

"Well, how are we this year compared to how we were last year?"

"Our stores of food are way up. Way up. Part of that, I'm sad to say, is that what we found that Jase was hoarding. And, since then, we've been careful to keep two people on stock duties at all times to make sure none of the rest of us are hoarding. As near as I can tell, we're not.

"So, the stocks: In no place do we have less than we did last year. In fact, we're doing better in a lot of ways. Adria taking over the fruit gathering and jamming has meant that we have more preserves than ever before, and we traded a goodly amount of that for extra cloth; we're all wearing newer clothes than ever before. And still have a surplus of preserves.

"We've got an excess of meat; this year's hunting and herding did beautifully, I'm sure helped by the incredibly rainy summer last year, but, still, we're doing quite well. I think we actually have enough of a food surplus this year that we could bring a new person in."

"How do the grain stocks look?"

"Better than ever. Enough that we can trade out for a lot of non-essentials or trade out for some and bring someone new in. In fact... Look, people, I don't know how to say this, but we could basically not worry about the winter vegetables out in the gardens and have such a surplus of food this winter that we wouldn't have to work. I don't think that we should, though—I think we should feast like we never have before. That will require us getting the rest of the food in, but... We likely won't have to ration food at all this winter. Do you understand what I'm saying? If we don't bring a new person in there will be no food rationing at all this winter."

"None?"

"None."

"Oh my God. I've never imagined. I'm starving. That's amazing. Feast now!"

"That's what I'm saying. We're doing amazingly well. More sheep. Another mule in addition to Sal. More food than ever. And we're all tired, I know that, but... but who's feeling worse about the work they've done this summer than the work they did any summer previously?"

"..."

"Right. No one. We're all happy with what we're doing, we're all better stocked, and we're no more tired than we ever were before. No one is hoarding food, we're all likely to spend this winter fat and happy. I don't know about you all but I am so pleased with this that I don't even know why we're voting, except that that's what we have to do.

"So. Before the vote, does anyone have anything bad to say about what we've got going on? Anyone want to have a king?"

"*KKKKKKKKSSSSSSHHHHHHH*... and the ...*KSSSHSHS*... are beginning to ..*kkkksk*... some improvement as well."

"What does the board have to say about it?"

"The board is more impressed with the progress down here than they are with the progress around ..*kkkkksssssshhhhh*..... though they're happier with the current state of Trenton than they are with Camden."

"Trenton's a damn secondary hub, and the board well knows that."

"Of course they do, but where do you think your coal and tires get shipped from, Drake? The board expects that actual trade will be coming in and out of...*kkkkksssshh*..."

"...*kssssssshhhhh* they know we've got ships moving trade through."

"Through the secondary port. When is the primary port going to be running?"

"When we get more longshoremen trained. We've stepped up our recruiting in the farmlands and we've got a few takers, but the local warlords are doing their best to clamp down on our recruiting efforts."

"So take down the warlords."

"Of course. That's the solution every time. Look, we've deposed ...*kkkksssshhhh*... don, and more other little duchies and kingdoms than I care to think about. But people down here aren't like they were up in the north, or up north there's enough shock troops to keep the people from reforming little groups. As soon as we get a power vacuum, some other little pissant group of warlords or coll*kkkksssssssshhhhhh*...or what-have-you forms up and starts over. And unless we start crushing them with troops, which I am getting more and more tempted to try, then new little*kkkkkksssssssssshhhhhh....*

"...by goddamned farmers?"

"Listen up, Gabriel, we're doing our best. Camden was in far worse shape than Trenton when we started out, and don't forget that our founders pretty much owned Red Bank when the Hemorrhage hit; they were able to cordon it off and keep it mostly—mostly—intact through the fall. We're goddamn jumpstarting civilization around here, these little *kkkkksssssssshhhhhh*"

"The board knows that, Drake. You're not telling me anything that we, or I, don't know. We do well appreciate what you're doing down here, that's for certain. But it's a drain on the Board's discretionary *ksh*. We're dealing with shortages in Red Bank and Trenton, the Board needs Camden running as a primary hub so that we can stop supporting you and we can all start supporting one another. As it stands, we're *kkkkssssshhhh* and we can't *kshk* keep doing kshhhhh what I'm saying? They're getting close to pulling some of your funds. You know you were supposed to have more of the farms in this area under your control by now. If you haven't decreased your demands on the supply chain by at least a tenth by the end of the year, they're going to have to cut it from you, and you're going to be dealing with the loss in supplies. Now, having said that, there were a few other things mentioned in the report that you sent up that merited my *kksh* here. What were they again?"

"Engineering staff. I'm not sure how committed my chief engineer is to our vision. Can you get any more staff down here?"

"Drake, *ksshk* the most *kksshhsh* in our *kkksshhh* you think *kkkksshh* up and *kkkksssssssshhhhhhh........*"

"Hello, Freeman."

"Hello, Professor Weatherby—or should I say, Dean Weatherby?"

"Indeed you should. The former Dean Pembrose suffered a heart attack last winter and I was, shall we say, elected to replace him."

"I fear I don't know your students."

"Oh, of course. Freeman, this is Shamokin, Clairmont, and he's new. You three, this is Freeman, and put up your crossbows, I shouldn't think he's an enemy of ours."

"Dean Pembrose never treated me so kindly."

"Pembrose was no true Upenner. His tenure as Dean was long, but he was from some place out west, Arlem or something like that; I don't know how he held on as long as he did. My boy, you never understood who you dealt with, did you? We're the University of Pennsylvania, and though we may have fallen since the old days, we're still the best damn University in the world. We understand more than you think."

"Oh. I... see."

"I see that you don't. Come, let's walk a ways. Where are you headed?"

"Towards the zoo."

"Lucky for you that our little rivalry with Drexel is at an end, then?"

"I had no idea."

"You've been on the far side of the river too long, Freeman. We took the Shaft and the rest of the university soon followed. Our merger is finally complete."

"Forgive me, Dean, but why are you treating me so? Dean Pembrose threatened—"

"I'm sure he did. Never mind him, Freeman. And never mind those shots. Those of the Fork are no longer allowed here. We've been expecting you ever since we spotted the plume of smoke today. You've finally come to defect, haven't you? No, you haven't. Well, a Dean can hope. Can you be tempted? We still have the best research facilities in the city, if not on the coast, and we can fight the Fork from here. In fact, I'm almost certain that if Pembrose hadn't prosecuted his silly little fight with Drexel for as long as he had, that we well would hold the place in the city that they've held up till now. Perhaps now that their little centerpiece is... incapacitated, we'll be able to take some territory on the far side of the Schuylkill back. And if you're on our side..."

"The Fork will stop at nothing to get me back, Dean Weatherby. It's not just the Fork that's incapacitated. Their manufacturing plant has suffered a small... setback."

"Ah, Freeman, when you're bearing this kind of news, how can you think that we could hold anything against you? The Fork has threatened us for too long, and now it's time for the Fork to be threatened."

"You know their home is far off, that they can mobilize massive forces against us here?"

"These things take time. I notice you said us. Will you be back?"

"There's someone I need to find first. Perhaps, after that, I'll come back. But it doesn't seem likely, sir. I have burned my bridges here."

"Literally, in some cases. I have research to do. I will let Shamokin and Clairmont take you the rest of the way to the edge of Drexel, if that's acceptable to you."

"It is, Dean. Thank you very much."

"Godspeed, Freeman. Thank you for balancing what you knocked out of true."

"To the beginning of all things!"

"The beginning of all things!"

"The beginning of all things!"

"Man, Rosa has the best beer in the city, doesn't she?"

"She really does. How does she keep it so fresh?"

"Enough with the looks, I can make some stuff work but can't keep beer fresh."

"Imagine if we could. We could have a pub like the Spectra near our house..."

"Don't talk too loud. She'll sap our credit and then where will we be?"

"Ready to trade for more batteries at half the price."

"Right."

"Oooh, she does have a band tonight. Look, she's got Christian on the banjo, and Washington on the fiddle—it's gonna be a good night."

"Sure is. Can't wait to dance. But before then, where are we at?"

"Oh, do we have to cover business tonight?"

"Yes we do. Alright, look, stop looking so glum, it's the three of us here and none of the rest of the Collective, we need to decide on some details before the next house meeting. Freeman, your sales are going well at the markets. It's halfway through the year and we've almost met our sales goals for the full year. How many batteries can you push out? Can we get more chargers going? If we can't, then where do we go?"

"I can't really push out any more batteries than we've got so far. The batteries aren't holding their charge as long as we'd hoped; I don't know if I'm diluting the tannins too far or what, but they're not as consistent as we'd hoped they'd be. We're prolly going to have to drop the price."

"We can handle that. Steve, we can handle that, right?"

"Yes we can Molly. The farms are producing as we'd expected, and I think we're prolly going to have to cut our expected intake down to nine this year rather than the projected eleven, but we should be able to handle it."

"What's that going to do to the hunting expeditions?"

"We've got enough stored that they'll be able to take trips out into the woods of the northeast. I think hunting will be okay, especially if they clean the game in the woods as we've been doing so far and eat on what they're hauling in, in addition to what we're storing at our quarters and sending to them."

"Good."

"Look, Molly, the band is starting. Let's stop with the planning and go out and dance, we don't get to do that enough anymore."

"Soon, Freeman. What's the outlook on more battery chargers?"

"Well, we've got ten in the sewers and eight on the roof. We could probably set some up outside the windows of the building, sticking down into the street, but if we do that then people might get some ideas of how to set up chargers of their own."

"As long as they don't have the books, or the knowledge, they won't figure it out. Alternators will just look like lumps from that distance."

"Alright, I can prolly get ten-twelve more set up. Molly, they're doing Toss the Feathers, we're not talking anymore, let's go!"

"Freeman! Stop—"

He crouched in the shade of the patchwork of vines as the hoofbeats faded into the distance. Sunlight dappled his face, and the sudden, focused brightness made his eyes begin to tear. He quickly scrubbed his face against his torn, filthy sleeve, not realizing that as he does so he was smearing blood—and not just his own—across his cheek.

Another horse rushed past. He wondered why they followed him. They've got what his family had, they've got the contents of the cart—they've got the disposable income of an entire village. Why should they bother trying to catch him too? What could he do? He's a now-unarmed youth. They're well-armed and possibly trained cavalrymen.

He can't hurt them. Perhaps he could go to their leader? Right. Their leader won't care. If he's going to put heavily armed tollmen on the roads, "taxing" the merchants who come past, then he's not going to care that they just slaughtered a family coming past. Maybe they're just completists.

Freeman looks up, at the imposing bulk of the Ben Franklin Bridge above him. They've chased him deep into the wastelands of Camden, where, according to his father—*FATHER*—even before the Hemorrhage, no one came if they could help it. Lord knew, he'd never met, and never cared to meet, the people who called this disgusting heap of rubbish home.

He had to think. They would realize that he'd gotten away from them, even if he could cross heaps of rock that horses never could. They'd be back soon enough, or he'd meet someone even worse...

He didn't even realize that he was climbing the vines until he was halfway up. Thanks to the yearly visits, and the exploring with Molly, he knew his way around Philadelphia and could probably lose Haddon's men in the maze of streets around Spring Garden, slowly work his way to the Full Moon party—if they dared cross the bridge, enter the city. Haddon's men weren't welcome in Philadelphia, they'd angered the Duchy of Fishtown, and they probably wouldn't chase him into the city.

The loose netting of vines he was hiding behind was awful to climb. Freeman's grasping hands tore and sent loose leaves and branches and shoots tumbling down to the street. But still he climbed, foot after foot, sometimes even gaining almost eight inches per foot he thought he was climbing; the webwork of vines was coming apart under his hands and weight, and he was not getting as near the top as soon as he'd hoped.

Every now and again the sun struck his face, and he had to will the tears back from his eyes. He had no choice but to climb.

He reached the bridge's lowest support beam as he was running out of breath, as the fire in his arms reached the point where he thought he'd fall. It might not be safe, but he had to rest. He swung back on the vines until he was above the extended part of the once-blue I-beam, then let go and fell bodily onto the beam.

Freeman let the fire in his arms recede. He knew he couldn't stay long, that just because he couldn't see through the webbing of vines didn't mean that Haddon's men couldn't see him from below. Besides, this part, and only this part, of the vine curtain was moving; it should be painfully obvious to anyone looking that something was going on here.

Freeman's eyes were tearing of their own accord. He scrubbed his eyes again, willed himself to stop, and resumed his climb up the vine staircase.

"I don't know if I want to do this."

"Louise, when you moved into the Collective this was explained as something that happened. None of us like this, but it is required for our survival. Are you with child now?"

"Not that I know of, but, I mean, I did my wifely duty while my husband was here."

"Yes. And that's why. You have four children already, we have taken them all in. Most of the families here have less children than that. Our census in the Collective only counts adults, not children; there's currently thirty-three adults and eighteen children in the Collective.

"You have to understand something: we all love our children. Those of us without kids think of the children of others as our own; those with children think of others' kids as their own. This is a huge sprawling family. As a family it is incredibly important that everyone not just survive but that everyone gets everything they need. We knew when we took you, Mary, and Shad in what it would take for everyone to survive this winter, we knew what we had and what we could handle. And we all need so much fruit, so much grain, so much meat, so many vegetables every day. One more mouth doesn't appear terrible until you look at it over the course of a winter, and a pregnant woman is another mouth—we make sure expectant mothers get larger portions than everyone else."

"But you let Holly get pregnant."

"We don't let anyone get pregnant, we just try to keep down the number of people pregnant at any one time. Holly was pregnant and missed out on drinking the tea for the first three moons, until she started showing. Once you start showing, if you're pregnant, you are excused from the lottery. But Louise, you don't know if you're pregnant or not. You might not be. More than likely you're not. If you're not it's just a cup of tea. If you are, well, you won't ever know. I promise."

"Why don't you have children if you like them so much?"

"I don't know. Maybe I can't have children. Maybe I just hit the lottery often enough. For a long time I drank the tea every moon if I didn't hit the lottery because I didn't have time for children; now, if I get pregnant, good. But only if I miss the lottery. Seeing all of you happy women with children makes me want them, especially because of my man—who I know wants kids and is disappointed that we don't have any—but I just haven't gotten lucky yet.

"Besides, what if you decide you don't want to stay? Leaving during the winter is no choice at all; Forever won't be able to take care of you and the kids now, that's why you're here. He doesn't know everything that's necessary to survive and doesn't have the stocks. But how are you going to take care of all that this summer if you're six moons in?

"You have four beautiful children, you need to take care of them. You're plenty young to have more children. This is temporary, nothing more. And once you're a full-fledged family in our bigger family we do have a list for women to sign up on; we don't just take people in. We have a list to be excused from the lottery if women don't have children and really want them, and if we have the resources at the end of the summer we absolutely excuse people from the lottery. This isn't forever. I promise. If you want more kids, you can have them. But for now, if you want to stay, you have to drink the tea."

"Okay."

"Dean Pembrose."

"Mr. Drake. After everything we've heard through the grapevine, it's good to finally meet you. And your companion is..."

"Freeman, sir."

"And we've heard plenty of things about you, yes we have. Well, faces to names finally. Can I get one of the undergrads to get you some tea?"

"Yes, please, Dean. Thank you kindly for your hospitality."

"Upenn is rightly famous for it. You, go fetch a pot of my private reserve."

"Yessir."

"Now, the tea should be coming, to what do I, a mere dean, owe the presence of two such august personages from the dirty side of the city?"

"Dean, we are looking to trade with you. The engineers of the Fork, led by Freeman here, are embarking upon a project of a magnitude which has not been seen in this city for years—"

"This would be the behemoth being assembled on the bridge, yes?"

"Yes, Dean."

"We have, of course, seen it. And there is something that Upenn has that you think you may need to finish it? Ah, here's the tea. Do you take honey?"

"Yes, Dean."

"Yes, Dean."

"And for me as well. So, what is it that you need from us?"

"Excellent tea, Dean. If it is aright with you, I should like Freeman to tell you of what we need."

"As you will."

"Dean, sir, we have need of some machinery from your chemistry department. None of your pyrex or kimex, of course, we understand its value and would never ask something so highly-prized of you. We have need of a few of your machines which may not currently work, a few machines which require electricity to function, which you certainly have better uses for than mere HPLC devices."

"Unfortunately for both of you, our HPLC devices are all in use by the university chemistry department. I doubt that the sciences department chair would enjoy my trading off some of their prized devices."

"Then, sir, we could make do with a spectrograph or two."

"That may be workable. What did you have in mind for a trade? Drake?"

"I understand that you have been prosecuting a rivalry with Drexel over the last few years."

"Indeed we have been. They have yet to understand and accept that both our academics and our sports are better than theirs and have not yet grasped the benefits of a merger with us."

"Well, Dean sir, we may have a few items extra that we might be willing to part with, and a few instructors—no, not instructors, that would seem to put them on the same level as your professors, and I should not care to be so presumptuous—perhaps, a few men trained in their use who could show your undergraduates how to use them."

"An interesting idea. Perhaps we should talk over more tea?"

"Freeman, I know what you're going to say. We can't start selling machines."

"Why not?"

"Because we don't know what people will do with them."

"Okay. Fair. Let me try a few things. First, we don't sell anything like a sharpening tool. We don't sell anything that's explicitly possible to use for violence. We keep the size of the pumps we sell down. We do everything in our power to make sure that what we sell can only be used peacefully."

"I don't know if that's even possible."

"Neither do I. But here's the second thing. Do you remember that thing we read in Rosa? The business about how producer's collectives can only work if they have a captive market?"

"Yes..."

"Look, this is our captive market. If we're the only people who can make and sell these machines, we don't even need to make an 'artificial' influence from the laws of the free market – for a while at least we'll have a natural one."

"What happens when someone else learns how to do it? When someone takes apart one of your machines to figure out its guts?"

"There is a whole host of skills I've had to learn to be able to do that. I don't know that it will be too easy for them to learn. And there's the other thing too."

"What's that?"

"We keep the means of producing electricity tight to our chests."

“Explain.”

"No one knows how we do it, right? Even the Collective just knows that the machines do it, not the theory. So we say it's demons."

"Demons."

"We'll lose some sales to the religious, sure, but you can come up with something. I know you can. We hide how we produce the power and only sell the batteries. Then we trade them cheap for recharging."

"That way people only have so much power at once. I see..."

"Right. If someone wants too many batteries and you suspect them... Well, we just don't have enough to sell right now to give you another. One, two batteries per household should be more than enough. Eventually people will want more and then they'll start trying to figure it out, but anyone disassembling a battery without serious foreknowledge is going to get hurt. And then the demon thing will take on a life of its own."

"What do we sell?"

"What we're good at. Sewing machines. Record players. Small pumps. Spinning wheels. Maybe a mill or two. No saws, no sharpening tools. No drills. Nothing of what we have been producing, or think we can produce, that people can use for violence."

"And what does this do?"

"Well, it'll let us not ration too hard this winter and seriously increase our seed stock this spring. If we can sell one sewing machine, we can probably get enough stock to plant the extra fields, and if we sell two suddenly we're in the gravy."

"Do you think you can get enough batteries and machines working?"

"Absolutely. Do you think you can convince the Collective?"

"Absolutely. *Devai.*"

"So. Where do we bury him?"

"I don't want to think about it."

"We have to. We've got to bury him before the ground freezes, and it's late October as it is. We'll be getting the first snowfalls soon. It has to happen now."

"You're right, I guess. When is Father Patrick coming for the funeral rites?"

"I still don't think it's important."

"Crissa does. She's what matters right now. For that matter, enough of us think it's important that it's going to happen. But when is he coming?"

"Two days."

"Jase always wanted us to get a new bed dug over by the far wall, right by Bainbridge Street. Why don't we dig out a new bed? We'll need it next year."

"Are you sure? I thought you were looking for a new group."

"True. But if I stay, we might still need it next year. We may as well get a bed dug at the same time. No sense in duplicating the effort."

"That's really cold."

"You're one to talk. You haven't cried yet."

"You knew him longer."

"True. Go get us some shovels."

"Reckon that's the best idea. Where should we start?"

"Right here?"

"Sure."

"What are we going to do? I know that you're one of the people who wants to take over the leadership. Hell, I think most of us want to."

"I don't want it. I'm no one's leader."

"But, Jase always suspected you."

"Jase was paranoid, like everyone who holds a position of tenuous authority."

"Don't talk about him like that."

"It's true, though. He was. He suspected everyone of wanting to take over the Gleaners, everyone except maybe Crissa. He thought you might a couple of times. And I know you want the group."

"It's true. I do. I can protect us, and I know the right way to go about doing it. I'd be good at it. I'm also as good a hunter as Jase was."

"You would be good at it. But I think there might be a better way. Molly's going to bring it up after the funeral."

"Molly wants to become the leader?"

"Not quite. You'll see when she brings it up. It's an interesting idea. It might actually work, and everyone might be happier with it than everyone would be with you, or me, or, well, any of us taking over Jase's old spot."

"Oh, this sounds complex."

"It really isn't. Damn, it's cold out here."

"That it is. You were right, we did have to do this sooner rather than later."

"Yeah. And I think the sooner we have him in the ground, the happier Crissa will be. I feel bad for her, real bad. I miss him, but I can't imagine what she's feeling."

"She'll pull through. That one's as tough as nails."

"You gotta be, don't you?"

Freeman strips his greatcoat off as he gets to the furnace. Even out in the supply yard it is warm, heat from the furnace pushing back the cold and damp late October air. The furnace room itself is likely to be stifling.

And, of course, it is. Freeman pauses for a moment, letting his eyes readjust to the new darkness, and returns the nods of the glassblowers who looked up when he came in, then back down at the work they were busy doing.

Like everything the Fork does, the furnace serves more purposes than it appears to on the surface. For the moment, Camden doesn't need the entire furnace's worth of slump, sheet, and blown glass, and the demand for forged iron is similarly low. So there is a production line of anvils and the other tools of the smithing trade lined up on the far side of the room, the smiths and glassblowers sharing the furnace's extreme heat to make finer works.

And above the furnace is a steam engine. This is what Freeman is here to work on. The theory is obvious; only so much heat is actually used in both the smithing and the glassblowing processes. The wasted heat is, well, wasted, and that's unacceptable; fuel is too dear, whether coal, tires, scrap wood, plastics, or other rubbish.

The steam engine was set up and connected to a drive train that heads out of this room of the furnace into the next room over, where lives the largest woodshop that Freeman has ever seen. Any number of saws, drills, routers, lathes, and planers attach to the central drive train allowing the artisans of the Fork to assemble the windowframes, desks, doors and crates of which civilization is built.

But, for whatever reason, the drive train isn't turning, and hasn't been for days. Freeman has been spending every moment he can here, trying to find the problem. The steam engine is drained and the drive train disassembled up in the catwalks, waiting for Freeman's ministrations. Before heading to the rafters, he stops at the assembly line. He left word here yesterday that he needed a few parts cobbled together, and sure enough, they're waiting for him in a box, linchpins and clips and a pointlessly complex gear, all milled down perfectly. He slips the box under his arm and heads up the stairs to the gearbox.

This gearbox is the legacy from a man apparently named Jones, the Fork's last engineer. Jones died several years back wherever the Fork is from, and the Fork has been without engineers since. Apparently, this steam engine is one of their last few remaining functional machines; there is a debt of machinery for Freeman to repair, and less time to do it in than he'd been led to believe.

Ah well. Freeman sets in to working on the machine, installing the new differential gear to replace the one that had shattered under the stress of constant operation. The new linchpins and clips slip on easily enough, and a few blows from the hammer ensure that the pins will stay in place. Then, faster than Freeman expected, he reassembles the gearbox, and the drive train is ready to be reattached.

The part of the drive train he'd pulled out was a six-foot steel rod, notched at one end and tabbed at the other, which attaches the train to the gearbox. Reinstalling it is a quick and simple lift, slip, pin, and hammer on both sides, and then the steam engine is ready to seal.

Freeman sits back and looks at the last few days' work, and realizes that he's never felt this satisfied with a completed job in his life. Perhaps this was the right job to take.

"Alright. This is all fine and good, but there are bigger issues at stake here."

"Molly, yer always on about the bigger issues. We're on about the food, and the transportation here."

"But that's not it. There's more here than that. Freeman, what are the Fork's plans in Philadelphia?"

"I am hardly privy to the Fork's plans. I doubt that I know more than any of you. As best as I know, the Fork have no plans for Philadelphia. Excepting trade, they have been content in Camden. I doubt they will try to extend power into Philadelphia."

"They're not native to Camden."

"No, and, before you ask, I do not know where they've come from."

"So the Fork are expansionist. They came from nowhere, and rose to have enough disposable food to not only eat well, but also to soak up all the free labor nearby. Including you, Freeman, depending on how the house votes.

"Do you really think that a group powerful enough to beat down all the groups who might be in a position to stop them has no designs on Philadelphia? Camden has a fine port, but if they can take the Navy Yard and clear the merge of the Schuylkill and the Delaware, they'd have a better one than Center City hands down. The Fork appears to be doing their best to repair Camden's port, presumably for trade, but it will only be a matter of time before their eyes turn upon Philadelphia."

"But if we can build up enough strength here..."

"But nothing. Your joining the Fork, even just in the day, will increase their manufacturing to a point far beyond what we'll be doing. We will be relegated to a vassal state of the Fork, or worse, in only a few years."

"But—"

"But nothing, Freeman. Look at the timing. Enough of you were here when Haddon was, out of the blue, desperate enough to try raids on Philadelphia freeholds. That was four years before the Fork showed. Then Fishtown collapses, two years before the Fork comes. We begin to come to power, and now the Fork is trying to undermine us. The Fork has been on the Camden side of the river for a year and a half now, and where are the other groups? No one has seen anyone flying Fishtown colors. Haddon is gone. *No one is rising to take their places.* Every time a group fell, up till now, be they the Sprawlers, or the Southies, or Abington, or whoever, whenever one group falls, six rise in its place. We all know that we are doing so well partially because there is no one else in Philadelphia trying to pull the boards out from under us. There should be any number of small fascists trying to carve out a corner of Philadelphia for themselves. Instead, we're unmolested. Until now. When the Fork is driving a wedge into our group."

"Molly, the Fork wants me to fix their machinery, not to, I don't know, what, infiltrate the Collective and try to bring it down? And, importantly, they're offering us massive amounts of food in return. Which will let us increase the number of families under the roof of the Collective."

"You don't even see it, do you?"

"I see food for the house, and progress for the city."

"Kids, this is fun, but we need to wrap up tonight's meeting. We will reconvene in one week's time. Everyone think about this question, there is no time for a vote tonight. We will not decide until we meet again. Dismissed."

Freeman stands and watches with not a little bit of pride as the families of the Fork's workers begin to move into the apartment building on Riverside Drive, the first of the umpteen buildings planned by the Fork and built from materials reclaimed by Freeman's machines. Even the ones he did not build are now completely and totally his.

Everything about this building serves the Fork. It is within sight of the Bridge, within sight of the giant moving factory being built even now. It is within sight of the first docks, built out into the river, that even now have docked sailing vessels, trading the wealth of the south and north for the produce of New Jersey. It is within sight of the rusting hulk of a battleship, also called the New Jersey, that slumps and melts into the waters of the river. It is within sight, and even easy walking distance, of the market, of the factories, of the heart of the Fork. And, unlike everything but the factories, it is easily defensible. Not that anyone stands against the Fork.

The fresh bricks glow in the noon sun, the tiles on the roof gleam with the light of the day. Even the glowing and the gleaming serve the Fork. Drake and Scotto and the rest of the directors got the first choice of homes in this building; the rest were put up for lottery among the Fork's workers. There were some mechanics to the lottery, but Freeman didn't pay attention; he handed his tickets one at a time to the children who gathered, letting them run the spare tickets to their families, dirty faces suffused with joy at the chance to live here.

Drake wanted him to live here, and that was enough to keep him at Spring Garden.

Not that these houses weren't far superior to where he lived. No mold, no mildew, no smell, heat, running water, company; Freeman preferred to be alone, and not to live in reclaimed materials. No matter that he spent his days perfecting that reclamation; he preferred to live in buildings that had their own history, that weren't suffused by the mixed dust of thousands of histories, and—*hoofbeats sundering the world*—he refused to live in Camden.

Which is not to say that the experience of watching people move into the new homes brought him no joy. The looks of wonder on the faces of the river-traders made him proud. The squeals of the drovers' wives as they turned on the faucets. His knowledge that it would be years—if ever—before these people had rain come through the ceilings onto them. His certain knowledge of their security—all these things made him proud to be part of this venture.

The second building was already in progress next door. A third was laid out and ready, and a fourth was in its planning stages. The third and fourth apartment buildings were to be on the other side of the docks, and some would be rented to the trading-captains who made their lives on the river. Peach, plum, and pear saplings were planted in the besidewalks. The Fork was willing to do anything to get people back to Camden; they would do whatever it took to get more people on their side, and if that meant building homes that would stand empty for most of the year, well, so be it. It wasn't just the residents of the new apartments: there were huge numbers of people living in the local tent cities, living in the burned-out slums of Camden, living ten to a hastily constructed lean-to. Camden was growing, growing fast and growing strong, and the Fork meant to keep it that way.

"You're really not answering my questions, you know."

"I know."

"Well, then, how does it work?"

"You realize that this is the equivalent of my asking you to spell out in six easy sentences the master plan of the Fork, right? Except it isn't, of course, because I work for you, not the other way around, and you wouldn't tell me."

"Right. This is true. But because..."

"I work for you I should tell you. Look, what I'm trying to say is that if there was a boss higher than you, and ten years ago he said, 'Go forth and rebuild Camden' and then came down now and said, 'how does it work,' it'd be a dicey proposition. For you. I'm not being coy, nor am I being retiring, nor slothful, nor trying to hide things. What I'm telling you is that except at the basest level—*that* boiler *there* makes the wheels go, and also makes the electricity, for example—the system is too complex for me to boil down for you into six easy steps."

"The that-boiler-there method works."

"Alright. See the boiler?"

"Haven't we been through that?"

"Around the top of the boiler, there's fourteen little nubs sticking off it, right?"

"The nubs with ropes sticking out of them?"

"Wires, but yes. At each of the nubs, there's a pole attached that sticks into the boiler. The end of the pole is covered in vanes, like a windmill. As the boiler heats water, steam comes out of it and turns the vanes, and the generators—those are the little nubs—make electricity.

"Which comes through the wires and runs out to different parts of the machine.

"Now you're going to ask which different parts. Well, for example, we separate glass from safety glass from thermoform plastic from thermoset plastic through use of spectrometers. Specs require electricity to work. There's one thing."

"What else?"

"You familiar with magnetism?"

"I played with magnets when I was a boy, but they've no use."

"Right. Well, we've got a sorter to pull out the metal, right? Once we've pulled the metal out from everything else, we need some way of separating steel and iron from the nickel and aluminum and copper and whatnot. Well, ferrous metals will stick to a magnet, others won't. We've got a huge electromagnet that pulls steel out of the metal bins and drops it onto a different belt for sorting and resmelting. Your boy's toy is where the ingots of iron that get turned into all sorts of what-have-you by the smiths come from."

"How do you get the belts to move, anyways? I'd assume that they'd come apart when the Fork turned, or stretched—not stretched, I know, but there's play between the cars of the Fork, and it looks like the belts should come apart."

"The belts are longer than they have to be. There are spare sets of rollers underneath each belt. When the sections, heh, stretch, the rollers are pulled out of position, letting more belt go free. When the sections come back together, the rollers go back into position and take the slack out of the belt."

"I guess Drake did make the right decision hiring you."

"Damn straight he did."

The sun is just beginning to flood the snow-covered city with pools of light when Freeman, Byron, and Sal take the sledge through the gates of the Gleaners' compound down to Fairmount Park for a day of hunting and woodgathering. Freeman's bleary eyes quickly sharpen as the icebound air hits them; he was up late the night before working through some problem sets—his dad's algebra lessons finally paying off —and almost, almost thinks he understands the Ohm equations by now. V=IR, I=V/R; despite driving the sledge around the trees and buildings of the city, his mind is more awhirl with letters and numbers and circuit diagrams than with the project at hand.

All down Broad Street until they hit JFK Place, Freeman is distracted by numbers and equations, until his ears pick up an unearthly singing. Sal's ears go flat. Freeman stops the sledge, and Byron reaches for his bow. Freeman's hand strays near the javelin. They stop, utterly still, until words finally reach them; it's just an Ave Maria from the church at Broad and Arch. Freeman taps Sal and they keep moving.

Freeman tried religion; so did most of the other Gleaners. Excepting Crissa, Keith, Lana, and Jase, most of the other Gleaners had lost interest. While there are people in Philadelphia who still follow religions, most of the non-Gleaners that Freeman actually likes seem to share the unspoken feeling that the world is creepy enough, and that the Hemorrhage is enough; the world needs no more unknowns. Why are we here? To make it through to the next day. To make the world a little better, to grow a little more food, to make it a little easier on the next generation—if it ever comes—tomorrow is good enough. Thoughts of the soul or God or what-have-you occupy little enough of their time. And with good reason—every family, every group, every person in the city knows someone who fell into a religious fervor, lost interest in farming or keeping warm, and wound up starved or frozen to death in the city. If you freeze, your corpse may never be seen again. Something—someone—is desperate to eat it.

Byron's already looking for deer or cattle or zebra or yak as they approach the Art Museum with one eye open—always—for any predator that might jump them, human or beast. There are more animals now in the city than there were before the Hemorrhage, that's for certain, but also more species. As bad at telling stories as he is, Keyin is still the resident historian, and he insists that this is because the zoo used to have species from other continents—Freeman's seen the maps and doesn't quite believe it—and that some of those species could survive here after being released from the zoos. Whether they're local or not, they're out there, and any number of people have lost arms, legs, hands, lives to the local wildlife. One must be very careful.

Freeman strays his hand a little closer to the spear. The Art Museum, at this time of year, is uninhabited, along with the rest of this part of the city.

Byron nods to Freeman and disappears into the trees. Freeman can of course joint an animal's carcass, but he's on firewood duty today. Which is fine, Byron's a better shot than he is. Hopefully Byron will bag something soon. Freeman crashes through the snow, Sal and spear ready, looking for fallen branches and non-fruiting saplings for wood.

There are some around, of course. He finds a cluster of Trees-of-Heaven, which he cuts up and dumps on the sledge even though they burn quickly. A storm broke an apple tree, and it looks like a nice one; its branches go on the sledge. And here, a treasure: a pitch pine lost a branch. Freeman ties a quick flag to the tree so they can collect the sap later, then moves on to find the next branch to load on the sledge.

"Dust, Freeman, didn't I tell you to be careful?"

"I thought I was..."

"Thought isn't good enough, Freeman. Who knows what you'd fall on? You might make it if you fell one floor, but you might not, and who knows if the door is open an I could get you, or if there's stuff underneat that you'd stab yourself with, or if there's even a floor down there and falling would make you go all the way to the street. Tap, and if it sounds hollow, don't step there. Hick."

"Just cause I ain't from the city doesn't mean I'm a hick."

"You're acting like one! Be more careful!"

"But I wanted to look at..."

"Then walk around!"

"Okay. Okay. Sorry."

"Don't sorry me, I didn't almost fall through the floor! I'm lookin' out for you."

"..."

"..."

"Do you know what this machine is for?"

"It prolly had something to do with the glass. Who knows? The only people who knew aren't here anymore."

"Maybe the books can tell us?"

"I can't read them. Can you?"

"Maybe. But I can't get to them."

"Then go around."

"Okay. Hmmm. Mmmm-oddd-errrrn. Modern. Lens. Desss-ig-n. Modern Lens Desigggn. Oh, the pages are all stuck together and black! Ugh. I can't read this."

"That's the way it is with most of the books in the city. Even if you could read them, if you knew what the, what, letters meant, the pages are all black and mildewed and gross. You can't actually read the letters. And the few that people can read don't last real long after they're out, no one knows why. They just turn all black and melty and that's that."

"Do people—eww—keep them dry?"

"As dry as they can, but that's not much dry."

"It happens to everything when you don't keep it dry. Grain, beans, books, apples, leather, metal... whatever you don't keep dry becomes unusable, uneatable, unreadable. That's why we oil the roof of our wagon so often, even though you all make fun of us. It keeps the water out somehow."

"I didn't know that that's why you oiled it."

"Dad told me not to tell. But I like you."

"I like you too, Freeman. Now come on, there's other things to see in here."

"Okay."

"Now, tap carefully, good. Hear that spot? Don't step there. Careful, careful..."

"All these stacks... they all used to be books?"

"Or something like that. They don't have the covers, though."

"Yeah, it's like they're... like books, but not books."

"Well done. Like books, but not books. Any other smarts from you?"

$V=IR$.

It had taken some doing, and some reading of far less technical texts, but Freeman finally felt like he understood the basic equations governing electricity. Which was good.

He'd thought that he understood the equations back around Candlemas, but more testing and further reading proved pretty well that he hadn't, so it was back to the books until it made sense. Now, planting was underway, and the demands on his time were growing bigger, and the amount of food that they had was shrinking, and there was little enough time for him to play around with what the rest of the Gleaners thought of as his little obsession that would never pay off.

Freeman was pretty certain it would pay off. The city around them had to be built by something. Perhaps it was by machines powered by this electricity.

How wonderful it must have been to live in the city in the old days. So much was taken for granted; he'd mastered the theory in the books that he was reading, but moving past theory into actually doing something was so difficult in this age. The book talked about things like light bulbs, batteries, breadboard, solder, and resistors as if they were common, easy-to-find things, things that grew on trees that fruited all year long.

These things sure did not seem to grow on trees.

He wished the Gleaners took him more seriously. The books that came out of the loft over the house on Second Street had already showed them things they didn't know—like the solar ovens he built that cut their wood consumption this year to half of what it had been before—you'd think that that alone would buy him some leeway, some time.

Which was unfair, Freeman knew, even as he thought it. The time that they had to grow food had to be spent on that. Winters were still difficult, even if the Gleaners lost less teeth and weight these days than they did before Freeman showed them how to can food.

Enough woolgathering. He turned back to the task at hand, lit by little more than a single candle. Tonight's task was to try to figure out how to hook up some stuff, even if he didn't have one of these batteries to do it with.

Jumpers, he'd figured out, were short pieces of wire, which somehow carried electricity down them from one thing to another. Breadboard seemed to be some way of connecting one part to another for this process called circuit testing. But circuit, he'd figured out, meant circle; apparently, every piece needed to be connected to another, with the circle starting at one end of the battery and ending at another. What does he have? A pile of jumpers that he made from the parts of broken machines, a few—broken? not broken?—light bulbs scavenged from one thing or another, and batteries, batteries that he assumes aren't good; he can't imagine that they're supposed to have this dry green foam on the outside that burns your hands if you handle them wet.

Little tubular things called resistors cut out of old record players, old computers, old televisions—all of these things were simply boxes before the books, now they're boxes with names, and with specific purposes, purposes well beyond Freeman's ken. He only had one more computer to raid, and it was Lana's favorite kitchen chair and she didn't want him touching it.

Freeman sat down with his color coded tubes and the book, and started trying to figure out how one of these circuits was made.

"Alright, Freeman, help me out with this here blanket. We want to keep the fleeces as clean as you-and-I can."

"Right. Is that why we've been keeping as much of the hay out of the pens as possible?"

"And also why they weren't fed last night. Last thing you-and-I need is for one of these puppies to scat on the floor and get it all over the fleece. Can't never get them clean enough once that happens."

"Right."

"They sound rather distressed."

"They are, but they'll be happier once they're shorn, long's we don't get a cold snap in the next few weeks."

"I remember watching people do this at home, but I never did it. Why did you wait so long?"

"You mean, until the Planter's Moon? Helps keep the tools in good shape. You did sharpen the scissors up good last night, right?"

"Sure did."

"Good. The sharper the scissors the less likely you-and-I'll hurt the sheep, we don't want to be doing that. Help me with Clover here, I'll show you on her and you'll try it out on one of the more docile ones. Some say it should be done it before they lamb, but I say that's why we crutch'em. We have to put more of the wool into the stuffing bin, but that's alright, stuffing does well enough anyhow. 'Sides, it's not like we can spare any wool for coats for these gals, and we want'em to stay as warm as possible."

"Why are we starting with Clover? Bess is far more docile."

"You never start with the blacks. White clippings in black wool we can deal with, but black clippings in white wool looks terrible."

"Ah. Easy girl, that's okay."

"Alright, so we start with a strip down the middle. Don't go too close to the skin, we won't get all the wool this way, but we're careful not to cut'em. Don't go as close as I am, I've done this before. Right. So, she's on her butt here, right? Now you flip her down, hold her head down, and shear around the head, being careful careful careful of her ears. She'll buck horrible if you cut her ears, don't do it. Then, each of the legs, like this—your hands are gonna hurt by the end of the day—starting at the knees and working your way up to the belly, go all the way around."

"Why this way?"

"Keeps the fleece in one piece if you do the legs before the back."

"Ah."

"Right. Now around the butt, then around the neck. That's the part that Crissa's really gonna want, she cuts those off and uses 'em separate for finer wool, there's less locking up there. Alright, now Clover goes down on her side again, that's a good girl, and we work our way across 'er side, then up and across, then up and back across, then up and back across, up to here, flip the fleece out, flip her to her other side —good girl—then again and again until the fleece is off. Boy! Get over here and lead her out to the pasture, she's hungry. And you—get this fleece onto the fleecing table. It's gotta be fast, we don't want it getting dirty! Ready, Freeman? Your turn now."

"How could this happen?"

"Sometimes it just does."

"But we clear our seed stock of black point. We shouldn't be getting a rust on the wheat crop."

"But we did. Now we have to figure out what to do."

"I've never seen this much rust on the plants. When did you notice it?"

"I started to notice a few days ago but it's been dry and I thought it might just be lack of water. It's on everything. When we've gotten rusts before we've been able to pull and burn the infected plants and we're usually okay but this is... It's everywhere."

"How are the sorghum and the barley? The corn?"

"They're okay. But our wheat is in serious trouble."

"Freeman? Do you know anything about this?"

"What do you mean?"

"Do you know how to fix this?"

"I know machines, not plants."

"Nothing in your chemistry knowledge? Nothing you can think of to fix this?"

"I'll look around in the books but I don't know anything."

"Dust. How much of the crop are we going to lose?"

"We might lose it all."

"Oh, starvation."

"Yeah. Literally."

"But this only happens if you don't rotate your crops or use bad stock. We got the kids to clear the stock and we're on a four-year rotation with the fields. This shouldn't have happened."

"Shouldn't but did. What are we going to do?"

"We have to have a house meeting to discuss this. Everyone has to be in on this one."

"People may have to leave."

"Or we're all going to have to go on smaller rations."

"On flour?"

"I know."

"Gods above."

"Christ above."

"Why is it so well distributed?"

"What do you mean?"

"Like you said, we put down clean seed. This sort of thing shouldn't happen, let alone so evenly distributed among the plants. I mean, they've all got about the same number of spots on them, and they all go the same distance up the leaves, and are on the same leaves on every plant. It almost looks intentional. Like they were all infected at the same time."

"..."

"Okay. That's something else to bring before the house."

"But who would do that? It would have had to be someone inside the house."

"It's probably just random. No one here would do that."

"We still need to bring it up."

"Figuring out what we're going to do for the winter is a higher priority."

Freeman had never been on the Drexel campus; for too long it was forbidden to anyone other than the Drexel alumni—as they styled themselves—and for too long was it contested territory. It was said that the Drexel-Penn rivalry predated the Hemorrhage, but even if it did, it had certainly picked up in the intervening years.

Little grew here then, and little enough grew here now.

Since the rivalry had ended, Penn was busy extending their farmlands into the former Drexel freehold; also, the lack of stealthy feet placing tripwires and digging pit traps under the dead of night had ended, along with the attendant push on both sides to keep anything that would decrease visibility from growing here.

There wasn't even any rubble. It had all been carted away as building material, fill, or just as a precaution to keep raids from sneaking up on the other side. This all changed, of course, when the Fork sold the Upenners gunpowder and flintlocks.

The Fork may have gotten a good price for the guns at the time, but they were certainly regretting it now as snipers fired at their dogs far behind where Freeman, Shamokin, and Clairmont were moving at a fast clip through the remarkably clear streets of Drexel's campus.

Freeman was, for the first time, glad to not be alone, glad to have Shamokin and Clairmont guiding him. Presuming he could trust Dean Weatherby—a major leap of faith—and that these two weren't meant to shoot him on the far side of the campus, they were leading him past traps that he couldn't even see, and that he'd have spent valuable time dodging. With any luck, even those of the Fork's dogs who weren't pinned by the rifle fire of the Upenners wouldn't be able to skirt the campus as quickly as he was now passing through it.

He shook his head as they passed the giant Student Union—as the sign above it named the building—which was once faced with sheets of glass that were the envy of the city. No one else had glass like it. Now, after the final, bloody end of the rivalry with Upenn, the story-high sheets of glass had been shattered and broken. The small squares of glass that crunched underfoot were in far smaller pieces than the labyrinth surrounding Liberty Place. Rust and rot were beginning to set in.

Why was it so much easier to destroy than create? And why did Freeman have to join the ranks of the despoilers?

He pushed those thoughts aside. Plenty of time later, if he survived, to ponder those questions. He wondered if Drake survived this morning. Probably, if he knew Drake, but even if he did, Freeman had done plenty of damage to Drake's reputation and rule this morning. He doubted that Drake would hold onto power much longer. He wondered what effect that would have on the city. Would this destabilize the Fork in the same way that they destabilized every other power structure that arose in the city?

What would become of the beautiful, sweeping, clean homes that they'd built in Camden? What would be done with the piles of fresh bricks, the pigs of steel, the fresh I-beams? Who would strip the Fork of its wealth?

Freeman suddenly realized that he'd been walking by himself for a few steps. He looked back, where Shamokin and Clairmont were melting into the buildings. One of them raised his crossbow in farewell, and then they were gone.

"Hey John, looking for cloth? We could use honey if you're looking to trade."

"Actually, no, Molly. I was looking to talk to you."

"About what? Can Freeman stay?"

"I hear he's into it, so yah, he can. Look, I was talking to Rick about Haddon, and he tells me that you've got some way to get back at them. My son still hasn't recovered from his spear wound, and I'm thinking it's time to go take something back from them."

"I did tell Rick that I was interested in getting people together, yes."

"What's your idea?"

"I say we get a bunch of us together to figure out how we get back at them. The spring's coming in, I hope your son recovers. Sometimes the warmer air helps wounds."

"John, my parents would take me to the ocean when I had a cut to clean the wound. Do you have any salt? Salt water might help some."

"I've got a bit of a salt store in. What should I do, rub the salt in?"

"No, not that, that'll just hurt. Just make up some salt water and wash the wound in it, like the way you'd wash lettuce to get the soil off."

"Whatever. What's your guys' idea for how we get back at them?"

"We'll talk about it at the meeting. We've got a few plans. We want to hurt them, but not badly enough that they have to raid again. Just badly enough that they can survive the winter without raiding us, but enough that they feel it and fear us. Fear Philadelphia."

"We don't have the strength to do that."

"We don't if we don't work together. If we try to hurt them as individual farmsteads, we can't hurt them enough to count, only enough to make them angry. You-and-I can't hurt them enough. If we go in as a group, all of us together, we can hurt them badly enough, overpower enough that they're not going to be willing to come over here for any sort of you-stab-us, we-stab-you tit-for-tat."

"And how are we going to do that, Molly. What's your great idea?"

"We all sit down and all of us figure out the best way of doing it."

"What do you mean?"

"Look, I don't know the best way to hurt Haddon without bringing their wrath down upon the city. I have to guess that you don't know either; if you knew, you'd go after them yourself. Someone in this city knows, though. We're not going to know who, though, unless we all get together and we all dump our ideas in a public setting. If we all throw our ideas out, we can decide on what the best idea is together. I'll tell you, I want to go and burn their fields. That's what I want to do. But if we burn their fields, they're gonna run out of food. If they run out of food, they have to go somewhere. And that somewhere is going to be this city. We don't want that. We want Haddon to hurt, but not that bad."

"So, what, steal their flocks?"

"A reasonable plan. But we should all get together to make sure that that's the best one. Look, we'll be meeting on the night of the new moon at the Customs House. Come that night, and we'll all talk about it, and come up with a plan that will let us hurt Haddon just enough."

"Who can I bring?"

"Anyone you know. The more people we have, the better."

"Do you think people will back down if they think their ideas are best?"

"Back down, no. The majority shouts people down. And recalcitrants will leave."

"Why'd you get us all together here, Molly?"

"Because of the stress in the house since Jase's burial. Because the stead is falling apart, and no one is talking about it, and we need to. Do you all want to see it the way I do?"

"Sure, Molly, why not?"

"Near as I can tell, we're not talking because we're waiting for someone to make a move at taking over Jase's position."

"Is that what you're doing?"

"No. I don't want Jase's position. Neither does Freeman. Just so that's out on the table. But Byron, Steve, Crissa, I know the three of you are looking at it. And maybe the rest of you are too, I don't know. But I know the three of you are. Unfortunately, there's eleven of us, and three potential leaders. When these things happen, there's going to be a fracturing. One of the three of you is going to take over, and the other two will strike off on your own, or with one or two supporters, and maybe some of the rest of us will head off without a 'leader' and try to find a new place. The house will break, and our life up until now will change, and drastically. Whoever becomes the "leader" will lead, what, four other people? Maybe? Four isn't enough to make it in the city, and they'll be absorbed, one way or another, into one of the other little groups, just like the rest of everyone who strikes out. And that's why no one has brought it up. Because as soon as it comes up, we fall apart, and we know we're not strong enough to survive, unless whoever it is wants to go all strong-arm on the rest of us, and, well, frankly, that won't work for that long."

"I don't think you're wrong, Molly. But we all have different ideas as to how our group should continue, and one of the eleven of us has to lead the group."

"That's not true."

"What do you mean?"

"I mean, why do we need a leader? Why do we need one person to tell us all what to do? We all, at times, chafed under Jase's leadership, I'm sorry to say. Aside from the whole hoarding thing he wasn't a bad guy, he just couldn't keep us all doing what we wanted to at all times. So, yes, I am here to propose a leader, just not the leader you think.

"I propose we all lead this group."

"That's not possible to do."

"Not true. I grew up in a village with forty people, and we were all reasonably happy, and we all decided on the village's goals in common, through talking it out. And our village survived admirably. Hell, you guys know how much Germantown brings to the markets, you know how well they do."

"That can't work, Molly. It's a nice thought, but we can't make decisions in common like that. One person needs to decide what happens to get anything done."

"Not true, Crissa. Look at the Full Moon Parties. They've been happening well, and with one person suggesting, and two people agreeing on a place, and then they go to other people, and discuss, and sometimes the four have to get together, but eventually three moons' worth of parties are decided at one time. It's far more efficient than it was before; we'd only get a few days notice as to where the party was going to be, and not everyone was happy with where it happened."

"But now people aren't happy with the parties' locations either."

"There's a lot of bees around that thing."

"Yes indeed there are. It's a good year for honey. You wanna do it?"

"I'm gonna get stung to pieces, ain't I?"

"Oh, I wouldn't worry too much. It's been a few years since someone I took over to the hives swelled up and died a horrible, choking death from bee stings."

"..."

"That's a joke, dumbass. I've only ever heard of it happening to people, and no one that anyone I know knows has ever met someone who died of it. It's just something that can happen but that's really rare. Besides, it's your fault we need more wax this year, so you get to help out."

"Like you complained about the canned food in the wintertime."

"Complained, no, but still. We've never needed this much wax. We hardly had enough to stamp out the foundations for this year."

"Yeah, these foundations. What's that all about again?"

"The bees produce more honey if you use some of the previous year's wax—well boiled—and press out very thin sheets of it, then stamp it with a hexagonal pattern. It removes from them the burden of starting the combs, thus less lost honey."

"How do you know so much about this?"

"My grandfather did this his whole life, Jesus rest his soul. He taught me everything I know about it. Now, you've got your screens on, and the gloves pulled tight, right?"

"Sleeves over the gloves."

"You're all in leather, you shouldn't get stung too badly. Let's swap out some of these trays. Now, approach slowly so as not to disturb them, good, and lay out that handful of hay in a circle around the hive. You got your magnifying glass? Good, start the fire going. Don't let it get too close to the hive."

"Why are we doing this?"

"The bees outside of the hive fly away, and the bees inside the hive go to ground. You'll get stung less—"

"Ouch!"

"Don't slap it! We'll get it out later. Can you breathe okay? Tell me if you start having trouble breathing. Anyway, you'll get stung less often if we're smoking the bees out. Now the lid comes off, and we take the first tray of honey away—shoo, bees—brush them off carefully with a brush, we don't want to hurt them—they're our little friends here, aren't they—and this is one tray of honey and wax. Thank Jesus it's been a dry year, this is a fantastic harvest. Take the tray from me and hand me the new one."

"Here you go."

"Okay, before we put this on, we're gonna check how the queen's doing. Take this deep tray off, and there you are queeny-baby, you're looking good today, aren't you? Larvae nice and white and plump, no discoloration, good. Looks like no mites, looks like no moths. No problems here. That many larvae and we're gonna have to move you off to a new nest, aren't we? Good, we get to up our production this year. Hopefully we can find a hidden place for the new hive."

"This top frame is damned heavy, you almost done? Ouch!"

"I shouldn't think that any sort of physical objects are worth this."

"Don't flatter yourself too much. It's not just your fans and spectrometers that we need from here. The Marches of Rowan have been staging raids on our supply trains, stealing from our farms, attacking our rent collectors. This has been coming to them."

"Jesus."

"Don't blaspheme. Besides, it's just through the shoulder. If he surrenders quickly enough and swears allegiance to us, our doctors'll patch him up before he can bleed out."

"Then again, he could rebuke the person trying to save him and get his throat cut, like that man just did."

"Also a possibility. All's fair in war."

"We're taking some casualties too, though."

"They've got good crossbows, but our flintlocks and crossbows are all better than theirs. They've got position, but we've got firepower, and they have no sense of tactics."

"Being on the other side of the wall should be enough."

"It's not, trust me."

"Ow. I guess not. Shit—duck—"

"That was close."

"This is insane. Can't we back off?"

"Freeman, you supported going after Rowan when you thought they'd stand down from a display of force with the guns. They didn't, and the Fork never, ever backs off."

"I've never seen the Fork do this before, though. This is ugly."

"It is. We try not to do things like this if we can help it. Sometimes we can't help it, and this is one of those times. But if we back down here, Rowan will think that they could face us, and then we'd have to fight them off in Camden. Everyone wants the machines that we have, the housing that we have, the food supplies that we have. Everyone includes Rowan. That's why they've been picking at us."

"Well damn! There goes the wall. Looks like the miners could get underneath fast enough."

"I'm pretty sure your explosives didn't hurt, either."

"I don't think so. My ears are still ringing and the wall is far enough away."

"Excuse me sirs, Mr. Drake, do we have permission to march on the college?"

"You do. Make it quick. They have good smiths, take as many of them prisoner as you can. Oaths of loyalty and a better house than any of them have ever lived in before should convert them to our side quickly enough. Besides, we've got most of the available women in this area."

"We'll do our best sir. Consider it done."

"Godspeed, gentlemen."

"And now the flankers that you kept in reserve go in and swamp the resistance from the back."

"And meanwhile, the front gates lose some of their support troops and we bring the ram into place."

"Looks like Rowan will be yours, Drake. They fight so hard it's almost a shame."

"Not hard enough, Freeman. No one can fight hard enough to withstand the Fork when it rolls."

"So why are we doing this again?"

"Because the cloth in this city is terrible, and I always used to dye cloth with my grandmother. The stuff from these oak leaves, and from the acorns, and from the bark, are called tannins, and you can extract them in water, and we can use the extracted tannins for all sorts of stuff."

"All sorts of stuff like what?"

"Well, they're useful as a mordant for cloth."

"A mordant?"

"It makes the dye stick to the cloth better. The cloth you get here is no good because no one uses mordants, so the dyes fade in, what, a year? At best? If we get tannins, we can make dyes that last longer than anything else that's locally produced."

"Oh."

"That's not all. You know how you have to leave your deerskins overwinter before they're ready?"

"Yeah, and half the time someone sneaks in and steals them."

"Right. We get a nice strong tannin solution, and we can tan the deerskins in a moon instead of in a season. And we can do it in the basement if we want."

"Really a moon?"

"Yep."

"Huh. This is a boring job, though, isn't it?"

"It's not so bad. I've had worse. Grab your scoop, we should strain this batch. They've been in for a bit now."

"Alright."

"You get more out of the acorns, and the lack of brown from the leaves is nice, but the acorns are more of a pain to collect."

"Is that why we've got them on a separate boil?"

"Sure is. We'll use the big drum with the leaf extracts for the deer hides, and we'll use the cleaner acorn extraction in the small pot for the dyes. The acorns get left in longer. Here, I'll stir and strain this pot, you wanna grind up some more acorns?"

"Sure."

"We've gotta get a windmill set up this winter for grinding grains and nuts. I can't believe how much time we spend at it. Do you know anywhere to get big rocks? And not concrete or asphalt. We need actual rocks, like granite or whatever."

"There's a few buildings that have fallen where we can find something like that."

"Oh good. We should prolly get the stones before it gets too cold so we can work them."

"You can take the mule. I don't know about all these projects of yours."

"Just wait until you see the cloth we can make. And wait until you don't have to grind grain by hand anymore. You'll see. Some of these projects of mine are pretty useful. 'Sides, you've found reading useful, haven't you?"

"Only for street signs. And maybe the occasional scrap of paper here and there, though I don't understand the whole 'work from home' thing. Isn't that what we all do?"

"Who knows, the old days were weird. Let's get those acorns in the pot."

Freeman twirled the hammer's haft in his hand, the slick-as-glass wood sliding over his skin, and wished, not for the first time, that he had the right arm to be a smith. Not that he couldn't work, of course, but he was no Peter or Gwyneth—and thanks be that the brothers had joined up. They were the true smiths here. Freeman set the hammer back down and turned to his side of the workshop.

It was really remarkable how much useful stuff Fishtown had left behind when they abandoned the Chestnut Street buildings. Sure, they'd taken all the intact glass out of the window frames, and dug most of the perennials out of the gardens, but they hadn't picked over the place nearly as well as the Gleaners had expected. Broken panes of glass, just waiting for a little bit of pitch to seal, were left behind.

Furniture far nicer than most of what the Gleaners had was left in the rooms, a few tools that needed new handles were left in the shed—the wastrels, handles were easy, it was the metal that was tough—there were even some wizened but edible roots in the cellars, along with a small pile of coal and kindling, enough that they wouldn't have to send out parties for wood for a moon.

But the real treasure was what they left in the smithy.

The Chestnut Street Compound was four buildings, with the enclosing wall starting off of the backs or sides of each building. Each building was far too large for the Gleaners to fill, but given time they could—and would—expand to fill them all, that Freeman knew. For now, one of the buildings, the one at the back of the lot, had been closed off; they'd glean it later to get stuff out of it, but it wasn't necessary for now. The second building, the one that said "Drugs" over top of it, that used to face out over Chestnut Street, was the main living space. With a huge downstairs and internal and external kitchens—stripped, of course, but still—and another building made of brick with huge windows and carriage doors, across the carefully dammed and sculpted stream, were the pens, supply, and smithy building. The fourth building was the parking garage across Eighth Street, which was a story unto itself.

After moving everything—everything—from South Street, they'd finally gotten around to opening up the huge brick monstrosity at the back of the lot, and what they had found made half of them weep for joy, and half of them wonder out loud what had happened to Fishtown that they did this. Half of the second building was intact animal pens, still with intact troughs and flaps for shoveling dung out, and the other half was a mostly-intact smithy. Sure, they'd taken the hand tools with them, but the furnace and anvils were still there, barrels of water and oil still intact, heavy workbenches clean and ready for the Gleaners to move in—or for Fishtown to move back.

It was here where Freeman was currently standing, looking over the half of the smithy that he'd been given to turn into his shop, staring at the pile of, well, stuff, that was his stock. It was chilly in the room, but he'd built up the small, banked fire in the forge and its warmth was now beginning to invade the room. The things that the Gleaners needed to survive the winter were now unpacked, food out, kitchens set up, animals bedded down, Rusalka in her new cellar, and everyone was now setting up their own spaces. Crissa and her bunch were upstairs, unpacking the raw cloth and getting their spinning wheels and looms set up, Peter and Gwyneth were inventorying which tools needed repair, and Freeman was about to start getting his shop set up in earnest—a far larger, better equipped shop than he'd ever had before.

"Wow, Freeman, I love what you've done with the place."

"Thanks, Kevin."

"This is awful."

"You should have seen it before I got it cleaned up."

"This is cleaned up?"

"Kevin—it's a sewer. The collected piss-and-shit-and-vomit of Philadelphia used to run through these channels. What do you expect it to look like?"

"True. And you cleaned it up?"

"As much of it as we needed."

"I see that you can actually see the bricks for, what, ten feet on a side here?"

"More like fifteen. We're hopefully putting in five more generators today."

"And this sluggish stream is what charges the batteries?"

"You know how we get better charging when there's a storm, or in the spring? Well, the faster the water in the sewer moves, the better charging we get. During the spring melt, the water is higher and moves faster, and during storms all sorts of water flows from the street drains and makes the water move better. That's why we've got to get it in now, during the seventh moon, before the late summer storms sweep through. Now where are your teams?"

"One's up at the manhole with the block and tackle, one's up with the braces, and one's ready to come down."

"Well, get the two who are going to be down here down here, and let's do this thing. Alright, you two, with the braces. Come with me. You see the X's chalked on the ceiling here?"

"Yep."

"I need those holes drilled through. They'll come up next to the kitchen. Go to town, and thank you very much for helping."

"Better than digging out the new plots. Its much cooler down here."

"True enough. Alright, you two. Let's get all the timber down first, we've got to build mounts for the generators before we can actually install them. I want to get this done today, let's get this stuff moving. Good. Kevin, grab a board and come with me."

"Sure thing boss."

"Alright. Again, I've chalked on the floor where the mounts need to go. Tools are over there, nails in the same place. There should be enough of everything. Get the nails down good, if the sewer floods I don't want to lose the motors."

"Won't the water wreck the generators if it does flood?"

"I've got waterproof housings for them now, and I'm going to build new floating mounts like those six over there once I've got more time."

"Then... the mount is going to look like a figure eight?"

"Well, two boxes, anyhow. So like a gas station sign figure eight, like two boxes stacked on each other. For now."

"Gotcha. Let's do it."

"How's everything up there going, guys?"

"We've got the timber down. What next?"

"Start bringing the motors down. Carefully. Drop 'em and I'll get Kevin to drop you."

Freeman worked the scraper carefully down the sides of the lead plates, gathering the scraped-off acid dust into a small, water-filled bin at the base of the outdoor work table. He had already finished his anodes, and was now working the pile of cathodes, getting as much of the dried gunk off as possible without stirring up too much dust. The deerskin gloves he wore to protect his hands were blistered from the several days work, and he did not want to see what his lungs would look like if he breathed in too much.

After the plates were scraped, they went into a metal pot that could be boiled to get as much of the acid off as possible. The anodes were already boiling, and he occasionally stopped work to top off the pot from the stream.

Freeman's first battery had come off without a hitch. With help from Matt the beekeeper, Freeman had fashioned a rather large wooden box with six interior compartments inside, each large enough to hold six anodes and six cathodes apiece. He had carefully, carefully, carefully welded a wire to the tab of each set of six, fit them together so as to not be touching but almoist be touching, and set the sets of twelve lead plates into the box, which had carefully been rubbed with beeswax and sealed with pine pitch and asphalt weepings.

After all six sets of dipoles were together and in the boxes, he brought water up to a boil and stirred in a little of his carefully husbanded battery acid dust, and a lot—a lot—of the tannins they'd extracted from the oak leaves and bark during the late fall. Enough that the water finally couldn't hold all of the tannins, leaving a white chunky powder on the bottom of the pot. This he, of course, saved.

The acid solution could bleach a newly-dyed piece of wool in less time than he'd have have thought possible. Wearing his hide gloves and moving with extreme delicacy, he filled each of the compartments in the box until they were overflowing. Then, carefully, carefully, he took six mortised lids, each rubbed with beeswax and coated along the mortise with pitch, ran the anode and cathode wires through holes drilled for them, and fitted the lids over each of the cells. Once the cells were sealed, he shook the box to release any air which might have been inside, then poured the excess liquid into the pot, leaving only a thin veneer of acid still on the outside of the cells. A little more pitch sealed up the holes that the anode and cathode wires came through, then the rest of the liquid was poured off.

He poured on a thick layer of melted beeswax, then, after giving it time to harden and cool, poured on a second thinner layer to be safe. The anode wires and cathode wires were then twisted together, and a soldering iron kept warm in the fire was applied to some solder to puddle the wires together. Finally, he took the final lid, also mortised, with two large metal poles labeled “+” and “-” in carbon black ink to keep confusion down, attached the wires to the poles, then nailed the whole lid down to the box. The box he carried down to the sewers and hooked up to a generator he had running in the underground stream and left overnight to charge.

The next day he gave Crissa her second electric spinning machine. She was already after him to electrify a loom—she said she'd need it, because now she was spinning more thread and yarn than any three other people in the city. The first order of business, however, was more batteries, and Freeman was ready to make them in spades. He scraped the last cathode and set the pot on the fire to boil.

"You know why Drake likes this thing—and, by extension, you—so much, right?"

"I assume it's because it's such a labor saver."

"Oh, don't be dense. Except in actually taking buildings down, this thing hasn't been a labor saver, its been a labor sink. You know how long it took to assemble, how many resources we've had to put into it. Drake had to ask for a special goods exemption for this project, and it wasn't one that we were all that happy about accepting, but Drake said he trusted you, and he trusted the project, so we decided to go for it. But it's not a labor saver. Granted, taking down buildings would be more difficult without this machine, but it's not integral to our plans laborwise."

"First you tell me that Drake likes the Fork, then say that it's a drain. Which one?"

"It's both. Damn me, aren't you supposed to be the smart one? Drake likes this machine not because of what it does to buildings, but because of what it does to people."

"We get everyone out of the buildings first."

"No, you get everyone out of the buildings first. We don't. Not that we think it's a bad thing, by and large, but you know as well as we do that it's not necessary to our plans to save the lives of the tribals that you hold so dear. No, even though the Fork hasn't killed anyone yet, except for the unfortunates who were crushed during its construction—and there were plenty of reports about that, believe you me—it is still what the Fork does to people that's what we like about it."

"And are you going to tell me what that is?"

"I shouldn't have to. You were the one who painted it black."

"I had to keep it from rusting."

"Why black?"

"Carbon black is cheaper than anything else, and I cut corners where I could."

"Well then, it's a lucky coincidence."

"So why does Drake like the Fork?"

"One word: fear. This machine, just like our organization, is something that no one can fight. That's why we wanted to keep the names the same. We are the fork in the path, the way to a good life and a salvation. Without us life just goes on, the path is straight, no changes. And this machine is the instrument of that break in the straight path.

"The new way that the path goes, the new road that we open up, is not one that anyone can fight. You can't fight the Fork, and you can't fight the Fork. Neither is something that anyone gets to choose. When the Fork comes to your town, we will drag you kicking and screaming out of the buildings that you live in, out of the sordid little dirt-farmer life that you led, out from your little internecine squabbles and into a group with one purpose: fixing the world. Bringing it out of this little Dark Age it's fallen into. And there is only one way out. That way is the Fork.

"Now, when the Fork comes to your building, and we announce through the megaphone—thank you for that one as well—that your building is coming down, and your home should now be with us, that's not something that you can fight either. You are going to walk our path, just as we are going to turn your building into the new city growing behind you. You will join us, or you will walk away. And you can't walk so far that we won't get there. This machine is far more effective than that megaphone is."

"Hello, Fishtown."

"Hello, the Collective. We are here to hear what you have decided about our future."

"Petitioners, what do you know of how we come to decisions here?"

"Only what we have heard on the street, which is that all of you come together and decide on what to do."

"Yes. That is how we here come to decisions. What we have found, over time, is that not all who come here wish to respect that method of decision-making. When we come to a point where there is a crisis, if it cannot be resolved, which is our preferred way of fixing it, then those who do not wish to abide by the will of all forfeit one half of their goods, and find a new place to go to. Their wives and children, or husbands and children, are not required to go with them. Do you understand? Each one makes her own choice."

"Heard and understood, Collectivists."

"Then here is our decision. If you, and your wives, wish to join us, then your wives and children may move in at the beginning of the Harvester's Moon. They are given conditional leave to move here, and we will protect them through the winter. You will, of course, be allowed to see them when you like, though of course only one at a time. We cannot be too careful."

"Of course."

"Over the winter, we are going to need more meat than we are likely to have with six more mouths to feed. We will require from you at least one doe or cow each moon, more if you can spare it. This is, of course, in addition to the supplies which you have generously already offered to us. Lest you think that we are being unfair, we will trade with you for these carcasses; we will trade bread or lettuce or grains or fruit jams or apples or potatoes. Though we require this of you, we will help you stay healthy through the winter, since you probably will not be able to stay at Fishtown once your wives leave."

"This is true. Where, may I ask, do you expect that we shall be able to live?"

"There is a house at Sansom and Third Street, a brownstone with a red door, that a new member of the Collective has just recently abandoned. As of earlier today, the house was still empty. It is winter-tight, and will be a place where you, Mote, and Forever can stay through the winter. There is even some firewood there for you to get started."

"I will have to talk to Mote and Forever about this, you realize."

"There's more. Come the last day of the Wind Moon, we will have a house meeting where we will decide whether or not your wives and children can stay with us, if they fit in well with our methods of decision-making. If we decide that they can, then your wives will be the ones to convince us whether or not we allow you to move into here. So, come the spring, if your wives wish it, and the Collective agrees with them, you will be allowed in, with provisional acceptances, at one-and-a-half-moon intervals. At the end of each moon-and-a-half, if the Collective decides that you do not fit in with us, we expect that you will move out quietly—and with your wives only if they want to go with you. Listen carefully: if we do not want you to stay, we will talk to your wives separately. You will not be allowed to talk to them yourselves. They must make their own decisions. This is the will of the Collective. Come back tomorrow, with your wives and chattels, if you wish to abide by it."

Freeman sent the pallet down to Jase, running the rope hand over hand through his burning digits, then started quickly moving the few remaining boxes from the corner of the attic to the window. They were moving faster, and more carefully, now, both because of the dipping sun and because the attic was no longer as stable as it had been. Just about an hour earlier, Freeman had almost gone crashing down into the kitchen with an ancient joist which had finally given way; if he'd been holding a box at the time, he certainly would have. As it was, there was a new tightening pain in his arm and a series of bruises blossoming over his ribs where he'd thrown himself out to land across other, fortunately more stable, joists.

The boxes at the back of the attic were heavier than those at the front, and received only quick perusals before Freeman moved them out and down to Jase. These were full of tools, tools that he'd never seen before and could barely figure out the use of, and also with—possibly—spare parts? He'd seen things that looked like them before: short, brown, stubby tubes, tacked down with silver to the green inflexible boards that certainly came from no tree Freeman had ever seen. He'd definitely seen the glass tubes, with the thin bare wires running through them, and the little black slabs with all the legs...

All the things were packed in clear bags of some slippery, shiny material, and all the bags were filled with what looked like soybean oil, though it smelled nothing like. What they did was make these boxes heavier than they looked, and made it much harder to get the materials out of the attic. Freeman moved handfuls over to the front window, the sash now utterly ruined, and seeing that Jase was done unloading the pallet, hauled it up to the third floor for Molly. She filled the pallet almost instantly, and Freeman sent the pallet down again to Jase after only one load from the attic.

And then, after a few more loads, everything was out of the attic, which was good, really, because Sal was going to have trouble moving this load as it was. Freeman hauled the pallet up, stacked the last of the insulation on it, sent it down, then climbed, finally, out of the dusty attic.

"Done?"

"Yep."

"Almost here too."

Freeman crossed to the front window, pulled the rope inside, then went to where Molly was filling a pot with silverware, carefully stepping around the fallen joist. Most of the drawers were out of the kitchen cabinets, and most everything was well unpacked at this point. Molly had, with her normal ease, dumped most of the junk immediately; the sink was full of plasticware and bulging cans of food, but, yes, no longer had copper pipes running to it from underneath.

Freeman busied himself with hauling Molly's piles of salvageables over to the window. And then, suddenly, they were done here, too, and were sending the last load of stuff—dishes, glasses, an acoustic guitar, a pot or two—down to Jase. Freeman threw the rope down to Jase, who caught it with a sigh of relief, and Freeman and Molly made their way out of the apartment into the already dark stairwell. They'd knotted a rope about the banister post for ease of access, and as soon as Molly seized it she dropped it again, and turned to Freeman. "Good job finding this one."

An extended kiss later, and they were out of the apartment, back onto the streets.

"You didn't have a skeiner where you came from?"

"Nah. We just bundled the yarn around our arms."

"Eh. That works, I guess, but you don't get color as consistent."

"Why not?"

"Not as much room between the loops, so the dye can't get into the fibers right."

"Alright."

"What did your family use for dyes?"

"Rose madder for red, indigo for blue."

"We don't bother with indigo, it takes too much to grow. We just hit up abandonded lots in the area for insect galls, they do a fine job."

"Really."

"Yeah. I've never heard of rose madder."

"It's a short plant, easy to grow. It grows wild around here, I'm sure I can find some. You dry the roots and then crush them to powder, and it does a fine job as a red dye. Also red Amaranth works for a good deep red dye."

"Never used that before either."

"Good plant. Tasty grains, and you can use it for red dye. Leaves are tasty too."

"We use pokeweed for deep reds."

"More purplish, really."

"True."

"And insect galls give you as good a blue as indigo?"

"I think so. And you don't have to wreck your land growing it."

"Good to know. How do you do yellows?"

"Onion skins."

"Ditto. How about mordants?"

"Mordants?"

"Things to keep the dye stuck to the fabric."

"I don't really bother."

"Really?"

"Really."

"But it's so easy to get a tannin bath going for before the dye, and even easier to make a salt bath for afterwards. And the dyes wind up much more persistent."

"I've never heard of that."

"We'll try that this year. You'll be impressed. The dyes will last three-four times as long."

"Huh. So, how about black?"

"We could never get blacks."

"I guess down in the Pines you don't really have walnut trees growing?"

"Not really."

"Walnut shells make a fine brown or black dye, depending on how long you leave the yarn in for."

"I think this is going to be fun."

"I think you may be right."

"Alright, guys, quick, before the waves wash it away, what is this letter?"

"S."

"This one?"

"T."

"Keep going..."

"P."

"No, look again, there's a little foot on it."

"R."

"Keep going."

"E-E-T."

"Which says?"

"..."

"Just look at the start of it. What do these three letters say?"

"Str."

"Right. Now, the last three letters."

"It."

"No, two E's together make a long sound, 'eee', like a kettle. Try again."

"Eet."

"Right. Now if you put them together..."

"Str-Eet.

"Street!"

"Exactly. So then, let's try both of the words together. Starting back here..."

"Sow-th, Str-eet, South Street!"

"Yes. Which is..."

"What it says on every street sign near our house."

"Exactly. Well done, Steve."

"What are some of the other streets?"

"Well, there's this one... Do the letters one at a time."

"P-I-N-E."

"Then again, the first half, then the last half?"

"Pi-ne. Pine! Pine Street is just north of our house."

"Indeed it is. Let's step away from streets for a little, and we'll do some other words. Who can sound this one out?"

"Su-un. Suun?"

"Try it with a shorter "uu"."

"Sun! Like, well, the sun!"

"Well done Molly. How about this, it's a little harder?"

"..."

"Try it by thirds, this time. Everyone together?"

"Cl-ou-ds. Clou-ds. Clouds!"

"Right on."

This wasn't part of Freeman's plan.

He burst through a wall of Virginia Creeper and stared miserably at the street in front of him. It was choked solid with rubble and vines, with trees and raspberry canes; a car's headlight poked out, perpetually winking. Freeman was beyond the map he knew.

It was just after noon, the sun was just to his left, and Freeman was heading north-and-west. He needed to be heading north and he hadn't expected to be stuck this deep in West Philadelphia. There were bridges to get across, but first he had to get to them, and he hardly knew where they were from here. These parts of the city had always been off limits.

He clambered over the car, thorns scraping down his sides, crushing the plants under him, knowing full well that he was leaving an all-too-clear trail behind him. And then suddenly, off to his side, there it was: a fire escape. He clambered up it, dodging rusted-out steps, to the roof of the building, and broke out into the sunlight.

The city lay before him, spread out like a glorious map. The river was in front of him after all, the sunlight gleaming off its curve like fire off guitar strings, herds of wild cattle and zebra visible as still lumps on the grassy banks. There was a plume of smoke to the east, the plume where the Fork's wreckage still burned. He determined his position quickly, the bridge he wanted was a little bit east of where he was, he was going to have to backtrack a touch. There was a jumble of greenery off to his side—that was the zoo—perhaps the best way to go? Perhaps up to the railroad tracks, and then down once he got to Fairmount Park, and east through the park through the bridge?

No, he'd be too exposed on the tracks; he had to assume that the Fork knew where he was, or at least where he was going, and that they'd be looking. Down to the streets.

He picked his way back to the fire escape in the sullen, oppressive, silent heat of the late summer afternoon, fixing the map in his head, transforming the beltways of green into streets and the brown buildings into walls, each streak of color a note in the labyrinth's symphony.

And then, just as he was beginning his descent to the streets—*hoofbeats sundering the world*—the distinctive clip-clop of shod hooves on asphalt. Anything was possible, but he had to assume that it was the cavalry. It had to be Scotto and Dawn.

Freeman scrambled down the escape, steps breaking behind him, ignoring of the racket he was causing. They'd never get the horses down this street, and they could well guess which direction he'd taken out of Upenn. They had some idea where he was already; the best he could do would be to head for the zoo and keep moving. There were obstacles there; he'd already ruled out the railroad tracks, but now he drew a double line through them—too easy to get the cavalry down them, not enough obstructions.

The only real surprise, he thought as he clambered his way over the rubble, was that it had taken them this long to bring out the cavalry. They'd have caught him far earlier if they'd had horses out while he was in the relatively open streets of Center City. They must have been overconfident, forgetting that he grew up as a street rat. He turned the corner, threaded between an avenue of oaks, and turned down another street clogged with bramble. The Fork could never separate the map from the territory.

Freeman ran down the side street, not as choked as it appeared to be, as the sound of pursuing hoofbeats finally became audible from the ground, and drew steadily closer.

"What are we doing here again?"

"Alright, we've got the superstructure set up here, right?"

"Sure. Dave's already got his hop vines planted under it. In fact, the superstructure has been taking up room since August."

"You know what, shut up. You agreed that this bit of land was too full of asphalt to do much in the way of planting. Anyway. Right. What we're going to do today is raise the windmill part of it. We've got this assembly here, this is going to get lifted to the top of the superstructure, where it will spin in the wind. We're going to use Sal here, good mule, to pull the rope, I've got the pulley set up on the wall, and we're going to mount this to the top of the structure. Once it's mounted, we're going to set up the stones underneath."

"Alright, I guess let's do it. You climb, I'll get Sal pulling."

"Go for it. Race you to the top."

"Pull, Sal, pull!"

"I'm up, where's the mill?"

"It's a-coming."

"Alright, good, tie off the rope, get one of the kids to bring Sal back to the barn, come up here, I need a hand getting it off the pallet."

"Yo, Weed, get over here, bring Sal back. Thanks kid."

"Bring a hammer with you, I forgot one."

"Of course you did."

"Not the most stable platform ever."

"You know, this is the first tower I've ever raised, how about you?"

"True enough."

"Once it's all in place, we'll get some extra supports on the bottom, but I wanted to make sure I didn't damage the hops before that happened, they're far more important."

"La la la. Ready to heave?"

"Sure. Alright. Good. Let's hammer. You get that side, I'll get this one."

"Now what?"

"Well, we've got the flat stone there, right? And the stone has a groove cut around the center, with bearings in, right?"

"Right."

"Then we've got the top stone, with holes drilled all the way through, lots of them, and the spokes coming out of it, right?"

"The circular one. Right."

"Well, we've got to get that stone on top of the bottom stone."

"So, you're saying, get Sal back."

"Pretty much."

"Yo, Weed! Yeah, get me Sal again. No, shut up. None of your guff."

"We can use the pulley though. Once we get the stones on top of each other, then we put together the already-built mechanism that turns the stones, and presto—flour. Flour that we don't have to grind by hand, and far, far finer flour than we're used to eating here. Trust me, fine, stone-ground flour is worth getting Sal any number of times, and stop giving me that look."

"True enough. True enough. But look: with figuring out the locations of the parties three moons at a time, if we're not happy with the location of the first moon's, we're all reasonably certain that the next moon's will be in a place that we like, and that we want to go."

"How does this apply to us, Molly?"

"We decide on scheduling in common. You, Steve, what do you like to do best?"

"Farm."

"Yet you still go out hunting, even when you'd rather be farming?"

"I am a good shot."

"But you don't like it. If we've got enough meat coming in, there's no reason that you can't say, look, I don't want to do this, to the group, and we can figure out someone else to go along. Jer, you're our best shepherd. You don't particularly love the work—none of us really do. If we all have a say in what we do, there's no reason that we can't get you off the flocks for three days a quarter, rather than the one day you have now. Yes, it requires more scheduling, it requires more work, its going to require sacrifice from all of us to get everything done. But, perhaps, it will require less sacrifice from any one of us than some stupid succession fight over who takes Jase's place will."

"How should we decide?"

"One of us brings something before the group. We talk it out until there's nothing left to say. Then we vote, in secret, with beans, like we did the night of the attack. There's eleven of us. So if there's more beans than people, we'll know that someone's cheating, and we can recast the vote. If six or more of us vote for something, then that's the way we do it, unless we can all come together and find a better way that more of us agree on. In fact, we should probably not even say six of us. We should say eight of us have to agree on something before we do it. That way, we minimize the chances that one of us gets marginalized."

"What if one of us disagrees, and disagrees strongly enough to leave?"

"Then we discuss. The main thing is to keep the stead together, to keep the house strong. We can maybe survive if there's nine of us, but that's the minimum. Less than nine and we can't do the work. It is of utmost importance that we stay together because that's our best chance of survival, and hell, people, we work well together. We know that. We know we're a good unit, we've been together here for between two and eight years. Freeman four, I've been here five, Crissa six, Steve since the beginning, Lana for six... We work well together, and none of us particularly like the people we'd otherwise go to."

"What if it doesn't work?"

"Well, suppose we survive the winter, then split. Come the summer it will be easier for us to find places to go. Every group is more likely to take people in the spring, when some have died in the winter, and the promise of food hangs in the air. Going and looking for places now is suicide, and none of us need that.

"Let's try this. Let's all put aside our leadership aspirations, and see if we can't do it. I think we can make it work, and we can make ourselves strong, and get past this."

"Let's vote with the beans? On trying Molly's idea 'til the spring?"

"I've got some right here."

"And that's ten and one. So. Now what? I know. Stand if you're willing to give it a shot."

Everyone in the room stood.

Freeman shuffled listlessly through the piles of machinery, screams of the wounded still echoing outside, billowing smoke from Rowan's burning defensive positions pouring through the smashed windows.

What sort—*hoofbeats sundering the world*—of people had he fallen in with? Drake spoke of the same sorts of things as—*a clenched fist pounding against the windowpane*—Molly had, back in the day, but their solutions to the same problems were far, far different. Molly—and, by extension, the Collective—were just as concerned with expansion and control and power as Drake and the Fork were, but where Molly preferred to bring people under her wing by showing them that yes, this path was better, and if you want to walk it we'll help you along, Drake... by any means necessary. Including, apparently, burning and slaughter.

Shouts from below: a new pocket of resistance? Drake had warned him of this; apparently, there were still raiding parties out, the campus was still dangerous. He moved quickly through the ancient, dusty laboratories, pointing at different machines that nameless navvies of the Fork came and collected, carried down the steps for him. Sometimes, it was a full bookshelf that needed to come.

Freeman wondered what the Fork would do with Rowan now. Probably destroy the walls and defensive positions, burn the fields, and abandon the campus; the Fork had enough to deal with in Camden without having to worry about taking on any extra territory.

Just as Freeman came to a locked door, his rage welled up in him white-hot. He came to, with Infidel standing at his side, a quizzical look on his face, and the door smashed down around him. This was a storage closet, and this was what he had come for. He indicated to Infidel "All of it" and kept striding down the hall.

There was nothing else useful here. He climbed the steps to the empty third floor, then leaned against the cool wall and closed his eyes. What had he fallen in with, and, what had he become? The Fork may have only done all this to Rowan using him as an excuse, but he was complicit in the awful slaughter still going on outside.

No, this wasn't his fault. Drake had said it himself. Rowan was raiding, as Haddon used to do, but in far more force, and it wasn't the sort of thing that the Fork would stand for. You don't hold back the incoming tide, and you don't raid the Fork. They were both forces of nature that could not be stopped.

But if this was the case, why did he feel so responsible for what had happened here? Because of the timing of the Fork's assault? Or because even before the wagons had gone for Rowan's food and seed stocks, they'd come here, with him, to the science building, to pick up whatever machines they could?

Freeman scrubbed his face. The navvies would be coming upstairs before he knew it, and he didn't want them to see him like this. He opened door after door, mentally catalouging what he saw. Any machines in the lab storage rooms were coming with, those were the most likely to be useful, if only because half of them would work and the other half could be converted into parts, parts that matched, and then they'd have half that half working. Yeah. Concentrate on the work, ignore the screaming horses and men. These parts were just what he needed.

These parts were just what he needed.

These parts were just what he needed.

"But how could this have happened?"

"What are we going to do?"

"How much of the wheat is ruined?"

"People. Please. We don't know what happened. We don't even know how much wheat we're going to lose. It's midseason; we might get all the grain in, we might lose some, we don't know."

"Midsummer just passed. When is harvest?"

"Early in the Green Moon."

"How fast will the rust spread on the plants?"

"I'm not sure. It depends on how hard the rust has hit the roots, and how wet it is. The more rain we get, the faster the splotches will grow. We have to slow watering on the wheat and hope that the year isn't too wet."

"Will it spread to other plants? Are we going to lose the potatoes too?"

"The rust shouldn't spread. It's like the powdery mildew on the tomatoes; each disease is usually tied to a specific plant. It might spread to the barley, but it won't affect the potatoes or the sorghum."

"If it's going to attack the barley, should we burn the fields now?"

"Well... that's the question. We've got a really, really bad infection."

"What do we do if we lose all the wheat and all the barley?"

"Yeah. Hunt more?"

"If we burn the wheat fields now and we don't lose the barley, can we make it through the winter?"

"We'll be on starvation rations come the Snow Moon. We'll have to up our hunting and wild gathering really a lot. Maybe if Freeman upped his machine output, or went to work for the Fork..."

"Can we survive without the Fork now?"

"If we don't lose too much of the wheat crop. I really don't want to fire it. We can pull the lower leaves off the wheat and we might still get a reasonable harvest. But... infections like this lower the size and quality of the seed we get. And we're not going to be able to store any of it as seed stock for next year."

"If we burn it now will we be able to put the winter wheat in early?"

"Not really. We could replant with beans, but we don't want to put wheat on that field for at least two years, not with an infection of this size. A few winters should kill whatever causes it, but... we really can't put down anything the rust will attack."

"We've also lost a quarter of our acreage for grain."

"Yes."

"And it might attack the barley."

"Yes."

"I move we burn the field."

"Seconded."

"Alright people, let's put it to a vote. But I recommend we don't do this."

"We cannot lose the barley. Bring out the beans."

"Alright. By the will of the Collective, we burn the wheat fields. Freeman, can you get us enough water to soak the other fields so we don't lose any more?"

"I should be able to."

"I came as soon as I could. What's wrong, oh my God, Molly."

"I found her like this in the doorway of the outhouse. I don't know what happened."

"There was blood everywhere, on her skirts, her thighs, she had been vomiting and there was blood in that. She's burning up with fever now and I don't know what's wrong."

"Did you send for Adria?"

"I did but she's not here yet."

"Molly, Molly, are you okay? Oh God Molly what's happening? Oh Molly..."

"This cup was in the outhouse with her."

"It smells like mint."

"That's what I was thinking. Pennyroyal?"

"I'm here, what's wrong?"

"Molly's vomiting and bleeding and she apparently just drank this."

"Oh dust no that's too much pennyroyal. Oh no no no. OK, Kevin, I need charcoal and my mortar and pestle. Go fetch it now. We'll try to wake her up. Freeman, stay focused I need you here."

"Ok."

"Freeman, was Molly pregnant?"

"Not that she told me."

"This looks like a miscarriage, an extremely sudden and violent miscarriage. I think she's definitely got too much pennyroyal in her system. I have to warn you, Freeman, there's a chance she won't pull out of this."

"Oh no no no."

"But there's a chance she'll be okay. We're going to have to wake her up and get her to drink a lot of water. You! Stop looking in here and go get us water. You! Go get warm water from Lydia, not too hot. And Freeman, close the door."

"She's going to be okay."

"If you help me set her up. She's going to get a lot of fluids on your bed."

"Fine fine just lets make sure she's okay."

"Good. Keep that up. On three, let's set her up, ready? One two three."

"Here's the charcoal Adria."

"Okay. Freeman, grind that as thin as you can while I get some tinctures ready."

"What are you giving her?"

"Dandelion and forsythia and honeysuckle to get things moving in her system. Charcoal to soak up as much of the toxin as we can. Linden and nettle to make her piss. And lots and lots of water so that she can cycle through as much liquid as possible."

"Willow bark for the fever?"

"Not with pennyroyal. They should never be taken together."

"Alright, Freeman, two teaspoons of the charcoal in her mouth once she's awake. She's going to fight, just do it. Steve, you make her drink while I hold her hands down."

"Ugh."

"Smelling salts for her. Go, Freeman, go. Molly stop fighting you have to do this if you can hear me Molly stop fighting you have to drink this you have to stop fighting Molly you have to do this please Molly do it for me you have to NOW Molly."

"Alright, people, settle down. We still have the most important order of business up for tonight, which is the addition of new people to the Collective. Now, I believe Crissa asks to suggest people for inclusion in the Collective?"

"Yes. The Hannah family of Bala Cynwyd asks to join the Collective; unfortunately they have stated that they are a unit, and shall not be separated. There are seven of them, three children aged two to eight, the parents, and their parents' parents. The request to join comes from the eldest of the household. I believe everyone knows the Hannah family?

"I'll take that chorus of assent as a yes. This request has been in the offing for several years; they originally requested membership when we were on South Street. Rosemary, the eldest of the family, has long been eager to get her hands on our dyeing methods, and, honestly, she is the best weaver I've seen; her cloth consistently demands top-notch prices. I have to imagine that the new looms, in her hands, will produce even better cloth than they already do. Dale, in addition to being a fine farmer, also has an amazing singing voice and a remarkable memory for lyrics. You all know the rest. Comments?"

"I understand that Rosemary rules the family with an iron fist. We can be relatively certain that everyone in her family will vote with her, whatever way she goes. Do we really want to place that much power in our decision making process in the hands of one family? Four voting members is easily a tenth of our voting body. Rosemary could wind up leading the Collective, in practice if not in actual fact. Do we want that?"

"I see by the conversation that this is a serious issue. Crissa, if you would sit, we will table this and call another meeting in two days' time to discuss the issue again. Is this contrary to the will of the Collective?"

"No." "No." "No." ...

"Excellent. We also have the issue of our three newest members from over the winter, who were given provisional acceptances. If Mary, Louise, and Shad could leave the room... Thank you. Any comments on these three?"

"A fine bunch, but I'm worried about Louise's husband. She has the habit of drawing her hair before her face after any time that he comes to visit, and shies away from even the contact of women. Have any others noticed this?"

"Yes."

"I'm fine with Louise, and I'm fine with her children, but I don't know about Forever. I'm worried about bringing him into the Collective. If he treats his wife so, he is unlikely to treat our consensus with any more respect."

"So, then, I hear a vote for allowing Louise. I think we all like her, but she will have to be part of the decision about her husband. We will likely have to protect her from her husband if she joins us, and agrees that he should not. How does the house feel? Bring on the beans."

"Twenty-nine in favor of Louise, and four against. Well, that's clear if anything is. Do any object strongly enough to leave the Collective?

"Then bring in Louise, and we will first discuss Mary and Shad, then the matter of their husbands."

"Could we come to order please?

"Thank you. As most of you know, I'm Molly, one of the members of the South Street Gleaners. You-and-I are all here for the same reason: you, or someone you love, or someone you know, has lost something to the Kingdom of Haddon. While they've stopped their raids for the winter, we don't know why they started the raids, and we don't know if they'll continue them now that the spring and summer are coming.

"Now, none of us here are of the Duchy of Fishtown or the Southie Sprawlers. You-and-I are all members of small groups or are independent farmowners or traders or whatever we are. And none of us, by ourselves, can stand up against the aggression of Haddon except in the heat of a raid. My group, the Gleaners, is one of the largest represented here, and we don't have the strength in arms to mount any sort of coherent response to the Kingdom of Haddon. I assume you are all in the same sort of place.

"Now, as I called the meeting, and the Gleaners have provided drinks for those who have gathered here, I would like to, at the sufferance of the group, retain my role as mediator of the discussion. Does anyone object?"

"I do."

"Yes, Farmer?"

"Yer a girl, Molly, and this is about war. Let a man stand."

"An interesting point. Does anyone disagree?"

"I saw her run one of Haddon's men through with a spear. She is as qualified to be here as you are, Farmer."

"Anyone second John's objection? No? Anyone to second mine?"

"Seconded. Seconded. Seconded. Seconded."

"Thank you. Please vote by raising your hand if you agree that I am capable of, and should, lead this discussion.

"Thank you all, that is more than fifty percent. In the interest of speed, if you have an issue with my leading the discussion—which does not mean that I will lead whatever we decide to do to Haddon—then you should feel free to leave now.

"Good to see that you're all staying. Now, we're all here. Who has an idea of what we can do to these bastards? Farmer Rick."

"Salt their fields so they can no longer grow food."

"Freeman, write this down please? Other ideas? Greg, in the back."

"Salting's too risky. Let's just go in and burn them down."

"Anyone else? Judy."

"Perhaps we can take Haddon's son prisoner. I hear he rides the patrols."

"You, in the back, and say your name please?"

"Richard, and a raid for livestock."

"Kurt?"

"Raid their grain caravans when they bring in wheat at the end of the summer."

"Anyone else? Mike."

"They draw their water from the Cooper River. Poison it."

"Anyone else? No? Then let's take the ideas in sequence. What do we think about salting their fields."

"We don't have—There's too much—Salt is too—Too dangerous—What do we get"

"PEOPLE! One at a time. Let's start with Rick, it's his plan. Rick, what do you have to say?"

Freeman snapped awake from a dream of capillaries and bones, treads and belts, hands and scales; ripped his head out from where it lay on his folded arms and stared at the center of the brick factory, the giant mouth-painted crusher, and felt the machine stare back at him even without eyes. Even without all his notes, he could finally see it...

He flipped over a sheet of paper he'd been using for working out improvements to the kiln and began sketching, snippets of designs he'd been sketching for a year now in margins suddenly detaching themselves from his memory, designs drawn in pencil now luminous, three-dimensional, glowing in his mind, slowly floating down and buzzing about until his pencil tacked them to the page, tacked them properly in place in the design. Small, disconnected bits now part of a grey and luminous whole.

Everyone at the brick factory had knocked off already; he really had no idea how long he'd been asleep, but the sun was still setting,so it couldn't have been that long. His pencil paused in its skritching—tonight was the Full Moon party. He was supposed to be there. But he could miss one, right? Especially on a night like this...

His pencil moved faster, sketching linkages, boilers, where the generators would go. Those freight containers near the bridge embankment at the old port; those would make serviceable cars, maybe you'd have to weld two of them together, but.

He drew new piece of paper after new piece of paper as the time wore on, time he hardly even noticed. The key was in the system of belts, and making the belts stretch; you could have the whole machine turn, and each of the cars stay close, close, close to normal with one another, not lose loads of material off the belts, if only you could make them stretch. Retractable rollers on springs solved that problem; joints that didn't allow more than a ten degree, no, make it eight degree, shift between cars would solve the turning problem. Three boilers, each generating electricity and motive power, the furnaces that fed them smelting different things: glass in one, metals in another, bricks firing in the third. Make everything serve two-three purposes, however many he could force out of it.

The blade from an excavator on the front, no, two, that folded down into a beak; that would work for ramming. Then raise the top blade to allow it to scoop. Use a block of fans to blow leaves, plastics, paper away, they would collect against the side, use a second set of fans to blow them back into collection chambers, they would just add to the fuel. Lose a plastic bottle or two, that was okay, plastic was hard to work with and burned well. Use tires for fuel; you'd need a few people working inside, just to sort tires out from the other metallic bits, but that was okay. Still, looking to keep people's role out as best as possible. Right. So, at one point, drop the metal. If it bounces off there are tire collectors in the line to pass them to a cooler furnace. Otherwise, the metal stays on the line to be slagged into pigs. Still needs two people, but. A grating underneath lets the metal in the tires melt down and be collected at intervals. Right. Sometimes you'd need coal, there isn't enough fuel in the city to run it, but that's okay too. There's still the coal barges from Allentown, from Carbondale.

How to separate out glasses, though: hold off on that one. He'd find it eventually. Wood floats, put in a tank, that feeds the boilers too. Once the tank empties, the stone at the bottom moves out, we've already pulled off the wood from the top with a rake.

He paused. He really had to get to the Party. The Collective was waiting for him. But the Fork lurked inside his pencil. Not for the first time, he was torn between the two.

"Hello, Scotto."

"Hello, Freeman. Back again, I see?"

"Back as often as can be. How's Camden treating you?"

"It's ugly. But it's getting better. How's Chestnut Street?"

"Getting better by the day. Listen, I know you're all about plums. Three rows over, two tables up, Clairmont Farm is in today. They've consistently got the best plums we see at the market. Aside from ours."

"Good to know. I see you've traded for some already."

"Yeah, they've got an old Singer I fixed up, and don't get here too often. They decided to swap for a bunch of batteries."

"Good on you guys."

"It works. Does the Fork need anything from me today?"

"We were wondering if you had anything new for us."

"I've got a coupla pumps I'm pretty happy with. And I've modded out a few more of those LED flashlights. They're good for almost a whole day on a battery."

"Excellent. We'll take the pumps. And we were wondering if you could do anything with this."

"Huh. Tub. Motor. Looks like it used to take electricity?"

"Yeah, that's what we were thinking. You think you can get it working?"

"Looks like a concrete mixer."

"That's exactly what it is, near as we can tell. We're getting to laying buildings in, and we're hoping to cut down on the number of people stuck mixing concrete. You know, the more not doing the prep work, the more work can get done."

"Absolutely. I'll take a look at it. I've got three pumps, that's nine bushels."

"Six."

"Eight."

"Seven."

"No, sorry, eight."

"Seven and a half?"

"Eight."

"Seven and three parts."

"Seven and a half in grain, eight in scrip."

"Five in scrip, three in grain."

"I think we can do that."

"Shall I have Infidel bring the grain over?"

"Sure thing. Here's your pumps."

"What do you guys do when the weather goes south?"

"I try to get a nice pile of stuff ready for trade next year. You know that, you're always scouting around during the spring to see what we've got."

"True, true. How about the rest of the bunch?"

"Most of our cloth gets made in the winter, then we trade out half in the spring, and spend spring nights getting clothes together for trade in the summer. That's when you get the best prices. Pumps, they're good at any time, though I have to say, if it wasn't right before the rainy season, I'd prolly have gone seven."

"Hand me the three-eighths wrench. No, not that one, the three-eighths. Dammit, this isn't hard, Byron."

"Isn't hard for you, maybe, Mr.-I-Don't-Speak-The-Same-Language-Man."

"Just hand me the damn three-eighths, it's smaller than that one. Perfect, thank you very much."

"There's no call for sarcasm, Freeman."

"Right. Coping saw? The one with the big loop and the thin blade? Thanks. Alright, look, so you know what we're doing here, this is Crissa's older spinning wheel. She doesn't much care about it, right?"

"Right."

"Okay, so this big wheel here gets turned by hand, and it turns the spindle down at the end slowly, right?"

"Right."

"Alright. When the spindle spins, you start stretching and twisting a lump of fiber into thread or yarn. What we're doing here is electrifying it."

"Right. You know, I don't actually need to know any of this."

"You will, if I get shot on a raid or sick or whatever and can't work on it. Someone needs to pick up everything that each of us knows, that's been our style since the beginning. Trust me, I never wanted to learn how to clean a deer, but there I was when it was time to learn, right?"

"Right. So, electrifying it?"

"Alright. This foot treadle here goes between the battery and the motor."

"When you say goes between, you mean...."

"The cold wire comes off the battery, connects to the treadle. When the treadle is up, the motor doesn't turn, no electricity goes to it. As you depress the treadle, it completes a circuit that allows electricity through the wire that goes from the battery to the motor. Then the motor turns. The hot line is connected straight."

"Sure. I'll pretend I understood that."

"That's fine I'm sure. Just so you can fix it if I can't. What's happening now is that we're cleaning out a mount for the motor to attach to the big wheel. This plate, disc, whatever, here, that we attached with the, yes, three-eighths bolt, goes through the center of the spindle. This disc attaches to the motor with this belt. The motor has to be secure or it'll waddle off of the mount, and then we lose the motor maybe. That doesn't want to happen, right?"

"Right. Okay. So, motor mounts here, tighten securely."

"Exactly. But, don't tighten down yet. While it's loose, slip the belt over this disc, and run it down to this disc. Always, always, always do this with the battery disconnected. We don't want the motor to start while we're working with it, I'm pretty sure you'd lose a finger, or if your hair got stuck, well, that would be really bad."

"Right. Always disconnected. From the battery or the treadle?"

"Better both. Now, belt's on, we tighten down the motor, belt is snug, good—play in the belt is bad—then plug in the treadle like this, attach the battery cables like this, and voila! The spinning wheel moves on it's own when you depress the treadle."

"You know, it's boring, doing this, but it's totally cool to see it move on its own."

"Before we begin, I would like to nominate Matt as mediator. Any seconds?"

"Second. Second. Second. Second. Second. Second. Second."

"I see. If it is near universal, then, do we have to put it to a vote? No. Okay. Then I accept, for the good of the house, and I hereby call the House Meeting to order. There is one order of business before us tonight, and it is the matter of Freeman's offered job for the Fork. The two competing viewpoints appear to be mostly Molly's and Freeman's. Do the two of you feel up to summarizing your viewpoints civilly for us?"

"There's no need for that, Matt. We may get boisterous in these meetings, but we've never yet actually started fighting. Yes, I can summarize my position. The largest question before us is whether or not we're willing to give up our autonomy. Now, Freeman is going to say that it's about the food, and that's true. A steady food source from the Fork will go a long way to helping us survive the winter, this is true. And yes, Freeman can still supplement his income by repairing machines for us to sell. Yes, this will not impact the trade in electricity for food that we've been gaining so much food with. Yet. We have never been in the habit of selling to only one group. We play each side off the other when the traders from Washington and Boston come in the spring and fall; playing them off against each other increases our profit, and not by a marginal amount.

"Fishtown requested that we trade only with them; we laughed at them. Even the remnants of Haddon, when they came back, we would trade with fairly. We have never denied one side or the other, but existed in the middle.

"Trading only to the Fork will make us dependent on one source, and therefore in their power. We will become the Fork Light, an extension of their arm, another hammer in their hand. What if we do it, and then they want more? We trade with them, use the steady income to increase the size of the Collective, and then they start making demands, demands like 'Only sell electricity to us.' We would not be able to say no without cutting back to starvation rations. This is just an example. I could talk for hours, believe you me. Instead, I will just say that I do not think this is a good idea."

"Collective, Molly is correct in some of the things she says, and not in others. Mainly, she is correct in the math of the trade. It will impact what we do now. What it will do is supplement it, not supplant it. I will still work on machines here. We will still trade to groups other than the Fork, though perhaps not as much. The benefits will outweigh the dangers, enough that, we could expand, or we could use the extra grain to become more comfortable. In the beginning, every time we went to expand, people worried about supporting extra people. This has not been a problem. We've been expanding steadily since we moved here, expanded to four times our original size. Four times! I look around and most of you were not here four years ago when we moved. Expansion has never been a problem as long as we back it up with trade.

"And we will trade."

"Freeman, I must ask, are there other reasons for wanting to work for the Fork?"

"Of course. My passion is machines, and they have the best, and the best facilities for working with them."

"Okay. I open the floor to debate. Yes, Maggie..."

"*kssssssh*.....*ksh*....*kkkk*...*k*..."

"*ksshssssh*...ake, we're not trying to say anything about the machine itself. The board well recognizes the value of what you've built here, and once all the kinks are ironed out they want the plans. We're, I'm, impressed with what you're doing. It's your Freeman that I'm worried about."

"Freeman's fine. His....*kkkkkkkkksssshhhhhhhhhh*....but now he's firmly with us. We don't have to worry about him."

"His attitude bothers me. He was overly rude, even almost hostile to me while he was showing me around the machine."

"He takes a light touch. You remember old McCullins. He was temperamental, but gave us what we needed to get started. Freeman's no different. These engineers, you have to treat them with a light hand. They're like artists."

"I don't think he's thinking about the Fork at all when he works."

"So long as he builds machines for us what does it matter?"

"Watch him, Drake. Watch him carefully. Speaking of..."

.......*kkkkkSSSSSSSSSSHHHHHHHSSsssssskkk*...."...I've heard a little of the problems you speak of, yes."

"Well, we need more troops up in the north. I've been instructed to bring three divisions of gendarmes and one cavalry unit back with me."

"That's more than half of my damn troops!"

"The Hudson Valley Company's got their own gunpowder and we need the troops. You'll get them back when we're done with them."

"You expect me to pacify Philadelphia after you take most of my troops away from me? How?"

"You've got your machine, haven't you?"

"I still need the men."

"We need them more. Train some of your demolition crews to be gendarmes."

"How's your whiskey?"

"I'll take a finger or two more."

"Scotto? Thank you. Take two divisions. Leave me with half my gendarmes. That'll be enough for what's going on here."

"But you requested extra gunpowder to deal with who you said were the last remaining resistance around here. What do you need them for?"

"No one knows what's in the Navy Yard."

"Ignore it. You said they ignore you."

"They're soaking up a fair amount of the trade from the Delaware Bay, and I don't like to think what goes on on the murderboats we see set out from the Yard."

"Murderboats?"

"You heard me. Freebooters. Pirates. Slavers. Who knows? No one knows what happens in the Yard. We haven't been able to get a man in."

"Alright. I'll leave you half the gendarmes, but I need more cavalry. How many horses do you have?"

"Two units of eight."

"Then we make it one unit of fourteen and I leave you two horses."

"That's....."

"The best I think we can .....*kkkkkkkkkssssssssshhhhhhhhhh*"

Hoofbeats sunder the air behind Freeman as he runs, the world shaking and blurring, through the rubble-strewn streets of Camden. His arms are torn from bushes, from vines, and when he can spare a glance at his shaking hands, he sees them dripping with blood. But he can't look at them directly, because the hoofbeats are getting louder and louder as he runs down the weed-and-tree-filled street.

He sees an alley coming up and knows, knows that the horses are coming too close, that he has to turn now or that's it. He's just to the alley when he feels the horse behind him, feels the blow of hot, moist breath on his neck, starts turning just as something slices the air next to him, grabbing his shirt, brutally ripping through it, but he's already turning, running down the alley, the horse's hooves suddenly receding as the cavalryman flies past where he had been just a second ago. He skirts a tree, runs up a pile of bricks, leaps a pit in the jumble of rocks. He hears the hoofbeats approaching again as the cavalry come around.

No time to think. Just time to get away from the pursuing horses. His arm is on fire. A turn and he's through a window, landing on a floor that should have been rotten but somehow isn't. Across the room, into a bedroom, then out the window and—

He stops short, suddenly, as "out the window" would quickly have been followed by "and into the basement two stories below." He turns, running, and leaps from this house to the house next door, window to window, bursting through the rotten sash and somehow clearing the broken glass on the floor. Across from this townhouse is another, and growing between these homes is a tree. He grabbed a branch and skids down to the ground, then cuts through the overgrown backyard, skirting a bicycle rusting in the grass and jumps a fallen chainlink fence, then cuts between two other houses.

Across the street. Down the block a little. Horses still coming. Again between two houses, find some place too small for the horses to go through, and too small for men to follow. Why were they following? His hands shake with the remembered force of the blow. The blood coating his hands and face and clothes has picked up dirt, sand, dust, splinters, he is filthy with gore and debris.

Out into the backyard. Skip down to the end of the block. Cut through the house, cross the wider avenue. The horses are coming up either side of the block. Is he leaving a blood trail for them to follow? That house, missing it's front door. Up the porch, boards breaking behind him, staying solid just long enough for him to push off them and move to the next set. Through the house, ignoring the grunted protestations of a squatter, out the back door and playing the backyard game again. Down to the street, this one choked with rusted-out cars. Run down the cars, no, too much noise, there: a factory, a broken window, and he's into it.

Here. Rest. Too much. Breathe. Forget. No, hooves approaching. Time to move again. Follow the belts through the factory, climb through spaces too small for grown men, let alone their horses, force them to dismount. No, that doesn't matter. Speed. Speed.

Why are they following him? What did he do? His hands shake again with the force of the spear's blow, the resistant-yet-soft feeling on the end of it, the spray of blood, more screams, because there hadn't been enough yet this morning. MOTHER!

These windows are too high. Look again. There, and up the pile of machinery, rust staining his already ruined pants, and out this window, onto the empty lot, and moving, moving again, moving away. Follow the bridge, rising high above the city.

"Honestly, Freeman, I'm really not sure why we'd want to build this... this thing."

"Drake, you want to build this thing because it will allow you to take down anything and turn it into useful materials. Plow through a forest, through a building, run it into a mountain or a hill, take down the bridge itself. Whatever you want to take down, whatever you want to turn into new materials, that will come down. You know how we're working on some buildings in Philadelphia, but people are stealing the materials we get, and our tools, and we're spending all our time either guarding materials or bringing tools to and from the site?"

"Of course. It's a serious frustration, you know that well."

"This will solve that. This is a tool that they can't steal, and it's a tool that ships the materials back on its own. We build it long enough and heavy enough and we'll transport the materials inside the machine, while they're being returned to a raw state, inside the tool that breaks them down. Far less guards."

"But manpower to build."

"Always manpower to build. But hell, it's not bad. Send me the trainees to work on the superstructure of it. I'll bring people in who can't weld, who can't work metal, and set them to working on the back sections of it that won't be under stress until they know what they're doing, then send them up to work on the front until they're good, then send them to you when they're masters. And they're not working on anything decorative, they're working on a tool, something that you won't have to look at daily, something that will just loudly and quickly provide tonnage of cinderblocks, of glass sheets, of steel pigs, of... of whatever you're looking for. Blocks of thermoform plastics.

"We'll separate the metals, we'll send tin and iron and copper and silver and gold and aluminum all to you, separated and pigged, and then the people here can turn them into whatever they want. Lord knows, you've complained about the difficulties in getting steel out of buildings that are still intact; this will turn intact buildings into those raw materials that you need."

"What will you build it from?"

"What I've got around. We might need some tires, and we'll need men, but we can take the shipping cartons on the northern docks and move them to the bridge, set all our workspaces up there, walking workspaces, in tents and enclosures, and move up the machine as we build it."

"I'm sure we don't have everything you need. Where do the materials come from?"

"We'll use the leavings. Yes, there are things that we'll need. But most of what we'll need I know how to get, and you won't have me bothering you for. We've done our surveys of Camden, Drake, and we know that we're going to run out of materials. The city is in too bad shape, it's been rotting for too long. There were too many buildings made of wood. There aren't enough raw materials here for what you want. Yes, this machine will take a huge amount of material, but it's the key to tapping Philadelphia for whatever materials we want. What do you want from Philadelphia, Drake? Do you want metal? Check, we'll get you that. Do you want stone? Concrete? Copper? Hell, control of the bridge? This will give you control of the bridge; it's a dam that will keep the Philadelphians from crossing it. This machine is the key to Philadelphia for the Fork."

Freeman carefully marked the building with chalk, giving the driver of the Fork the thumbs up on the point on the building's side to strike. The driver waited until Freeman had legged it far enough away to be out of the cascade of stone, then brought the Fork up to speed and rammed the building.

In the last few weeks this process had become rote, mechanical; which was really the plan from the beginning. But now Freeman was beginning to wonder about the plan.

The Fork needed materials for Camden, that was certain. Since the Fork had started up, building in Camden had stepped up; blocks of apartment homes were now going up all over the city as the Fork dumped tons and tons of fresh building materials onto the newly rebuilt city. Oversuppply of materials or no, the sight of the huge amounts of materials had inspired the navvies to new heights of building. The docks were a thing of beauty, gleaming fresh in the sun, and the newest apartments were, from what he had been told, the best places to live that anyone had ever seen.

But still. Freeman remembered gleaning, back when he lived near here in the city. He knew well that they were not pulling as much out of the rubble as they could. The Fork was, of course, incredible at pulling out resources, but he had to wonder about what the Fork was causing them to lose.

What the Fork could not pull out of the rubble was information, and there was information encoded in almost everything in the city. The mural that the Fork was about to strike, covered in soot and vines and flaking away, was one example. Books, another; the Fork could not discriminate between waste paper and paper covered in potentially useful information. The Fork found machines and melted them down to slag; the car that they'd eaten earlier in the day yet another example.

And, really, it was true that these buildings didn't belong to anyone, that there was no authority standing over the city and saying, yes, this is mine, and this is thine; but he still worried about the people who had to be moved out of every building, the hunters and scavengers and dirt farmers and thieves. Were they right in taking these people's homes away from them?

The Fork struck the building; a flight of pigeons darkened the air as they burst away from the shaking building. Small pieces of rubble fell to the ground. The Fork backed up to prepare for the next strike. Freeman could see the cracks spiderwebbing the side of the building; the Fork would eat soon.

A wailing rose from the newly homeless people watching; Freeman stood apart from the rest of the Fork and watched them, and the Fork, and the forces of the Fork. A few of the men on the side made as if to come at Freeman, as if he could stop it, could stop this new force on the earth; they were restrained by their family who nervously pointed out the squads of men with crossbows and muskets. People were taught quickly and harshly that you stayed away from the Fork.

Every machine that you used was an extension of yourself, a way of magnifying the strength in the human arm, or the speed of the human foot, or the sharpness of the human eye. Every machine that you built was even more an extension of yourself. A complete machine was a statement of hopes and dreams and wishes, this was something that Freeman understood. A statement, and a way of making those things come true, the machine was the instrument for constructing your hopes in a physical form.

So why didn't this dream feel like he'd thought it would?

"Alright, guys, so you know the deal by now. Write down any words that you don't understand, and I expect reports on the parts of the book that you do understand by next week. Those reports, as always, must include technical data on the writing, as well as information on plot, characters, whatever. Also, of course, what you liked and didn't like. Any questions?"

"Yes, Freeman, I have a question."

"What is it, Potter?"

"What does this book, this McElligot's Pool, have to do with engineering? I mean, it's a picture kids book. Shouldn't we be reading something a little more, well, related to what we're studying?"

"I could ask you the same question, Freeman. I was given to understand that you're teaching engineering here, and I find you teaching reading out of a book that I have read my children?"

"Hello, Drake. The answer is simple. You need to know, well, everything to be an engineer. For engineering, you must learn everything that runs up to it. On top of that, there are all sorts of other disciplines at the same level as engineering—chemistry, for one—that you also need to know everything for. Now, when I say everything, what I mean is that you must know to read, and read well, to be able to read through spec sheets, because spec sheets are massively important. You must be able to read physics texts to understand what the equations are describing. And you must know math to be an engineer, far more math than simple addition and subtraction, which most of you can probably already do in your head, if just from trading. Which is why I teach the math class after this, the one that most of you are in.

"So why Dr. Seuss? There's twelve of you in this class. We need books that we have enough copies of that everyone can take one home and read them. Those books are few and far in between. We have twelve copies of this, and it's excellent material for teaching people to read. I understand that you'd all like something more adult, but there isn't much that we've been able to find that's written for teaching adults to read. So we have to do the best with what we have. And what we have is McElligot's Pool. Any more questions? Good. Then I'll see you all either after the break, or next week, except for you, Drake, who I assume want to talk to me now."

"We need to talk about these classes. We're not getting anything out of them."

"To the contrary, Drake, you are getting something out of them. I'm learning, while I teach, which of the people you've got working for you are possibly engineer material. There's a few. Not as many as we'd like, but I have to teach them to read, write, and to do math before I can get them to start doing any engineering. Look at these papers. Look at Potter's. She was less than pleased about the book she was reading, but look how neat her handwriting is, look how she lays everything out in tables, look how organized her thinking is. Potter will be a fine engineer. On the other hand, we have Buckman, who does the minimum required. I will likely ask him to not come back if he doesn't start giving more than the least required work. You're finding out which of your employees are good thinkers. And, anyone that you teach this information to will be an extremely loyal employee, who will never even want to leave the Fork, because this is the opportunity you gave them. No, Drake, you're getting plenty out of this."

"I'm not happy with it."

"Alright, Mark. What's the problem?"

"I'm working too hard."

"Really Mark? Really? Because I don't see you working too hard."

"Steve? You want to take care of this?"

"Yes I do. Mark, what do you want to be doing?"

"I uh, I want to be cooking."

"Well, that's always been Lara's job. And she's too damn good at it for us to supplant her. But... well, Lara? Has Mark ever helped you out in the kitchen?"

"He burns water."

"Ah. Perhaps as a, I dunno, bread kneader? Vegetable chopper?"

"I've tried. He's just not very good at it. I've told him that. You're not methodical enough, Mark. I know you try really hard but you're better at other stuff. You're a fine gleaner. I know Adria likes working with you out in the streets, why don't you like that?"

"Because I want to cook."

"Alright. Lara. Will you please take Mark back as kitchen help?"

"I'll try. One night a week. If he gets better I'll keep him on."

"Mark? Does that work for you?"

"No."

"Well, that's my shot. Back to you, Molly."

"Mark, is this a big enough problem to you that you want to vote against the consensus?"

"Everyone else is doing what they want."

"That's not true, Mark. I'd be working on my machines full-time if I could. Instead I do everything else that we need to survive and work on the machines part-time. You could work in the kitchens part-time, but we need someone who knows how to use everything, someone who doesn't waste food in there. I'd take Lara's deal if I were you."

"Does anyone else have objections to the vote?"

"No. No. No. No. NO!"

"Alright. I say we vote on making this permanent. Freeman, please pass out the beans."

"Fourteen for, one against. I say we stand for consensus."

"Mark, you're not standing. I see. Do you intend to stay with us?"

"I don't think so."

"Then you should know the deal. One bag of personal effects. Your bedding roll. As much basic food as you can carry. And once you're out on the street, you're out. You can change your mind until you're out of the gate, but when you're out, you're out."

"That's not fair! I worked harder than that this summer!"

"You knew what the deal was when you signed up. We voted this in over the summer. It's really far more generous than Jase would have given you if you left."

"I wouldn't be leaving if he was still here!"

"I know that. We all know that. We'll be sorry to see you go. You're a good friend, brother, but you have made your choice I see. I move to close the meeting, in sadness."

"Second second second."

"And so moved. Godspeed, Mark."

Freeman slipped through the broken fence and made his way into the old Philadelphia Zoo. He picked his way as silently as he could through the trees, eyes about him constantly, hand on the knife in his belt, always on alert. The Zoo was someplace that you never went alone; the animals had been let out of their cages a long time back, and some of them—the zebra herds especially—had spread across Philadelphia. But deep in the zoo, many of the predators still lurked.

This was a dangerous place to be.

Despite, or perhaps,because of the danger, life abounded. Brightly colored birds flew from branch to branch, small things scurried underfoot, bursting away from Freeman's loud footfalls and ragged breathing. He slowed to a walk, knowing that the horses would have a hard time getting inside the zoo, and even now hearing their stamping wheel-about back where he'd entered. They'd be looking for a different way in. He was going to have to take a stand against them soon.

Freeman moved up to a jog, even though it didn't let him scan the underbrush as closely as he'd like. He passed cages aplenty, cages where small animals used to be kept, that were now colonized by birds who flitted in and out through their open doors.

The hoofbeats paused, and started coming nearer again. They'd find his trail through the tall grass soon. He was going to have to lose them, or make a stand, or... something, soon, or they'd catch him, and either kill him or drag him back to the Fork. Neither of these was a viable option. He started running faster.

He passed the boat, now standing on its side, in the middle of the pool covered in grey-green algae. Something moved in the pool, disturbing the scum on the top. There he could lose the horses if—yes.

If he could get up that hill, past that fence, he could get to the train tracks. From here, the horses would not be able to make it to the tracks, and they'd have to backtrack at least a few miles to find a place to get to them. He'd be exposed to the rest of the Fork, but he'd be able to escape the cavalry, who were his current problem. He hooked left, turning towards the tracks, followed the old trails of the zoo between the cages, drawing nearer to the tracks as the horses closed in.

As he passed the reptile house, he found himself at a dead end. Fences climbed on all sides around him. It looked, it looked like the best way was to the left, like that enclosure would lead him to the tracks.

As he reached the fence, he heard the growl behind him. There, in the darkness where the glass used to stand in the doors of the reptile house, were two glowing eyes, staring at him. Freeman stood still, willing himself not to breathe. The green glints, their owner obscured in the shadow, stared at him. Freeman leaned back, his pack against the fence. His hand on the knife. The knife that wouldn't do him any good.

"FREEMAN! YOU BASTARD!" Scotto and Dawn rounded the corner, horses charging, trapped between them and the fence. The eyes turned. A musket fired, missing him as the horse bucked. The eyes closed. The horses drew close. A blur of movement: the cheetah launched itself from the Reptile House and into Scotto's horse. Claws ripped. The horse screamed, fell. Dawn turned her horse towards Scotto. Scotto had his knife out. Scotto screamed, leg trapped under the horse. More blood. Claws flashed in the sun. Dawn unsheathed her spear. Her horse skidded, turning.

Freeman turned and went over the fence, running again, and never looking back.

They hoped to keep the violence down to a minimum, if they could, but they weren't too concerned.

It had taken most of the winter to put together, but eventually most every small freehold in Philadelphia had banded together, for the first and probably only time, with the intent of teaching Haddon a lesson. The Gleaners' compound was not the only one who'd been raided by Haddon's forces. Everyone had been raided by everyone, mind, but Haddon had been the most brazen. Everyone here had lost something to the Kingdom of Haddon. It was time for Haddon to lose something to them.

Haddon's main trade was in wool. They were known to have the best sheep around, and a surfeit of them. Enough that perhaps a flock or two wouldn't be missed—until tomorrow. They'd planned it out well.

The main body of men and women stood in the trees as the forward parties crept through the underbrush towards where the shepherds were quietly eating lunch, foolishly, in the shade near the treeline. A hundred or so sheep grazed quietly in the field. One or two sheepdogs patrolled; Haddon's men ignored the dogs, fools that they were.

The hoot of an owl, twice: that was the signal. The flanking force descended upon the shepherds as the rest of the men burst from the woods where they surrounded the sheep. There was a flurry of fighting far off, and a few knots of trouble where the dogs came at the men. Hurled spears took care of the dogs; dogs were far more effective close than far, as the Gleaners had learned to Haddon's dismay. None of the dogs even reached the assembled men of Philadelphia.

And then the shepherds were subdued, gagged, tied up, staked to the ground. None were able to raise an alarm.

A group of men scattered to get the wagons while the rest rounded up the bleating sheep. The sheep shied away from the dogs' bodies, but were still quickly herded from the field and towards Route 70, less than a mile away. The shepherds hadn't even put the Cooper River between them and the trees, and were more the fools for it. Haddon would not be pleased with these men.

The men came quickly with the wagons; they'd covered perhaps half a mile on foot with the herd. They quickly rushed the sheep onto the wagons, loaded what they'd stolen of the shepherds' gear in the wagons, then the overloaded train moved quickly towards the bridge. They were almost done with the raid. Yes, Haddon would not be pleased with this day's work.

They'd have to step up their patrols, but the mood on the way back to the city was jovial. A hundred sheep, forty men; each man would claim two sheep this day, and half of them would claim three. Many sheep would be traded before they even got to the city; most of the small freeholds couldn't support many more sheep than they already had, but the trades would be worthwhile.

The wagon train crossed into Camden, then onto the bridge, with no response from Haddon. Once they were into the city, it would be far more difficult for Haddon to deal with them. They knew the city, and Haddon did not. Haddon had lost their best men in various raids in the city, and now they'd lost a significant portion of their flocks. And anyone wearing Haddon colors was in serious trouble today in Philadelphia.

The rest of the sheep were divided by drawing beans from a bag. The Gleaners wound up taking home ten sheep, a fair haul for the day, and a fair reward for the time they'd spent setting up this raid.

"Alright. You—bolt this gear to the shaft. You two, keep holding while he gets the gear in place. The rest of you, you four with the axle, get that over here, get it to about the end of the driveshaft. Those of you with the rest of the gears, I want them in order, smallest to largest, each of you standing and ready to get it into place.

"Alright. First gear is in place. Good. You two with the new secondary shaft, get over here. I'll bolt it in place at the far end. Scotto?"

"Right. Tom and Mike, front and center with your gear. Get it up and over the shaft and as far down as it'll go. Let's move it, we want this assembled before the storm comes in. Freeman, you ready?"

"I'm tightening. You guys get it started, the shaft shouldn't move."

"You heard the man, let's get this on. Pat, you're on locking ring duty. You got the rings ready? Once Tom and Mike get the first gear in place, let's get the ring on. Come on you sons of mothers, the rain's gonna come, and we don't want any rust on this stuff. We've got to get it together before the storm starts. Move move move!"

"Alright, we're down. Let's get the next gear on the bottom shaft. First, where's that damned belt, we want to get that on. Alright, you've got the belt. This is the biggest one? Good. Let's get it on. You done with the lock rings? Yes? Alright, get that belt stretched. Shit, where's the crowbar? It's stuck."

"Right here."

"Thanks. Alright, Cooper, Marlin, get that next gear over here, come on, the rain's gonna start any moment, we need to get the lid down on this stuff, move! Okay, Pat, lock rings, good."

"Next gear on the top!"

"Next gear on the bottom!"

"Belt!"

"Lock rings!"

"One more set, you guys, and we've got this part done. Let's move it. *Devai*!"

"Alright. Now, everyone on the driveshaft, we've got to all move at once and get it in place. Not you, Cooper, we need you with the brackets to get it held down. You got the brackets and the nuts? Good. Everyone, at my mark. One, two, three, mark, LIFT, you people. Get it in place, and, good!"

"Cooper, you got the brackets? Let's get it in place, we've got to get the shaft in. We ain't got a roof yet and I'm sure you can feel it spitting. We want the cover on this, and we are not going to leave it undone. Oh, hell, give me one of those, the rest of you hold on tight. I'm letting go.

"Scotto, you should be able to let go of it now, and on three, back up one, two, three."

"Excellent."

"Excellent indeed. Now let's get the axle in place. Bring it forward. Don't worry about the treads yet, just get the wheels over top of them, we'll get it set later. Alright, on the treads, ready to go? Let's get a coupla more people over here and like *ligne nu*. It's gotta happen, that's some thunder up there. On three, lift!

"Good. Dammit, Cooper where are you with the brackets, let's get in here like right now and get those things on! We are not going to stand here and wait for you!"

"... and I would like to nominate Jeb for membership in the Collective. For those of you who do not know Jeb, he lost his wife earlier this winter to the plague that went around. Jeb himself was ill but made it through the winter. However, he cannot hold his freehold himself."

"What will Jeb bring to the Collective?"

"Well, Jeb made our butter churn. He is also an excellent tanner. Not the best in the city, but far from the worst. He's on a par with Byron. Jeb can, of course, also farm, and he is a fair butcher."

"Did he request entry to the Collective?"

"He did."

"Does anyone in the Collective speak against Jeb?"

"I do not exactly speak against him, but it is known that Jeb is a bit of a gambler, and he does like his 'shine a little much. If we bring Jeb into the Collective, we should extend his provisional period to a year instead of the normal four moons, and we should all keep an eye on him. He should also, I believe, be apprised of this so he can watch his behavior. Perhaps in a group setting ,he will find these urges easier to deal with."

"Do we all agree with these provisions that Molly has suggested?"

"Aye. Aye. Aye. Nay."

"Why nay?"

"I do not believe that we should accept Jeb into the Collective."

"If Jeb is to be accepted into the Collective, Dave, would these provisions be sufficient?"

"Yes."

"Why do you not wish him in the Collective?"

"Stories about him. It is said that he's fond of women, and sometimes too fond."

"Has anyone else in the Collective heard these stories?"

"Aye, I have. My friend Beth had to fight him off the once. He was too drunk to move properly, and she left him collapsed in the street."

"If Jeb is one who would take what he desires by force, perhaps he is not someone we wish to have in our consensus."

"Is discussion complete?"

"Yes. Yes. Yes."

"Then bring out the beans."

"The count is ten for, twenty-six against. Sorry, Manny, but that's pretty clear. There's little enough confusion there. Anyone else?"

"Yes. The Cooper family has requested entry into the Collective. They were driven from Jersey last year, they say, by some movement or another of Haddon. They arrived here with no food, no extra anything, and have taken up residence in Lydia and Matt's old freehold. They've mainly been supporting themselves by trading work for food. They could probably hold the freehold, but the short term of the Southies' tenancy on the land has well ruined the earth there."

"What will the Coopers bring the Collective?"

"Beekeeping. Guitars. Mike knows more songs than anyone I've met. Penny is a fine seamstress, and their children are excellent climbers for fruit. All can farm."

Freeman finished hauling the final table in from the farmyard just as the snow began to fall. They'd been lucky with the weather for the move, but now, now that they were finishing up the moving-over and starting up the moving-in, the winter was beginning to clamp down. In the thin light of the day, they'd hammered the stakes to hold the greenhouse in place down into the almost-frozen ground. Now that night was descending, everyone was getting busy with setting up their own workshops. Dinner had been a hurried affair at sundown, rather than the raucous, stretched-out affair that supper normally was this time of year at South Street.

Now that Freeman's four worktables were in the room, it was time to start setting them up. This one, deep and heavily scored with toolmarks, was his main bench; it would go against the west wall, under the window, where the evening and afternoon sun would shine well down into the workspace, and the morning sun would illuminate the contents of the drawers of parts acceptably. Freeman hauled the bench, cursing its weight under his breath—and this workbench wasn't even the heaviest.

There was, of all things, a vent in the south wall so it was here where Freeman hauled his heavy bench with the sealed top that he used for working with the noxious chemicals he sometimes had to use. He left a gap at the corner, between the two benches; his bookcase would go here. Molly'd be glad to have his texts out of their room. Hopefully the new room would be warmer than the last; they were at least glad of the books for insulation in the winter.

After hauling the bookcase into place, he hauled his secondary workbench—the one that took all his clutter—next to the first workbench, then dropped his assembly table, low and beaten, into the center of the L-shape that his three other benches formed. This one took some of his clutter, too.

The bins of parts were all piled in the middle of the room; Peter and Gwyneth would begin complaining if he didn't deal with those soon. But his back ached after the day's work, so he decided to get the books up on the shelf first. He caressed each one as he pulled them out of the crates; some of the books he'd mastered, some he'd barely cracked. He'd yet to find a use for this "Linear Algebra" book, but the calculus and physics books he'd worked through, and the ideas contained inside, had already borne fruit for the Gleaners; his improvements to the foot-powered lathe had all come from the Physics text, and the pulleys he'd made for lifting bales of hay had turned it from an all-Gleaner process into only two or three people—a serious reduction in workload for something that was no one's favorite task. Yes, these books had been useful. And he had great hopes for this text labeled "Chemistry."

Some of the other books had been less useful, but had still been enjoyable. Everyone enjoyed the small production of the Tempest that they'd put on last year, from the book of Shakespeare. Though they'd had to ham it up a lot for the archaic language to make sense.

The books away on the shelf, he started hauling the postal service boxes full of bundles of wire that he'd been collecting—heavy and light, flexible and not, braided and solid—and deposited them under his main workbench. There'd be time to sort them out later. For now, he just had to get stuff put away so that the smiths could get started. Wagon wheels needed to be fixed, there were tools they were going to need for the expansion of the gardens, and, if everyone agreed, for building the new wall and taking down the old one for the expansion of the compound itself.

"This is great. The two outside walls are west and south facing. Strong morning and evening light. We can grow reasonable grass here easily."

"Won't the sheep do too much damage to it?"

"Nah. Leave 'em on the roof most of the time, and only bring them down and up when the grass recovers."

"What do we do with the cars?"

"Well, yeah. Um. Well, there are lots of parts that I'll take. The plastic and tires will burn easily enough, even if we can't use the ashes as fertilizer. We can prolly make mattresses out of the seats. Hell, we can sit on the seats. We don't have enough chairs, we can find a few that look good and just use them to sit on. The metal, especially the frames, can go to the smithy."

"How do we get them out?"

"Push 'em off one at a time. We take out the intact glass and move that down, we take out anything useful, and then we shove them over the side of the building. Break the retaining wall, we can repair it later."

"That's extreme."

"Hell, if we do it over the side that faces the farm we'll help break up the concrete and macadam that's covering the new farmland."

"I hate to say it, but it's not a bad idea. And it sure beats carrying the cars down one at a time."

"That's what I'm thinking. The ones on the first and second floors, we can push those against the walls for now and deal with them down the central ramps one at a time. But the ones on the third and fourth floors? Off the roof. Scrap 'em."

"Most of the cars I've looked through aren't worth much more than that. For the most part, they've been destroyed by the elements."

"I like it. I like it a lot. We could build a wall out of 'em too."

"The metal's worth too much. We'll need it."

"Are you sure?"

"I'm pretty sure. We won't become a trade power without a good source of metal and this should keep us for a while at least."

"Hey, I bet we could keep the tires for use in the forges."

"That's not a bad idea. We don't want to use them for cooking if we can help it—anything that smells that bad can't be good for you—but they'll be perfect for the forges."

"Is there going to be enough dirt here?"

"We've used Sal to cart dirt in from the park before. We can do it again if there isn't enough. And grass seed is easy enough to pick up. Besides, sheep'll eat most anything. Put two inches of soil on the roof—and there may well be that much up here as is, I mean, look at those piles of compost—and we should be able to grow most anything."

"And we can take all our soil from South Street too."

"And there's more than enough there to cover this entirely with soil."

"This isn't a bad plan at all. Molly's good at this."

"Oh, we'll prolly still need the commons, but... I think it's solid. And the extra land for farming we enclose is also a beaut."

"I guess you're going to want to start with the batteries, huh?"

"That or the glass."

"We've never gone into the basements of the parking garages before. We don't know what, or who, lives down in them."

"There's stuff down there I think we need. The cars that are up on the streets, we can get batteries from them, they're okay, still sealed against the weather. But with only a few exceptions, which I've gleaned when I could, the alternators are frozen, rusted together. But the basements, the cars down there should be in better shape than the ones on the surface. They won't have been rained on as much, they'll be in better shape. There's even the possibility that there's stuff in the trunks. Maybe a guitar..."

"Oh, fine, let's go look. But at the first sign of anything weird, we turn around."

"Fair enough."

"Sal doesn't like the ramp."

"Sal doesn't like anything. Come on, it'll be fine. Let's get the torches lit and we'll both keep spears at the ready. The torches can go in the mounts on the side of the cart."

"Fine, fine."

"Smells dry. What do you think?"

"I think there'll be something living down here."

"Of course. It's possible it'll just stay away from us. Let's get a few more torches up if you're concerned."

"Sure. Are you sure about this?"

"We'll stay near the entrance."

"Okay. Hey, you're right, the cars down here are in better shape than they were up on the streets. Whatever this "Valet" thing means, they knew what was up."

"And how. Oh, look what's in the backseat of this one..."

"Well hot dust! There's is a guitar in there. How do we get in?"

"Door's unlocked, here let me get the back door for you while I get the trunk. See if there's anything else down there."

"Some coins, always useful. A lot of trash."

"Yeah, probably. Damn, this battery's in good shape, so's the alternator. I'm amazed that the little lever to work the hood still works after all this time, I didn't even need a crowbar to get the hood open. You got the tools?"

"You hear that?"

"Nope. Where are the tools?"

"On the cart. I'm standing watch, I didn't like that sound."

"Fair enough. Stand near me, you're making me nervous too."

"Are the bolts that bad?"

"They ain't great, but I think I got it. Sweet, one alternator. Let's hit the next one."

"Why'd you cut that hunk of, what do you call them, wires off?"

"So I know how the thing hooks up to the battery. Sometimes colors mean what it does. Not always, but sometimes, wire colors describe standards."

"Ah. Did we check the trunk of this thing?"

"Not yet. Let's look."

"What do you figure this did?"

"Maybe kept the rain off? It would be like a little tent if the fabric was intact."

"Maybe. They had some weird stuff. Nothing else here. Let's do the next one."

Freeman waved to the guard at the ramp of the Fork and started unloading his mule. The guards were used to his comings and goings; the Fork needed servicing at all times and he was often the one to do it. He supposed he should be glad that this was not out-of-the-ordinary behavior for him. He loaded the barrels and the tools onto a cart sitting by the exit, tied up the mule, and made his way into the Fork.

The Fork was always dark, and stuffy, and hot. It always smelled of burning tires. He walked along the conveyor belts, sweating and nervous. What if tonight was the night that they decided to check up on him, and see what he was really doing? Why couldn't there be a middle path between the Fork and the Collective? Why couldn't there be coexistence? And if there couldn't be, why did he have to sacrifice everything so many times?

He patted the side of the Fork tenderly, then kept pushing the cart. This machine had taken up so much of his life, had eaten his days like Philadelphia's buildings, and yet he loved the machine. But perhaps there were things to love more.

He came to the first boiler, and waited a few moments to judge the speed of the conveyor belt that carried the fuel into the boiler. He'd need about an hour, and the belt was moving slowly enough that he should only need about ten feet. He levered the barrel of gunpowder up onto the belt, then kept pushing the cart down the drive train.

Freeman felt what he was doing keenly, a knife in his gut.

The conveyor belts rolled around him, carrying bricks and dust and metal to places that they would now never reach. Here and there, steel pigs and copper ingots flew down the belts, working their steady way to the exit ramp. These were likely to be the last materials that the Fork saw from this, this monstrosity he built for them.

He had built this thing. It was his arm that reached out to crush Philadelphia, to crush the lives that were lived there. Its proper maintenance was his responsibility, keeping it oiled and repaired and fed. And its proper use was his responsibility. Stamping out the Collective, and all the lives therein, was not its proper use.

Perhaps, sometimes, when tools were being used improperly, there was only one solution. And this was the solution: to destroy what was being used wrongly. Even if it was your own arm.

He wished there was a different way. This machine was the first thing that he had actually put together, had built from the ground up. Yes, some of the parts were scavenged, but the generators that surrounded the boilers, the boilers themselves, the kilns, the smelter—they were all of his design. The belts were his. This machine was his.

Perhaps that's what Drake could never understand, that even though he had supplied the men and materials, had provided food and shelter for Freeman as he built this thing: the Fork had never been anyone's but Freeman's.

And perhaps Freeman had been right from the beginning. The Fork may have been the only way for man to reach the future that it deserved, to stop living dirty and cold, moving from one ruined building to another. Perhaps he had been right thinking that. But... now Freeman thought otherwise. This city didn't need another Hemorrhage.

Freeman reached the second, smallest boiler and levered the barrel of gunpowder up onto the belt, giving it about eight feet. Hopefully, this would give it enough time. He laid his hand on it, a farewell and a benediction, then kept pushing the cart.

As he kept pushing forward, he wasn't sure if what dripped down his face was sweat, or tears.

"Drake. Thank you for seeing me on such short notice."

"Freeman, good to see you. I trust you have good news for me."

"Yes. The Collective has decided..."

"Is everything okay?"

"Everything is fine. The Collective has decided that my coming over to work for the Fork on a full-time, paid basis is a good idea."

"Excellent! We're having some problems at the brick factory, we really need someone to take a look. We're not sure what's going on, there's some problems with the conveyor mechanism, and production has slowed to a crawl. We're barely getting any bricks out of it at all. They all have to be pushed through and pulled out by hand. Get down there right now and take a look at it."

"Drake, before we get any further, the Collective does have some requests. They've asked me to put them forth to you."

"What does the Collective wish?"

"First of all, they've requested that I have some time to finish some outstanding projects over there before I come here full-time. They're worried that once I start working here I won't have the time to finish up the looms and last few generators we need there."

"I see. And how long will this take?"

"I expect less than half a moon, but it's always hard to be sure. You understand."

"Freeman, I don't. I need you now. I need you—the Fork needs you —more than those farmers over at the Collective need you."

"Respectfully, Drake, the Collective told me to state that this was not a bargaining point. They wish me to finish my duties there before I start here. I'm ready to work all day and night to finish what I have to, but I still have to finish what we want before I come here. If you don't want me because of this, well, that's how it is, I guess."

"No, Freeman, we need you here. How long will it take?"

"If the machines are cooperative, about seven days. If not, a half moon. I'm willing to try to fix the brick factory today, but I cannot start full-time until I'm done over at the Collective."

"Freeman, this bothers me. This says to me that you have more loyalty to the Collective than to the Fork, and we're the ones who are hiring you."

"The Collective is my home, and I have to abide by the decision of the group, sir."

"...Alright. Please look at the factory today. What else?"

"The Collective wants one-tenth of my first year's salary up front so that they can work on getting people in to replace me. I still weed and gather fruit, like everyone in the house, and we have to replace that work, especially if I'm here as much as you want me."

"I think we can do that."

"That will make matters much better at my house. Thank you."

"Freeman, are you okay? This is more formal than I'm used to you being."

"I'm fine. It's just been... well... I'm fine. You don't need my problems."

"If there's one thing that I've learned it's that employee problems usually become employer problems. We can move you somewhere else if you want."

"Thank you, Drake, but no. My home is with the Collective, and it is there that I must stay."

"Thassome strong shit, eh."

"Rosa does a mean brew, yes she does. Dust. I don't know if I can dance the next round, what do you guys think?"

"Looks like they're bushsy overrere."

"Shure does. Damn that's strong shit."

"I need some air wanna come?"

"Yeah let's, that sounds like a good idea."

"Thass better. It's starvin' hot in there."

"Sure is."

"Look, Freeman, we need to, to talk."

"What about?"

"I'm starting to get con, con, consherned."

"'Bout what? Shtuff's going, going well, I thought."

"It is, I'm worried it's going too well."

"How can things go too well?"

"I'm worried about the Fork. Scotto. They're buying too much. I think the Fork's going to try for a power grab, and I'm, I'm worried, you know, that, that the stuff you're selling, that they're going to use what they're, they're, they're accumulating, to try for it. I'm worried you're part of their, their nefarious plan. Nefarious. That's a good word."

"Whadd ya mean?"

"I mean, look, the power structures in the city have always, what's the word, word you like, word. Fluc-shoo-ate?"

"Fluctuated."

"Right. That. Slowly in the city. Not quick. Sprawlers were up, Sprawlers were down. Fishtown rose slowly, right? But fell quick. And fell right before the Fork came."

"Fishtown fell apart from a, a what, a sickness. Plague. You know. Not any work by the Frok, no sorry, the Fork. Wasn't a power grab. Just something that happens."

"We're doing too well. If they are, they're going to see us as a, as a threat."

"Even if they do, they're across the river. Camden politics have never affected Philadelphia too much."

"What about Haddon? They sure did."

"..."

"Right. Haddon affected Philadelphia. Philadelphia affected Haddon back. We grabbed at them and won after they grabbed at us and lost. The Fork could grab at us. They're, they're getting too much too fast. Rising too fast. We're rising to match, well, not to match, but we're rising too. The area's too small. One of us will have to go. They can't stand us and we, we won't be able to operate with them around. Come a certain point."

"You're saying you-and-I should fight them? Fight them why? Fight with what? We can't fight them, that's not what we do. You shaid it yourself, we out-out. Out-what? Outcompete. That was it. Like the zebras and the cattle. Zebra territory shrinks cause the cattle move in, don't lose as many over the winter. Zebras lose. That's what we do. Why we don't eat the zebras."

"And they don't taste good."

"Taste bad. Uhhh... bad.. badd.... excuse me."

The conveyor belt system of the Fork was going to be the widest-ranging part of the entire machine. The belts that were being constructed out on the bridge were made of the widest set of materials possible; some were made of steel plates, joined by chains underneath, some made of canvas, some of plastic plates slightly narrower than the steel ones. Still others were made of rubber, and others made of aluminum, some of split and stitched-together tires. The composition of the belts depended on what material each belt would carry.

Right now, Freeman was directing a group of people getting a tire-rubber belt onto the set of rollers it would be riding on; this belt was going to be for the sheet steel they'd pick up from building ducts, from the chassis of cars, from burst, discarded cans from apartments and foodstores. The belt had been fashioned by the seamstresses of the Fork; tires had been stripped from rusted cars, sliced width-wise, and separated from their sidewalls. The remaining grooved strips of rubber had been machine stitched together with wire, using heavier machines than the seamstresses were used to. The resulting belts were now being carried by twenty-odd navvies and then hoisted, one at a time and ten across, up onto the roller mechanisms.

The navvies set one end of the belt down, and all brought the Philadelphia-facing end up and over a roller, then worked their way down the belt, bringing the loop of rubber up and over each roller in the conveyor system, then finally over the eighth and last.

This belt was not one of the ones that would twist with the Fork's movement, but rather the belt that ran straight to the storage bin before the furnace. Even still, it had to be tensioned. The roller closest to Philadelphia was the tensioning roller, and Freeman hefted a heavy wrench to loosen the roller. Three of the navvies pushed the roller west towards the city, and once the belt was tight, Freeman twisted down on the wrench to force the nut into place, holding the belt tight.

Now that this belt was tight, the belt before it in the system had to be adjusted. Each belt that led to a new one was inclined slightly, so that each belt would drop its load onto the belt after it. With the tensioning systems, the belts would have to be adjusted slightly so that no more material than physics required would fall between the belts and have to be picked up by hand or sweeper brush.

The belt before this was one of the belts that would expand and contract with the motion of the Fork. The belt was far too large for its roller system; a second roller system tied to a spring would rise and fall with the lengthwise motion of the Fork to alternately tighten and loosen the belt, dropping when the Fork moved forward, and rising back up when the Fork struck its targets or was stopped by the operator.

They were working the belts from the rear of the Fork to the front, getting each placed before working on the one before it, when materials allowed. This canvas belt in front had been finished before the belt behind, so it had been installed first, though its tensioning mechanism was not lifted into place yet. The rear end of the belt was the first to move, though; it fell a little shy of the rear belt. Loosen the bolt, push the arm, tighten the bolt, and it was ready. The team of navvies got up and moved forward now, still raucous from their break, and all grabbed the tensioning arm together and swiveled it into place.

Freeman on one side, and someone else on the other, positioned and tightened the blocks that would hold the tensioner in place, then hooked the springs down.

And then there were only about a hundred more belts left to put in place.

The hoofbeats of Haddon's cavalry echoing behind him, Freeman scales the machine, whatever it is, made of more rust than metal, gets to the lowest window in the factory, and looks around, knees shaking, looking down around the factory yard. Car below, he should be able to leap down and land on the hood. It should hold his weight, he isn't that heavy. Blood on the window frame where his hands grabbed it. No time. He vaults over, resoundingly crashes on the car, knees bending and buckling with the landing. He rolls off the car, barely missing a shard of glass the size of his leg that sticks straight out of the grass. Then back up and there's a building across the way and he's inside before he even figures out what it is.

Burst through an interior door, rusted hinges snap, door slams into the ground. Too much noise. He could see, a little, the sunlight filtered through the muck-and-vine covered windows. Shelves, rows of shelves, rows of boxes slumped from moisture and age lining the shelves. Dusty bottles. Rusted cans. He starts for the nearest aisle, jumps a sign that read 13B. Sounds of scattering animals, green eyes flickering away from his approach. Then through some black trays, mouldering newspapers, thin aisles, and in front of him a door. Once glass, now empty. And he's out into the street, makes a quick left turn. Horses still, sounding like they're behind him but nearing. Running down the street.

As the hoofbeats grow louder, he makes his ragged way between buildings, through buildings, past derelicts and over abandoned cars, trucks, here a flipped bus, tires dangling into the air. Across a street, another street, he doesn't know where he is, but he's going for the bridge, they won't come into Philadelphia. If he can make it to Philadelphia he'll be safe. Then a brick wall. Keep the bearings. Remember the frozen rainbow of the bridge.

Turn left down the street, follow the wall. He could probably scale it but it's newer, there's broken bottles embedded in concrete at the top, that's asking for a fatal gash in his leg or arm or chest, he keeps running. He steals a glance behind him, and he can see the man on horseback, Haddon's man, coming down the street for him. He can't run any faster but he somehow does and there's a break in the wall, suddenly, now right and down an alley and left and he's in a house.

There's no floor. Joists are whole, broken; some stretch across the house like ribs, some jut up like teeth. There's no time to turn around. He bolts down two joists, moving faster than he's ever moved, and he's in the kitchen. There's a floor here, soft, trying to give way under him, then suddenly the back door, rotting and broken. He doesn't even stop, just bursts through the door.

And he's in a backyard and running. He vaults a red and yellow plastic toy car, two feet tall and emulating the bus a few, several, however many streets ago. There are still hoofbeats. The bridge embankment isn't far from here. He can make it. He can hardly breathe. His hands and pants are covered in blood dirt splinters and rot. A right turn between houses.

Someone lunges at him, sooty hand attached to an arm draped in rotting fabric. Freeman somehow dodges the crow's wing and keeps going. He's almost to the embankment. A few more blocks. He crosses one side street and another, not even seeing any details anymore, just bolting past building after building and car after car. Then he's staring at the giant bulk of the embankment right in front of him and he turns and runs alongside, until he sees a drapery of vines and dodges behind it and stops, waiting for the hoofbeats to catch up to him, hearing his heavy breath even as he tries to still his laboring lungs.

"So, if we build this thing, this giant, what, wrecking machine plus recycling plant? Mobile recycling plant? Give me some ideas. What are we talking about materials, time, and people-wise? What is this going to take for us to build?"

"Well, that's a good question. I haven't taken a survey of the shipping cartons on the docks, but I'm guessing with rust and all, we'll need thirty-forty of them. We'll need hum, eight by four, then call it twenty-seven by two axles, so eighty-some axles. Eight tractor treads. There'll be four furnaces all told, metal, brick, cinderblock, glass, and plastic; it'll mostly burn the organics that it takes up, so it'll mostly feed itself. When it's not moving, it can probably function as a power plant for the Fork, too; we can charge batteries in ranks. The furnaces can run while we're getting it together. We can build those first, so that we don't lose that power. We can use the boilers stationary at first, while we build it, then hook them in later. You know we need a new brick factory anyhow. The one we've got keeps breaking, and its furnaces are hard to fix when they go.

"Each furnace is also a steam engine, so we've got that too. They'll generate power as they go. So, call it maybe three years once we get started if you give me a good team of men, twenty or so, and a few other people here and there for the bigger projects."

"That's a serious investment, you realize."

"Of course I do. But Camden was mainly wood. We didn't get as much in the way of materials as we wanted once we started taking Camden down in earnest. Philadelphia's a different story. Old City is metal, glass, stone, but we can't get at it. It's too difficult. If we do it this way, we can mine whatever we need out of Philadelphia, and have a surplus of the things that we already have some of. Drake, a surplus, can you imagine it?"

"It's a tempting idea, that's for certain. So, the boilers, where do they get water?"

"They're generating electricity, so they can pump water straight out of the river. And we can set up cisterns on the bridge so there's a water source to start the process and to act as an emergency backup in case something happens."

"Something like what?"

"Who knows? Emergency. You know as well as I that things happen to machines, that they sometimes just break. Say a pump goes and we're gonna lose water to a boiler. Or the hose rips down its entire length. Or there's a drought and we don't have a long enough hose to reach the river. Who knows? An emergency supply."

"What else will you need?"

"I'm going to need spectrometers. They'll be able to tell what a lot of the materials are, and sort them out. And an electromagnet. There's one I can salvage at a recycling plant in the city, which is where we can get two of the furnaces we'll need, just so you know. They're broken now, but we should be able to re-engineer them when we move them."

"What else?"

"Conveyor belts. Possibly a source of coal or tires for when we run into difficult buildings and need extra speed. A crusher to get cars down to size and masonry down to powder. A ram for the front. There's more things we'll need, but boy, will they be useful in the long run."

"And three years, you say?"

"Once we start construction."

"I'm going to have to talk to the backers, but I like the idea. Get me plans."

"The rust spread to the barley anyway."

"Yes. Despite burning the wheat field."

"Gods above."

"Yes. There's no sign of it on the sorghum, or the cotton, but the year's been so wet that it's just spreading through the soil and the roots are rotting out faster than the leaves are dying."

"How could this have happened? We clean the seed for black point, we rotate the crops, we do everything we're supposed to do and we're still losing a huge portion of our harvest this year."

"I don't know how it happened. It... it shouldn't have happened. It's just too damn wet this year."

"What does the distribution of the spots on the leaves look like?"

"Uniform. Across all the plants."

"Freeman, you saw the same thing on the wheat too, didn't you?"

"I did."

"Someone did this to us."

"How could someone have done this to us?"

"Sprayed the fields with something. Infected the seed. I don't know. But someone did this to us."

"We're too careful. No one could get in here."

"Then, I don't know, they spread the seeds of the disease on the wind maybe? But this was done to us."

"That's immaterial right now. We need to focus on what we're going to do. We've upped our cloth production and Freeman's been pumping out bikes like crazy, but I don't know that it's going to be enough to get both seed stock and enough food for the winter."

"How are the late beans coming in the old wheat field?"

"Well enough, but we're still short on food for the winter. We're not meeting our harvest goals."

"What should we do about the barley field?"

"Honestly, there's no signs of rust or rot on any of the other plants. I say we leave this one and let it go to harvest, get what we can out of it."

"Won't it spread the disease seeds to the other fields?"

"It might."

"And then we're facing this next year too?"

"Possibly."

"The field has to be burned then."

"Dammit! We are not going to have enough food for the winter if we burn the barley now!"

"We have to think about next year! There's got to be something we can do to survive this winter. We'll figure it out, but we have to look at the future too!"

"I am looking at the future. I am looking at having to reduce the number of people in the Collective or face starvation!"

"That's not going to happen. We will survive. I will take the job at the Fork."

"Another discussion, Freeman. Right now it's the fields. Which we have to burn."

"Seconded."

"Dammit people! Listen to me!"

He'd learned a bit more since the last time he had one of these things apart, that was for certain. Without the books from that attic, he'd never have gotten one of those record players he'd brought home so many years ago working, and even now it was proving problematic.

The problem was that there were so many things to work out. He'd started with the speakers, since they seemed the easiest; they'd never found an undamaged pair of speakers, but with enough time and practice he'd made a set of replacement cones for a pair of speakers. He was sure they weren't hi-fi or whatever the word was, but even the extremely rough paper that the Gleaners could make was enough that careful tapping of the speaker wires on a battery with very little charge produced an amplified clicking out of the speakers. That day had been a good day.

And then there were the players themselves. Freeman had enough experience with motors by now that figuring out if they were functional wasn't too hard, and getting a complete set of motors for one player happened in the fullness of time. He'd even repaired a few, that was fine. But the rest of it!

Five record players, and he'd found an intact needle that fit the one he'd gotten working—at least as far as the motors went. And, sure enough, if he connected the player to the battery, the platter spun, and he could put his ear near the record and hear voices, guitars, drums, all tiny and high-pitched, coming out of the needle, a scratchy voice of the past world coming out of the player for all—or at least him—to hear.

But that was where the ease stopped. This record player had an amplifier inside, but it was proving terribly difficult to make work. He'd tested out the board, component by component with a battery and a lightbulb and two tiny probes, changed out resistors and caps that weren't working, heating a tiny, tiny soldering iron in the brazier, saving everything—even the busted resistors—just in case. Then there was AC versus DC. One of the books told him how to make a chopping circuit; he knew it wasn't quite AC, but the board seemed happy enough with that current.

But then that last little thing...

There was this variable resistor connected to the board. He figured it wasn't important and just bypassed it, hooked everything up, and turned it on. Everyone in the compound came running as Janis Joplin's voice and electric guitars were heard for the first time in, well, the world. Then everyone laughed at him as the speaker cone tore itself apart. Even people in the basement could hear the thumping, tearing, staticy hiss as the mashup stopped working.

But now, now he had the variable resistor in place, a battery, and a new speaker, hopefully made more properly; he was using much thinner deerskin to attach the cone to the mount this time, and better paper. It was sunrise, and he'd been up since the day before getting it all ready.

Today was a day of gardening, and Byron's throat was too hoarse to sing. Today was a day for new things. Today, they'd have to see if they actually had the words to some of these old, old songs right.

Freeman started hauling the gear outside in the watery April morning and set up the equipment. Everyone would be going in for breakfast, and it was about time for Freeman to do the same. He hoped this would work, and be a fine surprise.

"It was, oh, seven years ago now, I guess. Deep in the winter. I was, seven? I guess I was seven. It sounds about right. Mom fell ill first. We didn't think much of it, everyone gets illnesses every winter, but this one was different. A hacking cough—horrible, deep, whooping, sounding like parts of her body were going to come out.

"Then when little James got sick, then we knew something was up. I did my best, bringing them tea, soup, everything you do, making what I could. Mom couldn't keep even the thinnest broth down. She'd eat, then start hacking, and then she'd just lose all the food, and then it wasn't just the food. She'd lose, oh, how to describe... like, she'd drink water, so, clear vomit, right? No, it was thick, stringy, ropes of pink-tinged white-clear-opaque stuff that came out of her.

"With James, it was the fever. Mom had one too, but we were too concerned with the rest, no, not true. We kept her near the fire, and under blankets, and then she didn't wake up one day, her skin burning, and we couldn't do anything. That was the day Dad started coughing, and the next day, the day after, little James' fever hit its stride. All the time, I hadn't been coughing.

"This was all down when we lived in Germantown. The neighbors came over to help at first, but as it grew worse, no one would speak to me. They painted a black 'X' on the door. I didn't know what it meant then, but I do now. You know what it meant. Stay away. There's nothing you can do. Except get sick yourself.

"Mom died about a week after getting ill. My aunt came by that day, but wouldn't come near me, just shouted towards the house. Dad was vomiting by then from the coughing, and for some unknown, ungodly reason, I wasn't sick. I just kept making broth and tea and whatever I could. But I couldn't hunt, and we ran out of venison. I killed our two chickens, knowing what I was doing, that we needed them for food through the winter, but knowing that I had to keep food in me, and in James, and in Dad.

"Baby James never had the vomiting, but he had the fever, and he wouldn't wake one day, and that day Dad was barely staggering around the house. I didn't feel powerless until I saw him crying because he was powerless. When he couldn't do anything about Mom, or James. When Dad was crying, I knew that it was over.

"James passed on two days after he passed out. That day, the last thing that my dad ever said to me, was that Mom had been pregnant, and that I would have had a new brother or sister, but now there was no family. He told me to go to my aunt's now, and when he got better he'd come and get me.

"Needless to say, he never did. I went to my aunt's, crying and practically clothingless, and she took me in. At first, she didn't want to, but after I'd stayed by myself two-three weeks in the cold spare room in the back, she did. She was heartbroken over what happened to Mom.

"But my uncle... he was a problem. He was too into the booze, and he'd barely come home. When he did he'd beat my aunt black-and-blue, and she wouldn't, couldn't do anything about it. I stayed there almost a year, then went to my grandmother's when I was too scared for my life, walked the ten miles in the cold Holly Moon air to her house. Stayed there. But she knew she was dying, and when it was time, she sent me off to her friends, who sent me to friends, who sent me to friends, and eventually, when I was ten, I joined the Gleaners. I've been here ever since."

The slope that led up to the train tracks was an empty, gravel-coated scree, rising at a tremendously sharp angle. There was nowhere easy for Freeman to climb up, he just ran and ran, away from Dawn, away from whatever had happened to Scotto, away from the cat, cheetah, puma, whatever. Every time he got partway up, he'd slip in the stones and be back at the bottom. Freeman gave up on getting up the slope, and ran alongside instead.

He could hear the hoofbeats—*sundering the world*—charging around the zoo, trying to get to him. Dawn was around, looking for him, maybe Scotto? Prolly not. More than one set of hoofbeats, maybe reinforcements had showed up. He ran below the tracks until the talus suddenly ended, and he was instead looking at a fifty foot high wall of concrete. It was time to give up on the train tracks. The bridge would be... dust. If the tracks ran straight, no curve, maybe thirty degrees off from here. He ran, jumping a low fence, until he came to a fence that recurved at an angle he knew he couldn't climb.

He turned right, away from the tracks, and followed the fence. Someone had to have cut it: there. Not a cut, but something massive, or multiple somethings, had crashed through the fence, partially flattening it. He carefully ran across the collapsed fence and was back on one of the zoo paths.

Keeping the bulk of the train tracks in sight, he charged down the winding zoo paths, keeping his breathing as shallow as he could and listening as hard as possible for the hoofbeats. They were somewhere near. And there they were, coming for him hard.

And then around a turn, and the gingerbread disaster of rust of the zoo's gates was in front of him. He charged for them, hearing the clack of hoofbeats, not even caring about stealth, just moving towards the river as fast as he could. He'd have to cross the Schuylkill Expressway, and if he could get down past it, he could escape the horses.

Freeman ran as hard as he could, dodging between houses, running down alleys, hoping each time he turned that the alley wouldn't be blind or blocked. The hoofbeats seemed to fade and grow, echoing and reechoing weirdly off the crumbling architecture.

Freeman came to a sudden stop as Fairmount Park opened up before him. The bridge across the Schuylkill gleamed red in the noon light, contrasting with the trees, and there was the Expressway, cars piled on the road, and the train tracks, rusted trains littering the tracks, and all he had to do was get down the... The sheer thirty foot drop.

There, down to the right: a fallen tree leaned against the concrete cliff. He ran for the tree, and there were the horses, and Dawn, coming.

Vines crawled from cracks in the sidewalk, going over the cliff. The horseman skidded to a halt, raised a musket. Freeman stepped to the wall, grabbed two handfuls of vines, and flung himself over. The fragments of stone flying overhead and the crack of the gun seemed to come at the same time. His feet scrabbled for purchase. The vines began to slip, to detach from the wall. He let go with his left hand, looked for a lower handful, skidding farther down the wall at every moment. A new handful of vines, this one solid. Letting go with the right, looking for a lower place to grab. Again. Again.

The vines ripped away from the wall. Freeman plummeted into a pile of rubbish at the bottom of the cliff. Something clicked in his knee, pain shot from his ass up through his body. The leaves closed over his head, blocking the sunlight. The horsemen were up there. He flexed his right leg, winced at the pain. Couldn't matter. He had no choice but to move. He gathered his feet under him and slogged through the leaves.

"People of the Collective! This is your final warning. You have seen, we are sure, what has happened to the buildings near you. The Fork has come, and taken the buildings. Sometimes we've taken the time to remove the inhabitants, sometimes not. Consider this your last statement from the Fork. We will be crushing down your wall tomorrow. We will be taking your buildings tomorrow. This is the end of the line. We have warned you and warned you, and now, we are through.

"Clever—you're shooting at us. You cannot shoot at the Fork and expect it to care. It doesn't care about your crossbows, your slings and arrows. It will shrug them aside as lightly as it will your little compound here. Come tomorrow morning, the Fork will be at your door, and when the Fork is at your door you'd best not be behind it. Stay if you like, or go, it is immaterial to us. We will crush your buildings."

"We won't leave, you bastards!"

"That's commendable. If I did not have the Fork at my command I'd be impressed. In fact, why don't you join us? That kind of loyalty is the kind of loyalty that the Fork looks for."

"We'll never join you, Drake. We remember you from when you came. We know that man standing behind you, that man who lets you do this to us. We know you, and we're not impressed. Bring your machine to bear on us. It will break its teeth on our walls and the strength of our consensus. The Collective has never stepped down before an outside force and never shall."

"What do you want me to do with this?"

"Talk some sense into them."

"I couldn't when I was there. Why do you think they'll listen to me now?"

"Just do it."

"Umm. People of the Collective. Look, I used to be one of you. I know the strength of your walls, and of your consensus, and the Fork won't care. Thank you all for turning your backs on me. Thank you for covering up your ears. Okay. Look, fine then. When this machine comes up against your walls, your walls will not stand. I helped build and reinforce them, and they're good walls, but not good enough to stand up to the Fork. It will... I'm not reaching them, Drake."

"You did your best to warn them, Freeman. They didn't listen."

"They're shooting at us again."

"Let them. We're too far off to be hit, and they're bad shots."

"They didn't used to be."

"They are now. Ah well, one more time, I guess.

"People of the Collective. A final time, your walls come down tomorrow. Stay or go, we don't care. We'll take down the walls, we'll tear up your farms and windmills, we'll raze your precious consensus to the ground with the buildings behind your walls. You will break on the Fork. You have once before, and you will again. Final warning!"

"They have once before?"

"Well, you left and joined us, didn't you?"

"What do you mean?"

"Just that the Fork has broken their consensus once before."

"I... see."

"Cooper, if you could leave the meeting room please? Thank you. Alright guys, the next order of business is to decide whether Cooper should stay in the Collective or not. Does anyone wish to speak for or against him?"

"I do. Cooper is among the first to volunteer for any extra work shifts. He's not the best at everything41 but he tries awful hard. And he knows all the words to *Mortal City,* which is a definite bonus."

"Thank you. Next?"

"I don't trust Cooper. He disappears for periods when he's supposed to be working, and when he comes in from his gleaning shifts, he often has less fruit than he should have. I'm worried that his, his excuses for why he doesn't have enough fruit are lies, that he's off somewhere."

"He's just a kid. He's probably daydreaming somewhere. He's a hard worker."

"I've seen him coming back from the east when he left to pick fruit in the west. I don't understand how that works. I don't trust him."

"Has anyone else noticed anything untrustworthy?"

"I have. He talks to himself constantly, and sometimes I've seen him rocking in the corners."

"Everyone does that. Okay, not everyone, but a lot of people."

"Personally, I'm not concerned about the east-west thing. He came to us after he was kicked out by the Sprawlers. If he was, what, spying for them? He wouldn't come back from the east. He'd be coming back from the south."

"What if he's not spying for the Sprawlers?"

"Who do you think he's spying for, the Fork?"

"..."

"That's ridiculous."

"There's too many of us here now to trust everyone. We have to start being careful about who we trust."

"Well, then, since he's such a hard worker, maybe we shouldn't just kick him out. Maybe we should give him another provisional term, another six moons. And we all keep an eye on him."

"Easier said than done. There's too much food coming in now."

"True. Still. I can't see someone who's working so hard for us as a spy. He takes extra shifts working, he's probably just sleeping it off somewhere. Let's not get paranoid. He's, what, fifteen? And the Sprawlers were never much for work. I say we give him another six-moon trial."

"Another six moons!"

"Alright. Bring on the beans.

"It's thirty to thirteen in favor of another six moons. Bring Cooper back in and we'll give him the news."

"Alright, Cooper, your provisional term has been extended. Is that amenable?"

"Absolutely. How long do I have?"

"Six moons. Alright, next up, we have to decide what we're planting next year. Steve's going to take the meeting over from me. Steve?"

Freeman directed the navvies to lay the thin, steel, open-topped box onto the chain-mesh conveyor belt, then signaled the next set of workers to begin lining the iron molds up on the plate. Once the molds were being set in the proper order, he began setting up the interior molds, with his workers watching. The interior block molds were cunning little contraptions; iron plate fashioned into circular tubes, jointed to form an oval when the spring that ran through the center was uncompressed. After they'd gone through the furnace, the springs had to be detached to remove the molds from the cinderblocks, and now that it was time to reset the molds, the assemblies needed reattachment.

The reassembled molds on the iron box left a sheet of H-shaped holes open to the roof of the factory. Each H had two of the oval assemblies placed between the arms of the mold, leaving gaps in the mold with the distinctive shape of the cinderblock. Freeman left the navvies to assemble the plates, then went on to start the cement mixer.

He'd found the mixer at the edge of Camden, in a yard surrounded by one of the ubiquitous, rusting chain-link fences, and two horses and a team of men had hauled it back here, to the cinderblock factory, to be repaired. Many of the mechanisms had only needed disassembly, cleaning, and oiling to be properly functional; the geared drive and the toothed rim of the mixer as the most obvious examples. The motor, of course, had needed to be scrapped, and a new motor was installed, one that would run on the direct current that came out of the batteries Freeman charged on the Delaware River.

Up until today, the cinderblock factory had worked mostly by hand power. Today, Freeman was beginning to change how materials were created in the city of Camden. Biting his tongue and ready to knock wood, Freeman bent down and flipped the switch on the wire that connected the battery bank to the drive motor of the cement mixer.

The motor hummed, the gear train groaned, and the mixer began to turn under its own power. The faces of the navvies fell open.

Freeman let them stand a few moments, their silent wonder far more important than any praise could be, then clapped his hands and started them working on getting the raw materials into the spinning circular opening of the mixer. It was faster and easier work than any that had ever been done here before.

Once the cement was mixed well, the crushed gravel from the tenement foundations of Camden was dumped into the slurry, changing the slurring susurrus of the mixer's work into a clanging, heavy sound. Then they attached the pour-spout and pivoted the mixer through a quarter-circle arc, swinging the heavy trough over the waiting forms, and tilted the mixer body to dump the cement into the forms. The cement, of course, spilled over the tops of the various forms, but holes in the base of the iron box let the slurried concrete fall into a catch-basin underneath, smaller workers reached underneath the conveyor with shovels, scooping up the concrete and dropping it into molds that were not quite filled. Other workers shoved thin sticks into the concrete, releasing air bubbles trapped within, and behind them worked men with squeegees, leveling each incipient cinderblock so that they would all be formed flat.

Once the forms were filled, Freeman pulled down the lever that would start the conveyor moving; the blast shield rose like the gates of heaven, and the last tray of handmixed blocks left the exit chute as the new blocks were carried in. It was still work, and hard work, but the days of handmaking cinderblocks were over.

"I believe that this discussion has been the hardest that we have faced as the Collective to date. Never before has a discussion gone into a third full session of House meetings. Unfortunately for us all, things have changed since the last time.

"The... disaster we found in the barley fields three days ago has altered the stakes of this discussion, and of Freeman taking the Fork's offer. The discussion has so far been a debate about the future of the Collective, and of the city of Philadelphia; it has been a discussion of long-term strategy. Now, as Steve will point out, that is not what we are discussing. Steve?"

"To make it all short, I reckon that we're gonna be running short of food by Candlemas. That's not firm, I mean, we can go on starvation rations before then, but food is gonna be tight. Prolly no matter what You-and-I do.

"Even if Freeman takes the job, and I must say I don't know how I feel about it, we're gonna be short. We'll be in better shape, y'all might not have to face starvation rations until April, but then there'll be greens, so. My best reckoning, we'll be in better shape if he takes it."

"Sadly, that's what the debate has come to. Does anyone else have anything to say? Molly?"

"No. I have nothing to say. We have to eat. That's the first thing."

"And there it is. Shall I call for a vote? Does anyone have anything else to say?"

"Yes. I do, Matt."

"Freeman?"

"Look, I know that I've been arguing in favor of the job. Yes, I want the job. I want to work on their machines, I do. But, as always. You know. The will of the Collective.

"If it should come that, after the winter, once we've recovered from all of this... Well, if you want me to take the job now and then leave once we've survived, to stop being there so much... Well. The will of the Collective. My future is in our hands."

"*Touching.*"

"*Not the time or place, Molly.*"

"Anyone else? Then I call for the vote. Bring out the beans. Black is for Freeman taking the Fork up on their offer."

"The will of the Collective will hold. This is still very close. Therefore. Like always when it's this close. Man. Twenty-five black, Twenty-three white. Dust. Okay. Well. I call for a second vote. That is: will the Collective split, or will the will of the Collective hold? Bring on the beans, black for the will of the Collective."

"And that's better. The three naysayers, as always, if you want to leave, our gates are open. Otherwise, we expect that you will continue to live with us, fully functioning members of our Collective. Freeman, the Collective has spoken: you will join the Fork."

The gates of the Collective opened for Freeman wide enough to let him and his bike through, then slammed shut, the silence of the guards punctuating the hollow echo of the closing of the gates. Freeman waved at Holly and Adria, but they sat stone-faced, peering out into the streets, ignoring Freeman's existence now that he was inside.

He parked his bike, leaning it under the roof eaves, and went inside to the meal hall. It had been a long day at the Fork, and the malice with which his grits were slung onto his plate made the day none the shorter.

He sat alone, as he was getting accustomed to, and quietly ate his meal. Conversations, thinner now that the Collective was so much smaller, rose around him, only to drop into silence when the talkers looked his way, or when Freeman made as if to join the conversation. Only Cooper would speak to him, and by the time Cooper sat down next to him and started chattering away, Freeman was in no mood for talking, and would only grunt when some sort of response was required of him.

Freeman finished his meal and stood up abruptly, stopping Cooper mid-sentence. He brought his plate over to the washbasin, rinsed it quickly, then set it on the rack to dry. Other people washing their dishes wouldn't even set their dishes in the same drain as his.

Freeman left the hall and headed over to his workshop. As with most days, there was a list of things the Collective needed. A generator down here, a windmill gone off true here, batteries to be charged, repaired, new battery orders to be filled...

Something shifted inside Freeman then. He knew that the Collective blamed him for what happened with Molly and Steve, with Byron and Joe and Crissa, for the schism in the Collective, for the funerals. But still, but still, to expect so much from him, and to give him so little in return, not even the shake of a head or a kind word.

To at least put their dishes in the same drain as his.

Freeman knew, at that moment, that his time with the Collective was ending. He got to work on the battery repairs, replacing a cell here and resoldering a joint here, all the time making a list of the things he would need at the Fork, and of the things they'd need here. He doubted that he'd be able to take more than a wagonload of materials with him; parting Collectivists weren't supposed to take that much with them, but, well, they were all busy ignoring him. He'd take what he wanted. They owed him anyways.

He brought wrenches out to the windmill farm, determined which one it was, fetched a ladder too. In the last rays of the sun, he adjusted one of the windmills in the forest that grew off the side of the Collective, threading himself carefully between the spokes that attached the windmill vanes to the wall of the building.

And then he was back in his workshop, quiet now that the smiths were no longer with the Collective. He'd need his books, that was certain. Even though the Fork had a library of their own he'd still need his books. His slide rule. His tools, oh, his tools. He'd need the selection of soldering irons, the wrenches, the socket set. It would be a shame to leave the drafting table here, but he'd never bring that with him.

He spent the rest of the night making a list, then headed up to his and Molly's room up on the top floor. As every night, it was a shock to see it so bare, to see it missing all of the things that he'd thrown away that were once hers. All the things he'd shattered. An empty room, on an empty floor, in a building that was no longer his home.

"Molly, I believe that you had something to bring up tonight?"

"Yes. I think it is time that we reexamine Freeman's relationship with the Fork."

"Oh God, not this again."

"Molly, we're doing well now, why bring this up again?"

"It's important. We agreed when Freeman took the job that it would be for a year, and that we would look at our state and the state of the city after that. It's now well past a year since he took the job. Our harvest is half in, and just based on what we farmed, we're in better shape than we were this time two years ago. Freeman took the job in a crisis last year, and we weathered that crisis, in no small part thanks to Freeman, and we have spent this year expanding and, frankly, so has the Fork."

"Molly, we're expanding, the Fork is expanding, is that so bad? They're in Camden. Really, is the two-city area really too small for you? Why don't you trust them, or at least agree that there's room enough for both of our groups to exist next to each other?"

"I don't disagree that the Philadelphia-Camden area is big enough for both of our groups to coexist. I worry that they don't think that. Do you remember how Fishtown's fields were sown with salt? No one was able to figure out who did that. And now, most of Fishtown's men have gone over to join the Fork. Their excavations and building in Camden is impressive, in large part because they've absorbed most of the populations of Fishtown and Haddon. They are achieving the kinds of things that we can't even dream of, and they're doing it faster than we can. What I worry is..."

"Yes?"

"What I worry is that they're now looking at us. I am not the only one to have heard the reports—starvation, some of you have seen it yourselves—to have seen the Fork's men scoping out the city, the Fork's estimators looking at tonnage of buildings and amounts of material that they can scrape out of Philadelphia. If the Fork decides to start mining our city for materials for their plan, do you think they will pay attention to things like our informal agreement on fruit trees, or sugar maples, or pitch pines? No, they'll raze our white oaks, our cherries to the ground. They will pay no attention to what we, what all of Philadelphia has built up."

"But what does this have to do with us, Molly? Freeman's contributions to our group have helped us not starve, have even helped us expand. We wouldn't have been able to support as many people here last year if Freeman hadn't been bringing in so much grain. And if the Fork wanted to close us down, wouldn't it have been easier for them to, I don't know, poison the grain that they've been paying Freeman in?"

"Perhaps it would have been, but we've been careful in how we accept Freeman's payments, always taking it in scrip and using that scrip carefully. Buying large amounts, all at once, and never from the same traders. There have been no reports of poisoning because the Fork can't map how we use the scrip that we use to buy the grain."

"Molly, you're being paranoid now."

"I don't think I am. Look, the Fork has their eye on this city, and we're a stumbling block for them. The reason we're a stumbling block for them is not because we're this huge juggernaut of a power structure, but because we are where Freeman calls home."

Freeman reached the third boiler, took a few moments to judge the speed of the track, and levered the third barrel of powder up onto the belt about ten feet from the ingress into the boiler. He hoped he had the timing right. Hopefully, when the first boiler went, the just-awoken engineers wouldn't have time to get to the third to see what it was about to be fed.

This boiler had been good to him. In addition to generating the power for the wheels and belts, this was the smelter. Inside the boiler, the ceramic conveyor belt moved along, dumping the metals into other ceramic molds. On other conveyor belts, molds that carried the new ingots out of the furnace and out to the waiting belts to be cooled and carried out of the Fork and down to Camden. He'd spent so much time here. He patted it, giving his farewells to this machine that he'd been closer to than any woman since Molly.

He pushed the cart with his last barrel down the path, along the train, feeling the hum and vibration of the machinery around him. The Fork could only discriminate up to a certain point, something dropped behind where it was looking would not be something it could decide about. Perhaps people were the same; ideas lodged somewhere inside and couldn't be dislodged simply by thinking about them, the hands and eyes and ears could not dislodge the wrong input if that input circumvented everything built to keep it out.

Perhaps the Fork had been that for him. Perhaps that idea—that must build, now and faster, and damn the consequences mindset—perhaps that idea had just jumped past what he thought. Perhaps it dug in, worked its way past the things that up until then had been the most important, and lodged itself so deep that it blinded him to everything and everyone that he had given up in the service of that idea, in the service of the Fork.

He pushed down the path, under the belts, and quickly now. He was running out of time.

The red light from the lamps flashed between the rollers of the belts, now behind the electromagnet, now through the crusher. And then Freeman was at the final boiler.

This boiler was the main motive force for the Fork. When it went, the linkages that ran the wheels, that ran the jaws, that ran the belts would crumple beneath the force of the blast. This boiler was the heart of the Fork.

Freeman climbed up the handholds on the side of the boiler quickly, scaling the side of the massive device. At the roof was an access panel, next to the boiler's exhaust pipe. He opened it and stuck his head and body out into the rapidly approaching dawn. He reached down to his belt and pulled up the pot of resin. He pulled on gloves and worked the resin between his hands, moving faster as he sensed his time running out.

Once the resin was properly sticky, he shoved the mass into the exhaust vent, praying that no one could see him. He dropped down, closing the hatch behind him out of habit, then left the gloves stuck to the ladder as he grabbed his hammer and flattened the pipe down.

Freeman dropped quickly to the floor, shoved the final barrel of powder under the boiler, as insurance for the linkages, abandoned the cart, and walked quickly along the drive train towards the Fork's ingress. Even now the giant fans blew, separating the leaves and litter from the rest of the materials; even now the belts against the far wall carried that rubbish to the boilers for fuel. Buffeted by the fans, he made his way towards the Fork's mouth. It stood open to the morning, and Freeman, soot-covered and sweating, emerged into the dawn, and, not even looking at the quizzical watchman, started his way towards the city, waiting to hear the explosions behind him.

The Fork would be coming for him soon enough.

"Are they showing any signs of movement?"

"No."

"Haven't we warned them enough? Do they not think that we are serious? Do they not realize that they cannot keep their puny little walls against the Fork?"

"Drake, I'm pretty sure they don't think we're serious."

"Fine. You know what? Starve 'em. I am sick of these tribals and I am sick of the dust-damned, Hemorrhage-loving farmers who call themselves a bloody Collective when they're just one more set of idiot layabouts standing in the way of progress. How much do we have to do to these people before they take a hint?"

"Maybe we do need to be more direct."

"More direct than what? We kill their crops, take their engineer away from them, wreck their standing in what the city calls a culture. Why will these stupid, stupid farmers not leave me alone? Why must they stand in our way at every opportunity? Don't they realize that we will not hesitate to crush them like we did Rowan? Like we did every form of resistance in Trenton, in Princeton, in New Brunswick? Absorb them like we have every bloody rotting set of farmers who has ever stood against us? That the Fork sweeps aside shit like them as easily as we knock manure from our shoes?"

"Drake?"

"Scotto, I am serious. You know what? They don't think we're serious, go down there with the gendarmes. Every time one of those farmers sticks their head above the wall, shoot it off."

"But we're going to crush the wall tomorrow morning. And... you know most of the gendarmes were taken north. We're going to need them tomorrow."

"I want blood, Scotto. I am sick of these people getting in my way. Send them in for a few hours at least. Pull them out at midnight. Get me blood, Scotto."

"What if Freeman finds out? He won't be happy about it."

"Oh, tie him up somehow. There's a fault somewhere in the Fork near one of the boilers, I'm sure, or just give him the evening off, send him home, whatever. Whatever recidivist, nostalgic affection he feels for them, if he can even feel anything, will go down tomorrow with the walls. He won't even notice if a few less rats stick their noses up at us before we crush their pathetic little dirt farm."

"I'm on it."

"Send him up here. I'll deal with Freeman myself, give him some busy work. He's probably down near the Fork, or in his little workshop or whatever, trying to figure out some new frippery."

"Got it. Gendarmes first, or Freeman first?"

"See if he's in the building. If he's here, get him up to me first, then give the gendarmes an hour before they go out. If he's at the Fork, well, get him this way, then the same deal. I want the Collective shot up, but we don't want Freeman to see it, to hear it, even to see the gendarmes moving. Do it all as low-key as you can."

"Consider it done."

"Send Marianne in with a shine and seltzer. Easy on the seltzer."

"Right."

Freeman slunk away from the door, where he'd had his hand paused in mid-knock for the last few minutes. He'd best get down to his fripperies. He didn't even notice the blood dripping from where he had his left hand clamped between his teeth.

Freeman leaves the warren of crates and boxes and shacks, of ramshackle lean-tos that litter the surface of the Ben Franklin Bridge, as the eastern sky is beginning to lighten with the dawn. All through the night, Haddon's horsemen had pounded back and forth across the free lane that runs through the center of the ancient roadway, and Freeman had spent the night dodging from shadow to shadow under the cold glare of the full moon, backing out of dead ends, moving from alley to alley in the shifting network of temporary paths, hiding from both Haddon's men and the equally terrifying denizens of the bridge. Twice during the night, Freeman ducked into some shadowy refuge as the hoofbeats tore past on the free lane, only to flee as unseen hands grasped at his shoulder or chest. Freeman bolted blindly both times, fear seizing his body, once bursting through a wall of wet, collapsing cardboard, once caroming off the wall of a wooden crate and then out the door, out in full moonlight into the center of the lane, then down the road and back into the warren through one of the innumerable, identical alleys as one of the horsemen, wheeling, fixed Freeman firmly in his sights.

But now, where the buildings of riverfront Philadelphia rise around the bridge, Freeman finds himself at the edge of the crate city and standing in the shadows of the dawn, watching a horseman peel back down the free lane away from the city. He runs from his spot in the shadows, tearing down the slowly lightening bridge, throws himself through the glassless door of some giant machine abandoned on the bridge in mid-transit.

Freeman lets his breath subside, waits until his shivering body can take no more of the cold that radiated from the rotten seats of the machine, then slips down out of the right-hand door of the cab. A line of concrete blocks, joined by metal links, runs into the front left-hand side of the machine; the free lane ran to the left of that. Freeman crouches his small body and works his way down the barrier, moving slowly, furtively, as the new heat from the dawn's fingers begins to take the chill from the air.

The Full Moon party should be at Race and Front streets. The closest bridge exit was at Fifth Street. Freeman pokes his head above the barrier carefully; there's a shape on the free lane—one of the horsemen. Freeman crouches and looks to the left, off the side of the bridge. There is a window across from the bridge, a little below the level of the pavement. Freeman is running out of time. He bolts as silently as he can across the bridge to the guardrail, creeps carefully across the barrier, stepping gingerly across the rails that run up the side of the bridge. The horseman vaults the Jersey barrier and is bearing down on him. Freeman looks at the arrow being drawn, looks at the window with who-knew-what on the far side, and flings himself across the gap between bridge and building.

Freeman strikes the window ledge with his thighs, the top of his body folds, his hands scrabble for purchase. He flips into the building, he hears the horse come to a scrambling stop on the bridge. He stays low, and looks for the exit to the room. He hopes that the horsemen won't enter the city. They can't care enough about him to risk an inclusion, can they?

There are steps in this building, thankfully metal ones. Even still, he skirts down them carefully, keeping near the wall. And then he's on the ground floor, the rotten door standing kicked open, and he's running toward Race Street, the bulk of the bridge rising above him. He can hear the sounds of the party winding down ahead of him, and runs faster and faster towards that haven.

When he gets to the party, Molly is still there, yawning at the dawn, and he throws himself, weeping, into her tired, strong arms.

"What is this? Why is there a building inside the building?"

"It's a courtyard, apparently from so long before the Hemorrhage that those cars you see everywhere, with the wheels, you know, they couldn't move on the streets anymore, so they moved the building and the fountain into here. But that's not what we're looking for. Come on."

"But, but I've never seen anything like it. Where is it from? It feels even older than Philadelphia. It smells of, not mildew, but stone and dust and..."

"It is, dummy, it's from across the Atlantic Ocean. Far across it, there's this land called Britain where it's always summer, never rains, and you never grow old or die. The traders talk about it."

"And that's where this is from?"

"Yes, it's just like Fiddler's Green except it's real. And we know it's real because these buildings came from there. Now come on!"

"Okay."

"There used to be weapons on display here, but they're not around anymore. People came in and looted them."

"I see. This was a display of 16th Century swords, whatever that first part means."

"You can read?"

"Can't you? Can't everybody?"

"No, I never learned how. Could you teach me sometime?"

"I can try, but it does take a while. You can't learn it all at once."

"That's okay. Now, look, carefully, after me, carefully put your hand here on this window edge, and reach out with your foot, and there's a platform right here. You-and-I're going to go up the steps. Can you do it?"

"I think so."

"Yep, that platform right there. Now your left hand on the railing, and that's it, and we can go right up to the roof."

"Oh. Oh my."

"Have you ever seen the city from anywhere like here?"

"Never. It's so, so green, so beautiful from up here."

"Look out towards the sunset. There, that's the Schuylkill River, and that alongside it is Boathouse Row. Upenn and Drexel still fight over it, sometimes. Down there, those grazing lands, that's called Fairmount Park. That's where the zebras and cattle and buffalo and wild horses graze. We hunt down there, so does everyone who doesn't have grazing land. There's deer out in the forests, but you have to be careful. There are big cats there too, big cats that escaped from the zoo a long time ago. Here, why don't we sit down and watch the sunset?"

"It's gorgeous, all red and yellow fading to purple... you can really see it from here, really see everything. It's amazing. Thank you for taking me up here."

"No problem. It's a little cold though."

"Is that better?"

"Sure is."

"Your hair is really red in the sunset. It's pretty. It shines like, like copper."

"Oh, Freeman, come here already."

"..."

The sides of the boiler sat unfurled, leaning against the sides of the freight container like an opening flower. Freeman finished running his rasp against the edge of one of the petals, ran his fingers down the now-smooth side of the boiler, then patted it gently. He motioned to the workmen above, and they began pulling on the rope that ran up to Cooper's specially-built scaffolding next to the Fork's outer skin, raising the curved metal sheet up into position. Two workmen below helped move the thick iron sheet into place, then handed Freeman his welding torch.

They called it a torch even though it technically wasn't; the tip of the torch was a rod of metal which would melt under the flow of electricity coming from the serially-connected bank of batteries sitting on the cart behind Freeman. He pulled his mask down over his face, then began welding the sheet to the boiler, tacking down the corners first, then working his way across the joint. It was slow going; he still wasn't getting quite as much amperage out of the batteries as he should be, but despite the lack of power he was able to proceed.

Then, seemingly suddenly, the gently curved outer sheet was welded down. There were three more skins to be welded down, but the batteries would have to be recharged overnight before there was enough power in them to weld another seam. Oh, sure, there might be enough power there, but Freeman hated leaving a seam half-finished, especially since the seam that gave way the last time they made a boiler. Fortunately it hadn't been under max pressure at the time; unfortunately it had meant a ton more work to be done.

One of the workmen hitched the wagon up to a mule and ran the batteries back to the generator banks at the Fork's main wind farm. The rest of the workmen climbed off the scaffolding, leaving the ropes tied in place to support the boiler skin, and entered the Fork; even though they were done with the boiler proper for the day, there was no shortage of work still to be done here.

This boiler, like the other three in the Fork, was made of three parts: the actual combustion chamber, the furnace, and the boiler. The combustion chamber itself was already complete, but there were some other parts that needed to be done; specifically, the ductwork for both carrying fresh air into the burners and for letting smoke escape. Problem was, they couldn't work on it until after the boiler was constructed; if they did, they'd find themselves trying to lift the giant sheets of iron around the ductwork, and if they didn't smash the pipes, they'd drop the boiler parts.

So, instead of working on the furnace as they'd originally planned, they got started on the generators. The boiler would eventually have eight generators placed in it, all in the upper portion of the boiler approaching the steam vent. Each generator had three sets of paddles, all light-weight wood attached to the same shaft, in ranks that shrank in width as they got farther from the generator itself. This way, each of the two rings of generators would be able to get the maximum amount of torque from the boiler's furious boiling of water. This is what they would work on today: the giant pile of uninstalled vanes lying in a pile near the generators.

Freeman took one of the smaller sets of vanes from the pile, and picked up one of the generator shafts. He inserted the vane into a slot in the shaft, pushing it through until two holes in the center of the vane were lined up with two holes in the shaft, then set two copper lugs into the holes. He passed the assembly to the nearest worker, who set the lugs with a hammer, then passed the assembly on to the next worker for the next set of vanes.

This process would continue until all the rotors were assembled.

"That is a lot of food."

"That is a lot of food. Molly sure can trade, can't she?"

"She sure can."

"Look, I know she ain't pleased about this gig you've got with the Fork, but I have to say, Freeman, we're all really excited about this. You haven't been there that long, and this is going to keep us well fed this winter. With this kind of a stock for eating, we're going to have no problems at all getting a seed stock together for next year, you know that right?"

"I thought so, but wasn't positive."

"You saved our bacon, Freeman."

"I just wish Molly was speaking more than two words at a time to me. I miss talking to her."

"I know. Don't worry. She'll come around. She's not sniffing around anyone else's fenceposts, and she's still hanging around in your room, right?"

"The nights that I don't spend in the workshop we do spend together. Not, well, yeah, that, but she'll put her arm around me in the night. I know we'll get through this somehow."

"And don't think she doesn't see what you're doing. She was as worried as the rest of us, maybe more—you know how she is—and she's been a lot calmer recently. At least about food."

"What hasn't she been calm about?"

"She's worried about the Fork. She's worried that if they get the market over in Camden built up, then the free traders won't stop at Penn's Landing anymore, that they'll all go over to the Camden side of the river instead. That the free markets will dissipate, and that the Fork will either take all of our business or charge such a high levy for trade that we won't be able to afford to sell in their markets. She's actually been talking with people, quiet-like, about issuing our own scrip to match the Fork's. She thinks we have a good enough name in Philadelphia to pull it off."

"But, we can't back the scrip. If anyone called it in, we'd have serious problems."

"She wants to back the scrip with cloth, not grain. She figures we can do that."

"And she might be right. We do have a bit of a stockpile."

"What are you two talking about down here?"

"Nothing, Crissa."

"Come on up. We're getting a supper together, and it wouldn't be right if you weren't there, Freeman. Molly's getting people from outside to come in. It's looking like it's going to be a regular hootenanny up here."

"Is that what all the noise is?"

"Sure is. We're getting the food together now. You two get up here, we're going to have some fun tonight. The Bookbinders are coming, and Allen's going to be doing the dance calls. It's practically going to be a market night here today. And we owe it to you, Freeman."

"Hardly. Everyone decided that I should go work for the Fork."

"True enough. True enough. Even still, though, we owe this one, and this winter, to you. Now get upstairs and get ready for the party!"

Had their powder gone bad? Perhaps a bead or three of sweat had fallen into the bag, or the pan; no more musket balls chased Freeman across the old expressway. Arrows had fallen close, but Dawn had always been a better shot with musket than with bow. Freeman dodged behind a rusted-out car leaning against a tree that had burst through the tarmac, leaned against the hood, felt the rust crumble beneath him, and took a few moments to get his breath. He was on the old Schuylkill Expressway, now clogged with the last traffic jam that ever filled its wide lanes.

He risked a glimpse around the side of the car. Dawn had met up with—he couldn't tell who from here—someone, and they had wheeled their horses around and were riding hard to the east, moving fast for the ramp down to the roadway. They must have thought they'd easily corner Freeman in Fairmount Park; they could probably get their horses down the scree-covered embankment next to the highway, but were playing it safe.

He had a few more moments than he'd thought. But what if more followed?

Freeman started moving again through the crumpled blacktop of the reforesting highway. He'd left his final cache at a bridge that crossed the Schuylkill, and once he reached it he'd be able to move as fast as they. But first he had to deal with the horses.

He skirted around cars, trucks, vans, all filled with the rotting detritus of the lives of those who'd lived before the Hemorrhage. They'd gleaned through here once or twice, but for the most part, what was contained in these cars, so near the river's floods and so exposed to the elements, did not survive long enough to be useful.

Freeman jumped the Jersey barrier and kept moving. All the cars were pointed the same way, and he'd always wondered what the point of the barrier was if the cars would all head in the same direction. No matter. He skirted two cars and hunched his way down the grassy hill that led into the park. He could again begin to hear the hoofbeats of the Fork's cavalry, and he began to move faster. He was going to have to face them before he'd be able to escape. But what could one unarmed man do against two cavalrymen?

There was a game trail here, carved by deer or cattle or zebra. He started his way down the trail, making sure to leave a clear trace of where he'd been—if he had to face them, better at a place he chose.

In the woods loomed the ruins of an old stone house. He noted it and kept running down the path. A few hundred feet more, then he jumped from the path and moved as silently as he could back to the house. Perhaps there would be something there to help.

Freeman eased his way carefully through the door of the house and skimmed the contents of the house. There wasn't much here to begin with, and the roof had fallen in, covering the entire floor in shingles. There wasn't anything here to help him.

He left the house and was about to move away through the woods when he saw the power line running to the house. He followed it down into the leaves with his eyes and kept a straight line going across the landscape. It ran to that pole, probably, and then to that pole, and from there to the pole straight across the path.

There was a tangle of brush right near where the power line ran. He hadn't seen it on the path; neither would Dawn. He took the power line in his hand and gave it a tug. It was hard to move but might do the trick. And at least he was in the woods if it didn't.

Freeman ran as silently as he could to the tangle of brush, and dug through the leaves until his hands slipped on the insulation of the power line. He pulled on his gloves, propped his feet against a tree, and sat to wait for the cavalry. By the sound of their hoofbeats, they wouldn't be long.

"My Gods! What's happened here?"

"We don't know, the building somehow caught fire."

"Is everyone out? Where's Molly? Dust take it, man, where's Molly?"

"She went back in to try to find people."

"How long ago?"

"Freeman, come back, you can't go in there—"

"Don't tell me what to do. Molly! Molly! Where are you?

"Keep coughing tell me where you are I can find you if you cough—

"Where are you—

"Dust are you okay do you know where Molly is?"

"No—huuuh—I came in here after her but the beam—"

"If I lift the beam can you crawl out?"

"Maybe, I can't feel my feet, I don't know."

"I'm going to lift. Start moving, MOVE, someone come down here and help!"

"Maybe here—wet this and put it over your mouth to breathe, it will help."

"Molly? MOLLY! Where are you? chhhuuuhh MOLLY!"

Bodies on the floor. One was Molly. She was breathing shallowly. Freeman grabbed her slight frame by the arms and hauled on her, dragging her to the exit as the flames consumed the Betsy Ross house around them.

"I'll get her from here, man, she came in to get me out. Go back in, see if there's anyone you can help, we're missing, dust, I don't know, twenty? Fifteen? We can't count, there are more trapped inside, see what you can do."

Crissa's face on the floor, her hair smouldering, loomed out of the orange darkness. He doused her quickly with his canteen, then started hauling on her arms. A beam had fallen across her legs. He shoved the beam off her, barely feeling the coals blister his hands. He started pulling her out of the basement, not noticing that her feet were gone. A figure loomed from the darkness, took her hands from him, and he headed back in, his head going light and his breath going shallow. Sparks flew from his left as another beam crashed down into the hellish basement. There were dark figures on the floor.

"Come—hhhhuuuhh—this way, there's more, come quickly!"

"Freeman, we need to get out of the building! Stop! The steps are collapsing!"

"They may still be alive!"

"Freeman, they've been in here the whole time. And the steps are collapsing. You-and-I need to leave this building right now. Like *ligne nu*, Freeman. Just do it. I know you want to help them, but if you stay any longer, you will die too. We must leave right now."

The steps began to crumble behind Levi as he ran up and away from the fire. Freeman risked a glimpse back, watching the house and his life burn. This was it.

He started up the steps, feeling them beginning to give way beneath him. And then he was out in the cold October air, gulping down giant coughing lungfuls of breath.

His hands began to ache dully. Someone handed him a canteen. He moved a few steps from the conflagration behind him. The house was collapsing fast now, bricks falling from their crumbling mortar mounts into the basement behind him. Someone was pulling a blanket over—Crissa, no, Crissa!

He slumped over to where Molly sat against a wall, fell to the ground next to her. Tears ran down her face, and his. He put his arm around her, and she shoved him away.

The Betsy Ross House burned in front of him, taking his life away with it.

Freeman had spent the last forty-eight hours awake, running back and forth, supervising the machinery of this giant rolling factory, and now stood in the shade of Drake's mobile pavilion with Scotto and Drake, waiting for the first load of stone to be deposited onto the deck of the Ben Franklin Bridge. There were mules, wagons, teamsters, and longshoremen all waiting and ready for this, the day that they finally saw the Fork shit out its first load of new material.

Everyone but Freeman was excited. Below the pavilion stood the teams of navvies he'd had working with him on the Fork's construction, and they were chattering briskly back and forth, ready to see their handiwork pay off in spades.

Freeman wasn't excited. Freeman was tired, tired and punchy. The last two days' worth of alertness and work had taken their toll on him, and he was ready to head back to his apartment on Pine Street and sleep the sleep of the just.

He wondered how just it was. Whenever he set foot in Philadelphia now, he had to have a cadre of gendarmes surrounding him, guarding him from the street folk who wanted to do him harm. Which was odd; it was a long time since anyone had it in for him. Perhaps the residents of Penn Medical would have struck out at him if the weight of the Fork hadn't been behind him, keeping him safe.

Freeman watched the Fork, and saw the conveyor belts near the plant's orifice begin to roll. The navvies grew quiet and restive, jostling back and forth to be the first to see the cinderblocks roll out of the plant and onto the wagons, ready to head to their new home. A group of longshoremen moved up into position to load the newly minted blocks onto haywains to be moved into Camden.

There they came: fresh grey cinderblocks, rolling off the production line and into the waiting arms of the longshoremen. They were too busy to cheer, but the navvies at the base of the pavilion erupted, hats flying into Freeman's view, shouts of joy echoing through his ears. Drake turned to shake his hand, saying something, but his words were drowned out by the throbbing of the Fork and the screams of the navvies.

It was rather anticlimactic. Soon enough, blocks of glass and steel beams would also pour out of the machine, along with blocks of aluminum, iron pigs, copper bars, the occasional silver plate, clay ready for mixing, blocks of plastic... any materials that could be reliably recycled from the ruins of the city would roll into Camden on the backs of the haywains, and all out of his machine.

Freeman remembered, now, the joy of the harvest, the deep sense of accomplishment and community that rose in his body when the crops were all in, when the sheep were all sheared, when the wood was all chopped and stacked for the winter. How they would all stand together and celebrate. And now, here he was, standing apart from the men he'd worked so closely with for so long, celebrating with Drake and Scotto as they congratulated one another and talked about where to go next.

Freeman slipped from the pavilion and landed among the men that he knew so well, and so little–did he even know any of their names? As they realized that he was standing among them, their shouts faded and their applause petered out, and they stood, waiting for his cue. He looked from one to the other of their young, mustachioed faces, and as a grin crept across his face, he applauded them and their labor.

And their faces lit up, even more than they had when the cinderblocks started pouring out of the Fork, and the looks on their faces when they saw he was proud of them made this day all the more worthwhile.

"Freeman, what are you saying?"

"I think it's pretty clear, don't you? We've got a nice little thing going here, but Philadelphia was not built—the original Philadelphia, not this little fever-dream vision we've got going on now—this city was not built by everyone getting along and agreeing to everything that everyone wants, and moving slowly and carefully and making sure no one's feelings get hurt. The Fork understands how you have to build a city to put a culture into it. And they're building a city, and that city will be what Philadelphia once was."

"After all this time you still don't get it. We don't know what the Hemorrhage was, but what if it came out of how they built the city in the first place? What if the communities just sickened, if the cities built up all over just turned on themselves? What if what the Fork is doing now is what led to the Hemorrhage? What if the autocratic, petty warlords that ruled the cities of the old world made the Hemorrhage happen?"

"Molly—"

"Don't you Molly me, not after what you're saying. Do you even believe in what's happening here? Do you even believe in what we've built, or are you just going along with what's happening because this happens to be where you live?"

"Molly, we have a responsibility to try to fix the world. You've told me that. We're trying to fix it in every way that we can. The Fork is not going to bother us here. If I go and work with them it lets what we're doing here get stronger..."

"You're wrong. The Fork is evil, Freeman. They're Haddon, Fishtown, the Sprawlers, they're just another bunch of petty warlords, but with pretty toys and far more firepower. And if we become a serious concern in the city—dust, we are a serious concern. We've got more people than anyone but them, we've got more manufacturing power, we're a serious trading rival, if we keep doing what we're doing they're going to try to destroy us. Why can't you see it? The only thing we can do is build our consensus as strong as can be, and hope and pray and trust that what we're doing is the right thing."

"And there you have it, Molly. If the will of the consensus is that I go and work for the Fork, what else can I do? We take from them and become stronger in the taking."

"But you're making them stronger than you're making us! You're not working from within to destabilize them, you're letting them bend your will to make them stronger than us, which they already are, to make them able to destroy us! Any temporal gains that we make when we expand from the resources you gain from them will just come back and fall apart when they come for us. And come for us they will, with whatever resources they have, some of which you will have built for them."

"Why do you think that they're so evil? They're just doing what they can."

"Because it all comes down from Drake, or whoever is running Drake. One person runs the show, one person who hides wherever he's hiding, and he wants us gone. They need you, so they're doing this to drag you away from us. They will use this job as a means to split our consensus down the middle, no matter what we do."

"Molly, we have to trust the consensus."

"Freeman, you should have said no. You brought it before the consensus, you mean to take it, and I don't know that the consensus will stand against you, even with me on the other side of this issue. And if the consensus falls apart, we will lose each other, and I don't want to lose you."

"You won't lose me."

"If the consensus falls apart, I will. I already feel myself losing you to them."

Freeman gingerly locked the door to his workshop behind him, twisting the key carefully in his bandaged hands. The willow bark poultice made his hands slippery, and each minute movement on the door twisted through his body, making him want to scream.

The windows rattled in their frames as he sat next to the forge, its fire banked as the smiths were not here, might never be here again, and placed a book on the desk next to him. He read on vector forces and tried to forget the day. Tried to forget the four fresh graves, dirt mounded up on top of them, ready for tomato seedlings next year.

Forget the two preachers who presided over the funerals, a Christian for Crissa and Byron, a priestess of the Great Mother for Peter and Lara. More had died in the fire, but they were not of the Collective and therefore would not be buried on the farm.

The windows rattled as sleet and wind pounded at them. A pounding came at the door. Freeman ignored it, threw some detritus on the fire to make it burn hotter. His hands hurt. He put the book into his lap and curled up against the forge.

Freeman was not religious. Even still, he preferred the sermon of the priestess of the Great Mother; she talked of the circle of life, which they'd all experienced first hand. It was more comforting to think that his friends were all around him now.

No one had figured out how the fire started. Everyone had their theories. Most everyone had come around to Molly's view that the Fork was responsible. Freeman had his doubts. The Collective had been swayed by her argument that no fires had ever run over before, and that it happened when Freeman wasn't at the Full Moon party.

The pounding at the door stopped. Whoever it was had given up.

The Collective had seemed empty since the fire. Byron's laugh, Crissa's bad attitude, Peter's solid presence, Lara's incredible cooking; the Collective would not be the same without them. Freeman didn't know how to live in a Collective without these people around him. Even if they could survive without Crissa's genius with a loom.

A window frame rattled with more force than before, with more force than just the wind would give. Freeman ignored it, kept staring at the book as if he was reading it.

Freeman had to stay with the Fork now, that was for certain. Without Crissa's cloth, there would be no other way for the Collective to trade for enough food to live. If the food he'd brought in had seemed essential before, well, that was nothing compared to now. Which would, given time, stall the rumors that the Fork had burned down the Betsy Ross House while the Collective was inside.

The window pounded again. Freeman thought he could hear a voice over the wind, but put it down to his imagination.

This was probably the end of the Full Moon parties. In all the history of Philadelphia, such a tragedy had never happened during a party. Fourteen people killed by the fire. It was... it was unthinkable.

"Freeman! Freeman open the door! Dammit Freeman!"

Freeman turned and looked. There was a clenched fist pounding against the cracked window; a flash of lightning showed red hair silhouetted against the sky.

Freeman looked down at his book. He could not deal with her right now. There would be time tomorrow. She blamed him. Maybe she was right. He had no way to know.

Freeman ignored the window, but could not help but see the knuckles of the fist slowly slipping down the glass, dragging against the rain-runneled glass, the fist of a person slowly and finally giving up.

There would be time to talk to her tomorrow. Freeman tried to focus on his book.

"Hi."

"Hi."

"..."

"..."

"Thank you for taking care of me. I know Adria's been keeping you out since I've been awake."

"I wanted to come in, but she told me it would be too much. I've been coming in while you were asleep to hold your hand."

"She told me."

"Do you want to talk about what happened?"

"I... I do."

"*Devai.*"

"I... I missed my flux two moons in a row, Freeman. And I started vomiting in the mornings, couldn't keep food down. And I panicked, Freeman. I just didn't know what to do. I thought I'd make some pennyroyal tea, just deal with it. And since the tea I'd been drinking didn't do it, I made an extra-strong cup... and I guess it was just too strong..."

"I thought Adria kept the pennyroyal locked up pretty well."

"She does. I traded for some privately after she wouldn't give me any last year."

"Why didn't you tell me?"

"I... I didn't know what to do, Freeman. You've been so distant recently. Spending so much time with your machines. I didn't know if you'd be able to be a father to our child, I didn't know if you'd be able to pull yourself away from everything. And as much as I like April and Kestrel, I didn't want to be a single mother. I don't think you're going to stay here with us. I think you're going to leave and I don't want to be left, Freeman. And my responsibilities right now are so great that I just don't even know that I'll have time to be a mother. I... we just can't have a child now."

"Molly... I didn't know. I thought, I thought I was doing the right thing. I thought I was doing what I was supposed to be doing for the best of all of us."

"You are, but... You are doing the right thing. But you're cutting me out. You-and-I've never been this distant before. And I was hoping you'd notice, but you didn't, and I've just been more and more alone and I couldn't, couldn't do it, and I just freaked out."

"But we need the machines, we need the grain..."

"But I need you, Freeman, and you haven't been around. You're so much not around. You're just not who you were, not even a year ago. You're turning into one of your machines and I need you, Freeman."

"But you need the machines too. So I can't do anything right here? You need my products for your little trading empire, but you need me around all the time too?"

"No, Freeman, what are you saying? I need you around some. Some. We all need what you make, but I need you, too. I love you, Freeman, and I need you."

"You're not being fair to me, Molly."

"Me? I'm not being fair to you—"

"Freeman, are you disturbing my patient?"

"I think so. I'll leave."

"You-and-I're not done with this discussion, Freeman. You-and-I need to talk about this."

"Alright, so let you-and-I suppose for this moment that the Fork isn't, what, poisoning us, because Freeman calls us home. What if you're right, and then what if we pull Freeman from them? They will stop at nothing to get him back, right? Then we're looking at something truly terrible happening to us when the Fork decides to destroy us to get Freeman to be a, a free agent."

"I somehow don't think that if Freeman left the Fork, that he'd then go back as long as there was at least a clear chain of causality leading from the Fork to the Collective's downfall. Would you, Freeman?"

"If it were clear enough, then no, Molly, I wouldn't. I would stay with what was left of the Collective—if I survived this theoretical Hemorrhage. Then, of course, I would stay away from the Fork. If there was this, as you say, clear chain of causality."

"So then, what do you say to that?"

"What I say to that is that I don't know how we'll have enough grain next year to support us all. Yes, this year we can survive, and the winter will be easy. But what about next year? One of the reasons this winter will be easy is that we're moving people off the farm and into cloth production. We've increased our yields of grain by moving more cloth into the trade market. But that's not guaranteed. What if a ship sinks, what if the traders don't come next year? We knew we could survive because of Freeman's extra grain, all of which he brings in by the Fork. It's guaranteed. Next year, there could be another hailstorm, there could be no traders, there could be rust, sickness among the plants. Among us. There could be a dearth of tomatoes, of fruit, the bees could sicken again and the scurvy could come back, no matter what we tried to do. And then what? Freeman wouldn't be bringing in his sure supply from the Fork. And that's a supply that we need, desperately, to survive."

"Surviving now is good, but we can put people back on fruit duty, back on honey duty, back on farm duties. I will go back to farming myself. People, come on! We should all go back to farming—we've become dependent on the Fork for our survival. We've never been dependent on any outside group before. Dust, we've never even been dependent on any one person before and now we're dependent on an outside power that means us ill. I tell you for true, if we do not stand up to the Fork now there will, will, will be dust to pay later. The Fork will come for us."

"Molly, there is no proof of that. There is no proof that the Fork is behind any of the ill luck that has befallen any of the other groups in the city. Haddon, well, they were always too secretive, who knows? Fishtown was just a succession struggle, they happen all the time to groups around here. The Southies and the Sprawlers were always at each others' throats, we knew they wouldn't make it too long. You can't hand us any proof. You are just an oracle spewing out dire warnings that we are to take on faith. And I, for one, prefer grains to faith."

"Are we done? Then I call for the beans. Molly, why don't you pass them out. Black for Freeman keeping the job with the Fork, white for Freeman staying with them."

"And now the counting."

"I see ten against, and forty-three for. Freeman, if you agree, you will stay with the Fork. We have the lesser consensus. Will we all stand for the greater consensus?"

"I'm sorry, but I can't."

"Everyone but Molly, then?"

A hand on his shoulder.

"I'm sorry Freeman, but I'm going to have to ask you to stay here."

"Excuse me, Infidel? I was just inside doing some last minute maintenance, and I am quite ready to go home. Also, remove your hand from my shoulder. Thank you."

"Freeman, word has just come through the pneumatic message tubes that Drake would prefer you to stay here and speak to him."

"What is this about?"

"There's word that someone smelled smoke at the main building of the Fork back in Camden, and tried to get in. Apparently, someone broke their key off in the door of your office, where a fire was raging. They're trying to get it under control now, but they haven't been able to. The last person to leave the office with a key to the building was you, and they want to talk to you."

There was a pile of rebar near his hand. "Infidel, what are you even implying?"

"I'm not implying anything. They said specifically they were including that much information to 'overcome our loyalty to you.' I am just to hold you here. Scotto is coming to take you to Drake."

"I don't even know what to say."

"You could start by taking your backpack off. That's an incredibly heavy load you're carrying around. What do you have in there? Freeman, is what they're saying true? Did you set fire to the Fork intentionally?"

"Why would I do something like that?"

Infidel moved closer to Freeman. "That's a fine question. What the —"

There was a tearing sound, a ripping; near the back of the Fork a flower of fire bloomed, tearing through the structure of the machine, ripping metal to shards.

Something that may have been a person flew off the bridge, smacked a building with a meaty thud. Freeman's hand was moving without conscious control to the rebar. He grasped it as Infidel swung his head back towards him, lifting as the second boiler blew, a mushroom cloud of steam lifting above the petals of fire now ripping through the superstructure of the machine, a hot wind issuing from its gaping mouth. The rebar was swinging through the air, just above Infidel's lifting hand, as the sound of taut conveyor belts snapping and rebounding echoed through the machine's hungry interior.

The rebar struck Infidel's ear as the shock of the blast staggered them both; Infidel went down and Freeman fell to his knees, the ring of the blast striking his body as the shock of the strike rang through his elbow. He was acutely conscious of the Collective members watching; he hoped that they saw what he was doing. He got back up, raised the rebar.

"Freeman, please, don't." Freeman brought the rebar down across Infidel's knees, crushing them as mercilessly as the Fork crushed the tribals living in the parking garage. As Infidel howled, Freeman dropped the rebar, fell back to his knees, vomited up whatever was in his gut. After the racking heaves subsided, he heard over the hiss and burble of the third boiler's explosion and Infidel's cries the sound of men coming down the length of the bridge; some coming to fight the fire and some, certainly, coming for him.

Freeman turned, and started running from the Fork, only barely registering the sight of Lydia's, Matt's, Dave's, and Michael's right hands raised in fists above the bullet-pocked wall of the Collective as he began to flee for his life.

"Freeman, stop following me around."

"No, Molly, we should finish this now."

"Get your hands off of me, Freeman."

"Fine. Look, everyone is watching us. Can we just go off to the side and finish this discussion, and then I'll leave you alone, but before I do that we have to finish this."

"Fine. What do you want?"

"I want to know why you got so upset at the idea of your running the Collective. Our running the Collective. Whatever."

"Because, Freeman, that's what everyone in this damn city has done since we've been around. Fishtown. The Southies. Upenn. Drexel. The Fork. Every little collection of power, of control, has been run by one person, and when something happens to that one person, the whole thing falls apart. We thought Fishtown was stable, look at them now. They're a small group of men on horses who know that if the city rose against them, they'd be crushed, so they're eking out a living on a tiny plot, and growing weaker every year. I want to build something here that will survive us, Freeman, something that doesn't depend on one person, or two people, to stay stable. So when you say that I run it, it means that I'm failing at what I am—what we are—trying to do. You know—you *know*—that I don't put up with people who call it Molly's Collective, or 'my' Collective."

"But it is yours. You put it together. You seized the reins when Jase died and you put the Collective over us, and we like it, and everyone's happy, but it was your idea. You put your Quaker upbringing on us, and we're happy with it, but it is yours. We're all used to being told what to do by a lord, a father, a grandmother. You can't take that apart in a few years. Everyone looks to you, to me, because we're all taught to look to someone."

"Then we're failing, Freeman, we're failing at what we're doing."

"No we're not, Molly. We survive the winter. People voted against your plan—"

"Only to vote for what you wanted."

"Only to vote for what we needed to do to survive the winter. And we did. And we're still expanding. We might get the old compound at South Street back this year. If we do, we can start to take hold of a serious piece of Philadelphia. We'll have a huge part of Old City, more than any group has controlled in this part of town for years. We're not failing, we're succeeding in spades."

"No, Freeman, you're confusing survival with success. We're surviving, and surviving well. But it won't outlive us if we run it. If something happens to you, or to me, or to both of us, well, things can go wrong in a moment. Then what happens to the Collective? The Collective is family, Freeman. We're this huge, arguing family, and a family can't be taken down with a jot of poison or an arrow or a season of sickness."

"How do you know that it can't survive our leaving, not that that's in the cards? It's rolling along well enough that we're both mostly out of the day-to-day, and we're just working on the machines, or improving our cloth, or trading, or... we are succeeding."

"But it isn't. Because people still call it Molly's Collective. And I am not the leader, even you think I run the show. I don't. I'm just another person in the process."

"No, Molly, you're special, and we wouldn't be where we are today without you."

"But I'm not, Freeman, I'm just a woman, another person in the chain. So are you. Neither of us are special. We've got skills, but they don't put us above anyone else here."

"Then why were you so upset when I joined the Fork?"

"...right, Freeman. I'll talk to you later."

"To the Collective,

"By the time you read this, we are far gone. Which is how it has to be.

"I know that this is a hard loss, especially after we had to place four of our best in the cold hard ground yesterday. Leaving the Collective is the greatest betrayal I will ever make. It is not what I wanted. But it has been coming for some time. I think we all saw it.

"I wish I could sit down with each and every one of you, and that you-and-I could talk it out together, and find a way, person to person, to make it work. Or at least make it happen differently. But you-and-I cannot, because that's not the way it can be.

"We all know how it is. With the fire, we've lost our standing with the city. We've heard the mutterings and seen the glares. We've lost the city to the Fork.

"Perhaps if we'd stood up to them sooner... but no, I realize now. If we'd stood up to the Fork, if we'd taken Freeman and his machines away from them, they would have found another way, or done exactly what they did sooner. If you don't trust anything else in this letter, if you don't trust my intentions with the Collective now, if you think that I was working against us this whole time, trust this: the Fork are not your friends. The Fork have it in for you. The Fork burned the Betsy Ross House. Everyone saw how the fire suddenly burned brighter, burned fiercer than it had moments before, everyone saw how the fire suddenly leapt and caught the building. Everyone knows how careful we are that that never happens. But it did, despite our precautions, despite our eyes and hands and experience making sure that exactly what happened didn't happen.

"The Full Moon Parties are done now. All that is left for Philadelphia and community are the Commons, the pubs, the trees and markets. The Full Moon Parties were the only place where we came together to do things other than work or drink.

"Perhaps I'm wrong. Perhaps the community of the city can survive. Perhaps it wasn't the Fork. But they have shown that they do not have any interests but their own in their hearts. They have what they wanted: they are the power in the city. The people of the city will distrust one another, hands will be turned against hands. People will turn against one another: it is already happening. We had to turn against you, because there will be no survival in the city if we are here. For the Fork to ignore the Collective, we need to remove enough of our strength that the Collective is completely finished as a power. A dozen of us leaving, a fourth of our strength, will do that.

"I love you all, I love Philadelphia, and leaving is tearing my heart from me. This is never what I wanted or hoped for. This is the hardest, worst thing that I have ever done.

"And finally, Freeman: this is where we were headed. I wish that you had never found that storehouse of books. Yes, we used that knowledge, and used it well to strengthen what we had, but it also tore us apart. We ate well for a time, but now none of us will. The Fork may well have still come, but they never could have expanded so quickly if you hadn't stepped up and handed them the keys to building so fast.

"Whatever you do, Freeman, whatever happens, I hope you stop working with them, or at least see what they are when you continue the work. If you must work for them, realize what they are: a group that will not be satisfied until they put the entire city, perhaps the entire land, under their thumb. If that's what is required for this future of yours, then I hope you're happy with your choice. Let it be said that I am not.

"Farewell, all, and good luck. For any interested, we go north to find a place without the Fork, where we can build a consensus again.

"Love, Molly."

Freeman was surrounded by trade goods and the sound of hoofbeats.

"Yes?"

"You're on the Kingdom of Haddon's road, and we are the toll collectors. None pass without paying the toll."

"You've got an awful lot of spears and arrows pointed at us for toll collectors."

"Don't give us any of your lip. There is a ten percent toll for crossing this road."

"Then I suppose we'll go around."

"No, you're already on the road. And the toll goes up with smarm."

Freeman's hands clenched tight on his spear.

"So then, you admit that you're not toll collectors, you admit that you're bandits."

"Fine then. The toll now includes your woman. Now put down your bows and let us search your wagon."

"You know, somehow, I don't think I'm going to do that."

"Fine. George?"

Suddenly the air was full of every awful sound he could think of—hoofbeats sundering the world, screams, the cries of horses, the twang of bowstrings, grunts, screams, cries—and something crashed through the drapes of the of the wagon, something sprayed across his face.

"Sonofabitch shot my horse!"

"Free..." An arrow, two, three, sticking out.

"Mom?"

"Someone help get this out of my shoulder."

"You help me get this out. Damn that hurts."

"Someone see if the woman's alive, see if there's anything in the wagon."

Freeman spun towards the back of the wagon, heard the man dismount, held the spear with both hands. A red curtain dropped over his gaze as the rear curtains opened, and he jumped, weight behind the spear, slamming into a body in front of him, seeing eyes open in shock as the spear rent the man's chest. Blood blossomed out as he fell into the man. They both rolled into the dirt.

The sun went out. A horse reared over his head. Freeman rolled to the left, letting the spear go. The horse's hooves landed on the chest of the man Freeman had stabbed, making a horrible wet crunching sound.

"What's happening back there? Someone? Roy?"

There was a sword at his belt. Freeman scrabbled, pulled the blade, and slashed at the first thing near him, the horse's belly. The horse screamed and ran. Freeman rolled back to the shadow of the cart. Two horses, one shot, one stabbed and running. Four men, two horses? The yelling man was chasing the horse, someone else should be coming—

A bearded figure came around the right of the wagon. Freeman swung the sword, hitting the man's bow and hand. The sword was jarred from his hands as fingers and bow splinters flew at him. The man grabbed at Freeman with his half-hand but missed.

Freeman spun and started running. Camden was before him.

An arrow skittered in the dust at his feet. Freeman broke off the road and into the shadowy forest to the south side of the road. One of the horses was now under control—the sound of hooves on the roadway was sharp. Freeman slipped in a puddle and went down, got up soaking and kept running. Camden wasn't that far, he'd be able to lose them in the streets. If he could see through the tears that kept trying to blind his eyes.

Freeman watched from the thicket as the cavalry broke from the tangle of cars on the Schuylkill and headed for the trees. Dawn shouted as she saw the spoor Freeman left on the trail; the horses curved in a graceful arc towards the forest. Freeman tensed his arms on the cable and waited as the horses drew closer, waited, waited, then pulled with everything he had left, flexing his legs against the tree, pulling the cable as taut as he could.

Dawn's horse crashed through into the cable. The cable ripped from Freeman's grasp, taking skin with it. The horse went down, its front legs caught on the cable, its breast and head slamming into the ground with a scream, Dawn flying off the saddle and into the ground with a sickening crash. The second cavalryman was following too closely and his horse tried to shy away, but couldn't turn on the narrow game trail. The horse half-reared, half-stumbled, and the second man fell from the saddle and slammed into the ground with a mighty thud. His horse broke into the trees. Dawn's horse screamed in pain and terror. Freeman launched himself from where he stood and fled for the river.

After a few moments, or maybe five minutes, of directionless fleeing, Freeman slowed to get his bearings. From here he could see the Expressway, so he was headed the wrong way. He turned so his back was to the road and started jogging, the surest way to get to the river, checking every now and again that the road was out of sight. He bound cloth around his hands as he moved, stanching the flow of blood from his palms.

And then suddenly, the trees ended and he was at the river. The bridge was to his left. He started along the riverbank, watching for the Fork, occasionally glancing at the herd of zebra grazing calmly on the far bank. Once, he would have been looking at them as a source of food, and soon he would again, but right now, they were a sign that he was still alive, that there were still living things in the world, that he

468

hadn't killed everything.

He skirted the foundation of... something. He was stumbling along now, the adrenaline finally having left, so far past even his fourth wind that it was all he could do to just remain upright until he got to the bridge. He had to get to the bridge.

The backpack was heavy on his glass-scored body.

The hoofbeats of the Fork, and the hoofbeats in his head, were silent. Perhaps the Fork was too busy trying to save what they could from the wreckage to send anyone else after him. But now, the sun was jewels on the river, birds were singing in the late summer sun, and he was leaving, leaving after having fixed everything he could, in the only way he knew how.

Seemingly suddenly, he was staring at the bridge embankment. He scrambled up the bank, made his way up to the roadway. There, in the thicket, he'd buried a bicycle in leaves. He scrabbled with his bandaged hands, found the bike, pulled it out of the humus.

He turned the combination on the lock and unchained it from the old piece of metal. The chain went into the saddlebags with the books and food and clothes he'd packed away. He gave the cloth and pitch wheels a kick, then started out across the bridge.

He stopped at the center of the Schuylkill. He had never found a matching piece of paper to the one about the Eastern Gate, and did not know what the Northern Gate was. But it was right that he not leave this time by the Eastern Gate; he had accepted his responsibility, finally, after so long, realized what he was doing, and did his best to fix it. Now he had to leave Philadelphia to make it without him. After all, he was just one person in the city. The city would have to choose its path without him. He gave it one last look, then remounted the bicycle and started off.

He'd be able to find her. After all, she had gone to the north.

Afterword

Hey! Thanks for reading my book and coming along on Freeman's journey with me. Molly and Freeman (and the rest of the Collective and the Fork) have been with me for a long time, and I'm proud to share their story with all of you.

I can't easily count all the influences I've had as an author, but aside from the texts mentioned in the book, the three biggest textual influences on The Fork are Robert de Clari's 'The Conquest of Constantinople,' Jorge Luis Borges' 'Labyrinths,' and Roland Barthes' '*La mort de l'auteur.*' Deleuze and Guattieri's 'A Thousand Plateaus' probably deserves an honorable mention.

de Clari's 'Conquest' is a medieval memoir recited by the illiterate author to a scribe who wrote down his story. In addition to being a striking primary source on the Crusades—dude was a random French knight and doesn't really do anything important through the story—it's an interesting window on how people have, for the longest time, retold their stories to show themselves in the best light possible.

I was thinking rather too much about both memory and authorship when I built this novel, and about the way the things we consume bang together in our heads to generate new ideas. I always imagined Freeman lying in bed in some random stockade in Ohio, twelve or fifteen years after the events of this book, thinking about the things he was going to say when he finally told his story the following day. This book is Freeman's anamnesis.

I'm sure you've noticed the variant page numbers. I wanted to take the idea of the death of authorship to its logical extreme, and let you, dear reader, deconstruct the book to your liking and read it however you should want... but also force you to take an irrevocable step and physically destroy the book to do so. The left-hand set of page numbers would let you put the book in chronological order, if you wanted. However, the book is structured quite intentionally, with Freeman progressively remembering far harder things near the end, and alternating those hard memories with extremely mundane memories as he tries to escape thinking about his past. Reordering the book away from the intent requires an irrevocable step. If you want to take that step... well, I'm sure you've got a pair of scissors, and the binding is *right there.*

A number of people read this book in its various larval stages, and their contributions made the book far better than it would have been without them. Tom Shore, Hilary Gross, Matt Phelan, Jeff Fein-Worton, Marc Wicoff, Snehal Bhatt, Langdon Herrick, Pieter Waters, Jason Cook, Scott Nieradka, Beth Hinners - thank you. This book would be significantly worse without your input. There are a few people who deserve specific thanks: Kate Hoopell listened to me yammer about this book for a long time, and helped me realize that this wasn't a short story, but was a full blown novel. Nora Temkin helped me work through a particularly knotty plot problem when we went to visit my expat mother in Panama, and was also there reading the book as I finished the first draft. She was the first person to get really angry at me for what the characters went through—Infidel, in particular, owes Nora a big thank-you. Huge thanks also to my lovely wife, Katie Ziesman, for doing a yeoman's work on the final round of line edits, and for cheerleading me through finally publishing this thing. You all helped make this book into what it is today. It would be a far poorer book without your help. And of course: any errors are my own. I'm 100% positive they're there.

The final influence on this book that I think worth mentioning here is the hundreds of examples of postapocalyptica I've consumed. One thing that I've noticed about them is that in many of them—not all, but definitely the majority—the text either starts out with, or eventually tends towards, a strong authoritarian, white ethno-nationalistic, or otherwise fascist/fascist-light message. I wanted to provide an antidote to that, and thus we have our Rosa Luxembourg-quoting friends Freeman and Molly.

I'm writing this afterword, and publishing this book, in the middle of the COVID-19 pandemic, and staring down the barrel of man-made climate change. I don't think we'll have a Hemorrhage, but the main reason I think that is the remarkable changes I see happening now, on local and community levels, even if our leaders are laser-focused on messing things up as best as they can. I hope this book helps inspire you to build community, to build soil, to garden, to throw parties, to bake bread, to raise animals... to live intentionally. If Freeman has one greatest sin (and let it be said, he has many), it's to forget that his actions have consequences, and to focus on what's in front of him instead of acting for the larger cause.

I firmly believe now, as I did when I wrote this book, that:

What gets us through this, is us.

Thanks for reading.